I0772377

1226 PINE LANE: THE SCARLET ADAMS MURDER

1226 Pine Lane: The Scarlet Adams Murder

KIT SPAYD

Kit Spayd

COPYRIGHT

DEDICATION

This book is dedicated to the more than 600,000 individuals that go missing every year in the United States, and the countless number worldwide.

ACKNOWLEDGEMENT

Nick and Mike, this book would not have been possible without the advice, insight, and guidance from you both.

PROLOGUE:

Landon Harper

"Hello, my name is Landon Harper and I run a true crime podcast. I was looking to speak with a Detective Schaffer."

"Yes, please hold. I will see if he is in his office." The secretary.

"This is Schaffer. What can I do for you."

"Hi Detective. I am."

"I know who you are, I heard your podcast before. What can I do for you?"

"I was hoping to interview you."

"Ok, did you have something specific in mind?"

"Actually yes. The Scarlet Adams murder, and the other bodies that were found in the Innerborough Creek."

He went quiet, and I was thinking he wasn't going to do it. I had done a lot of research and such so I really didn't want to be turned down. This case deserved to be recognized and talked about.

"Ok. When?"

Holy hell, he said yes. "Uh, whenever you're available."

"March 1st."

"Ok, sir. Thank you. I have a small office if you wouldn't mind coming there?"

"What's the address?"

I gave him the address and we agreed to noon. I had a feeling that would be the date and time since that is the anniversary of when she was found. I had so many questions, and heard the stories growing up, but I wanted to hear from the one who was there. The one who knew her, the one who made me want to start this podcast in the first place. He doesn't know, but I am Chick's grandson. My grandmom remarried and we took her new husband's last name. After my grandfather passed away, he adopted my dad legally, and the last name was changed to Harper.

I had no idea how to tell him, or even if I wanted to. I knew it was a way to be connected to my granddad. I asked so many questions about him my whole life so far.

March 1st, and I was ready for him. I moved the room around about ten times, until I put it back to the exact way I had it set in the first place. I could hear the door open at the end of the hallway, and knew it was him.

I was nervous as hell, and even shaking a bit. This was the first time I was ever going to meet him in person, and I was anxious. A knock came to the door, and I opened it and greeted him.

"Detective. Please come in."

"Thank you, Landon."

We sat down and he started at me for a minute and said, "Why didn't you tell me you were Chick's grandson?"

"How did you know?"

"Boy, you forget I was in internet crimes for most of your life."

He has no idea how long I have been following what he does.

"You're Frank Junior's kid. You look just like him."

"Yep, guilty."

"Ok, so what do you wanna know?"

"I heard the stories growing up, obviously living in Carriage Ford my whole life, about the bodies. More specifically about Scarlet. I want to know how I can help. I want to get this solved for you, for her. Something told me I needed to do it, so I need to."

"You're what a junior?"

"Senior."

"You know she was about your age when she went missing. You're seventeen?"

"Yep, Eighteen next month. I know that too, I think that's why I am so drawn to the case. I mean I feel bad for the others that were found but I don't have a connection with them."

"And you think you have a connection with this case?"

"Well, yeah. I have seen her."

He looked dead at me, like he didn't know if he should believe me or not.

"Seriously, kid?"

"Yeah. I see her when I drive on that road. She was wearing a black long sleeve shirt, jeans, and Fila sneakers."

"Who told you that?"

"No one. That's the problem no one will talk to me about those things."

"That's because those details were never disclosed to the public."

Well at least I wasn't as crazy as I thought now, apparently, I'm just slightly crazy.

"Let's get this interview started. And then we can recap and talk a bit more about these sightings you have."

I hit play on the background music. He laughed. It was a radio dispatch, and sirens all playing lowly while I started my greeting.

"Hey everyone and welcome back to Behind the Tap True Crime Podcast, I'm your host Landon Harper. With me today we have a local icon, a hero if you will. Detective Mike Schaffer."

"Thanks Landon and hello everyone."

"Detective, I invited you here today to talk about the Scarlet Adams murder. What can you tell us?"

Schaffer

"When I made detective back in 1995, I was young, dumb, and eager. I started off my career as a beat cop but didn't want to stay there long so I studied a lot, and it got me far. I was the youngest detective in Weston ever, and I really enjoyed it at first. I worked with Detective Frank Miller, we all called him Chick though, for a short year and a half until I was transferred to computer crimes, which was new back in the day. The department wanted "young blood" in that division, so guess who got to go? Yep, you guessed it, me. I know I'm here for a True Crime Podcast interview, and I wanna give that to you, but I have to tell you that after you hear the story you may not like the outcome. My first unsolved case has stuck with me even to this day, that's why I asked to get transferred to the Cold Case Unit. I have not slept a normal night's sleep in over twenty-seven years, and I was hoping that getting back in to test for new DNA, look for new evidence, maybe, just maybe, I will get some closure for me and their family. I worked on this case for a few months, it was damn near impossible to find anyone willing to talk to us, any hard evidence, shit, nothing was helping us.

It was crazy, I knew what a tight knit community it was, but I never expected the secrets that would come from such a small town like Weston, and the surrounding area. Judge Majors and I, do you know her? Well anyway, Detective Miller and her had a history so they didn't work well together. She wanted to help any way she could with this case, which was rare for a judge to be as involved in a case like that, right?

So, here's the thing, a murder like this didn't happen in our area. It just didn't. We had, I think back then, maybe fourteen thousand residents, in a seven-mile radius, it sounds like a lot I am sure, but it didn't feel like it.

Everyone knew everyone, at least for the most part. There were new people that moved in every year, but they seemed to fit in just fine with everyone. No one was violent, hell the most violent crime we had was a carjacking of a car that no one was even in. I mean, if that doesn't tell you how safe it was to live back here then I don't know what will. We took it personally.

Frank though, he didn't sleep for days after she went missing. It was like he had his own personal stake in it and did everything he could until he couldn't. So, now I get to try to unravel twenty-five plus years of memories, heartbreak, you name it, it's gonna be in those boxes."

"Detective Schaffer, do you believe the answers really are in there? Those boxes?" Landon asked. He was the one conducting the interview for the podcast.

I sat there for a minute thinking of how I was going to answer him.

"Well, Landon, I will tell you this when you hear the story, I want you to tell me if you were able to figure out who could've done this. It has been torture for me trying to figure it out. This will be as much a mystery for you as it has been for us, and the families. There are so many unanswered questions, so many unknowns. And you know, it shouldn't be that way. It should've been easy, it's such a small town. But it never was. I remember the missing person posters that were up for days, the search parties that were out looking day in and day out. Nothing. When we did find something, it was heartbreaking, because what we found was not what any of us ever expected. "

"Did you ever think there was more than one person involved?"

"Of course, what do you think we are? Stupid? Nah, I trusted Miller and his process. Miller knew a lot and he knew what to do. He was on at least over eighty cases before I came along. Back in the day when he worked for the city, he was the best detective. Everyone wanted him, he was an ass, arrogant, pompous, but never missed a thing. He could run circles around even the most senior detectives in the department. Probably why most hated him, but damn did they respect him. I remember him telling me this one case about this young girl, just graduated high school, was killed in a hit and run. No one ever found the driver. Wanna know the most ironic part?

"Yeah, of course." He was on the edge of his seat.

"The young girl that was murdered, she and her family moved into the same house that the high school graduate who was killed, lived in. Talk about eerie. So, to answer your question, I have too many suspects and not enough proof."

Over the next few hours, I spoke about her story, what her family told me over the years. What we read in notes, her notes. We compiled it all together and came up with a pretty compelling story for Scarlet. One I believe has helped get her voice heard to hundreds, if not thousands of people. When we were finished, I hadn't realized how much time went by. I looked out the window and it was pitch black out. I wasn't sure if anyone would listen to this, especially with how long it was, but damn I was hopeful.

"Wow! Detective Schaffer, that was a very powerful story. I am trying to wrap my thoughts around everything you said, I think I can say everyone who is listening is doing the same thing. I am sure I know the answer to this already but, what did you hope to get from this podcast? If anything." He asked.

"Honestly, I hope that someone hears this and realizes that it's still not too late. It's not too late for you to come and talk to me. We all just need that closure, twenty-seven years is a long time to hold in a secret, so I know it has got to be weighing on you. Call me, come see me, I don't care how you do it just do it. Make this right. Don't go to your grave with this secret. Because Scarlet Adams has already gone to hers and what would she say if she was here right now?"

"That's a heavy statement Detective. I hope everyone is listening, and that if you do know something, email Detective Schaffer. Isn't it time to close this chapter? Detective Schaffer, thank you for sharing her story with us today."

"I never know if I am doing her story justice or not, but I do make every effort to get it told. If she can't tell it, I will for her, in her words the best I can. I have permission from her family to share her story, to hope that at some point during the story it could trigger something in someone. Maybe they don't realize they saw something, that happens sometimes. But I hope everyone will take the time to listen. What you're doing here is a good thing Landon and I know you wanna help. I appreciate it. Shoot, you might even be able to help me."

"How so?" He turned his head to the side with a curious look on his face.

"Well maybe telling her story to someone who hasn't heard the whole thing yet, might just catch something that we missed. Might just help me solve a twenty plus year old case. Maybe you can do what Chick and I couldn't. Hey, who knows?"

PART ONE:

Scarlet Adams

Chapter 1

July 4th, 1990, in Havre de Grace Maryland was typical for a small town in the US. Some of my favorite times when we were living there were the parades down Union Avenue, and the concerts in Hutchins Park. Mom and dad would always have the neighbors over for a BBQ, and I can still smell the burgers and dogs, that without fail dad would burn every time.

Mom would always get on his case about it, she would say "Joe Adams, how in the world do you manage to burn them every time we cook-out?" they would all laugh because it was true, and dad would reply with "My sweet Ramona! It's because I am too distracted by your beauty!" and then he would walk over to her, grab her, lean her down and kiss her.

It was awesome, and kind of gross, that my parents were that much in love with each other. My mom was so beautiful, she had long black hair, green eyes, she wore a lot of dresses and always had her jean jacket on. My dad was handsome, he had blonde hair, blue eyes, and was tall. I was a happy kid growing up here, our town was one that people should write books about.

Most of my family lived there, or near Chesapeake City. So, we celebrated every holiday together, many weekend BBQs, and birthdays were not missed by anyone ever. We were very close, and it was comforting having all your family near you, especially growing up as a kid.

I remember this year vividly, why? It was the year my mom was diagnosed with cancer and ultimately was taken from us by it. I was eleven years old, and it changed my life getting that news.

I remember my parents sitting me down in the kitchen and telling me things like "You know we love you" and "What we want to tell you isn't going to be easy to hear."

It was something that I never thought I would have had to hear from them until they were super old. Life changed for all of us the day mom and dad told me. They didn't tell my little sisters because they thought they were too young to know the details. But I guess being eleven made me an adult? I don't know.

So, it was not easy watching her after she really got sick. At first, it was like nothing was wrong. She was still able to play with us, hang out, and even take us places. And suddenly everything just changed. It was like when *Superman* runs into the phone booth as *Clark Kent* and then comes out like 5 seconds later as *Superman*. Well, that's what it was like when it hit, except it wasn't as heroic as *Superman*, it was more like a horror movie that was disturbing, dark and terrifying. When you watch someone, you love get sick, and start to become a different person, it's scary as hell and at eleven years old, the most crucial time in an adolescent's life, it was indescribable.

Like I said, at the beginning it was like nothing changed. Mom took us to see *Teenage Mutant Ninja Turtles* in the theatre. It was awesome, we ordered popcorn and snacks. Mom always went and bought snacks before a movie because she always said, "It's too expensive there, so we will just grab some before we go." I knew things were starting to get different though, because she did let us buy snacks that day.

I sat with her one night, brushing her hair that she was slowly losing, and was going to paint her nails for her. At her request of course because I was the best around. We talked about the future and how she wanted me to be happy in all the choices I made, and how she knew that my sisters were going to be in good hands because there was no better big sister for them. We talked about how I wanted to go into the *Peace corps*, because I wanted to help people and how I wanted to go to school to be a therapist for young people like me, who had to deal with their parents being sick.

She said to me "Don't ever let that sparkle dim, my sweet, beautiful Scarlet." Those words would follow me forever.

I never really knew what it felt like to be that sad, I mean I lost my dog when I was eight, he came back home though after a day of being missing. I made posters and hung them all over the poles in town, mom helped me. We looked for hours for him, Murphy is my best friend, and if we hadn't gotten the phone call from the *SPCA* the next day, I don't know what I would've done. So, I knew what that felt like.

This feeling was different though, this was something that made me feel like I was on the *Gravatron* for too many times in a row. I wanted to be sick from school every day, so I could spend it with her.

My little sisters were oblivious to what was going on, they just thought they were being spoiled by my mom and dad all the time. It would really make me so mad that they didn't even care to notice that she was getting sick. Looking, well, different. She got so skinny, and the medicine they gave her everyday made her sicker. I hated this life; I hated it so much. It happened so fast; within a few short months she was gone.

I ran away one night; I had no idea where I was going. I had no money, and only left with my pj's and slippers on. I ended up at the new promenade, a place we went to almost daily because of how new it was. I felt at peace here, listening to the ripples splash lightly against the river rock down below. I could hear the ducks quaking, as if they were having a conversation with each other. The stars were so bright, and the moon was waxing. It was cool by the water, but warm everywhere else in town.

By now, everyone knew mom was sick. I couldn't go anywhere without someone asking "Hi Scarlet. How is your mom? How are you doing?" it never ended.

I would watch my dad try to avoid answering people, but he didn't want to be rude, so he would talk to them for a few minutes and then say goodbye and rush us out the door or across the street.

I promise my life wasn't always sad, this is just an especially crucial time for me, and I wanted you to get a better understanding of how we ended up here outside Philly. I'll get onto that part of my story later, right now I want to finish telling you about my mom. When the time came for the nurses to come to the house, that was the first time my sisters asked what was wrong with mom. I remember looking at my dad to see why he wasn't answering them, and he was crying and holding mom's hand.

"Daddy, what's wrong with mommy? Who are these people here?" Avery was seven, and Violet was only five. I knew that I needed to take them to my room so I could try to explain, was that fair for me at eleven? No. Was any of this fair? No.

When I took the girls up to my room, they had a ton of questions the entire way up the stairs, it was kind of annoying, but they didn't know any better. I sat them down and told them mommy was sick, and that she was getting special medicine to try to help her.

Violet asked "Should we get her some ginger ale and crackers? Like she always does for us when we don't feel good?"

I shook my head and put my arm around her and explained that I didn't think that would work, but it was a nice thought.

It wasn't until Avery spoke that they both understood that mom was not going to get better from this sickness.

"Letti," that was my nickname from them "Does mommy have the cancer?"

My heart broke because, something that I knew about for months and had time to learn about and enjoy time with my mom, the girls only just figured it out.

"Yeah Avery, she does." I felt my heart break again when I told them, and seeing the looks on their faces made it so much harder.

It was hard pretending to be an adult, but I think I did a good job at it. If we're being honest, I hated every damn minute of telling them about our mom. I hated that she was sick, that my dad was so sad all the time, and that at eleven I had the weight of the world on my shoulders.

This was August, and school was almost ready to start. I didn't wanna go, but I knew I had to. I wanted to be home with her, but it wasn't her, so it felt weird when I was around her. Her home nurses were nice ladies, especially Nurse Myers, Lucy, she was always checking on me, like it was her job too. I knew it was her job to take care of mom, and she did that too, and she always saw me before she left. She made sure we had dinner, or lunch depending on what time of day it was, she asked how our summer was going. She tried to make things a little normal for us. I didn't know much about her; except she was so nice and a really good nurse. She brought us dinner a few times, which unfortunately mom couldn't eat but we all did and she was a really good cook. My mom was too when she was better. I miss the times when she would be singing in the kitchen with the windows open, the breeze was always so cool coming off the water. She loved Classic rock, so it was always playing in the house even while she was sick. I could hear her every once in a while singing some *Journey*, or *Kansas. Carry on my Wayward Son* was her favorite song, she pretended to play air guitar, which made us all smile, and even a little hope that she was starting to feel better.

Unfortunately, that was not the case.

Dad, and all my family were there one morning, I remember how everyone was pacing around the house, like they were waiting for something. Sadly, something happened. On September 12th, my mom passed away from cancer. It was a quick spreading cancer; it only took a little more than three months for it to take over her and she was tired. Tired of the medicine, tired of fighting it, tired of being sad. I felt my heart break that day, I think even some of me went with her. My dad came to me after it happened, I was sitting with Avery and Violet in the backyard. I saw him and I told myself that he was coming to tell us she was going to be ok, that he couldn't possibly be telling us bad news. Boy, was I wrong. I know it was hard for him to tell us, I am sure he was scared, so were we.

CHAPTER 2

I remember walking down the stairs and my mom-mom was crying, a lot. My Aunt Joan, who is my mom's sister, was sitting on the bottom step, she heard me and looked up. She had me sit by her and hugged me. I think I knew she was trying to make me feel better, but I was relieved in a way. I was relieved that my mom wasn't in pain anymore, and that these nurses could leave. I hoped my dad would not be as sad now and that my sisters would remember how awesome our mom was.

The first night without her was eerie, all the nurses were gone, there was no beeping from the machines anymore, I couldn't hear the music. Why wasn't the music playing anymore? I remember walking into her room, and it still had her small, which I didn't expect at first. The bed was made, the afghan that my mom-mom made for her was folded and sitting at the end of the bed. I grabbed it, sat down on the bed and pulled it up to my face. I inhaled as I did and started sobbing, knowing that she was no longer in pain but now I am. I am hurting, I feel like I can't breathe, and that the world isn't spinning anymore.

My mom was my best-friend, and the best woman in the world. No one will ever be able to take her place.

The weekend of my mom's arrangements was a blur, there were so many people in my house the morning of my mom's viewing, I don't even know if I knew them all, to be honest. One woman, she was old, came up to me and my sisters and was like "Hi, girls. I am sure you're confused and all. And it would be completely understandable if you were. No one blames you for any of this, and everyone loves you." Why did old people talk like this? I guess I'll never understand, until it's my turn one day, I guess.

Dad stood in front of the line, and then me and my aunt and two uncles were next. Avery and Violet sat in the front row of the seats with both sets of grandparents, and they colored. How I wished I could sit and color with them.

I said, "It's nice to meet you," and "Thank you so much," more times than I can remember that night. Most of my friends showed up with their parents, which was awesome. All her nurses came, Dad seemed to struggle but thanked them all for coming.

The entire town was there at one point, and I thought the entire state because there were so many people there. My mom was a Professor at the University of Maryland, she taught Art History. She was just mom to me, but to other people it really seemed like she was a queen or something.

Like I said, EVERYONE was there, and if they weren't there on Friday night, they attended Saturday. There were so many military personnel there too, my dad was a communications officer for the Army at Aberdeen Proving Ground (APG). It was very overwhelming, but I could see that dad was honored to have so many people show up for mom.

Her funeral was something I would remember for the rest of my life, any kid would, right? There was so much pomp and circumstance, I wasn't sure what that meant at the time, I only say that now because I heard other people say it throughout that day. It was cloudy, I remember everyone thinking it was going to rain but it never did. It just stayed dark and cloudy all day, kind of gloomy some would say. I felt like it was an episode based on Eeyore from Winnie the Pooh with how gray it was, and it made it sadder.

That was the only viewing and funeral I went to, I am happy I never had to attend another, because it was for sure the saddest, I have ever been, like ever.

The time after that was different in our house, even though dad tried to keep it as normal as he could, he had three daughters he was trying to care for and not really knowing what to do with them.

He would say things like "Your mom was always better at this than I am," or "I wish your mom were here."

I wanted to say, "Yeah she was," or "So do we dad, so do we." I know it wasn't easy for him, but I like to think I did an ok job helping with my sisters, I wasn't the expert that my mom was, but I helped them with things like hygiene, and schoolwork, and when Avery had questions about everything it seemed, and so I helped with all of that.

Once the dust settled after that, everyone's lives went back to normal for them. It never did for us, at least I didn't think so. Dad was lonely, and luckily for us he never started drinking or taking up any bad habits, he just got sad. I didn't know what to say to him, I am the kid not the adult. I walked to my principal at school, and she was trying to help give me some advice and tell me to give him some time to heal and grieve. Sure, he lost his wife and love of his life, I lost my mom and now I feel like I lost my dad. No one seemed to want to listen, my family would stop over from time to time, my mom-mom was here all the time, which was nice because she reminded me so much of my mom. That also made it hard for my dad, I think. Other people would try to come over to get him to cheer up a bit, and it would work for a few hours, but as soon as everyone was gone, he was alone again. I could see it when it hit him, it was like a lightbulb going off in his head, and he would sit in the family room watching *NYPD Blue*. It was funny watching him watch the show, he would yell at the TV and try to tell them who did it, like every episode. It made me smile and laugh, and I remember he caught me one night.

He heard me giggle and turned around and saw me behind the kitchen counter peeking my head out.

"Who's there? Do I need to call for Sipowicz and Kelly to help investigate?"

I laughed even more, and I heard him get up and come over to me. "Who's there? I mean it, come out with your hands up."

I came from behind the counter with my hands up, he walked over and hugged me so tight, it was the first time he had done that since before mom passed away. I think that night helped him snap out of it, to come back to me and my sisters.

The next morning was different, Dad woke up before I did which wasn't common these days, and he had pancakes and sausage, OJ, and chocolate milk. The girls were so excited to see this, they only got cereal or toast when I made breakfast.

"Morning dad! What's all this?" I was hoping that the dad we knew was back, back to his old self.

"Morning kiddo, breakfast?"

I smiled and heard the girls coming down the stairs.

"Guess what? Daddy made breakfast. Sorry you're not getting the usual cereal or toast today," I said laughing and joking with them. The smiles on their faces were so big, they both were so excited and grabbed a plate and filled it.

"Ok, slow down. There's plenty here!" Dad even sounded like his old self, which was so nice to hear again.

We all sat down and had breakfast with each other, it had been a long time since we did that. Typically, it was me and the girls and dad would be at work still, or in his room, or in the garage tinkering with something. Like I said, today was different.

"Scarlet, I wanted to talk to you later. Ok?" I was scared when he said that, because I wasn't sure what he could want to talk to me about, we hadn't talked about anything real in forever.

"Ok, dad." I was a little nervous about what he needed to talk to me about, since he hasn't had much conversation with me since mom.

After we cleaned up from breakfast, and the girls went out to play I asked my dad if he wanted to talk now. We sat down at the kitchen table, and I remember how nervous I was about this, how uneasy I felt.

"Scarlet, I want to thank you for keeping it together with your sisters. I know you probably think I didn't notice but I did, I promise. I know it wasn't fair for me to put that on you, I am the parent, right? I want you to know that you mean the world to me, and I am going to make sure you never have to go through that again. Ok? I know there's more I should probably say, but I'm not sure what that is yet. Please know that I am dad, I am back, and we are a family always and forever."

Hearing him say these words made me cry, I didn't even realize I was crying at first honestly. I felt like I was in a different world, it was just me and dad talking, well he was talking and I listening. I was so happy to have him back, I knew he would still be sad, but I knew he was always going to be there for us.

"Ok dad!" I got up from my chair and wrapped my arms around his neck, "I love you dad. We missed you so much."

Dad hugged me back, and from that moment on I knew everything would be ok. It was ok, he was dad again. It was such a relief too, because I really was afraid, I was losing him. The first holidays were the hardest, but we were managing, we were figuring out a new life without mom. It wasn't easy, but with dad having his head back in the game we were good.

We made new memories, new traditions, and always made sure to include mom somewhere in those. We started a new thing at dinner, it was a way for us to check in with each other. We would go around the table and ask each other what the good part of their day was and if they had a bad part. It was something that no matter what, we always made sure we did it, whether we were at home eating or out at a restaurant one of us would start that.

When it was the last persons turn, they would end it with "And Mom's would be watching over us, and she didn't have a bad part," this made it easy for me and my sisters to help heal the loss of her.

CHAPTER 3

November sixteenth, 1992, my thirteenth birthday. I was excited for this day to come. Dad said I could get a second hole pierced in my ears as soon as I turned thirteen. Well, it's here and I hope he remembers. I really need to wash my clothes, I have nothing to wear, ugh. I opened my closet, and it was nothing but dresses and skirts, and even though I had no problem wearing either, I just really wanted to wear something else. No, no, no, not warm enough, not cute enough, I give up. I had a pair of jeans that I got from my aunt and Uncle so I think I will wear that, and I am going to see if my dad will let me borrow one of his button-down shirts. I noticed that a lot of girls were wearing them, with T-shirts underneath and big jeans with their sneakers.

"Happy birthday Letti!" Behind me the girls barged into my room and tackled me to the floor, they were so excited for my birthday too apparently.

"Thank you, girls. Is dad awake yet?"

They both giggled, "MmmHmm," and ran out of the room just as fast as they ran in.

I could hear them all trying to whisper in the kitchen, they were bad at keeping secrets. Mom always said that if you wanted the town to know a secret to tell one of them and the town was sure to know quickly. I found my *Ugly Kid Joe* T-shirt so I decided to wear that, and still ask dad if I could borrow one of those button down shirts he had, he's got so many of them.

I made it known I was coming down the stairs, this way the girls thought they were being sneaky and could surprise me.

"Oh, why is my birthday on a Monday? I guess I just have to make the best of it. I wonder where everyone is, hmmm."

As I walked down the last two steps, I could hear Avery shushing Violet, "Shhh, you're going to ruin the surprise Vi."

"Oh, be quiet, I can't help it Avery. I can't wait for her to see our presents," my little sisters were the best you could ask for. Over the past two years we have become much closer, and I really have no idea how anyone can ever complain about their little brother or sister, mine were the best.

I came around the corner and pretended I couldn't see them, "where is everyone?" they jumped out, dad included and yelled "SURPRISE!" When they ran over to hug me, I could see they decorated the kitchen and living room, and dining room.

It was the best day ever so far. "Dad! You did this all for me? This is so awesome!" I knew dad was getting back into the swing of things, and this was just more proof that he was his old self again.

"Yep kiddo, well I had a little help!"

I remember how proud Avery and Violet looked when dad said that, and they should've been because it was a memory that would last a lifetime for me.

Dad made French toast and home fries, my two all-time favorite breakfast choices. There was a bag too with tissue paper popping out and a balloon tied to it. "Letti, this is yours from daddy and us. We don't have any money, so daddy had to buy it for you, but it's from us too!" Avery was all too eager for me to open it, as she handed it to me. I looked at dad to make sure it was ok to open, and he popped his head back in an affirmative manner. I sat on the stool at the kitchen counter, pulled the tissue paper out, and looked in. There were three wrapped presents. I took the first one I saw out and started to tear off the wrapping paper.

"Oh my gosh dad, this is the cassette I wanted. Yes!"

Dad remembered me telling him I wanted the new *Beastie Boys* tape, they were the best band, dad even liked them. The next gift was an *UNO* box, which I also wanted, and the last one was a small box. As I opened it, I could see it was like a jewelry box of some sort.

As I opened it, I could feel them all staring at me like they knew something I didn't, well they did because they knew what was in the box.

I started to cry instantly; they were mom's silver stud earrings that she would wear daily. I looked at dad and he was smiling, so proud of this gift.

"Read the card." I opened the envelope that was with the box, "My Scarlet, these were your mom's as you can see. I thought they would be perfect for when we go to get your second piercing done this weekend."

I hugged my dad so tight and cried in his shirt, he was the best dad ever, and I knew thirteen was going to be an incredible year.

"So, we're going to get my second hole? You remembered! Dad you are hitting homers left and right today!"

One thing dad loved was baseball, and I did too because he did. We watched the *Phillies* play all season, while most people where we were from rooted for the *Orioles*, dad took a liking to the *Phillies* when he was young, so we all just kind of did too.

We wanted them to go to the *World Series*, but the stupid braves did, we didn't like them at all. We wanted the *Blue Jays* to win, so when they did win, we were happy. Ok, back to my birthday day.

"Hey dad, could I borrow one of those button-down shirts you have?"

He looked at me confused, "Umm, you'll have to show me kiddo."

I ran upstairs quickly and grabbed the first one I could find from his closet, sprinted back down the stairs, and showed him. "This one dad."

"Oh, one of my flannels? Yeah of course, but I think it might be a little big on you. Don't ya think?"

"It's how all the girls are wearing them though," I put it on to show him. It was a little big, but it looked so cool.

"It looks great on you, kid."

I smiled, and walked around to model it for my sisters, "What do you think? How does it look?" They were not impressed, but they also wore dresses pretty much every day, so their fashion sense was a bit behind mine.

Dad drove us to school that morning, it was my eighth-grade year, and middle school was not as hard for me as it was for others. Maybe because my mom died when I first started so maybe people took pity on me, who knows. I know I am not complaining, because it's better than the alternative. I was first in line to get dropped off; my friends were waiting for me. It embarrassed me more than anything, but it was nice.

"Bye Letti!" my sisters exclaimed as I waved goodbye.

"Oh hey!" I said as I walked up to my friends. Real quick, let me tell you about my friends. There's five of us, all grew up together, our parents are all friends. They were all there for me when my mom died and have been there for me since. Let me tell you them one by one.

First, my absolute best friend is Melinda Barr, she is a little taller than me, super skinny, she always had on the most colorful pants and a shirt that matched one color in the pants, slip on shoes, and her hair was pulled back on the side with a clip.

There's Gabriella Clark, her mom was a seamstress, so I am sure it would be no surprise to you when I say that she wore everything that was a McCall's pattern, and I mean everything.

We have Jen Walker, who was our sports girl, or some would say jock. She played every sport she could play, if they let the girls play football, she probably would play that too. Sweatpants, sweatshirts, sneakers, every day for her style.

Heather Fraser, the pretty one everyone said. I think we were all pretty, but whatever. Anyway, she wore the best clothes anyone could ever buy. Her dad was something big at the University, so he earned his kids love by buying them pretty much whatever they wanted. If she saw something in Seventeen, she needed it immediately.

Oh, I forgot I'm the fifth *Beatle*, just kidding. I don't think I ever told you all what I looked like. So here goes. I am about five feet tall, I have long reddish blonde hair, my skin is pale, I am not skinny like Melinda, but I am petite like mom always said. I am hoping this is the year I can "grow" into myself, if you know what I mean? I explained my style, and even though it's a new style for me it's one that sticks.

So, now you know who we all are! I can continue with my story now. Oh wait, I forgot to mention the boy I like. Even though I am sure he doesn't even know I exist, Rich Greene is easily the cutest boy in school. I've known him my whole life too.

I had probably everyone wish me a happy birthday, teachers too. Even got to use a gym pass, woop woop! I had mystery club after school today. What's that? Good question. It was a club where you had to use your spy skills and survival skills to solve mysteries. We would make up these mysteries, even though it was all harmless things we would think up, like if Mr. Jones changed his front window at the florist.

We would come up with a scenario and write down all the clues and hints, questions, whatever we needed to make the mystery club fun.

May sound silly, but we were young, and it was boring in Havre de Grace when it wasn't tourist season. I mean, it was a nice break from having all those people around, but it got boring. We made the most of it.

We were all talking about my birthday during this meeting, and my party this weekend. Today we met at Gabriella's house, it was closest to school, and it was cold, so we wanted to walk as little as possible.

Dad called around four forty-five to let me know he was on his way, and we were going to dinner for my birthday. I was excited that we were going to Burke's, we rarely went out to eat so it was a treat to go. Dad pulled up and I got my stuff to head out.

"Thank you, Mrs. Clark. Bye girls!"

"Byeeee."

I waved to my dad as soon as I walked out on their front porch. When I got to the car door, I could hear my silly little sisters in the back seat making faces on the windows after they would blow hot air on them. Dad just laughed and greeted me.

"How was your day? You ready to eat?"

Shaking my head yes, I proceeded to tell him about my day. We drove off and started to make our way to the highway.

Burke's Restaurant was about forty-five minutes away, in Baltimore. It would be a fun car ride, and I learned a few new things about my dad on that ride. We listened to music, sang super loud, and told silly jokes.

Avery wanted to play the plate game. For those that don't know what that is, it's when you try to find a license plate from every state in the US, or one from far away. It helped pass the time and kept them occupied for a while. During the wintertime, Baltimore didn't have the fishy smell like it did during the summertime. It was nice to pull into the city and not have that smell smack you in the face.

Dad found a spot in one of the parking garages near the restaurant, so we didn't have to walk extremely far. We walked in and dad gave his name and how many of us there were. We had a table by the big windows so we could see the harbor lights reflecting off the water. Even saw a few boats in the distance. It was the perfect day.

CHAPTER 4

When the waitress came over to take our order, my sisters still had no idea what they wanted even though we had been there for ten minutes already, dad and I just chuckled about it. This was definitely one of the coolest places we've ever been to. It was dimly lit, the walls were decorated with family crests, huge dark wood-colored chandeliers hung from the high ceilings. It was an experience to say the least.

"Daddy, can I get fried popcorn shrimp?" Violet asked.

"Yes, of course Vi. Get whatever you want if you will eat it."

My sisters were notorious for ordering something they never had before, especially Vi. She nodded her head to dad and smiled like she was so proud of herself.

"And you sweetheart?" the waitress turned to Avery now, "Um, I would like Fish and Chips please. Thank you."

Avery was most certainly one of the sweetest kids I have ever met, I know I said that before, but it was a fact.

My turn, "I would like the lobster and steak, medium well, please." I was a little anxious ordering this one because it was a huge meal, dad looked at me impressed as did the waitress.

"And for you sir?"

"Hmm, let me get the Oyster Dinner, please. Waters all around as well please, thank you."

We sat and talked more about how school was today, mystery club, my party coming up this weekend, which took an unexpected turn.

"So, kiddo, I wanted to talk to you about your party. I know it's been a hard two years for you, for all of us, I loved your mom more than anything else. I know how proud she would be of you, and how you have handled so much with your sisters especially during last year."

I was so confused why he was saying all of this, again. We just had a similar conversation.

"Ok. Thanks dad. Are you ok? You said all this to me already before. I am not mad or upset with you if you're thinking that way."

He shook his head when he answered me, "I don't know how to say this. Here goes, do you remember Nurse Lucy?"

When he said her name, I was happy, she was a great nurse for mom and was so nice to me and the girls, and dad. Oh snap, dad likes her. Ewe, dad likes her.

"Yeah, I remember her. She was super nice to me and the girls. Why?" I kind of already had an idea where he was going with this.

"Well, she and I have been talking for a little while now. When I went back in August for my annual checkup with my doctor, I ran into her," I giggled, "Letti, please. We had a cup of coffee after my appointment and sat catching up on the past 2 years. I wanted to see if it was ok if her and her two boys came to your party. They are around your age. And..."

I interrupted, not rude like, just because I had a question that I needed to ask before I forgot,

"Sorry, is she married?"

"She is widowed like me. She lost her husband in the Gulf War, about six months after your mom passed away."

Oh, that's depressing, I thought to myself.

"Oh, that's a shame, Dad. I feel bad, that's like worse than how mom died. I at least got to say goodbye to mom, her sons never got that chance. Yeah, I would like that." I think I just made my dad's day by agreeing to them coming.

The rest of dinner was a lot of fun, even though the staff came out to sing happy birthday with ice cream and a candle lit sitting at the top of it, I still had so much fun.

"Make a wish Letti!"

At that exact moment I had no idea what I wanted to wish for, because what I wanted could never come true.

"Hmm, ok." I blew out the candles a made a wish, which I can't tell you what it was because then it won't come true.

"Alright girls let's get to the bathroom before we head home, we have a little bit of a ride ahead of us. Scarlet, can you take them please, so I know they used the bathroom and didn't just splash in the sink."

I love how dad put things so plainly, "yep, ok girls let's go." When we were done, we walked back to our table but didn't see dad.

"Hey girls, your dad is out front. It started to rain so he brought the car around." The host pointed out front, and we could see dads' headlights pulling up.

"Thank you!"

"You're welcome, and Happy Birthday!"

I smiled at him and me and the girls ran out to the car. The weather was crappy, as *GnR* put it, cold November rain, even though the song had absolutely nothing to do with cold, November, or rain. I don't remember the last time we had this much fun. When we got home, it was after the girl's bedtime and close to mine. They were way too big for me to help dad carry either one in so I had to wake up Avery, dad could carry Violet in. They were both so groggy, I took their shoes and socks off, but they would have to sleep in their clothes from that day.

I was just about to head to bed, and I heard a knock on my door, "Hey kiddo, just wanted to say good night, and to thank you again for being ok with Lucy and her boys coming on Saturday. Happy birthday, I love you."

I don't know why I cried so much after he said that, but I cried, and I cried a lot. I was not a fan of crying, I really thought I didn't have any tears left after mom, but apparently, I was wrong. I am quite sure I cried myself to sleep that night, I woke up and my pillowcase was still a little damp, gross I know.

I couldn't wait to tell my friends how dinner went and the fact that dad has a girlfriend, and that it's Nurse Lucy.

Fast forward to school now, "Wait what? Are you for serious?" Melinda was buggin out, Gabs was not really interested, Jen talked about how cool it was, and Heather was asking dumb questions.

"What if like, they get married. You would have a mom again, and she's a pretty mom just like your mom. And if anyone gets sick, she can take care of them. I think its sweet."

Heather was harmless when she said those things, it was like she lived in a romance novel or something. It really drove Mel crazy how Heather said things that were inappropriate or not the right time to say them.

"Christ, Heather, really? This is what you think to say after Letti tells us that." Mel shook her head in utter disgust, and the other girls agreed with her on this one.

"Scarlet I wasn't trying to be rude or insulting, I am sorry. I hope you know that I wasn't trying to do that?"

"I know Heather, you just have bad timing sometimes and I think it just sounds rude. But I am ok, I didn't take offense." I tried to pat her back, so she understood I wasn't mad, because I really wasn't, the thought crossed my mind after dad told me so it's not crazy for her to say it.

And I also understood where the girls were coming from too, it was innocent on both their parts. The rest of the week flew by, I had two tests this week, a ton of homework, never ever understood that, cleaning, and decoration shopping for Saturday.

I walked down in the living room, where dad was watching *NYPD Blue* as usual, "Hey dad!" He was taking a sip of his tea when I alerted him.

"Hey kiddo. What's up?" I sat down on the other side of the couch, "Nothing, I was wondering what kind of food are we having on Saturday, because the fridge is empty and the pantry is bare," I didn't know what he had planned so I figured maybe he forgot about that part.

"Oh, well everyone is bringing some kind of dish, and I am just ordering pizzas from *Little Caesar's*, and your mom-mom is bringing the cake with her. I promise Scarlet, that's taken care of. I know you think I forgot, didn't ya?"

I gave him a half-sided smile, eyes looking around, nodding my head yes look, I am sure you all know what I mean.

"Yeah, maybe just a little bit."

He nudged my foot with his on the ottoman, "I got it covered sweetheart."

"Ok, cool. Well, I am going to get some sleep because I have a big day tomorrow, with getting my ears pierced in the morning and my party later. Night dad. I love you!"

I walked over and hugged him and went up to bed.

"Love you too."

CHAPTER 5

"Rise and shine girls! It's party day! We have a lot to do, and we have to get to the mall to get Scarlet's ears pierced. Come on, let's get going!" Dad was adamant about all of us going to the mall for me to get my ears pierced, which didn't bother me, but I knew the girls would want theirs done, and we didn't have time for that today. Today was such a huge day for me and my social status in middle school.

If today was an enormous success, then I would be recognized as one of the popular girls, and at thirteen who didn't want that? Dad and Aunt Joan had so many cool things planned, everyone was going to love it. I really hated having my birthday in November though, it was either freezing cold, or rain and freezing cold, but my family always made it so incredibly awesome for me. Everyone else had birthdays in the spring or summer, lucky. This summer for Avery's birthday, we went all the way to *Six Flags* because it's where she wanted to go and it's always the nicest weather for her birthday.

"Ok, dad, I think we are ready to go. If we get there by eleven, will we have enough time to get home to set up?" I was nervous that we would be late getting back, and even though I wanted my ears pierced again, I really need my birthday to be the best this year.

"Yep, Aunt Joan has set up an eleven o'clock appointment for you, which is why I said we have to get going!"

My Aunt Joan was super awesome, she was my mom's older sister, she had five kids, all of which were older than me.

We all got in dads' car and drove off to the mall. We got to the parking lot, and go figure it was packed, it always was.

"I hope they aren't running late, dad."

I was worried of course that it would take longer than we thought, we got to the kiosk that did the piercings, dad told them my name and the girls were ready for me within minutes. I was nervous, but they made such a big deal over the earrings that we were using that it took the nerves away.

"Ok, what do we think of this placement?" the one girl put the dots on with a marker, to indicate where they would put the piercing gun for the studs.

"I think that looks great. What do you think dad?"

Dad walked over and checked out both sides, "I think that looks good, as long as you're happy kiddo!"

I was so tense now; I knew it was the sound that would get me and then the pain after the fact.

"Ok ready, count of three. One-Two."

There were no three counts, they just did it. It didn't take me by surprise because I was expecting them to trick me like that.

Ow, there's the pain.

"Oww, that hurts. How do they look?" I turned my head side to side to show them off, and one employee handed me a mirror to look at them. I looked right, then left, then right again. I was so happy with how the studs looked, I started to cry.

"Aw, my girl. Come here." Dad leaned in and hugged me as if trying to take away the sadness and pain.

"I'm sorry. I just miss mom so much."

Dad looked down at me and shook his head yes, "I know sweetheart, and nothing I say or do will ever change that. I know how excited she would be that you were able to use her earrings to get this done. She always said for you thirteenth birthday she would take you to get them done, I did that for her."

Hearing my dad say that made me cry even more, I had no idea mom wanted to do that and Aunt Joan and Dad made it happen for me. I was loved by her even though she wasn't here physically.

On our way out of the mall the girls wanted soft pretzels from *Auntie Anne's*, they had the best soft pretzels and lemonade, and dad always got them for us whenever we came here, which hasn't been for a while since mom died. The girls were dancing as we walked out and over to the car.

"Thanks daddy," both girls said. It was only eleven forty-five, and we had plenty of time to get home.

As we pulled up to the house we could see mom-mom and pop's truck in the driveway and Aunt Joan and Uncle Ben's car on the street parked. I knew it was PARTY time!

"Dad, what do you want us to do when we get in? I just want to help with as much as possible before I get dressed for it."

Dad was getting the mail and grabbing the newspaper, "Umm, how about you get the girls to get the balloons ready, and you can ask Aunt Joan and mom-mom what they need help with. Thanks sweetheart."

When I walked in, I could hear them all talking and laughing, "Hi everybody!" They all turned and got overly excited.

"Oh, there's the birthday girl! How did the appointment go?" My mom-mom was one of my best friends, as she was also my mom's. She was short, with reddish blonde hair like mine, but was cut short, she always dressed so nice for her age, was stern but she was usually nice to everyone.

"It went so well. Look at how awesome they look!" I turned my head side to side to model them off. They of course made a huge deal about it, probably a little more over the top because of my mom not being here to make a big deal, which I appreciated.

Uncle Ben and Pop were setting up the tables and chairs downstairs in the basement, getting ice ready, and doing all the "manly" things, that's what they called it, mom-mom said it's because they couldn't cook very well so they needed to do the simple stuff, ha-ha! It was almost two o'clock and time for me to start getting ready.

I had the most perfect outfit picked out, black bike shorts, a black mini skirt that went over it, a red top that shows my belly button, I don't think dad's going to be happy with it, white bobos sneakers and ankle socks. I called it the *Kelly Kapowski* look, and it was totally rad looking.

I wanted to do my hair like the girls from *Beverly Hills 90210*, but I didn't have that much talent, so I just did it half up half down, some hairspray and little bit of teasing and I was looking out of this world. At least I thought so.

When I walked down the stairs, everyone's mouths dropped in shock and dad was speechless.

"Wow, Letti, look at your hair," Violet laughed when she said that, so I guess it looked dumb.

"What's wrong with it? I think I did an excellent job on it. Aunt Joan?"

Aunt Joan looked over at us and was hesitant to answer, "Yep, it looks good to me kiddo. But don't go by me I am old and totally out of style."

I laughed because she wasn't wrong, but I really liked my whole outfit including my hair, and I wasn't letting Violet or anyone ruin that for me today, no way.

I could hear the cars pulling up and my friends and their parents walking up the driveway, "They're here!" I said in my best Carol Anne voice, that's the girl from the movie *Poltergeist* in case you didn't know.

Oh, that's another thing you should know about me, I am obsessed with all thing's horror. Last year my cousin Tiffany, who is seventeen, was watching me and my sisters, her boyfriend came over and they wanted to watch *IT by Stephen King*. I was terrified of clowns and had no idea that the movie was based on one. I am sure you can imagine that I didn't sleep at all for like three nights, I swear. Well maybe not three nights, but I know I had a tough time that night.

After that night though, when I realized I survived, I started to watch horror movies that were on TV. We had a VHS player, so I would ask dad if we could go to *Blockbuster* and get a new movie every weekend, I would get a new horror one and the girls would get ones like *Honey I Shrunk the Kids*, or *Aladdin*, you know, kiddy movies. Now that I was thirteen, I was able to go to the movies and watch the PG-13 movies that were playing, so when one comes out, I'll be able to go to one, plus all my friends are already thirteen and have been to one.

Getting back to my party, I was super bummed because he hasn't shown up yet. Who? How could you forget? Rich Greene, the love of my life even though he doesn't know it yet. We were all dancing and playing twister, air hockey, and just having a fun time, when he finally showed up. There was most of the eighth-grade class here, and I felt like I was on cloud nine.

"Uh oh, it's a slow song," Heather was hinting that Rich, and I should dance, but I didn't want to ask him.

It was my party and I wanted him to ask me. When he didn't come over, I got super sad, so I got some punch and just watched everyone else dancing. How do I not get asked to dance at my own party? Suddenly, I felt a tap on my shoulder and heard someone clear their throat behind me. Yep, you guessed it. It was Rich, and yes, he asked me to dance. Tears in Heaven, by Eric Clapton was playing, and somehow that song became "our' song. Little did we know what the song was about, we still loved it anyway. We talked while we danced, just small talk really.

We agreed to hang out tomorrow, so we could get to know each other better. I never in my life thought that he would ever be interested in me.

I am beyond excited for tomorrow now.

"I like your earrings."

Oh my GOD, he noticed them.

I touched my earlobe, "Thanks. They were my moms, I just got them done today."

He was shaking his head like he knew that.

The song ended and we went back to talking to others at the party, but there were times when we would notice each other and smile shyly to the other one, we knew everyone saw but we didn't care. Nurse Lucy got there late, dad said she was running late at the hospital but would be here. I was happy that he invited her and her sons, and excited to meet them and see her again. I could hear Murphy barking at someone new coming in, it was a friendly bark, he wouldn't hurt a fly, well he did once but he was trying to save it, I think.

I could hear a lot of talking, laughing, and knew it had to be them. I went upstairs to check it out. When I got to the kitchen, I could see dad's smile from the doorway, something I haven't seen in a long time.

He saw me right away, "Scarlet, come on over here for a minute. I want to introduce you." I went over to him, and Lucy was just as pretty as I remembered her, "Hi Nurse Lucy. Nice to see you again!"

Her sons really were close to my age.

"Thank you, Scarlet, it is so nice to see you again as well. These are my sons, Justin, and George. Boys, this is Scarlet."

They both said hi at the same time and looked kind of uncomfortable being there. I really didn't blame them; I would've felt the same way.

"Did you guys wanna come downstairs and hang out with us? We have some games and stuff were doing." They both looked at their mom, who urged them to go and have an enjoyable time.

They followed me downstairs, I introduced them to everyone, and Justin was very friendly, George was a little shyer. Gabriella was also the shy one of my groups, so naturally they started talking to each other. Everything was perfect.

I bet you're asking yourself "When does the bad stuff happen?" Sorry to say, but it doesn't, at least not here. After today, things start to change a lot for me and my family, this is when it gets good, I guess you could say.

The party lasted until late, and my friends were spending the night too, we were going to watch Encino Man, it was the only one we could agree on.

All my other friends left by eight, including Justin and George, which I think they had a fun time. We all got in our pj's and laid out blankets on the floor in the basement.

My dad came down to check on us, "Hey girls, everyone ok? Are you all settled in?" They all said yeah and thanked him for asking. I wanted to get up and say goodnight and let him know that it was the best birthday ever.

"I'll be back down guys, I wanna go say night to my dad and the girls."

Walking up the stairs, I got a little sad that my mom wasn't here to experience this, but then this wouldn't have been this if she were here, it would have been amazing none the less though.

"Hey dad! I wanted to say good night and thank you for everything today. It was the best birthday ever!" I know he wanted to cry when I hugged him, I could feel him get all tense, but he didn't, he just smiled at me and said,

"It really was, wasn't it!"

I saw the girls were having their own sleepover in the living room with my two little cousins, so I ran in and kissed them goodnight. As I was walking down the stairs, I stopped quickly and turned back to my dad,

"Oh, I am happy Lucy was here today. I like her sons; they are cool." I know that made my dad's day and saw the big smile on his face after I said that.

I ran back downstairs, and we all gabbed and gossiped about today, and what will my day with Rich bring tomorrow? God, how will I even sleep tonight, I am so anxious.

CHAPTER 6

I don't even remember falling asleep last night, and by the looks of it it must have been late, because the rest of the girls weren't even awake yet and it was ten o'clock. I had no idea what time I was supposed to hang out with him, but I knew I needed to look my best.

"Hey, get up you lazy bones!" I went upstairs to start to get cleaned up for my date today, my sisters were up and making pancakes with dad, oh I do love pancakes.

"Mmmm, they smell good, can I have some too?" Avery and Violet giggled,

"Daddy said you have a date today. "Ohhohhh" they teased but had no idea what they were teasing me for, but it was cute.

"It's not a date, he's just a friend. That I would like to date!"

Dad just rolled his eyes, I knew he was not ready for me to like boys yet, but he was cool about the whole thing. It also helped that his dad was the Chief of Police, and his mom was one of my teachers at school. So, there wasn't a whole lot of chances for us to get in trouble without getting caught. Suddenly, the phone rang, and the room went silent.

I could hear a stampede coming up the stairs, "I'll get it," "I'll get it" my friends were nuts. Mel and Jen were fighting over who was going to answer the phone, but dad got to it first, it was funny to see.

"Hello? Yes, she is, may I ask whose calling?" He knew damn well who it was, "Sure, let me get her. Scarlet, are you available to take a call, it's from Rich."

Oh my god, dad.

"Yeah. Thanks dad. Hello?"

"Hi Scarlet. How are you?"

"Oh. I'm fine thanks. How are you?" Everyone was on the edge of their seats listening to our conversation.

"Did you want to go get ice cream with me. My mom said she could take us if it's ok with you and your dad."

"Sure, let me ask my dad. What time?"

"How about twelve o'clock?" "Ok, let me ask."

I put the phone in my stomach, and screamed into a dish towel, "Dad is it ok if I get ice cream with Rich around twelve? His mom would take us."

Dad smiled at me, I knew it was ok, but I didn't want him to think I was too eager to go, leave them curious right? "Yes, that would be fine. But he will walk up to get you when he gets here."

That was a no brainer, mom always told me never go running when a boy calls for you, let them run after you.

"Rich, ya there?"

"Yeah."

"My dad said it was ok."

The grandfather clock in the hallway chimed twelve times in almost slow motion, and my heart sank.

I didn't say anything about coming up to the door to get me, because I wanted to see if he would just do it. I think dad was confused why I didn't say anything, but I knew it was the right move. And it was, because it was almost noon now and he walked up and rang the doorbell.

"I'll get it," Violet was sprinting to the door, and beating everyone there.

I could hear her invite him in, "Letti will be ready in a minute."

I don't think he knew that people called me that, close people anyway. I walked out and said goodbye to everyone.

"Hi, I am ready!"

We walked to his mom's car, he opened the door for me, I had no idea boys were supposed to do all this. I liked it though. We didn't say much to each other on the ride there, his mom did most of the talking. I think she was nervous for the both of us.

The ice cream parlor was not far from my house, so it was a quick ride. When we got there, it was packed, but it usually was on Sundays. He opened my door, AGAIN, when we were ready to get out. His mom told us she would be back in an hour, so we had some time to talk. I was really hoping we would do a lot of that. We ordered, I ordered rocky road, and he ordered a hot fudge sundae {solid choice}, and we took a seat by the window. There wasn't much of a view, but it was ok because I was only looking at him anyway.

"So, Letti, huh?"

I wanted to laugh that that was the first thing he brought up, "Yep, my littlest sister, Violet, couldn't say her S's for a long time, so my mom taught her to say Letti, and it just kind of has been my nickname ever since. Only people close to me call me that, honestly."

He took a spoonful, nodded, and said "Well, can I call you that?"

Um, I think my heart just jumped out of my chest. He wants to call me that. WAIT, does that mean because he wants to be close to me. ALERT! ALERT! What do I say?

"Well, sure, but does that mean you want to be close to me?"

"Yeah, I mean I have liked you since the fourth grade, and when you finally invited me to your party, I thought you might like me too" I wasn't sure if that was a question, a statement, an observation, I was utterly lost.

"Yes, I like you. I have for a while too."

This was the awkward time in a love movie when the kids have no idea what to do or say now that that was out in the open.

I felt like I needed to say something, and I guess he did because we both started talking at the same time, "So what do you" "You go ahead."

"No, no," every sentence we said at the exact same time every time, it was so funny though and we both started laughing hysterically.

"Ok, for real, what's your favorite kind of music?" I always wanted to know what he listened to when he was in his room hanging out.

"I love Hip-Hop, Motown, style. Especially *Boyz-II-Men*, they are the bomb." He had good taste in music, hm what else.

"Ok, what kind of movies do you like to watch?"

"I love all kinds. Sports, comedy, action, thrillers. I saw *Batman Returns* over the summer with my older brothers, and then we started watching *Twin Peaks*. My mom wasn't happy we were watching it, well more like wasn't happy I was watching it. It's a good show, and I went with my sister and her boyfriend to go see *A League of Their Own*, around the fourth of July this past summer. I really like going to the movies. How about you? Music? Movies?"

Oh goody, I thought he'd never ask, "Well, music, I love the Seattle sound, like the grunge *Soundgarden, Pearl Jam, Mudhoney, STP*, you know bands like that. And movies, the scarier the better! I love horror movies the most, and then probably comedy second."

He looked surprised when I told him that, I started to worry when I saw his reaction.

"That's actually not at all what I thought you were gonna say, but that's really badass!" Ok that was a better response than I thought originally.

We kept eating our ice cream, and filled every minute with words, questions, getting to know each other, I didn't realize how much I liked him then I did that day.

His mom came almost exactly an hour later, and we weren't ready to go but we knew she had papers to grade and didn't want to hold her up from that. When we got to my house, I was nervous to say goodbye to him, not sure why.

"Ok, Scarlet, were here. Please tell your dad I said hi and I am sorry I couldn't attend your party, from what I hear it was a fun time." She said looking in the rearview mirror at Rich, and he was blushing bad.

"I will Mrs. Greene, thank you for the gift, and thank you for taking us for ice cream. I had a fun time."

She smiled and waved as I was getting out, he came around and opened my door, again, and walked to my front door. I had no idea what was going on again, I was secretly wishing he would kiss me, and wouldn't at the same time. Suddenly, he started to lean in, and I turned my head, and he got my right cheek.

Oh, no what did I do? Did I just totally ruin that? Ugh, I hate me sometimes.

"Thanks Letti, I had fun. I'll call you later?"

"Yeah, I'll be home. I had fun too, thank you."

Once I walked into the house I screamed out of excitement, and my dad and sisters came sprinting in the foyer to see what was wrong. Didn't mean to startle them.

"Scarlet, what's wrong? Are you ok?" I just leaned against the door and smiled and recalled everything we just talked about and even that awkward head turn that hopefully we can pretend that never happened.

Eek.

"Nothing dad, I am wonderful. It was the best day ever."

I went up to my room to call Mel, she needed to hear about this, and I couldn't wait 'til tomorrow to tell her.

"Hey, it's me. Yes, oh my GOD, it was the absolute best day ever. He was such a gentleman..."

I went on and on to Mel about our date, I am sure she was annoyed by the time I was done, but she was a trooper and listened to me, or pretended too either way I didn't care, I just needed to tell someone.

It was exactly what you would expect from a young love relationship. We split our time between our friends and each other, we didn't want to end up like "other couples" that forget about their friends completely and then if they break up, they have no one to comeback to, yeah, we weren't doing that. We really liked each other, and genuinely enjoyed spending time with one another. It could've been because we didn't spend every second, we could be together, we gave each other space. Our friends started to get along and hang out too. Which was cool because we could see each other a little more often. Mel started to really like his one friend, Pete, he was cool, he was very preppy, even more so than Rich is. He liked Mel, a lot, but then again who wouldn't, she was an amazing person and absolutely model gorgeous, and oh my best friend!

The months went by, and we were all becoming good friends, the eighth-grade formal was approaching, and his friends all asked my friends, and we all went together. We celebrated holidays and birthdays together as a group. It was so crazy to think that my birthday brought all of us together.

We all knew graduation was coming soon, and we would be starting High School. I was starting to get really bummed out, Rich was going to a private high school, which was about an hour away.

Not because he was a bad kid, but because he was wicked smart, and his dad wanted him to get the best education around, and apparently what we had was not nearly as important as his education. Sure, I agree but I don't have to like it. We spent every day together that summer, which made it so much harder when he had to leave at the beginning of August, almost three weeks before we started school here. I can honestly say that we really did love each other, I'm not sure if we were in love because I have never had a boyfriend before him, but I do know what love feels like and I know I love him. I thought I did, but what do I know at thirteen?

So, on the weekend before he was leaving, we went back to the ice cream parlor, and just reminisced on our brief time together. We promised each other we would write, and he would call when he could, but I think deep down we both knew that this was the end of the road for us {*see what I did there?*}. We walked back to the promenade and spent a lot of time there holding hands, skipping stones on the water, listening to the ducks. It was sweet for two teenagers who knew nothing about young love.

The day came for him to leave, and I couldn't bring myself to walk down to say goodbye, my heart was breaking, and I didn't want to feel that again. I swore to myself I wouldn't love someone like this again, because even my insides hurt me.

I cried and cried for what felt like days after. I was sad because I never walked to his house to see him leave, I knew that last weekend was probably the last time I would see him as my boyfriend, and the next time we would just be friends. God this hurts like hell.

CHAPTER 7

1993 I started high school, something I was not looking forward to. Rich was gone, the girls were still dating or talking to the boys. The year itself was an exceptionally boring year, except for the *Phillies*. They were the highlight of that entire year. They made it to the world series, sadly did not win, but did they play like no other. Dad and I went to a game that summer, it was so much fun.

The stadium was old, big, and smelled like stale beer. Vet Stadium is what the locals called it. Dad bought me a Dykstra jersey as an early present for my birthday.

Dad and Lucy were spending so much time together, which none of us minded. I never heard from Rich. So much for being in love, how foolish of me to even think that is what it was.

It was not until the next year, 1994, that things started to get interesting.

I don't think anyone from the nineties can say that their high school experience was boring, we had the best style in clothes, hands down the best music, maybe not the best movies the eighties can take credit for that, we had awesome lives, malls were at their peak, fairs were pretty much everywhere all the time, rap music was kick-ass awesome. I could go on and on, but I am sure you get the hint.

Most everyone knew everyone in our high school, we all grew up in the same town, or area, so we didn't have a bunch of kids we didn't know, unless of course you were new or a transfer student. We all walked through those doors on the first day and were Warriors, that's our mascot, and your experience here was how you made it for yourself. I was never into sports, but I love theatre and singing, so I knew I would be trying out for the play and chorus.

What made things harder was that we were all still friends with his friends, they didn't talk to him either, at least they told me they didn't. If that were true, I'll never know. Homecoming was right around the corner, and I will sadly be going stag. I am sure I could ask someone to go, but truthfully, I have no desire to go with anyone. I am strong enough to go by myself, plus not all my friends will have a date, so I'll be in good company.

Dad and Lucy were getting serious, they would take turns staying the night at our house and then at hers. I think the girls were a little confused, because she wasn't mom, and they didn't realize that you can love another person, it's just a different love. They were never mean to her, they were just too young, I guess.

I remember mom told me one time when she was brushing my hair, "Letti, if your dad meets someone, please promise me you will give her a chance? And you'll help your sisters navigate through your dad meeting someone new. Explain to them that the love dad and I have will never be the same as what he has with someone else. And we want him to have that, we don't want him alone forever trying to understand three girls."

She smiled and hugged me when she said it, that was one of my last great memories of mom. One of the very few where one of them didn't come running in on us. It was just her and I, God, I miss her so much.

Homecoming came and went, it was a dance, we had fun. I was dateless, and still no word from him. Ugh, this is torture. I decided that I would go pick up the girls after school one day this coming week, since the elementary school was across the street. Maybe I would run into Mrs. Greene? I told dad that on Tuesday I would walk the girl's home, so he didn't have to rush home to get them. We must walk since we are so close, the bus doesn't go to our house.

"Oh, Scarlet, you're the best. Thanks kiddo."

The girls were excited too, because they knew we could stop at the park on the way home.

The girls were still in school when I walked down to their school, which I knew already.

I walked in and saw Principal Stewart walking into her office, "Scarlet Adams! How nice to see you! How is High school going? I assume you are getting your sisters after school?"

She was the nicest person and new every single kid that walked through those doors, she had been principal for over thirty years, and everyone was happy with how she was.

"Hi, Principal Stewart! High school is ok, it's really big. Yep, I am here for them. Is it ok if I stay here until they are done?"

"Oh, why yes of course. I can also let their teachers know that you're here. This way they don't dilly dally."

We both laughed at that statement because it's one thing my sisters did all the time. Dad always said that it shouldn't take fifteen minutes to get out of school every day, but with them it did. The girls came to the office, and we were able to leave a few minutes early, thanks to Principal Stewart.

I was hoping we would, because this was about the same time that the middle school let out, so maybe I would see Mrs. Greene, who knows. Struck out there, I didn't see her car, I am thinking she wasn't in today. Boo. Maybe another day. We stopped at the park, as promised, for about twenty minutes, I had to get home to let Murphy out. I know I haven't said much about him, just know he's the best dog, and he's still here. When we got to the top of our street dad's car was already there, and so was Lucy's, which was not normal this time of day.

I was curious as to why they were here already. The girls didn't even notice, which is no surprise. We all walked in together and I could hear them in the kitchen. Justin and George were here too, what the heck is going?

"Hey Dad! Hey Lucy! Justin, George, 'sup!"

Everyone said hi and the girls were hugging dad when he asked everyone to come into the living room. Uh oh, I don't like where this is going one bit. Dad and Lucy sat next to each other on the chairs, we sat on the floor and the couch, waiting in anticipation for what they could say.

"We know you're all probably thinking "what the heck is going on?" and we totally understand that thought process," nailed it dad, "we wanted all of you together so we could tell you all at the same time."

They kept looking at each other, and I am sure Justin, and I had the same thought, since we both looked at each other as they were holding hands.

"So, we have been dating for a while now, and we really do have very strong feelings for each other, and we would like your blessing, all of you, for us to get married."

You should know this important fact. Around Valentine's Day, in 1994, my dad took nurse Lucy out on a date. Which I was so happy for him, well after that date they really started dating, and now they are boyfriend and girlfriend {*I'm pretty sure they still call it that at their age*}, they haven't talked about moving in together or anything like that, but I can tell you that the boys and I have become close like siblings because they are here all the time. We don't go to the same school, they are in a different High School in Chesapeake City, but Lucy brings them over every weekend, or we would go there to hang out. Dad's happy, and I like her a lot. She's amazing with Avery and Violet, she has the patience of a saint that's for sure. Dad and Lucy told us the story that day in the living room.

George really didn't have much to say, he never did, "Sure, you're the adults, why do you need our permission. I like Joe, and the girls. It would be cool to have sisters."

I smiled at him, that's the most he's said at one time like ever, I think.

Justin was so cool about the whole thing, "I look at them as my little sisters already so just seal the deal and its official. I like Joe too, mom, you know that. I am also going to be heading off to the work force in a few months anyway, so whatever you guys want I support that."

Justin graduated last year from his high school, so of course he wouldn't have an opinion on this, he doesn't have to change schools. Yes, we were the exception to the blended family, we all got along, and we all wanted the best for our parents. It was nice, until dad started talking again.

"Justin I am glad you brought up the work force thing. How do I put this? I have been trying to get a transfer out of APG for a few years now, and well one just so happened to fall on my lap. I was offered a position as a museum curator for Fort Mifflin, and I will take the next year to travel back and forth for training there."

We all probably should've known where this was, but none of us had a clue, so we waited for him to tell us.

"It's in Philadelphia."

Oh, no he didn't just say that. I hate my life, this sucks more than Rich leaving. Why? And is that even a real position?

I wanted to be happy for him, but I wasn't.

I was mad, so mad. "Letti? You, ok?"

Dad tried to console me, but I didn't want that right now. I wanted to be pissed, I had every right to be. I have had a rough life for only being fourteen years old. Lost my mom, my dog ran away, my boyfriend went off to some school an hour away, my dad tells me that we are moving. I didn't even blink when he said he wanted to get married. I like Lucy, as I said. I really did not want to leave my life here.

"Can I go to Mel's?"

I know dad wanted to talk, but I wasn't ready for that. I needed to vent, to talk to my best friend.

"Um." Dad looked at Lucy, and Lucy urged him to say yes.

"Yeah, that's fine. Just uh, be home by five. We are going to dinner to celebrate."

Yay me.

CHAPTER 8

It was not the smartest move for me to walk to Mel's, but I was so angry at them. It wasn't right around the corner, but I didn't care, I needed to just get out of there before I lost it. Living on Green Street, and her living on Fountain Street, it was about a fifteen-minute walk. I didn't even call her to tell her I was coming over, so I hope she's home, or I see her along the way. Shoot, what's today again? Damn, it's Tuesday, she has volleyball practice today. Well, I certainly can't go to school, who would be home? Heather, I'll go to Heathers I know she's home. But, if I do that then Mel's gonna be pissed at me for not telling her first, oh the crap we teenagers must deal with.

I guess I'll head back home then. I was walking back down Pennington Ave., which is one street over from mine, and I was overcome with such sadness and immediately started missing mom. It's not that I didn't want dad happy, I just didn't want to have to move. I am almost fourteen and I don't want to have to start my life over in high school. Maybe if I explain everything to them about how I feel, maybe we won't move. Wishful thinking, I know.

I saw the house as soon as I rounded the cross streets and knew that I wouldn't be looking at it forever like I planned. I'll have to call my cousins who live in Chester County in Pennsylvania, which I have no idea where that is, and ask about the area and what they think. It would be kind of cool to live in the same place that our favorite Baseball team plays, that might be the only positive thing I can think of.

So, maybe I was a little dramatic earlier, maybe I could've talked about it more instead of running out, but I am literally a teenage girl filled with angst, drama, anxiety, and lord knows what else is yet to come. I got to the house, and walked in hoping everyone would just forget about my outburst and chalk it up as a hormonal thing.

"Hey, you're back!" Justin seriously was the coolest guy I knew and couldn't help but like him.

I nodded my head, "Yep."

I had no idea what else to say, I wanted to say yeah captain obvious, but I figured I probably made everyone mad enough already, so I won't press my luck.

I went back to the living room where everyone still was, and made myself known to everyone I was back, even though I'm sure they heard me.

"Hi, I'm back. Did I miss anything fun?"

I was so appreciative of the fact that both dad and Lucy knew that I was sorry for how I was acting earlier, and that they welcomed me into the conversation like nothing had happened. I knew damn well that dad would want to talk to me later about it, but they let me off the hook for now.

We all were ready for dinner now, after talking and hanging out as a family, which was nice. Dad and Lucy made reservations for *MacGregor's*, which the food was dynamite, for five but we wanted to walk so we left a little early to give us time to get there. The girls, like I said before, get a bit distracted on their way anywhere, so it was a necessary evil to leave a little early.

I turned back at one point and looked at my family, and I couldn't help but smile. It was something missing for a long time since mom, and it felt right. Was I thrilled about leaving here? No. Was I excited to be part of this family? Yes! You're damn right I was. We got to the restaurant, and sat down at the big corner table, one that I always wanted to sit at because it was always the big families that got to sit there. We were that family, finally!

This was a core memory for me, and I promised I would cherish it forever in my mind.

"So, where exactly will we live? Like in Philadelphia? You know I don't know much about it, we only go to Uncle Dave's like once every three years, so I don't remember much of the area."

Dad was shaking his head, "No, not in the city. A suburb outside. And most likely not where they live, it's a bit far from the museum. There are a bunch of small towns we can look at, we will make this decision as a family, as one unit. Now Letti, you will just be starting Junior year, George you'll be a sophomore, and the girls will be in elementary and middle school, so we will have to find an area that has a good education for all of those. We can't afford private schools, so we will do a lot of research on those. Maybe we can start this weekend. I can stop at the library and see what the Atlas has by way of maps."

Ugh, now I really had to tell Mel what was happening, I'll call when I get home later, then I'll tell everyone else. This was going to be big news for the town, and for my circle of friends. It was not going to be easy to have to say goodbye to everyone, but I knew it could be a good thing for all of us, a way for us to start as a new family together.

How do you start over in the middle of high school? I knew we still had until next year, but I had a feeling that it was going to fly by, so I needed to spend as much time with my friends as I could.

CHAPTER 9

As soon as we got home, I ran up to my room so I could call Mel and tell her everything. I knew it wasn't going to be easy to tell her, but since we were going away this coming weekend, I knew it was mondo important to tell her.

"Hi, is Mel there?" No one ever bothered to ask who it was when I called the Barr's, same when Mel called here.

"Hey, what up?"

I was still trying to figure out how to tell her.

"Yo! How was v-ball?"

She has been playing volleyball since we were in middle school, and she was good, she was back up Libero for Varsity, and Libero for JV.

"It was good, was practicing digging, and I think I messed up my wrist, but it's all good. What up with you?"

"Well, it's been a helluva day to say the least." Here goes, wish me luck.

"Ok, what's going on chickee?"

"I don't know how to say all of this so I'm just gonna say it. My dad and Lucy are getting married!"

Before I could say the bad part of the news, she was screaming into the phone with excitement.

"I knew it! Do you remember when I said a while ago that your dad and her would end up together? I was right! So why do you sound so bummed out, we were hoping for this. We were hoping for this right?"

I took a deep breath in and exhaled, "Yes, I am so happy for them. But that's not the part that's hard for me to say."

"Ok, so what is?"

"Well, we are moving." The phone went silent, I couldn't even hear her breathing on the other end.

"Mel, you there?"

"Yeah, I'm here."

Her voice was shaky and cracking, I knew she was crying and so was I.

"I know, I'm sad too. It's outside Philly, not sure where yet. Dad got a job offer at some museum, as the curator. So, we must start going up in the area to look around for a house, with a good school district they said."

I wanted to throw up, I felt sick to my stomach telling her this, I know this was not going to be easy for her either.

"Well, this is bull, I can't lose you. You can't move that far away. What am I going to do without you? We are supposed to do this whole high school thing together, and then college."

"I know, I know. I was so mad too, now I'm just sad."

"I don't even know what else to say. Like, how long? Did they say?"

"Probably over the summer, right before junior year starts, so we have some time still. I really would love it if you could come with us a few of the times when we go up there. You'll have your license by then too, so you'll be able to drive everyone up to hang out! So, we have to make sure that this next year is the best year ever. Plus, I know they will be ok with you guys coming with us to check out the places and the houses."

I was trying to think of the most positive things that could come of this, but we knew it was going to suck, a lot.

"Where are they thinking?" she asked.

"I have no idea. My dad said in the suburbs outside Philadelphia, but I don't know what that means. I only go to Uncle Dave's every once in a while, so who knows."

It went silent again, I knew she was sad and so was I. I didn't want to leave here; it was my home.

"Alright, well I gotta get off here and take a shower and do my homework, I'll see you tomorrow ok. Night."

"Ok, yep tomorrow. Night." After I hung up the phone I could see my dad in the doorway, not wanting to interrupt.

"Hey, kiddo. Was that Mel? How'd she take the news?"

I shook my head, "Not great. She seems mad right now. She's never gotten off the phone that fast before. It's not like I made this decision, it's not like I want to move away."

Dad could tell I was getting more upset just talking about it, so I guess he thought now would be the time to bring up my outburst earlier.

"I know this is bad timing, but I just wanted to check in with you and just see if you were as mad as you were earlier. Look, I know this is not ideal for you, or any of you, but this is a wonderful opportunity and in a lot of ways we can start over, start fresh. You can meet new people, one of us can bring you back down here anytime you want on the weekends. I'm sorry Letti. I truly am. And I hope you can forgive me one day."

He hugged me, and turned and walked out of my bedroom, closed the door behind him and I started to sob into my pillow. I felt as if a piece of my childhood walked out with him. I hated those types of nights, I've had them too many times in my life, especially before today. I knew it was going to be a bad night trying to sleep, so I just wrote my horror movie script ideas down. I tended to do that a lot to help me forget about the sad things. I had no real plot yet, just a bunch of ideas that were all different story lines, none of them jumped out at me saying "this is the one," but it helped me get tired, so I did that when I couldn't sleep.

My alarm was blaring in my ear, six-fifteen was always too early for me, but this morning was especially hard, not only did I not sleep well last night, but I have to face my best friend after what I had to tell her yesterday. Fun times for me. I quickly got dressed, ran down grabbed a banana and an oj, yelled to dad to have a wonderful day and started to head to school. The walk to school was peaceful for me most days, I loved watching the leaves on the trees change color during the fall, it was one of my favorite times of the year. It was usually mild during September and October here, and I made sure to soak it up for as long as I could.

I got to school before everyone else, and sat on the bench out front, dreading when they all got here. I wasn't sure if Mel would've said anything to anyone, or if she just got off the phone with me and that was it.

"Scarlet!" I was never happier to hear that voice!

"Mel!"

She was running up the stairs and hugged me so tight she almost knocked me over.

"So, I thought a lot about it last night, and this could be the best thing in the world. New boys, new place, new you. Like, ok I'm kinda jealous actually!"

"Hey girlies whatya talking about?" Jen asked.

Mel looked at me and I looked back panicked, I wasn't sure if here was the place to tell them, but I guess they will find out anyway. So, I told them the same thing, and they were all excited, bummed but excited for dad, me, Lucy, all of us. We promised we would meet after school so we could talk some more, everyone was going to come to my house, which was fine by me.

CHAPTER 10

When the final bell rang, I met Mel and Heather outside of my Bio class, they were across the hall in Spanish. We picked up Jen on the way down the hallway and met Gabriella outside on the stairs. I was going to miss this so much when we moved, I wanted to make sure I enjoyed every minute of us being able to spend time together. As we were walking down Freedom Lane, I saw Mrs. Greene outside in her garden, it took me off guard and I stopped walking. It was the first time I saw her since Rich left, it's been a while since I've seen him and honestly I don't miss him at all. I heard he has been home, but he never made an effort to contact me, so I moved on and obviously so did her.

"Letti, Mrs. Greene is out, you should go talk to her."

Lord knows I love Gab, but she had no idea how bad of an idea that was. Mel was shaking her head no, and the other two were oblivious to what was happening at first.

"I can't, I don't even know what I would say. And honestly, I don't want to open those old wounds. He hasn't called me in months, and I think that's for the best."

Gab leaned over and hugged me, she was such a sweetheart all the time, and she didn't mean anything by that.

We got to my house, and it looked like Lucy was there, and her trunk was open. We ran up to see if she needed help with anything.

"Hey Lucy, can we help with anything? We don't mind."

She seemed surprised and elated that we were there. There were a ton of boxes in her trunk and back seat.

"Oh, girls, that would be terrific if you wouldn't mind." We all grabbed a box, and brought it into the living room, until there wasn't any left.

"Thanks girls, can I make you some lemonade or popcorn?"

I shot a look at the girls, and of course they all said yes, "That would be awesome! If you don't mind?"

"Of course not, I offered silly! I'll bring them down as soon as they are done."

How did I get so lucky to end up with her as my future stepmom? I have heard so many horror stories about evil stepmoms, but she was not anything close to what other people dealt with. She really seemed to care for me and my sisters, and really love my dad.

While we all sat downstairs gossiping, talking about the future, boys, what we were going out as for Halloween next week, Lucy came down with lemonade, popcorn, chips, and brownies. We all thanked her and continued with our teenage girl talk. These memories were ones that I knew would stay with me when I was having a tough time in my new life, the ones that would get me through everything. These were my best friends, and it made me so sad thinking about leaving them. I was sitting there and could hear the girls running into the house from school, and I realized I never even bothered to see how they were taking all this news.

I will make sure I check in with them tonight at bedtime. The girls were getting ready to leave so we could all get ready for dinner, homework, and bed. I think we were having meat-loaf, mashed potatoes, corn on the cob, gravy, and brownies. I loved the fact that we would have more home-cooked meals, since Lucy and Justin were good cooks. I think Justin was planning on looking into some schools up north when we started our search for the next Adams house.

As the months went by, we took a bunch of visits up to Pa. We went to some nice areas; I think they were a little too nice for us, but Dad and Lucy disagreed. We looked at houses in Carriage Ford, Eslin, Conrad, some places I couldn't pronounce but they were nice too, so many nice places, we really liked Weston, all of us agreed that this could be the place, which was rare because one of us found something we didn't like about the other places. But Weston seemed to be it.

I asked dad if I could bring the girls with us next time so they could see it too, but he said that we should wait until we have a house first so they can stay somewhere and enjoy time with me, which made sense, I guess.

I forgot to mention a few of the holidays, nothing big happened during them but I wanna talk about my Halloween costume, my fifteenth birthday and Thanksgiving. Halloween we were famous girl band members. We went as the Bangles, yep, I know there were four of them and five of us. Jen refused to dress up like that, so she went as a softball player. Not very original for her, since she has been playing softball since the womb, and has about fifteen different uniforms.

My fifteenth birthday was boring, nothing big this year and no boyfriend, but we had a cake that Justin made and was delish, and dad made dinner. Lucy and I were going to get my hair done that weekend, and me and my sisters went to rent the *Sandlot* on VHS since it was finally at blockbuster and had a sleepover with my girls. It was a good birthday.

Thanksgiving was up next, which was nice it was the first time we had a full-blown dinner for turkey day since mom passed. We had everything from the turkey to the cranberry sauce, to homemade rolls. It was awesome.

Christmas at the house was sad, we knew it was the last one here, so dad and Lucy went overboard with decorating, the girls loved it, I did too secretly. It was the fourth Christmas without my mom, and it wasn't any easier this year as it was the past three, the only difference was the people that were with us. It was nice having them here. The holiday break was filled with family from both sides, my parents, and now Lucy's.

My grandparents seemed to like her, but my mom-mom and pop, my mom's parents, were leery as expected. But I think they saw how happy we were and how much the girls and I liked her, that they gave her a chance.

After New Year's we all knew it was time to decide on a house up in Weston, and we thought we had found the most perfect one, it was on Oak Lane, and was owned by an old married couple.

Like super old, at least in their fifties it seemed after dad described them. They didn't have any children and the house was gigantic and getting too big for them to care for. So, I am thinking they are old. We went up to look at it around Valentine's Day, which was also dad and Lucy's anniversary, and it was big they weren't kidding.

It had a creek that ran behind it, that apparently, we would own to the middle of that, a monstrous back yard, two farms that were across the creek we wouldn't own but super cool. It almost seemed like it was a part of a town that time forgot. It was perfect! We knew that 1995 was going to be a great year for us. I was excited, nervous, sad, every emotion possible all wrapped up inside.

CHAPTER 11

I couldn't wait to tell the girls about this place, and how big the house is. I was quite sure this was going to be the house that dad and Lucy were going to put a bid on, I knew nothing about real estate so I'm going on what I hear them say. Dad said we could take the ride up there in a few weeks, so I have to make sure I plan it with the girls as soon as possible. About a week after we were up there dad and Lucy told us that the couple accepted their bid, but they couldn't move into the mobile home they purchased, so probably around May or June, which was perfect in my opinion because that gives me time to hang out with my friends a bit longer.

We went up during spring break of my sophomore year, April 1995. It was a little cooler this time, one; because I had my girls with me, and two; dad took us to one of the local spots for lunch. Apparently, you could get the best sandwich around, so that was enough for dad to want to go. When we walked in it was not exactly what we expected, it smelled fantastic, the fries and cheesesteaks wafted through the air, it was packed. I think we all thought it was going to be some fancier place, but it was just like our sandwich shops back home, that was comforting.

Everyone looked at us when we walked in, it felt like they knew we were from out of town, but they were friendly. We ordered and sat down at two of the tables, grabbed some sodas from the fridge, and waited for our food. A cute boy brought out some of our food, followed by an older woman with the rest. One bite and I was hooked, the fries were crispy and salty, the cheesesteak was nothing like home. It was overloaded with meat, literally falling out of my roll, which I absolutely should've gotten a small one not a large, what was I thinking. We all got cheesesteaks, mine was fried onion and ketchup, the onions made it taste greasier which was amazing!

"Uh, dad? I think I need to take the rest of mine home because I cannot finish this."

Everyone laughed because no one could finish theirs. Dad walked up to the counter to get some to go boxes and struck up a conversation with the owner. He called me up to meet him, "Scarlet, come over, I want to introduce you."

I got up and said hi to a gentleman standing waiting for his order, and he nodded his head at me.

"Scarlet, this is the owner of the shop, Mel."

I couldn't help but laugh and look at my Mel behind me, "Hi, nice to meet you."

"You as well. Your dad tells me you guys are moving here from Maryland. That's great. What do you think of it so far?"

I wasn't sure how to answer that because I have only driven through some areas and other than the house this is only building, I have been in.

"It seems nice enough." I know I looked totally awkward standing there while they continued to talk.

"Scarlet, what grade are you in?" Odd question from an old guy.

"Er, I am a sophomore."

His eyes lit up, "Great my son, Chris, is a junior. He's back on the fryer today. Let me grab him so at least you'll know one person when you move up here."

Ugh, here we go. I was not the best at meeting new people, especially boys.

I turned around and shot a look at the girls, like please save me. When I turned back around, I saw this super cute boy coming toward me, and I thought my heart stopped for a second.

"Scarlet, this is my youngest son Chris, Chris this is Scarlet. She's moving here from Maryland with her family in the summer."

I could feel the girls staring at him through me, and I had to take a minute to catch my breath.

"Nice to meet you. The fries were good."

Oh my god, you dumbass, really that's what you say the first time you meet him. Can I just crawl back into my hole now.

He smiled and chuckled as he responded "I'm glad you approve. I'll be seeing you again, I'm sure. Gotta get back to making good fries."

He winked as he said that and walked away after shaking my dad's hand.

Someone please press rewind that so I cannot say that again. I walked back over and put my hands over my face and was dying of embarrassment.

"Who was that?" Jen of all people asked who he was, we never thought she paid attention to boys until just now.

"That's the owner's youngest son, Chris. I just told him that he made good fries."

Shaking my head, the entire time I recapped the conversation, which was minimal because of me and my foot in mouth syndrome.

"And then he responded with "I gotta get back to making really good fries," like what? Why? Why did I say that?"

There was a roar of laughter from them, which of course everyone, yep including Chris, turned, and looked at us. I wanted to run out of there like *Flo-Jo*. When we were done there, we went to the house so the girls could finally see it.

Dad had planned with the old couple for us to explore the property more so the girls could see it firsthand and not from the van.

It was spring in PA, and there were daffodils everywhere. We pulled up in the driveway and the girls ooohed and ahhhed over the house, as we all got out of the van.

"Dude, this house is huge. I mean which is a good thing because there's a lot of you guys."

Heather seemed a little envious when she said that, but I knew if I asked her, she would deny it and just compare it to her mansion.

I know it may come off as me not liking her, but I promise I do she just can just be a little too competitive at life sometimes, and it gets a little old after a while.

Dad walked up and knocked at the door, which was weird because we all had doorbells back home. The woman came to the door, and she welcomed us in immediately.

"Thank you so much again Mrs. Lawrence, we really appreciate you taking the time for us to come by."

She smiled, the creases on her cheeks got deeper and longer, her eyes smaller and her nose wrinkled up, "The pleasure is all mine. Mr. Lawrence is out back; He has something he wanted to show Miss. Scarlet."

She looked down at me and smiled, she had such a grandma feeling and it made us all at ease. Mr. Lawrence was a large man, his hands were like the size of bear paws, his feet were like bigfoot, he was just large and kind of scary.

We went out back, down the rickety stairs of the deck, through the gate which opened to the back yard. It was breathtaking back there, a willow tree stood in the center of the yard, surrounded by many tall, strong oak trees. I assume that's how they came up with the name of the street. The breeze made the willow branches move in unity with each other, it was most definitely my favorite place so far here. Oak Lane, huh, fitting.

I could see him standing by the creek bed, with a stick in his hand and throwing something with his free hand. I walked up to him, as I said hello, he turned and nodded at me.

"Hi Mr. Lawrence. Mrs. Lawrence said you wanted to show me something?" He stepped down a few steps and pointed to the water.

"You see this? This is where my daughter spent most of her time as a young girl drawing pictures of this beautiful space. I hope you find the peace here that she did."

I leaned over to see what he was talking about, and I could see this flatter rock popping out of the water. It looked like it was a seat and that it was just big enough to sit on it and think about life or draw like his daughter did. I have no idea why he wanted to show me, but I am glad he did. Knowing this was here made me look forward to coming back to spend some alone time at.

"Thanks, Mr. Lawrence, for showing me that. I will come here often, I know it."

The girls all loved the house, I showed them where my room would be, and of course everyone else's. It was a great memory for me, and I was excited at the idea of the girls being able to stay at the house, because my room was at the front of the house and was huge.

After about an hour and a half dad hollered and said we needed to head back. As we walked out of the house Mrs. Lawrence stopped me and said something that I didn't quite understand at that time, "Scarlet, your wish will come true. Maybe too soon though."

It was eerie at first when she said it, and it wouldn't be until later that it would be clear as to what she was talking about.

"Ok, well thank you Mrs. Lawrence. I'll see you later."

I walked out and down to the van and couldn't shake what she said. I didn't understand either, but it was something I thought about a lot afterward.

As we pulled away from the house, the sunlight bellowed through the willow tree out back as if it were glowing, it was the most beautiful thing I had ever seen, and suddenly, I started to cry and became filled with emotion. I thought about how much my mom would have loved it here, even though we wouldn't have had to move if my mom were here. Dad and Lucy picked the most perfect for us, it was old but had character. The willow tree was my favorite so far, even though I would quickly find many other things that would become my favorites.

CHAPTER 12

I didn't realize it was only an hour away from home, I thought it was hours. So, by the time we got home it was only a little after dinner. When we pulled up it was just getting dark out, and I asked the girls if they wanted to sleepover, Mel and Gabs were able to stay, but Jen and Heather both had to go home, they had a youth group thing early tomorrow morning. I could never get into the youth group; it was just not my thing. I asked my dad if we could order pizzas and wings for dinner, and he called about twenty minutes later. I couldn't help but think about what Mrs. Lawrence said to me, and how I still don't understand it, maybe I'm not meant to right now. I was excited about the idea of going back to that thinking rock, that's what I am going to call it, and do a lot of my writing there. It was very private and beautiful, there were birds everywhere, some sang, some knocked, some screamed, it was nothing I have ever seen or heard before in my life.

Lucy was anxious to hear how everything went, we told her everything. I mean everything, Mel was first to tell her about the boy from DiMada's and the entire embarrassing moment between him and I. I didn't tell anyone about the thing with Mr. Lawrence, I guess I felt it was private and only for me. I asked how their day was while we were gone, and Lucy had a busy day.

"Well, funny you ask, I ran into Judy Greene while you all were gone. I took the girls to the park, and we happened to run into her walking her dogs. It was a little awkward at first.

I told her how we were selling and where we were going. And you know, she said the most interesting thing to me."

I was hanging on her every word at this point, "Ok, what was that?"

Lucy sat down after pouring a glass of lemonade, "When I told her the area, she said Rich, her son, goes to a school somewhere not too far from there. Letti, do you know where he goes?"

You could have heard a pin drop in the room or knock me over with a feather.

"Uh, nope. I had no idea it was even in another state. Apparently, there's a lot I didn't know. I am so totally cool with that too."

Everyone knew I was upset; I mean of course I was, but a part of me didn't care to hear anything about him. At least I knew now to avoid him if I ever saw him again, and since I can't drive, and neither can he I'm certain the odds of me running into him are slim and none. I guess now I have to find out where he is going to school and stay clear of that area. The doorbell rang and I thanked God it was the pizza delivery guy, we were starving.

The girls ran down, and George came up from the basement, I wasn't sure where Justin was.

"Where's Justin?" Lucy was getting the plates together for dinner and answered from the kitchen "He's on a date."

We all looked at each ither shocked, my mouth dropped, and Lucy laughed, "You catching flies Letti, ha-ha?"

We all always say things like that when people do silly things, like when your mouth is wide open someone would say are you catching flies, or if you looked deep in thought someone would say penny for your thoughts, you know things like that.

"WITH WHO?" I couldn't help but practically yell that out.

"Some girl in one of his culinary classes, they are partners in class and apparently are hitting it off he said."

"Well, that's exciting news for him. I am so glad to hear that because he's always whining about not meeting anyone, and I always tell him he won't meet anyone when he's sitting here."

After dinner Lucy took us to *Blockbuster* to see what new movies were out for rent. I loved going there, there was always something new to rent and we typically ended up coming home with a movie of some sort. When we pulled up, we could see that it was packed, typical for a Saturday night, and we sprinted in the doors, I immediately went toward the horror section, Mel when to comedy, and Gabs went to romance yuck. George was looking at some documentary true crime movies, I can safely say I have never been to that section.

"Yoooo, *My Girl 2* is finally available, can we get that? Dude, you know I've been dying to watch it."

Mel loved comedy and I don't think I was in the mood for horror, so I was on board for that, "Yeah, I'm cool with that. Gabs you good with that?"

"Sure, I am perfectly content with that."

Gabriella had the sweetest voice, almost high pitched, but didn't hurt your ears when she talked. She was the nicest person anyone could meet and a loyal friend. She was most definitely my second-best friend, for sure. I knew with the friends that I had I would have them for life, no matter what. I could be an hour away or a plane trip away, it wouldn't matter to them, and it wouldn't matter to me. It did make me wonder how it was going to be for me at the new school and meeting people. I never had a problem with that, but I also never had too either. Like I said before, I've known everyone in my schools since we were little, so this was very new and very scary.

We grabbed candy and popcorn as we were checking out, and sprinted back out to the van, "Last one to the van gets the floor tonight."

I yelled to Mel and Gabs, and we ran even faster, Mel got to the van first, then Gabs, then me. I may or may not have let them win, and no one will ever know.

Once we got home, we went downstairs to get ready for our sleepover, and even George asked to watch with us. I think he liked Gabriella, but he never said so he just acted like it. He never cared about hanging out with us unless she was there. It was kind of cute, and weird, but he was awkward and so was she, so it might've just worked for them if we weren't moving an hour away. We started the movie and so far, it was ok, not really my type but it was cute. I did love *Jamie Lee Curtis*, since she is the scream queen and the leading role in *Halloween*, among other movies, so I figured I'd give it a chance, and *Dan Akroyd* was in it and he plays in *Ghostbusters*, so I'm sure it's going to be just fine, even though the first one made me cry more so because it was just a year after my mom died that I watched it.

"So, what'd ya's think?"

I was almost asleep when Mel asked us that, and it startled me awake, "Oh, um, it was ok. It wasn't as good as the first one, but that boy was super cute in it."

Mel and George both shook their heads when I said that I don't know why they were surprised I said those comments often when a cute boy was on tv. We could hear the door open upstairs, and knew Justin was home from his date, secretly we were all waiting to hear about it. He came down and sat with us and made small talk.

"Um, excuse me Justin, I don't want to do small talk. I wanna hear about your date" I said with the cheesiest grin I could muster up.

"Ok, that face isn't terrifying at all. It was nice, she may be a little too nice for me. I think maybe we will just stick with being partners in class."

What a disappointment for him. "Well, that sucks, but c'est la vie, right? Right!"

"What were you guys watching?" I rolled my eyes, "*My Girl 2.*"

"Oh, ok. I know that wasn't your choice. Mel?" Mel put her head down and we all started laughing, "Guilty."

We stayed up late that night, talking about the day and what the future looks like. How scared and upset I was about leaving them and knowing that in a few months I won't be able to do this as much anymore.

Gab said something that broke my heart, "Letti, I am afraid that you're going to meet all these new people and forget about us back home. I mean, I know it won't be your home anymore, but to us it will be. What if that happens?"

They both got on the floor with me now, and we embraced in a big bear hug, "That's never gonna happen, I promise. You are all my sisters, and I can never live without you all. You're all so important to me."

It was a wholesome moment we shared, and we all knew that would be one of the last times we would have this with just the three of us. We all slept on the floor that night, not sure if it was on purpose or we just cried ourselves to sleep there, whatever it was it was a comfort that I would miss sooner rather than later.

<h1 style="text-align: center;">CHAPTER 13</h1>

Yep, I am fast forwarding to the week of us moving. Why? Because not a whole lot happened over the past month and a half, and the story is just about to get good!

Sunday, June 12th, 1995, was the first day that the moving trucks showed up at the house. We all knew now was the time we really had to start getting our stuff packed. It hit me like a ton of bricks that this was the last week I would be living here, the place I grew up in. Where I learned how to tie my shoes, ride my bike, kiss a boy, kiss a girl, skip stones along the water. I learned so much here, I was kind of excited for what I would learn in PA.

"Dad, am I supposed to use the yellow markers or the orange? I don't remember what you and Lucy told me."

Lucy was so organized, which was awesome for sure, but I forgot a lot of what they told me for color coding stuff, especially mine.

"You have orange, Avery has yellow, Vi has pink, George has green, Justin has blue, I have black, and Lucy has red. Got that?"

What the heck colors were for everything else then?

"Yep, got it." Everyone else yelled too that they "got it." Lucky for us school was already out for the summer, so we had a lot of help from our friends and neighbors.

All my girlfriends were here to help, and yeah it was hard, but we made the best of it. I ate so much take-out this week, I think I gained like ten pounds. We had gone up to the house a few times over the past two weeks, and I met a few of the neighborhood kids, who all seemed nice, just a little different than my friends here.

When the girls were over on Wednesday it was basically the topic of conversation, "I dunno how they are different, they just are. They seem like they are fast, like they talk fast with this weird accent, they move fast, I don't know how to explain it."

Mel didn't seem phased at all by the stories, mainly because she was sad, she just didn't say anything about it.

"Oh, I mean we are more laid back here, I guess. I am sure you'll get the hang of it Scarlet."

Gabs being the sweetheart of the group was always trying to find the positive in every situation, it was one of my favorite things about her.

We had one last big sleepover Thursday night along with everyone else in the house. It was packed, and I thought dad and Lucy were going to have a nervous breakdown because of the number of kids in the house. There were kids sleeping everywhere, it was funny.

I'll admit I was emotional that night, I knew it would be different after this. It sucked, but I knew it was inevitable. I don't think I realized how nervous I was until right now. My friends were so amazing, and everything you could imagine being at fourteen years old. We kept telling stories, and remembering fun things we did.

"Jen, do you remember when you broke your arm on the monkey bars in third grade. We all thought you were going to have to get it cut off, because none of us had broken anything up until then," Mel retold the story and Heather interrupted, "Oh shoot, yeah. And when you came to school the next day, we thought they put a fake arm on you. God we were dumb."

"I don't think we were "dumb" Heather; I think we just didn't have a clue." Heather just sometimes didn't know how to talk to us, I mean really none of us did, but she just put her foot in her mouth often. I am sure you have a friend, or two like that, right? Either way, I am gonna miss the hell out of them. As we sat there reminiscing, I couldn't help but think of the good times I had with my mom living here.

Oh, damn, we're leaving mom. In that moment I felt sick to my stomach, thinking about mom being here without us. Will we come back to see her on her birthday, for the holidays? We always go to see her, and I even walk there sometimes. Oh, no, I don't know if I can do this. Who will put flowers on her grave when it's her birthday? Who will visit her on the holidays? Yeah, of course my family will go like they always do, but we have made this a tradition since she passed away. So what now?

"I'll be back in a minute" I knew I needed to talk to dad about this, because I was even more sad now and having a lot of doubts about this. The thought of leaving my mom here was breaking my heart, it started to bring up the pain that I felt when we lost her. I didn't want to leave her behind.

I was walking up the stairs and the railing came off the wall, which of course I fell backward because I lost my balance and landed on my hand. My mom asked my dad for years to fix the railing, and the last night we are here this is what happens. It was a sign from her, but I didn't know it was supposed to a sign or a warning.

When I hit the ground I heard a crack, and the worst pain I've ever felt in my life, at least physically. Everyone heard me, it was so loud, the fall, the crack, me screaming in pain.

"Oh my god, Letti, what the hell? Are you ok?"

Like a flash Mel and Heather stood up and rushed over to me, I could hear dad and Lucy running to get to the door to come down, and they hurried down the stairs.

"Letti, honey, what happened? Someone get the car ready, we're going to the ER." Dad was usually a little over-dramatic when we got hurt, but this was the one time I agreed with him. I knew it was broken. I just knew it. Man, this sucks so bad, what a way to start off my new life. I hate this.

Justin got the car ready and helped dad get me up the stairs, which I was ok if I didn't move my arm. Thank God it's my left arm because I'm a righty.

"Dad, I got it. It'll be easier if I go up by myself. Thank you,"

I wanted to make sure he knew I was ok, but I was in so much pain. Everyone in the house was in the living room and hallway now wishing me good luck and hoping that it wasn't broken.

"Thanks everyone. I'm sorry for ruining the last night you're all here. I am so mad."

My whole life when I get hurt, I get sad and then mad afterward, not sure why but I just do. I remember mom telling me this story from when I was six. I was sledding out back of the house, we have a slope in back that you can sled down, and it was a lot icier than I thought and the sled kept going as I came down and I slammed face first into the walnut tree. I broke my nose, and lost three of my teeth, which luckily, were baby teeth. Oh, and speaking of that, you know how they say kids have that "awkward time" in their childhood? Yeah, well I hit mine at seven, when I had adult front teeth, two on top and one on bottom, and my class picture I didn't smile because I didn't want anyone to see my mouth.

It was so embarrassing, just like this but now I must not only rely on everyone around me to do everything for me, but I also must move to an entirely new state, with strange people, new places, ugh why me? As we drove to the hospital dad kept asking me questions about how I was doing and such. I just kept telling him I was fine but wasn't looking forward to the outcome of this.

"Hi, I need to have my daughter seen. I am pretty sure she broke her arm, hand, or wrist. I am not sure."

That was the first time I heard Lucy refer to me as her daughter. I was taken back by it and wasn't sure how I felt at first. My dad looked at me concerned on how I was going to react to her saying that, but honestly after a few minutes of letting it sink in, it wasn't that bad. I have always felt that Lucy was a great mom and good person, especially for my dad. So, it could've been worse right?

"Hi, I am Jackie, your triage nurse. I am just going to get some vital signs from you and get your side of what happened. Ok. Mom, dad, if you both want to come back to this little room back here, we can get that all done and then come back out and wait to get sent back. Sound good?"

I looked at both assuring them it was ok. "Ok!" We all walked back to the room, it was small, but I wasn't staying there, I told the nurse what happened and what my pain level was currently. That was it. She walked us back out to the waiting room until someone came to get us.

Before Dad even was able to sit down, another nurse called my name as he came out of the electronic doors, "Scarlet Adams,"

"Right here,"

"Great come on back."

We all walked back, and we were in room ten, which ironically was mom's favorite number.

"Ten, my lucky number," Lucy smiled as she said it. I smiled too, of course it is. I knew my mom was sending me signs all the time that Lucy was right for all of us, and this was just another thing to add to the list.

"Knock knock."

A head peeked around the door, "Hi, I am here to take you down for x-rays. Ok?"

Finally, I cannot take this pain anymore.

Walking down the hall there were other sick kids, or something was wrong with them anyway, and when we got to the x-ray room, I knew my sigh of relief was heard by everyone. Whatever, I didn't care, I just wanted it cast.

"Hi, Scarlet. So, I want to get x-rays of your left arm, all the way from the hand to the shoulder. I have to maneuver it to some positions that will absolutely be uncomfortable and may hurt. I am sorry if that happens, I just have to make sure we get as many accurate pictures as possible. Ok?"

I nodded my head and let her do what needed to be done. She was so right, it hurt. Finally, after we were done, she took me back to the room and I was more dramatic than I should have been, I didn't care I was over this.

"How'd that go kiddo?" I know my dad knew that was not a walk in the park.

"Umm, well that sucked a lot. But we're pretty sure it's broken. Just don't know where exactly yet."

It wasn't long before the doctor came in with my results, "Hi there. I'm Dr. Long. Looks like we have some breakage going on in our left wrist and hand, huh?"

As soon as she said that my head dropped down, I became more depressed.

"Great." I could not have been more sarcastic, and everyone in the room knew I was frustrated.

"I know, I'm sorry. We will get it cast up for you and get you home as soon as possible ok. Shouldn't be too long."

Sitting here with my dad and Lucy made me miss my mom a lot.

I could hear her saying "Now Scarlet, be nice to the doctor ok, they are just doing their job, And, Joe, I have told you too many times to get that railing fixed."

Mom, I miss you.

Now, don't get me wrong I loved having Lucy, and she taught me how to do my makeup, so I don't look like a clown, and how to dye my hair from the box. She wasn't trying to replace my mom; she was just a good addition to our family.

Sitting there waiting patiently to get my cast on, I watched my dad with Lucy, and he was so happy. I know I've said it before, but I am so glad he found her so when I am no longer in the house and I am off at college or get married or whatever, he won't be alone and my sisters will have a "post mom", I don't like how step-mom sounds because it comes with such a stigma so I'm making up the word "post mom", that obviously means the mom that comes after the first mom but is super nice, and takes you places, and treats you like you're one of her kids. You're welcome!

About ten minutes went by and, two nurses and the doctor came in so we could get started on this casting deal. If this part hurts, I'm gonna cry again. They were bringing in all kinds of tools, and talking fast, all I could think of was that were going to cut off a limb, ha!

"Ok, Scarlet we are going to get you all set up so we can get you out of here. I'm just going to need you to sit very still and lean back on the pillows. We will talk to you through the entire process, and let you know what we are doing when we do something. Ok. You ready?"

I know I wasn't, but I had no choice, "Yep, let's do this."

I am going to spare you the details of how this all went down, I'm pretty sure you know how the cast goes on and that whole thing. When they were done, we were able to go home, thank God, and I could finish my last night with my friends. Now, I only had to figure how I was going to navigate with this stupid cast on. Ugh, well maybe dad will finally fix the railing since someone finally got hurt.

CHAPTER 14

Everyone was waiting for me when we got home, I could see them staring out the window in the family room when we pulled into the driveway. Vi and Avery sprinted to the door to greet me with huge smiles on their faces, cheering and jumping for joy that I came home. I smiled when I saw them, of course, while dad and Lucy laughed at their silliness.

"Woo Hoo, yay! We're so happy you're ok Letti! We were all worried. Your cast looks cool, can I sign it first?"

Avery was inquisitive of the cast on my arm, and she twisted just a little too far and it caused a sharp pain to shoot up to my shoulder, unfortunately I winced and let out a painful cry.

"Avery be careful sweetheart, we don't want to cause any more pain, ok kiddo?"

Dad was trying not to sound stern, but he knew how much pain I was already in, and I honestly appreciated it. Avery looked as if she were about to cry and ran off up the stairs up to her room. I could hear her little voice crying as she ran up there and I knew I needed to go check on her.

"I'll be right back."

I am pretty sure everyone knew where I was going, and I think they all expected it. I saw her door was closed and I tapped on it and waited to hear her respond. She didn't say anything, but I could hear her whimpers through the door. I opened it and saw her sitting on the floor on the other side of her bed. Her little head was just peaking above the mattress, her blonde hair shining from her little desk lamp.

"Hey little sister, can I come in?"

No response, so I went in anyway and sat by her. Her face was buried in her arms that were crossed over her knees, and she was so sad.

"Avery don't be sad. Dad was just looking out for my arm since it's still fragile. You didn't do anything wrong."

I tried to nudge her to get her to pop her head up, but she just nudged me back and shrugged me off.

"Ok, well if you don't want to talk to me then I will leave you alone. But that means you'll miss out on being the first one to sign it" I didn't know what else to say to get her to respond at all.

As soon as I said that she started to pop her face out of her arms and looked at me from the side.

"Wait."

Finally, I didn't want to do it that way, but I knew she would just be so sad all night, and I really didn't want anyone else to sign it first.

"There you are! You wanna sign it?"

Avery exposed her whole face, and she broke my heart with how sad she was, I wasn't sure if it was just from the cast thing or if it was something else that she didn't want to talk about right now. I certainly know how that feels.

"You got a marker?"

Before I could even finish, she was already over in her art stuff looking for the perfect color. She skipped back over to me, now with a big smile on her face, even with her eyes red still and her nose sniffling with two markers in her hand.

"Ok, what do we got?"

She opened her hand and showed me the colors she picked, green which is my favorite, and purple which was hers. It was awesome she picked that.

She opened the purple one first, "Letti, can you put your arm on the bed, so I don't hurt you again?"

Her little voice was so sweet, and sincere, of course I piled up her pillows and put my arm on them on the bed to make it easy for her to write. Her facial expressions had me laughing, she was so focused, and her tongue was sticking out of the bottom part of her mouth. She smiled when she heard me laughing. I put my arm on the pillows, and she wrote her name as gently as possible, and was so proud when she was done.

"All done, Letti! Thanks for letting me be the first."

She leaned into me and hugged me so tight; it almost made me cry and made me realize I don't hug them enough.

"You're the best, Avery!"

You would've thought I just told her she was my favorite, but Vi would be heartbroken if I said that so I made sure I didn't say anything too crazy as to not start a fight between the two of them. We walked back downstairs, and everyone was standing around the kitchen, and all cheered when they saw me. Mel practically jumped on me. She was so excited, and of course dad almost had a conniption, but I was fine, and I half expected it anyways.

They all signed my cast, of course the girls were obnoxious and wrote so big there wasn't much room for many other names, but it was whatever since I didn't know anyone yet where we were going. Which, ugh, we still must do that this weekend. I never got to talk to dad about what was on my mind, and I knew at this point it wasn't worth it, but I would talk to him about him eventually.

CHAPTER 15

We all went to bed, again, knowing that tomorrow was going to change so many lives. We all knew it would be one of the last times we would do this, and it was a super sad reality for me, and I think it was for everyone else too.

"Welcome to Pennsylvania. Pursue your happiness," Avery interrupted the license plate game that we were playing to read our new states sign.

"Yeah! Are you so excited Av? I know I am!" I wasn't as excited, but I wanted the girls to see that it was ok, and we were all going to be ok because we were in this together.

Behind us were Justin and George in one moving truck, and Dad in the other. Us girls ended up all together, thank God. I had no idea how much further we had to go, but it felt like we were driving for hours, at least the girls started the license plate game, so that helped time go by. The coolest one we saw was from Quebec, I think that was the farthest one too. Lucy and I got to catch up a lot on if I had spoken to Rich at all since, he was at school. Of course, I haven't, and I didn't care to either. That's a big fat lie, I hated that he never wrote back to me and never visited when he was home a few weeks ago. I guess I just wasn't for him.

I am so hoping that I will meet cool new kids, and maybe even a boy or two. I was so anxious about how things were going to be for me, and the girls of course, but they were so young and could bounce back fast. I was a teenager, and these were the most crucial times of my life so far.

"I think we are about twenty minutes from our exit," Lucy smiled and was trying to hold back her excitement, but she wasn't doing a great job!

The girls squealed in the back seat and started counting down the time, which I would've rather gone back to the license plate game.

"Hey Lucy?" I know she heard the sadness in my voice, so her reply was very soft and low, "Yes Scarlet?"

I was staring out the window and a tear started to fall down my check, "Do you think dad will take us back to visit mom on special days?"

Lucy's expression went to sadness immediately, and it was like a lightbulb went off that neither of them even talked to us about that.

"Oh, Letti. Yes of course, I will take you, your dad will. Justin can. Whenever you want. I am so sorry we didn't even talk about that. I feel terrible."

I knew she was sincere in her response, and I was satisfied with that, sad, but that was all I wanted to hear. Things started to look familiar now as we drove on the backroads leading to the house. We passed by DiMadas, *McDonald's*, some convenience stores, pharmacies, and *Acme*.

"Ok, we're not too far now. Are you girls ready for this?"

The girls had not gotten to see the house yet, so their excitement was highly anticipated by all of us, because we knew how genuine it was going to be.

"Ok, we are coming down the hill, so you guys gotta close your eyes real tight, ok? Don't open them until I tell you to!"

As we pulled into the driveway, the realtor was waiting for us outside and waving as we pulled up.

"Ok, ready. On the count of three open them. ONE! TWO! THREE!"

Dad was at the car and me and Lucy looked back to see their reactions. Their eyes were wide, and their mouths dropped in awe. Lucy and Dad, we're obviously so happy the girls reacted the way they did, and honestly so was I.

"Welp, here we are. Home sweet home! What do you think girls?"

The girls couldn't open the doors fast enough to get out and go exploring. The house was bigger than I remembered it being, the air was so fragrant with flowers, maple trees, and honeysuckle. The sky was a different shade of blue than I was used to, kind of like the color of a blue jay, it was so beautiful. There were farms around, horse farms mainly, but you could hear a few cows, and some chickens, it was very different than Maryland, at least where I grew up anyway.

Being here I knew would be different, but I wanted to make the best of it and was hopeful that it would be an easy adjust-ment. It was difficult having a cast on, and trying to take my stuff to my room, which was awesome because I had my own bathroom connected to it. The main floor had a kitchen, living room, game room, kitchen nook (whatever that is), full master bathroom and the master bedroom that had French doors which lead to a walk out porch where you could see the woods and the creek that ran along the property. That was where Lucy and dad would be.

There was a huge laundry room and I guess it was like an office or whatever you wanted it to be. Then you come upstairs to the second floor, and there is another kitchen, living room, two bathrooms, two bedrooms. One was mine and the other the girls were sharing. There was a cool door though that was between our walls, so the girls could come in anytime they needed me. The third floor had a bathroom shared between two bedrooms, which were gigantic. One had a library that was set into the wall, and both had secret crawl spaces. Justin and George had the upstairs, and I'll admit they were cool rooms. The windows were so big, like I didn't even know that they made them that big.

At the top of the stairs was a small door, which accessed the crawl space behind the bedrooms, the girls loved the idea of a secret room. When I got to my room, there was a note on the windowsill. I had a feeling it was from Mr. Lawrence; I couldn't wait to open it.

The window was different this time though. I sat down on the seat and opened the letter. I was right, it was from him, and only for me to read.

Miss. Scarlet,

I hope your trip up was a safe one, and that you are your family are settling in well. I left a few things for you, which are in the back shed with your name on them. I built you this window seat because my daughter always wanted one, and I finally had the time to build one. I hope you enjoy it as much as you enjoy the things I left for you, and the secret place I showed you. I don't have many words of advice for you, but my wife, Florence, did. She says "be careful who you trust. Look for signs and listen when you hear things." I don't know what any of that means, but she was adamant that I tell you those things.

Ron Lawrence

Ok, well that couldn't have been creepier, ok actually yeah it probably could've been. This seat is awesome though. Weston was not like home, even though this was home now, the sounds, smells, bugs, everything. I was hoping the people weren't so different than my people back home. I say that often, so get used to it, just kidding about the whole get used to it bit. Our new home really was beautiful, it was older than the one in Maryland, but it had a lot of character. It had a large barn door that led under the porch, which I have not explored yet. It was white, with black everything: roof, shutters, siding, mailbox, you name it. We had so many trees, which was comforting because we had so many back home.

We all brought in as much as we could, but we were all exhausted from the packing, the night before, the drive. Dad ordered sandwiches from DiMada's. Justin and I went with him to pick it up when it was ready. He was there, and still cute as before.

"Hey Joe! Scarlet! I don't believe we have met yet. I'm Mel, I own this joint!" he was referring to Justin.

Justin walked over and shook his hand and introduced himself, "How do you do sir? My name is Justin."

I saw Chris in the back again, and he was looking to see who his dad was talking to.

"Oh hey, Scarlet, right?" I shook my head, and Justin gave me a side eye and smirked.

"Yep. Chris, right?"

He smiled, and his eyes got bluer, "That's right. Good to see you again! Am I making you good fries today? Or just ok ones?"

I knew he was joking, but it was mortifying, especially now that Justin was here to witness the moment. Of course, the jerk started laughing uncontrollably and I wanted to punch him.

"No fries for me today, thanks though."

Chris started to walk away, "Ok, well next time then."

I just nodded my head, since I had no words for what was happening.

We got to the car with the food, and I waited for it, Justin got in and there it is "Good fries huh? I thought you were joking before when you told us about that. I can't believe it happened for real. Did the girls laugh as much as I did? I can imagine Mel, the smartass she is, was falling on the floor laughing."

I just rolled my eyes and stared out the window.

"Letti, you know I'm just kidding right?"

Of course, I knew that it still sucked hearing it and seeing just how embarrassing it was for me. "Yeah, I know you are. He does make good fries though!" There was a rumble of laughter now coming from inside the car.

The first night in the house both girls ended up in bed with me, they feared being in a new place. I tried to explain that it would be ok, but I could understand how they felt. It was eerie for me too that night. There were strange noises, I don't know if it was just the house settling since it was over one hundred years old, and apparently part of the original hospital for one of the sawmills that used to be here.

Dad said all the old houses around here were all built around the same time and where people who ran and worked in the mills lived. Cool? Yes, but creepy at the same time. Dad told us about some stories at dinner tonight that Mr. and Mrs. Lawrence told him during the time he came up here. When he had stuff to do for his new job he stayed here, they were nice enough to let him stay so he didn't have to pay for a hotel. The infirmary part was cool, and there was a beautiful old stone home across the street from us. The large stone house was the owner's house. Which made total sense, it was like the size of Heather's house. Literally was the size of mansion, and well-kept by the family. Dad said the family has been there for six generations, that's insane, but kind of cool.

Our house was big too, but the downstairs used to be a garage and the upstairs, where we live, was the original home. It was a long night, between the girls kicking me in the bed, and the noises, and my damn cast, sleep wasn't meant to be for me. Hopefully, I can sleep in the morning, after everyone else gets up, since I can't do much else anyway.

CHAPTER 16

The sun shined bright through the window, and bounced off the walls like a spotlight, it was almost blinding. The girls were up early, and I could hear them running in and out of the house and into their room, they were so loud. I guess I wasn't sleeping today. I got up and started unpacking some of the boxes that George and Justin were nice enough to bring in for me. Unpacking fifteen years of memories was not for the faint of heart, it was not easy, and I know if my mom were still here, we wouldn't even be in this situation. But I am here and now I must make the best of it.

Everyone in the house was busy as bees putting stuff away, bringing in boxes, it was utter chaos. I walked by the girl's room to see how they were making out, and they had a fantastic game plan. Avery would put the boxes on the floor, empty them out and Vi would put it on the correct side of the room for which girl was living.

"You girls look like you got it done the right way. Awesome job!" They both just smiled at me and kept on unpacking.

I think George and Justin were upstairs because all I could hear was loud rock music, and boxes being flung to the center of the hallway. I walked downstairs to see what dad and Lucy were up to, and she was unpacking the kitchen and Dad was working on the bedroom and living room so they could get good night's sleep tonight, they both slept on the floor last night, so I can imagine they wanted to get set up as soon as possible.

"Hey! Can I help with anything?"

Lucy looked up and let out a long sigh of relief, "That would be wonderful. Could you put the silverware and plates and all away? If you can't reach or if your arm starts to bother you just holler, I will help. I just want to get the rest of the bathroom things in all the bathrooms. Thanks Scarlet."

Everyone was exhausted, you could see it on our faces, but we knew we wanted to get in and start to make it feel as normal as possible. After I was done with that, I asked to go for a walk just to explore and to give my arm a break, ha-ha see what I did there. Anyway, no one minded so I walked down our little dead-end street with Murphy, yes, he is still here I know I haven't talked much about him because, well, he's a dog and he doesn't do much except eat, sleep, and you know. But, trust me, he becomes a lot more important later.

Walking down the dirt path was breathtaking, the trees were so tall, and I honestly have no idea what types they were, there were so many birds, everywhere were birds.

I could hear water running, it was loud and sounded like it was fast, like a waterfall or something. Murphy caught the scent of something and broke away from me, holy crap I panicked.

"MURPHY, STOP! STOP NOW! GET BACK HERE!"

I yelled and yelled to him to get back, while I was running after him. I ran through some brush and almost went head-first into the water. I could hear Murphy barking, and voices. Do you have any idea how hard it is to walk a dog with a cast on my arm, a place you know nothing about, and then must chase after him through the wild, dude not a fun time.

Once I composed myself, I saw Murphy finally, dumb dog was in the creek.

"Murphy, damnit, get out of the water. You're in so much trouble."

I was so mad at him, but he was a dog and literally my only friend here. I tried not to pay attention to the people in the water and up at the waterfall, which I knew that's what it was I heard. Yet of course they sure noticed me.

"Hey down there. Your dog's cute."

I rolled my eyes because who says that, wait, remember you're in a new place and new people are everywhere.

"Thanks. He's friendly, and in a lot of trouble." I knelt to look at him and make sure he wasn't hurt; it was hard with this damn cast.

I could hear a voice coming closer, "Hey, ya need some help?" as I looked up and saying, "Is that a question, or?"

I couldn't finish my thoughts because he was so cute, and I was speechless, which never happens.

"Um, it was a question," he replied laughing.

"Sorry, no I am good. Thanks though."

There were about six people there, they all looked to be about my age too.

One of the girls ran down when the guy was talking to me, "Hiyee! I'm Carmen, I am your neighbor. You must be the new girl. From Maryland, right?"

Jesus, how did she know all this, and which house was hers?

"Hi, yep that would be me. I'm Scarlet. And this," I looked down at Murphy, "Is Murphy. Nice to meet you."

She was adamant on introducing me to everyone there, yay me.

"Let me introduce you to everyone. Guys, come down and meet the new girl and her dog."

I know the sigh I let out could be heard by them and was not interested in the least on meeting anyone right now, but Carmen had different plans. She reminded me of Gabs. Everyone started making their way down to where we were. All of them hootin and hollerin as they made their way. Murphy was excited to be getting so much attention, I however was not thrilled by any means.

"Guys, this is Scarlet. Remember I told you about the new girl moving in? Well, this is her, and her cutie pie dog Murphy!"

Yep, exactly like Gabs, that's a little comforting. There were three other girls and two guys there, all were good looking and very outgoing.

"Scarlet, this is Ryan Campbell," handsome, built, black hair, dark skinned, tall, "Josh Drexler," average looking, blonde hair, green eyes, super tall, kinda built, "Tori Singleton" drop dead gorgeous, brunette, hour glass figure, "Rachel Carter" oh, the hippie of the crowd, "Kim Allen" red head, blue eyes brighter than the sky, seems annoyed by me being here, "And last but certainly not least, Matt Singleton, yes he and Tori are brother and sister."

Well, he was hot, medium height, nice build, brunette, blue eyes, his smile was the first thing I noticed, everything else just fell into place after that.

Shortly after Carmen introduced me to everyone, I could see Kim hanging all over Matt, I get it that's your man, I'm not here to take him. She was not happy with my mere presence.

"Nice to meet you all, I am going to take Murphy back home now. See you all later."

I could hear them all saying goodbye as I turned and walked back up the hill with Murphy.

"I hope you're proud of yourself. I for one am mortified," I was speaking to Murphy as we got to the trail back to the main street.

Our home was the first on the street, or in this case right now walking back, was last. Some of the neighbors were out enjoying the weather, and they waved as I walked past them, I waved back of course. One nice woman walked down to introduce herself to me and Murphy.

"Hello there. You must be from the new family? I am Mrs. Burns. What is your name?"

I didn't know how to take all of this in, "I am Scarlet Adams. Nice to meet you." She was kneeling petting Murphy, who was loving it up.

"And who might this handsome fella be?" I rolled my eyes at him, knowing he was in so much trouble when we got home.

"This is Murphy, and he is in a lot of trouble."

She laughed and continued petting him, "Oh, don't be too hard on him. No dog can resist the falls, it's just so much fun for them!"

I didn't want to be rude, but I was ready to get back to the house.

"Well, it was nice to meet you Mrs. Burns, but I gotta get Murphy home so someone can get him cleaned up. I will tell my parents I met you and hopefully they can meet you too."

"I would love to meet them. I know Florence and Ron very well, there was a lot of love in that house. Especially after their Sandy tragically passed, just an awful thing. It was so nice to meet you, Scarlet."

Ok, so how does one leave a conversation with that and expect someone not to ask what the hell they are talking about. I must find out what happened now.

This town is eerie, which I felt that from the first-time dad brought me here, but now it's curiously eerie to me. I'm going to see if Dad or Lucy heard anything about her and how she died. God, I hope it wasn't in the house, man, I don't wanna think about that ever. I mean yeah, I love horror stuff but not in my house, so I'm praying nothing happened in the house.

I looked down at Murphy as we were getting back to gate, "This is your fault. If you didn't run away from me, I wouldn't be so freaked out right now. Pain in my butt."

He wasn't in trouble, but I was really freaked out. Getting back into the house, I tried to get a towel for him first, but he was almost dry already.

"Hey Justin? Could you help me with Murphy please?"

I heard him up in his room and knew that Murph would only listen to Justin when it came to a bath.

As he was coming down, he could see how dirty he was, "Murph, buddy, what mud pile did you come from? You're filthy dude!"

We both started laughing, "I took him for a walk down that trail at the end of the street and he overpowered me since I only have one working arm. Jerky took full advantage of it!"

Justin took him outside to the hose on the side of the house and started to clean him up for me. In the meantime, I needed to find dad or Lucy, and ask them about the history of this house. Hopefully, they knew and could tell me that we had nothing to worry about, and in fact the house was not haunted at all. Please, please, please let them say that.

"Hey girls, have either of you seen dad or Lucy? I gotta ask them a question."

They shook their heads no, so I went back into their room. I could hear them talking and laughing.

"Knock, knock. Can I come in?" The talking stopped, "Of course Letti, come on in," Lucy answered back. As I walked in, they were putting away their clothes and such, it was nice to see them so happy with each other.

"What's up kiddo? Looks like somethings on your mind." Dad could read my face well.

"Do you guys know a lot about the history of the house? Like did the Lawrences talk about their daughter at all?"

The looks on their faces were not reassuring at all. "Well, by the looks on your faces I'm gonna say you don't know. Awesome."

"I don't know much of anything, even when I was staying here, they were very private and kept to themselves. They are nice people though, so maybe we can ask around and see if anyone knows. That is of course after we get to know the neighbors a bit."

"Funny you say that dad, I met some local kids and one of the older ladies who lives a few houses down."

Both looked surprised and confused that I said that. "Wait, where did you meet local kids? And who was the lady?" Lucy was curious now.

"Well, I decided to take Murphy for a walk down that trail at the end of the street, and he broke loose from me and ended up in the water, and there were a bunch of kids there my age, and then when I finally got him, we were on our way back home and Mrs. Burns was outside and walked down to meet us. She asked if we were the new neighbors and that it was a shame what happened to Florence and Ron's daughter."

I don't think I took one breath during the entire time I said that. Both looked at each other concerned.

"I will make a few calls later and see what the deal is with that. No need to worry."

Both Lucy and I were happy with that, and now anxious to hear what the story was about that.

CHAPTER 17

The kitchen was ready enough to have a home cooked meal, so Lucy and I decided we would make chicken fettuccine alfredo, with garlic bread and a salad. Oh, it was going to be glorious having a home cooked meal, it's been probably two weeks since we've had one and I know we were all tired of take out and fast food.

"I am so excited for this meal, and thanks for letting me help Lucy! It's been a while since I've made dinner for the family, so this will be a nice treat. Should I melt the butter before I put it on the rolls? For the garlic bread, I mean?"

"Yes, I would recommend that, it makes it much easier to swipe it on there. You don't have to melt it fully though, maybe just a few seconds in the microwave, that should do the trick."

I looked up at her and smiled, and wanted to say you got it mom, but I wasn't sure how she would feel about that, or even how I would. I should talk to dad about that first, I hear the girls call her it all the time which doesn't bother me, but I don't know, I ask myself all the time if its ok if I call her that, or would mom be upset? Ugh, this is hard, but whatever I'll be good. Ok, I'm just gonna ask, its time, right?

"Hey, Lucy?"

She was chopping cheese to add in for the alfredo sauce she was making, "Yeah, kiddo? What's up?"

Breathe in and out, remember its ok, "I was wondering if it would be ok to," what's your deal girl, just ask.

"To what honey?"

"To make some of these plain and not add garlic?" You idiot, you totally chickened out.

"Of course, whatever you like!" Welp, I guess I will ask another time.

"So, tell me more about these kids you met. Were they nice? Older? Younger?" I was so happy she asked if I was waiting to tell someone about the whole ordeal.

"So, I wanted to take Murphy earlier for a walk," as soon as I said the word his head popped up immediately, "No, bud it's not time for that. Anyway, we went down that trail at the end of the street, it's back there by the way.

As we were walking, we could hear a bunch of people talking and laughing and stuff, so I went further with him and then we heard splashing and Murphy took off and it was super hard for me to hold onto him because of this," I nodded to my cast, "I finally found my way through the brush and stuff and of course there he was hamming it up for all of them. Loving all the attention," we both looked at him and rolled our eyes but laughed.

"They all seemed to be my age, there were a few girls and boys, I don't remember their names except Carmen, she's a girl, and Matt, he's a guy!"

There's that look I was hoping for, every girl hopes for it from their mom. The "oh a boy huh?" look. "And he was cute too!" Lucy was like a little kid filled with excitement, and it just made me so happy that I could share that with her.

"Awesome! But they seemed nice?" Lucy was of course protective of me.

"They seemed like it. Well, one of the girls didn't like the fact that that boy Matt was talking to me, but other than that yeah, they were all fine!"

It was so nice being there in the kitchen with her, just being a normal family finally after a few weeks of chaos, things were starting to fall into place. Standing there in the kitchen and listening to everyone unpacking was the best sound I heard in a long time. I was looking forward to everyone eating since I helped make dinner, and it smelled delicious. I happened to look out the living room window and could see the same group of kids walking by the house. Murphy was outside and ran right up to them, go figure.

"I'll be right back. Murphy's out on the road."

I walked out of the kitchen door onto the porch and jogged to Murphy. "Murphy, we bothered them enough today. Come on buddy lets go back home." This dog was giving me gray hair.

The kids were all laughing and petting him, not bothered by him at all. Matt was talking to him, "I think your big sister is upset with you buddy, she's coming over fast. And here she is, oh hey again!"

"I'm sorry, he must really like you guys. Come on Murphy, let's get home."

Matt stood up and looked at me, "Well at least he seems like he likes us."

What? What does that even mean? How do I respond to that.

"Yeah, so anyway, we're gonna head back in the house. Good to see you again." If that wasn't the most awkward conversation I've had in a long time. Last time it was that weird was when I first talked to Rich, ugh how embarrassing that was. As I walked away, I could hear their voices get lower as they went further down the street. I walked on the porch and saw them walking up to the house right across from us. I didn't know which one of them lived there, but I was curious now and even a little excited that someone my age lived so close.

"Murphy, what are you doing to me boy, huh?" He looked at me like I was crazy, and I knew he had no idea what I was saying.

"Sorry about that. What can I do now?" I knew Lucy saw the encounter and was waiting for her to say something.

"How about you grab the dressings and set the table for me."

"You got it."

I couldn't help but think about what Matt said to me, when Lucy walked in and interrupted my thoughts.

"Were those the kids that you ran into?"

I shook my head yes, "Yep. They seem nice, and Murphy likes them that's for sure."

"Well, our Murphy likes anyone that gives him pets, and attention."

We both laughed, he really did like that attention from anyone who was willing. I finished setting the table and started to round everyone up so we could sit down and eat. I walked in the girl's room first and they didn't get much further than the last time I saw them. No rush for them, I guess. I went up and grabbed George but couldn't find Justin. "Hey George, where's Justin?"

"I don't know, he went out back after he finished putting up his posters. He got done unpacking a lot faster than me."

"Ok. I'll look out back. Thanks Georgie!"

As I was walking back down the stairs I felt this cold spot around the middle step, it scared me a bit. Then I felt like someone ran by me fast going up the stairs. Creepy. I didn't like that at all.

I went out back to see if Justin was there talking to a girl. I didn't want to interrupt at first, but dinner was ready, and I knew we were all starving.

"Hey big bro! Dinner's ready."

Justin acknowledged what I said but kept talking to her. She was pretty. She had long strawberry blonde hair, redder though, was wearing a long patchwork skirt, an olive-green tank, and a bunch of necklaces. I noticed she didn't have shoes on either.

"I'll be right up. Letti, this is Rachel, she lives over at the house across the street. The big stone one."

"Oh, hey, I think I just met your sister. Pretty like you."

Rachel blushed and placed her hair behind her ear, "Aww, how sweet. Yeah, most likely, she was back at the falls with a bunch of her friends. Not really my scene, but it's all good."

Her smile made me smile, which was super weird.

"Ok, well nice to meet you Rachel, and Justin, I'll see you up at the kitchen."

"Bye, nice to meet you too!"

I couldn't help but laugh under my breath at him and how completely different she was than he is. It was cute, he looked shy almost when he introduced her to me. When I was walking up the steps, I saw something out of the corner of my eye. I thought it was a person, but I wasn't sure because it happened so fast. I stopped to see if I could figure it out, but I didn't see anything. So, now I am seeing things. Great. I just shook my head and kept walking.

When I got to the kitchen I could smell the aroma of dinner, I could almost taste it smelled so delicious. That could be because I was starving and it was one of my favorite meals, but who cares I couldn't wait to eat it.

"Justin coming?" Lucy asked.

"Yep, he said he'll be right up."

"Ok, well let's get ready then." Lucy directed all of us to start filling our plates.

We all sat down, and I was looking around at everyone looking so happy and thinking to myself this couldn't get any better. I really wish I could've joined in more of these after this day, because after today everything changes for me and my relationship with everyone living in the house. I didn't plan it, it just happened, but I think that's what a teenager does right? Learning things on their own, meeting new people, going on adventures, I am sure you all did when you were teens.

"Sorry I am late. This smells and looks delicious. Thanks for making dinner mom, and Letti for helping!" Justin was abnormally chipper, he typically was filled with teen angst and seemed to hate the world, but after talking to Rachel he was not the Justin we knew. It was eerie, I didn't like it.

"Oh, it's ok. What was keeping you? If you don't mind me asking." Dad asked him.

Justin looked over me with a surprised look, "Wait, Letti didn't tell you?" I remember the look he gave me, kind of like "ok cool, respect little sister."

All eyes were on me now, "Big bro, it wasn't my story to tell. So, I figured you would want to." We both smiled at each other.

"Well, I was talking to a young lady, her name is Rachel, and she lives in the big stone house across the street."

The girls looked out the window at the big house, Avery said "Ohhh, the really pretty mansion looking house?"

"The very one kiddo. I think Letti met her younger sister earlier when she was back in the woods with Murphy."

Murphy perked his head up and we all told him "Not right now Murphy."

Every time he heard his name, he always perked his head up, like he was going somewhere, or getting a treat, or eating, or pretty much whatever he thought in his dog head, so we always told him "Not right now Murphy," he was the best dog ever.

Believe it or not this was one of the last meals we all shared as an entire family, everyone had something or was somewhere else. I know it had to have made the girls sad, and Lucy and Dad, but it was just how it was now. Me, George, and Justin all became super busy because of school, friends, work, and after school things.

Dad started "the good and bad part" when we were all almost done eating, this is when we all tell our good part of the day and a low or a bad part or something we didn't like. I don't remember if I explained that already. It was one of the absolute best things about being in this family. We added Mr. Myers and of course we still said my moms, when we first did it with Lucy and the boys, they thought it was such a cool thing. We did it the first night at McGregor's and have been doing it as a family ever since.

We had a rule that anyone who didn't help with dinner has to clean up, I always made sure I was making something, so I never really had to clean up. I always did though because we always had fun doing it. Sometimes choices you think you make today are the right ones for your future, but that only happens in movies and tv shows, writers can rewrite the script. No one can rewrite real life, and you're going to learn so much about me, and the people that get introduced in my life that I never got the chance to meet.

CHAPTER 18

That night I decided to take a walk out back to my rock, really to think about what it was going to be like living here and what the people were like, this place was so new, smelled new even. I wasn't sure what to think of the kids I met earlier, because I only met them for a few minutes. They seemed fine, but I'm not sure if they are my scene. I heard the phone ringing but didn't realize what time it was. I heard George inside holler my name, which meant it was eight and that was Mel!

"Coming." I yelled to George, got up and again I saw something by a tree that was at the bottom of the driveway, this time I could see it a little better. It was a girl, maybe a little older than me, and I couldn't quite make out what she was wearing or who she was, but it really freaked me out. I ran inside ready to pee myself and grabbed the phone from him.

"What up!!!!!" I obnoxiously said to her as I put the receiver up to my ear.

"Yooooo, what up!" she replied.

I started to tell her about how it was today, the kids I met, what everything has been like so far.

"Oh, and Justin was talking to a girl. Really too, not his type, which is probably best for him now that I think about it. The house is kind of creepy, like not House creepy, but like *The Lady in White* creepy.

I feel like I should have "Have you ever seen a dream walking? Well, I did," playing in the background."

She laughed hysterically at me, "That movie scared the hell out of me. Do you remember we watched it at Gab's 9th birthday party sleepover. Oh my god, I thought we were gonna get in so much trouble for watching it when her mom came down."

"We all pretended like we were asleep" we said together laughing.

"Oh my god, that was the best. But yeah, you're right that movie scarred me for life."

The phone was silent for a few seconds, and I knew I needed to tell her what I saw today and just now when I was walking in.

"Mel, I gotta tell you, and don't you dare laugh at me when I do. I know it's going to sound crazy, but I swear I saw like an apparition today and then just now before I came in to get the phone."

"I told you; you shouldn't have moved there. I knew that place was going to be off. I felt when we were there at spring break, I even told Jen when we were in Math class after we went back. She didn't see it and she probably thought I was crazy, but I'm telling ya Letti it's a weird place. Weird energy."

"There's this older lady, she lives on my street, and she stopped and welcomed me and Murph when we were walking back from the woods. She said something about Mr. and Mrs. Lawrences' daughter and that she died tragically. What does that even mean?"

"Dude, was she like murdered? Oh my God, maybe that's her ghost you're seeing. You need to find more info about that Moi pronto."

"I know, but like, literally it's been one day I need to wait to meet more people, duh. Maybe I'll take Murphy down to Mrs. Burns' tomorrow and see if she can tell me anything else. Ok, Chica, I am exhausted, so I am going to try to go to sleep now."

"Ok, well don't let the ghost of Sandy Lawrence get you tonight."

"HAHA, whatever. Good night!"

"Night, call me tomorrow."

We hung up the phone and I was so mad at her for saying that because now I am totally freaked out and I sleep in her room. Ugh, this sucks big time. I avoided windows and mirrors tonight because I was ridiculous and acted like a child. I laid there and it was awesome how the moonlight lit up the room like Mr. Lawrence said. The sparkles on the ceiling looked like stars, there were popcorn ceilings in every bedroom, it made it look so cool.

I was thinking about everything I wanted to do tomorrow. I needed to hang up my black light, my posters, and just take my time going through my boxes. The boys offered to help, so I think I might take them up on that because my arm was sore from all the pulling Murph did today.

I whistled for him to come sleep with me tonight, he always made me feel safe. In about twenty seconds he was in my room, I patted the bed "Come on bud. Come lay down."

I realized I hadn't found any radio stations yet, and lord knows I couldn't fall asleep without Delilah. I leaned over and grabbed my clock radio and started scrolling the know looking for her. Oh, there she is, a little comfort. "Can you feel the love tonight, it is where we are..." I drifted off, and didn't remember doing so, but I woke up at two-thirty feeling like someone was standing over me. Murphy was sound asleep, and I've always heard that dogs can sense when the supernatural is around.

So, I fell back asleep, and woke up later that morning to the smell of coffee and bacon. I stared over at the window seat that Mr. Lawrence built for me he said, and I couldn't help but wonder why he would do something like that. I really wanted to go talk to Mrs. Burns, but I knew I had a ton of stuff to do.

"Ok, Murphy let's get this room going, huh?"

"Letti?" Avery knocked, "Can I come in?"

"Hey, good morning. How was your sleep?"

"It was ok, I made it all night, so I think that's a start, right?"

"Avery, I told you, you can come in my room anytime, that's what the door is for."

"I did, I came over night, but Murphy was on the bed and there wasn't enough room for me."

Well, that makes sense as to why I thought someone was over me, because Avery was, well at least in the room. So, mystery solved on that part. Still unanswered questions about the ghosts that I saw. "Oh, I'm sorry sweetheart, I was little lonely last night so I had Murphy with me, but next time just push him over a bit, he will move for you."

"Ok! Thanks Letti. Mom wanted me to come and see if you wanted to eat. She made bacon, eggs, toast, home fries, coffee, and some weird looking meat. It's like hard on the outside and mushy on the inside. I don't like it." She made the cutest sour face.

"I'll steer clear of that then. Thanks for the heads up! I'll be out in a few if you can let her know for me."

"Ok!"

I pulled my hair up in a ponytail and threw on a hoodie and my sweatpants and walked out. I was walking through the living room and George was watching some science show or something, eating his breakfast.

"Morning Letti."

"Morning Georgie."

"Do you want my help today? I am done my room now, I just wanna finish hanging up the solar system but I can do that any time."

Did I mention George is like a genius or something, he's so smart seriously smarter than anyone I know.

"That would be super cool if you could. I can't hang things with only one arm," I held up the broken arm not that he didn't forget or anything, I just tried to remind myself that I had it.

My arm was not as sore today, only faintly. I got to the kitchen, it was an old farm house kitchen, you know where the pots and pans hang from the center of the ceiling, a humungous island underneath, a porcelain double sink, well I think it's porcelain I remember dad and lucy saying that, a stove that you could cook for an army on, and those saloon doors when you walked in from the living room to there. It was probably my favorite room in the whole house.

"Morning!" Lucy and Avery were the only ones here.

"Morning sweetheart! How did you sleep?"

"I slept ok. I had Murphy with me. Not now Murphy."

"Actually wait, it is now Murphy. Its breakfast for you too."

"Oops, sorry buddy. I was thinking later, if it's ok, I would take Murphy for a walk to see Mrs. Burns again. Would that be, ok?"

"MmmHmm, sure. Maybe I can walk down with you, I would love to meet her since she wasn't here the last time your dad and I came up. But she left us this beautiful house plant."

Huh I wondered where that came from and why it was here already when we got here.

"Oh, that's sweet. I thought it was from the Lawrences, oops. I was going to ask her a little more about their daughter, do you think it would be too forward of me to do that?"

"No, I don't think so. I can also help ease the inquiry as well. But let's eat, and get some more of these rooms unpacked and we can head there around one, sound good?"

"Yep, sounds good."

The three of us continued to eat and talk about things we wanted to accomplish today and such. It was nice, because Vi finally joined us too. So, it was just the ladies of the house.

CHAPTER 19

Dad was at work, his first official day on his own, no more training and he seemed psyched for it last night when we were talking at dinner. Justin was who knows where and Avery was in her own little world out back exploring. Luckily Vi, Lucy and George were here to help me with the rest of my stuff.

"Ok, I think that it's! Thank you everyone for helping me!"

They all of course were happy to do so, and I really couldn't have done it without them, and if I had it would've taken me all summer because of this stupid cast.

"Did you still want to go see Mrs. Burns, Scarlet?"

Hell, yeah, I do! "Yes, I would love that, do you think she's home?"

"Oh, can I come too?" Violet asked in a desperate tone. I know she was feeling some sort of way not meeting any-one her age yet and I kept reminding her that she would. We found the playground down the road within walking dis-tance, and I promised we would go there one day this week to check it out.

"Of course, short stuff, but you have to walk Murphy."

"Deal!" She was so excited to go, I think it's because she didn't wanna be in the house by herself, which I can't say I blame her because I am not looking forward to ever being by myself here.

Lucy yelled up the stairs to George's room to see if he wanted to go as well, he declined because he was finishing hanging his solar system up.

"Ok, shall we then?" All three of us, and Murphy of course went out the door to see if our nice neighbor was outside. And yes, she is, I could see her working on her flowers. She had a beautiful lawn that she took care of, and she was old, so it was awesome to see her out there. Not that she wasn't capable, she just did her thing. Everyone else seemed to be at work, which made sense since it was Monday, so the street was empty.

There was an old man who lived next door to us, we haven't met him yet, his house his very old. It may be the same age as ours, I just don't think he's been taking good care of it. Some of these homes around us were so old, some were run down, and some were well taken care of. Ours was right in the middle, the Lawrences seemed to do the best they could with it only being them and it being such a big house.

As we got closer to Mrs. Burns, Murphy started to bark friendly at her. She stopped clipping the hedges and saw him. Once she did, she knelt to greet him.

"There's my buddy! What's up Murphy? You look a lot cleaner today!"

"Yeah, we are avoiding the woods today." I looked down at him and he ignored me. "I want to introduce you to my stepmom and sister. This is Lucy and this is Violet."

"Hello, Mrs. Burns, it is a pleasure to meet you," Lucy extended her hand to shake it.

"And so that must make you Violet? So nice to meet you. Would you like some fresh squeezed lemonade? I just made some for my husband and I, and I made plenty."

We both looked at Lucy to make sure it was ok.

"Of course, we would love that. Is it ok for Murphy to come? We wouldn't want to impose him on you and your husband."

"Oh nonsense, our Toby passed a little over a year ago, so it would be lovely to have a dog in the house again. Come on up, let me show you the house and introduce you to my husband."

Fresh squeezed lemonade, I don't think I have ever had that before, but I was excited to try it. We walked up the steps and the gate closed behind us.

"You can let him off leash if you think he will be ok running around?"

I leaned down and unclipped it, you don't have to tell him twice. "Go ahead buddy, be free!"

We all walked into her house, it smelled musty and floral like at the same time, it was not the most pleasant smell, but I guess they were used to it.

"Larry, these are our new neighbors. This is Lucy, Violet, and I told you about Scarlet. Oh, Murphy is outside running around like a chicken with its head cut off. They come to get some lemonade."

When we walked in and saw Mr. Burns, we were a little taken back. He was in a wheelchair with only one leg, he was an old guy, lots of wrinkles on his face. Gray hair and beard, big fat glasses, and a hat that read Korean War Veteran with a bar that was in the middle of it.

"Hello there." He had the lowest voice I ever heard, it was a comforting voice, it reminded me of my pop pop's, my mom's dad, he spoke so low all the time because my mom mom was loud enough for both, Mrs. Burns reminded me of her.

"Hello Mr. Burns. How are you today?"

"Please call me Larry. And you girls can call me pop if you'd like, that's what most of the kids call me."

He was such a cool old guy, and Mrs. Burns was even cooler. There were pictures of them when they were young, pictures of what I assume is their children and grandchildren.

"Are these family?" Violet asked as she was looking at the pictures.

Mr. Burns, Pop, rolled over to her, "Yep, this is me and my honey when we were first dating," he picked up the frame and smiled, "isn't she a beauty."

I knew it wasn't a question he was asking; he was stating a fact.

"This one is our four daughters when they were teenagers. Let me tell you how full of life this house was when they were all teenagers at the same time." He laughed and joked.

"What are their names?" Vi asked.

From left to right he named them, "This one is Michelle, she is the oldest of all of them. The next one here is Charlene, she married Mel DiMada they own the hoagie shop in town. Don't know if you've tried that place yet, if not you should."

"We did, Dad got it the other day. It was so good!" Vi replied.

"Oh good. Ok, next is Cheryl, she is the baby of the group. And last but certainly not least is our Angela, she was in a bad accident before this picture was taken. Here help me get this album from down below there."

I leaned down, grabbed an old heavy photo album, and placed it on the table next to him. He turned to his left and told us to take a seat, Lucy was in the kitchen talking with Mrs. Burns. He opened it up and he slowly went over page-by-page which girl was which. There were pictures of them throughout the years, some with other people, most with just the four of them.

"All girls huh? You never tried for a boy?" I asked.

"We had a baby boy between Angela and Charlene, we lost him at delivery sadly. The girls don't remember much because they were so young." It was quiet for a minute and then he continued.

"Ok, and this is what our Angel looked like before the accident. Isn't she beautiful. Just like her mom." He was looking through to the other room and could see Mrs. Burns, and the smile grew across his face. It was sweet and I was curious as to what happened.

"Mr. Burns," he looked up at me, "Sorry, Pop. If you don't mind me asking, but what happened to her?"

He looked surprised that I asked, "You don't know? I thought they would've told your parents. It's a long story, but my Angela and Sandy Lawrence were involved in a hit and run when they were seventeen. It was bad for the whole town. I'll tell you the story another day, unfortunately it is time for my meds and a nap. Why don't you come over tomorrow, and I can tell you all about it. How's ten am?"

I shook my head, "That would be great!"

Mrs. Burns walked back in with Lucy and lemonade, "You girls wanna sit out on the porch with me so Pop here can take a break? Come on, follow me. Murphy seems to be enjoying himself."

He was of course, he was basking in the sun in the middle of the yard.

"You bum." He picked his head up, glared at me, then laid back down.

"So, Scarlet, have you met the Carter girls yet? They live on the corner there," she pointed, "and then there's Carmen, who lives right there," she pointed just up the hill a few houses, "And a whole bunch of them are always walking back to the waterfalls. They go swimming and have fun. They typically keep it clean, so I hope that doesn't change."

"I did. I met a few of them the other day when I met you. And then my brother met Rachel, and they all seemed nice. Carmen was the friendliest of the group."

"She's a good kiddo, her family owns the Gas station at the top of the hill, and they all work there and help take care of it. Heck, it's been in the town for as long as I can remember, and I'm pretty darn old." She laughed and smiled.

We all listened to her talk about some of the history of the town, especially our part of town, which was the oldest. She told us how each of the homes that we saw were all part of the manufacturing district, which were wool mills. She told us who originally lived in them and that ours is where the infirmary used to stand but it burned down back in the early 1910's, which was super amazing to hear. This made me wonder if the apparition I have seen is someone who died here.

"Mrs. Burns, did anyone die in the fire?" I was curious and I figured she might know.

"Nope, it was empty. Which was rare because it was one of the first times in history that no one was there, and all the staff were either outside or on lunch break. Eerie in a way. But there were some people that died in there. Larry swears that he sees people all the time just wandering around. I tell him he's too senile for that."

Hearing her say that made me feel less crazy, but also made me want to tell him about what I have seen. I plan it tomorrow when I come back to hear about what happened with Angela and Sandy.

We stayed a bit longer to talk with her, when their daughter Charlene pulled in their driveway, and it was then that I had the realization that Chris was Mrs. Burns' grandson. How did I not put that together, duh. I got nervous again because he was so cute. He looked up and saw me, smiled, and yelled up, "Oh hey there new girl! What ya doing here?"

"Visiting with your grandmother. Shouldn't you be making good fries?" They both laughed and none of the other women knew that they had even met before.

"You two know each other?" Mrs. Burns questioned.

"Oh, yeah Grams we go way back. HAHA!" he replied.

"MmmHmm, way back." We both grinned at each other, and he had an arm full of food for them, so I walked down to get to the gate.

"Thanks Scarlet."

Uh, holy crap, he remembered my name. I was not expecting that. "You're welcome, Chris." Were we flirting right now, because if so, he was just as bad at it as I was.

We could see the moms and their facial expressions back and forth, as Mrs. Burns introduced Lucy and Charlene, and then myself and Vi.

"Pleased to meet you Mrs. DiMada, your dad just showed me some pictures of you and your sisters when you were all younger."

"He didn't tell you to call him pop?" Chris asked.

"He did, but I didn't want to be rude since I only just met him and your mom."

"Chris, Scarlet met some of the kids from your grade yesterday, down at the waterfall. Uh, Carmen, the Carter girls, and who else Scarlet?"

All eyes were on me now. "Um, one of them was Matt, and I don't remember who else, except the ones already mentioned."

"Let me guess, most likely Kim was there because she's never five feet from Matt. Uh, Victoria and Josh, Carmen and Ryan, and Quinn.

Poor Quinn, always the seventh wheel, she really needs a boyfriend, or girlfriend, or whatever. She tries so hard to do whatever to fit in with that crowd and I will never understand why, they treat her like shit."

"Christopher don't talk like that in front of ladies. You know better and if pop would've heard you, he would have said the same thing," his mother reprimanded him.

"Sorry mom, my apologies ladies."

"It's ok." Lucy replied on behalf of us.

I didn't care what he said, I was enamored by his looks right now.

"Scarlet you wanna help me with this stuff?" He lifted his arms a bit and nodded to the kitchen. "I can show you how to cut a hoagie properly, and cheesesteaks."

"Sure. Teach me something I don't know." I was trying not to be sarcastic, but he didn't know me yet so he had no idea what I could do and how good of a cook I was.

"Letti knows how to do that stuff," Vi interrupted.

Chris was impressed, "Oh, really? Well, show me what you're made of then Letti."

"No no, you don't get to call me Letti, just my close friends and family."

"Well, I hope that one day I can become a close friend so I can call you Letti one day."

"Maybe, if you're lucky." Now I was trying at flirting.

"Touché!" he said with a devious smile.

Oh, that smile just got my attention. I think I'm gonna like it here.

"Pop asked me to come back tomorrow so he could tell me about the Lawrences' daughter and your aunt. Do you know anything about it?"

We were cutting the sandwiches and wrapping them for the freezer. He responded a bit hesitantly, "Some. No one really talks about it. My mom cries about it sometimes, and Aunt Angela is a living reminder of what happened. I just know it was right after graduation, there were a lot of teens and partying one night like right after and there was some accident. A lot of people think it was on purpose, I don't know, pop can tell you more. Maybe I'll come by so I can finally hear too."

"That would be cool if you came too. He said like ten am. Can you come then?"

"Yeah, I should be able too. I would love to hear about it for sure. He told you to call him pop huh. He must really like you. Usually, he tells everyone that after he has met someone a few times, not the first time typically."

Being there with him was comfortable for me, I couldn't understand why. It was like we knew each other and not just from meeting during spring break, but like we knew one another for years. He was easy to talk to too, and on the eyes, it just came naturally for me. I think for him too. We kept talking and picking on each other while we were prepping their meals for the week. It felt like home, or at least what home was going to feel like.

Violet came in and interrupted to let me know she and Lucy were heading back home and they would take Murphy if I wanted them to and that I could stay.

"Um, I think I'll stay a little bit and help. If that's ok with you?" I glanced at Chris looking for confirmation from him.

"Yeah, that would be cool. We can catch up some more if you want?"

"I would like that. It's not going to be easy being the new girl around here, I can tell that already."

"Why's that?" he asked.

"I don't know, the one girl acted like I was bothering her by being there. She kept giving me dirty looks. I guess it was the Kim girl you mentioned earlier, because she was all over that guy Matt."

He had a pained look after I said that. "Yeah, you will want to steer clear of her warpath, she is a bit obsessed with Matt Singleton. He and I used to be best friends, until they started dating last year. It was weird cause Kim is not his type at all."

"How so?"

"She's kind of scary, very dark, very mean, her friends are I swear witches or something."

I laughed, "Sorry I know that's not funny, but maybe opposites do attract?"

He was walking by me, and his arm slid against mine, "maybe they do?" with that devious smile again.

"Well, looks like we're all done here. So, I should be heading home. You know it's a long walk," I said jokingly.

"Ok, tomorrow at ten am sharp I will see you. Have a good night, Scarlet."

"You too Chris. Goodbye Mrs. Burns and thank you for the lemonade. Nice to meet you Mrs. DiMada."

"Bye, Scarlet," they both said from the other room.

Walking home was quick, but I was on cloud nine after this day. I was looking forward to tomorrow even more since he will be there. I was excited to tell the girls about today.

CHAPTER 20

When I got to my house, I saw that dad was home, and I was excited to hear about his first official day by himself. It was still something I knew I had to get used to, being out of school so soon. In Maryland we would still be in school for the next two weeks, so coming home and not being able to call Mel or one of the girls right away was different. I know I'll get used to it, it's just all new right now. I couldn't wait to tell them about me and Chris and our day date tomorrow at his pop's.

I know it's not an actual date, but I can pretend it is. "Hey Dad! How was your first official day?" He was sitting at the island in the kitchen and Lucy was standing next to him with her arms around him and his around hers. It made me so happy that they found each other, I hoped for a while that dad would find someone and when Lucy came back into his life.

"Oh, hey kiddo! It was great, very different being by myself. It's a slow time of year for the museum, but they said it starts to pick up in the next week or two. So, we will see how that goes. I think your mom and sisters were about to start on dinner, did you want to help them or help me with trying to hang that back gate up properly?"

Dad knew I loved to work with my hands, and anytime he needed an extra set of them I was the first to volunteer. But, at the same time I really enjoyed helping Lucy make dinner too. I was torn.

"Can I do both? I can help you dad, and then come back in and finish up with dinner and setting the table and all. Would that work?" I looked at both for an answer.

Lucy shook her head yes, "That would be alright with me. I can get the girls started on a lot of things and by the time you come back up we should be ready for you!"

"Awesome! Let me go get changed, dad, ok!"

As I was walking into my room, I felt uneasy and like someone was standing there but wasn't. It was cold, like not when you see your breathe cold but when you get the chills kind of cold. It was freaky and I did not like it. I was hoping that talking to Pop would help answer some of the reasons why these things were happening to me.

When I walked back out, it was gone. No cold spot, no uneasy feeling, nothing. I could hear the girls and Lucy in the kitchen laughing and having fun, George was in the living room watching some sci-fi show, and Justin was nowhere to be found. I assumed he was off working on his car or looking for a job. I was very wrong in my assumption; there he was out back at the picnic table talking with Rachel again. They saw me as I was walking down the stairs to help dad and waved.

"Hi guys!" I hollered out back to them. "What's up?"

"Hey Letti. Not much, just hanging out. What are you up too?"

I pointed to the gate and dad, "Helping dad with this gate."

Rachel looked at Justin surprised, "Do you need to go help too? I can wait here if you do."

He shook his head, "Nah, they love doing that stuff together. I always ask but they always tell me they got it covered. So, I don't bother really."

"Oh, ok. Well, that's cool, and sweet that they do that together." She said.

"Yeah, after Letti's mom passed away the two of them became close, and she tried to fill in for Mrs. Adams whenever she could. I felt bad for a while because she put so much pressure and stress on herself, but she always tells me she doesn't mind. She is always helping my mom too, and I know my mom loves that because she always wanted a daughter and now, she has three. It wasn't easy after my dad died, but we all got through it and once we got with the Adams' we were just whole again."

Rachel stared at him wide eyed and as if he hung the moon, stars, and universe, hanging on his every word. It was kind of gross, but maybe this girl would be a good fit for him since she was not his type.

Dad and I got the gate rehung in about twenty minutes, which was a record for us because typically we take at least two hours to get anything done like this. We were both hungry and we didn't want to mess around.

"Alright kiddo, we got it. Thank you as always for your help. I'll clean up the tools, if you wouldn't mind taking my glasses in when you go in?"

"Ok dad, not a problem at all. I'm gonna walk down and just say hi to Justin and Rachel, ok?"

"Yeah of course."

Our back yard was gigantic, and beautiful. We had the biggest Oak trees I have ever seen in my life, and lilies every-where, orange ones. The creek was alive with fish coming up every so often, and there was a blue Heron, which if you've ever seen one in person is like the size of a Pterodactyl and even looked like one too. Mr. Lawrence told me that if we see them in the water then the water is clean because they don't drink or eat out of dirty or contaminated water. Our neigh-bors to the left of us had the cutest farmhouse, which was apparently the first house built here, but I'll have pop con-firm that. The old man next to us wasn't out ever, his house was dark again, and so far, I haven't seen anyone coming or going, gotta ask pop about that too.

We had the remains of the waterwheel, which was not useful but still cool. "Hey!" I said as I came upon them.

"Hey," they both replied. "All done with the gate. That was a fast one." Justin commented.

"I know right. Dad said he was hungry, and he didn't want to mess around. But I figured I would come back and say hey! Rachel you should stay for dinner!"

I thought Justin's eyes were going to pop out of his face, he looked at me confused as to why I would say that, but then a smile started to form, and I think he was thankful that I asked, and he didn't have to.

"Yeah, that would be cool if you could stay for dinner," he smiled at her.

"Ok, as long as it wouldn't be a problem."

"Absolutely not, there's always so much food left over, and we always have extra space at the table. I'll go up and finish helping and let them know that you're staying."

As I was walking away, I heard him say, "She still hasn't gotten to the point to call my mom, mom yet. I can't imagine how hard it has been on them. My dad and I weren't close at all, we just had our differences, but I do miss him. I am lucky mom found Joe, he's a good man and good to her. Any who, I am happy you said yes to staying for dinner, you're gonna love the family and they are going to love you."

When I walked into the kitchen, I could smell fresh biscuits being baked, and the sauce was bubbling, and the aroma made me even hungrier. "Hey hey!" I exclaimed as I walked in.

It was just Lucy, no surprise the girls bailed on her, "Where are the girls?"

She put her hand up and waved it away, "oh they left me a while ago," chuckling she replied.

"Why am I not surprised. Well, what can I do to help? And where should I put dad's glasses?"

"I'll take them sweetheart, and if you wouldn't mind cutting some tomatoes and cucumbers for the salad that would be so helpful. I'll have more stuff but as you can see the girls haven't cleaned up their mess from making the biscuits."

"I'll take care of that too!" man I wanted to call her mom, but I just couldn't get the words out yet, one day.

"You're a life saver Letti!" She kissed my forehead and took dad's glasses downstairs to their bedroom, so he had them when he got out of the shower. I loved that she did that all the time to us kids, it was such a mom thing to do, and it made me remember how important it was to have that with a mom.

Lucy came back smiling, as always.

"I forgot to tell you; I asked Rachel to stay for dinner. I figured you wouldn't mind because you always have so much food left over."

"Wonderful, of course I don't ever mind. And I can't believe Justin was ok with that, he hasn't said anything about her to me really except for dinner last night. But he has spent all day with her, so I'm curious to see where this goes with the two of them," she was taking the lettuce out of the fridge and that's when she turned the tables to me, "And what about you and Chris, you two seemed a bit flirtatious today. I wasn't sure if you were coming home or not, you two were hitting it off so well."

I could feel the redness take over my cheeks, "Oh my god, he is so cute, and I like talking to him. I don't know if it is anything, but I know I can't wait to see him again tomorrow!"

"He's coming tomorrow?" she asked.

"Nope we are meeting at pops at ten am. Pop wants to tell me about the history of the houses, town, and the Lawrences daughter. Do you think I could talk to you about something later? After we eat dinner and all."

"Of course, Letti, whatever you need I'm always here to listen!" She walked over and hugged me, I almost started to cry because it was the most unprovoked hug I have received in a long time.

CHAPTER 21

We all sat down for dinner, Rachel too, and it seemed almost normal. I say that because we haven't had a lot of that in the past few weeks. Dad was driving back and forth to here from Maryland for the new job, which caused him to miss a lot of dinners and end of the year school events for the girls. None of us were mad or anything, we knew it was necessary, but we did miss him being there.

"So, Rachel, what grade will you be going into in the fall?"

"I will be a senior, and I am anxious to graduate."

"Do you have plans after graduation?" Lucy asked.

"I do, I plan on attending community college for my gen-ed courses, and then when I am finished with them, I will be heading to Penn State local for being an Art Curator."

I don't think anyone was surprised when she said that. She had a free-spirited demeanor about her. She was nice and seemed to like Justin. When I tell you she was not his type, she wasn't. He would date girls with black nail polish, makeup so thick it looked very dark Goth type. Not that there was anything wrong with that, I dressed like that most days minus the makeup, I am just pointing out how different she is compared to the other girls he has dated in the past.

I remember this one girl he was dating, back in Maryland, she was a real daredevil, she would climb up the railroad tracks above the hidden bridge tunnel, near Warren Street. It was scary, because she would just stand there staring down the tracks, like she was waiting to play chicken with a train. I couldn't understand why he was dating her, but I was happy when he stopped.

We all talked about the summer coming up and what we were hoping to do, how dad's first day on his own went, what the girls did, and more questions for Rachel.

"So, Rachel, you're going to be a Senior this coming fall, so exciting! Are there any pointers or advice you can give to Scarlet and George? Any clubs, or after school activities they should look at?" Lucy was always looking out for us.

"Uh, I mean it all depends on what they like to do. What do you guys like?" She looked back and forth at George and me.

"I love Science, and math." George replied.

"You would probably want to look into the Mathletes group, I'm not familiar with all they do but they are all smart. And we have Science honor society which would also be cool for you. Wait what grade are you going into?" Talking to George.

"I will be going into ninth grade this coming school year."

Nodding her head, "Ok, cool. Yeah, I don't know if they let freshman into those groups. My sister knows more about that stuff than I do. I can bring her over one day this week, you two would get along well!" smiling at George.

"That would be so sweet of you, Rachel. I think that would be nice, don't you George?" Lucy asked.

"Sure." He responded.

"I would love to meet her again. It was quick so we didn't get to talk at all. We just said hello. It would be nice to get to know some of the kids my age before school starts." I said.

"What grade are you going into Scarlet?" She asked.

"I'll be a sophomore this coming year. Kind of sucks coming in so late, but I am trying to keep an open mind."

"Oh, cool. There are a lot of Sophomores that live near us. I am sure you met a few yesterday, but I'll make sure you meet them all again. And I'll make sure you know who to steer clear of. I'll make sure you know all the ins and outs before September."

"I would love that!"

We both smiled at each other, and I started to feel a little better about starting the summer here. I was hopeful that the next two school years would be easy as well, and that the kids would be just as nice as Rachel. It was bad enough I had to move in the middle of summer, but to try to make friends when all these people knew each other since they were kids, well that sucked.

Justin, Rachel, and I were all sitting on the front porch, which had a beautiful view, enjoying the cool late spring air. Summer was only a few weeks away, and we had no plans as of now.

"Letti, what's that kids name you're meeting up with to-morrow at the neighbors, again?" Justin asked.

"Chris. Why what's up?"

He shook his head, "Nothing just couldn't remember. Rachel, do you know him?"

"Of course, I do, he's only one of the most popular guys in school. Every girl wants to go out with him. He had a girlfriend up until Valentine's Day, when he found out she cheated on him. He hasn't dated anyone since, which I can't say I blame him. Scarlet, do you have a boyfriend?"

"Nope, I had one for a little while, and I've been on dates and such, but growing up with the same people you get to know everything about them, so it makes it hard and awk-ward to date them long term."

"Yeah, I totally understand that." As Rachel said this, she looked at Justin with a shy smile and dreamy eyes.

He smiled back and his cheeks were so red from blushing. I had never seen this before from him, and I knew it was time to head into the house and call Mel.

"Ok, well, on that note I'm gonna head in and call Mel. Rachel good night, big bro I'll see you when you come in."

"Night!" they said in unison.

I walked into my room, and picked up the phone, dialed Mel's number and it rang three times when she finally picked up.

"Helloooooooo!"

"Yo, what up?"

"Not much, I saw it was you calling. How was your day? What'd you do? Any more spiritual encounters," laughing she said.

"Haha, very funny. My day was good, actually it was pretty great. Remember that kid from DiMadas? Chris?"

"Yep."

"So, apparently my old neighbors are his grandparents, so guess who spent the afternoon with him and will be meeting him tomorrow?"

"Shut up! Dude he's so hot. You're so lucky. I'm never going to meet anyone here, not like that. Everyone is so boring, and we know everyone here. I need a Scarlet to move here, but you know as a guy."

We both laughed hysterically at that statement because it was true. It took me moving to Pa to meet a guy that might be worth my time.

"So, what's his deal?" She asked.

"I don't know much, but the girl that Justin met, Rachel, well she said that he had a girlfriend for a long time, but she was cheating on him, and they broke up around Valentine's Day. And, he has not been seeing anyone since. So, who knows? Maybe tomorrow will be the start of some sweep me of my feet relationship."

Again, we both laughed.

"You never know. Did he ask you to meet him?"

"Nope, his pop wanted me to come over and talk with him about the story of the Lawrence girl, and Chris invited himself after I told him I would be there."

"Nice, see there's a chance Letti. Did you tell him to call you Letti yet?"

I replied "No, you know that's a special name that not everyone gets the pleasure of calling me. But, I mean, sure at some point I would like him too."

We talked for about an hour that night, about what we wanted to do this summer, and when Mel and the others would be coming up. It made me so sad how much I missed them, especially her.

"I miss you so friggin much. I know I need to give this place a chance and literally it's been like four days, but I am so homesick, even though this is my home now. I don't know, it just sucks a lot."

"Girl, I know, me too. I walked by your house and saw the new people moving in. I was stalking them almost, to see who they were. I haven't seen a person, just moving trucks and stuff. Hey maybe it'll be my "Chris" that moves in."

It was time for me to get ready for bed, and my arm was killing me from the past few days. I was so excited to meet with Chris tomorrow, he was cute and super nice. I was hoping that I would meet some nice kids my age, and so far, the few I have are nice. Or so they seem anyway.

CHAPTER 22

When I woke up my arm was a lot sorer than it was last night, and it really hurt to move it. I guess when Murph pulled it the other day it messed it up, which sucks because now I have to tell my dad and Lucy, and I do not want to have to go back to the hospital for it. I figured I wouldn't tell them anything, at least until after I met with Chris. No way was I missing spending the day with him.

I grabbed breakfast, just a toaster pastry, and a cup of OJ, and waited until I saw his mom's car pull down the street. Avery was staring at me, looking at me like she wanted to say something.

"What's up? Why are you staring at me like that?" I asked her.

"Letti, I think I saw a ghost last night. It scared me and I don't wanna go back to my room again. I don't like it here." She spoke.

When she said that I knew exactly what she was talking about since I've seen it too. I didn't know how to answer her though. I didn't want her to think she was crazy, so I was trying to think of how I was going to respond.

"What did it look like?"

She looked at me with those big blue eyes, all wide like. "Well, I think it was a lady. It looked like it anyway."

"Ok. Well can I tell you a secret?"

"Uh huh."

"I've seen her too. A couple of times. I think it's Lawrence's daughter. The one that passed away. I have seen her too. I don't think she wants to hurt anyone. But I will know more after today. I am going to the Burns' house to hear about some of the history of the town and our house. I promise little sis, I think you'll be ok."

I had hoped that she felt a little better after I told her I saw the ghost too, she seemed it anyway.

"Ok, kiddo. I'll be back in a few hours. I will be home for dinner I think, if not tell dad and Lucy that I will call if I'm not."

"Ok! Have fun!" Avery yelled to me from the kitchen.

When I was walking down the steps, I could see that they were there already, and my heart started racing. I was so nervous. Mrs. Burns was outside pulling some weeds from her garden when she saw me and hollered down to me at the gate.

"Come on in!"

I opened the gate and could see that Chris was standing by the bay window looking down grinning at me.

"Morning Mrs. Burns."

"Morning Scarlet. They are inside, waiting for you. And my husband is in rare form today, so good luck!" she said while winking her eye.

"Ok, thanks for the warning."

I walked in and could see that he had photo albums laid out in every room and was sitting at the table talking with Chris.

"Morning!" I greeted.

"Good morning, Scarlet. Ya hungry?"

"No, I am good thank you. I ate some pop tarts before I came."

"Pop-Tarts? That's not breakfast. Christopher make the young lady a sandwich. You like eggs, bacon, and cheese on an English muffin?" he asked me.

"Uh, sure. That's great. Thank you, Christopher!" I said picking on him.

"As you wish," smirking at me.

Ok, I like the sound of that.

"So, where did we leave off yesterday?" Mr. Burns asked.

"You were going to tell me about your daughters, Sandy Lawrence, and the history of the town."

"Ah, yes. Let's start with a little more history of the town. Especially our part of town. Ya know it's the oldest section, where we live."

"Nope, I did not know that. That's cool. So, there are a lot of haunted houses around here. Is mine?" of course I had to ask.

"Yep. Sandy walks around there all the time. Ron would always tell me about the stories of when she would show up. It was always when something bad was going to happen. It was weird, how it always timed itself out. One month she showed up for a few nights in a row, and then after she left their basement flooded and it had a bunch of old sentimental stuff in it originally, but for some reason Ronnie knew to move it onto one of the shelves he had built."

I didn't think that was weird at all. Ironic maybe but not weird. It wasn't until this next story he told me was when is started to think something was weird.

"Another time she showed up and within a few hours their dog died. Just dropped dead. That was weird. His name was Murphy, he was a good ol' dog. Everyone in the neighborhood loved him. Kinda looked like your dog."

Ok, what? That is weird. "When was that?"

"Uh, I would say probably about 8 months or so ago. He buried him out by the willow in the back. Most of us do that when our pets die, we bury them in the yard, plant something on top of them and then it grows to high heaven. Crazy."

The way he explained things was comical to her because he was so animated with his facial expressions and hand movements.

"So, my dog is Murphy."

"Ah, so it is." He scoffed and shook his head.

Chris walked out with my sandwich, which smelled delicious. I took one bite; it was even better than I thought.

"I can cook ya know. I make the best fries in town remember," he smiled at me, and good lord he was so cute.

"I remember, and thanks for always reminding me," I said annoyed.

The next few hours I sat and listened to Pop talk about his daughters, the history, the accident, and being in the war. It was cool learning about the place we just moved to, since living in Maryland my whole life, we never really knew about many other places. He asked me a lot of questions about there, so did Chris.

"Do you have a boyfriend waiting for you back there?"

"Nope, well I had one, but he was sent to an all-boys school. I don't remember the name of it, but my parents told me it's not that far from here. Not that I want to see him ever again. But that's a whole nother story."

"Gotcha. Well, his loss I guess, then, right?" Chris said staring out the window.

"Right!"

"Pop, it looks like it's about to storm. Scarlet maybe I should walk you home."

I was confused, I lived right down the street, I could see my house from here. But I wasn't arguing.

"That would be great. Thank you pop! I really enjoyed my day." I gave him a big hug and left with Chris.

"Thanks for walking me home, but you know you didn't have to, right?"

"I know, but I wanted to. I also wanted to ask if you wanted to go to Devil's Hole with me sometime/"

I had no idea what he was talking about, and I think he could tell that by the look on my face.

"Duh, sorry. It's a place we all go on the weekends sometimes, we go swimming, fishing,"

"Partying," I interrupted.

"That too." He laughed.

"Yeah, that would be cool. When were you thinking?"

"Well, this Saturday? If not, I totally get it, I just figured I would ask. Plus, it would be a good way for you to meet some of the other kids from school and the neighborhood. I know you met some, but there are so many people that go there. It would be cool."

"Oh. Um, my two best friends are coming up from Maryland. I am sorry."

"Well, bring them too. It would be fun. I can even bring some of my world-famous fries," he chuckled.

"Haha, you're so funny. I will ask them and see if they are ok with that."

"Cool! Well, here's your house, umm would I be able to get your phone number?"

"Sure, you got a pen?"

He patted himself down, "Nope."

"Hold on." I ran into the house and grabbed a pen and ran right back out. I took his hand and wrote mu number on his palm. I always wanted to do that. He smiled at his hand and then at me.

"Cool. I will call you."

I was hoping he would. I went inside and was like floating around the house. Lucy was in the kitchen unpacking more boxes.

"Well, hello there! How was your day? Looks like it was pretty good by the smile on your face."

"Mom, it was amazing. Pop talked about everything, told me that our house is haunted, Chris asked me to hang out this weekend. Oh crap, I gotta call Mel and Gabs and make sure they are ok with going." I didn't even realize I called her mom at first.

"That sounds like a great day. Where did he want to go? You know we don't know much about the area yet so I don't want you going anywhere that you can get in trouble."

She didn't even mention that I called her mom, did she even notice? I am sure she did, I've never called her that before. What do I do now? Do I keep calling her that? I can't go back to Lucy, right? Ugh!

"What's for dinner? Can I help with anything?"

"Just hoagies from DiMada's. Justine is going to pick it up in about an hour. Did you want to go with him?"

"I don't want to seem like I'm desperate to see him. I shouldn't do that right?"

"Sweetheart, you're fifteen, enjoy the flirting while you can. I am sure he wouldn't complain, seeing you twice in one day. I would!"

"Thanks, Mom!"

"You're welcome sweetheart!"

I heard in her voice that she was about to cry but she waited until I left for my room to start. It made me happy that I was finally able to say it to her. I grabbed my phone and hopped down on my bed and dialed Mel's number.

"Hello!" She said.

"Hey! What up?"

"How was it?" she asked.

I sat and told her about my entire day with him and Pop, and I told her about how he asked us to hang out Saturday night, but I wouldn't do it unless her and Gabs said yes.

"Sure, I'm down. I am sure Gabs will be too. If there's boys, there she will be down too."

"Awesome! I can't wait for you two to be here, I miss you guys so much. I feel like it's been months since I've seen you."

I got off the phone with her so I could run to get dinner with Justin. He was waiting for me in the car, music blaring.

"Big Bro! Good song." We both started singing Black Hole Sun, belting it out with Chris Cornell. Damn he has a great voice.

We pulled into the lot, and I could see his mom's car was there. We walked in, smelled like fried onions and oregano. I could see him in the back by the fryer.

"Uhh, is that my girl. Scarlet?" he yelled from in the back.

Justine looked over at me and started laughing hysterically, I pushed his arm and told him to hush up. Everyone was looking at me now, ugh how does this guy manage to embarrass the hell out of me every time I see him. I waved.

"Adams pick up right?" Chris's mom was the one working the counter, she was very nice.

"Yes ma'am." Justine said.

"Scarlet, did you enjoy your time with my dad today? Chris said he did."

"Yes, I did very much. Your dad is a cool guy and full of stories."

"Yes, he is!" she laughed. "Chris also told me that you might be hanging out with him this weekend at Devil's Hole? That sounds fun!"

Justine looked at me again, "Yep, he asked. I have friends coming up from my old town. So, I have to make sure they wanna go. But yeah, it sounded cool."

"Here ya go!" Chris placed our order on the counter. "Twice in one day Adams, I'm beginning to think you like me!"

"In your dreams," I laughed as I said it.

"Yeah right, you absolutely like him. Don't even pretend Letti." Justin really knew how to embarrass me even more."

"Can we just go now." Now I was just mad and ready to be home.

The ride home was quiet, and he apologized and told me that he would be at Devil's hole this weekend too so if I felt uncomfortable that I shouldn't.

CHAPTER 23

One of the hardest things about being in a new town was not knowing anyone and having to relearn how to become friends with new people. I felt awkward just walking up to someone and saying "Hey, I am new here, wanna be my friend." First no one did that in the nineties, and second, it's just weird. Lucky for me I met one of the most popular guys so that was certainly going to help me meet new friends. I hoped at least.

Don't get me wrong I loved having siblings, especially two my age, but they were siblings, and I didn't wanna hang with them all the time. I couldn't talk to them about how my day was with Chris, Justin made that obvious, so I needed friends. I was excited for Mel and Gabs to come up this weekend, and excited to hang out with Chris and his friends. I really had no idea what to expect, since he didn't tell me much about the place. I don't really drink, so it'll be interesting.

The rest of my week was boring, I was unpacking and decorating my room pretty much the entire time, it took me a little longer because I still had this damn cast on. I went to talk to Lucy about when I was supposed to get it off, and how I should keep it from not getting it wet this weekend.

"Hey mom, when is this stupid thing coming off again? It's really cramping my social life." I thought it was funny, but then again, I always think I am funny.

"Um, I'm not sure on the exact date, but if you at the calendar on the closet wall there it should have it, I think its July maybe right before the fourth."

Yep, she was right, totally forgot that it was then. The fourth was not a favorite holiday of mine ever since my mom passed away, but maybe that'll be different here? Who knows?

"Yep, thank God. Next question."

"Shoot."

"How do I keep it from not getting wet?"

"Well, don't go in the water for starters. And I have a plastic cover we can put on it."

Ugh, the embarrassment that I would suffer would be unbearable.

"I will just make sure I stay away from the water."

"That's fine too. I don't blame you; I wouldn't want that on my arm either. How embarrassing."

She totally gets it.

"Thanks mom. I am going to head out back under the willow for a bit, did you know Lawrence's dog is buried under it? Apparently, a lot of the neighbors bury their deceased pets under plants and trees. Weird, like a real-life Pet Cemetery. Creepy!"

"That makes great fertilizer for the plants. So, I can't say I am surprised."

Yep, she totally gets it!

When I was sitting out back the breeze was so cool under that tree, and I guess from the creek too. I could hear the girls playing in the treehouse, and George was looking for bugs, He was some genius. He could name over three hundred different types of insects oh and identify them too. I for one am not a fan of bugs, but it was cool when he showed me a super neat one, like the boxelder bug. It was black with orange on its back and big red eyes. It was cool to look at. Justine started working at DiMadas during the day so he left a bit ago, which was cool because he really wanted to go to culinary school, dad and Lucy just couldn't afford right now. He was a pretty good cook too, which surprised me that he didn't cook more often at the house.

I was so excited to take the ride to pick up the girls, Lucy hadn't yet started work at the hospital, so she and I went, while George stayed with Avery and Vi. It was nice to just have some one-on-one time with her, since we never got to do that. We talked a lot about what pop told me, she was surprised by pretty much all of it. But she did tell me that she saw a ghost too. She wasn't sure what or who it could be, but after I told her about what happened to Sandy, she knew it had to be here, just like Avery and I suspected.

How cool is it that we move to a crazy old town, like backroads stuff, into a haunted house, with pets buried everywhere. I think should send this to Stephen King, because it would make one heck of a story that only he could write. It took about an hour to get to Havre de Grace; traffic was terrible because everyone was going there for the weekend apparently. I was fidgety in my seat, waiting impatiently to get to Mel's.

"Ah, there she is!" I literally opened the door before Lucy could even stop the car. "Oh my God, I missed you!" Yeah, I was probably a bit dramatic, but if you left your best friend of fourteen years, you would be too.

"LETTI!" She yelled out, and Gabs was sprinting out the door to meet me.

We all hugged for what felt like forever.

"Oh my god I missed you guys so damn much. I can't wait to hear everything and for you guys to hear everything. Was Heather and Jen super upset they couldn't come this time?"

"Yeah, Jen was mad at her parents for making her go to that soccer camp. And you know Heather's family is always at Virginia Beach this weekend, so she was pretty upset that you planned it for now. I told her to get over it, and there would be plenty more weekends." Mel had no patience for Heather ever since I left, which made me sad because I loved them both so much and was hoping it wasn't me that kept that friendship going.

"Bummer. But yeah, we will have plenty of weekends coming up. I am gonna run in quick and say hey to moms and pops, be right back!"

I loved Mel's parents; they were like my adoptive parents, and I missed them just as much.

"Hello?"

"Is that who I think it is?" Mrs. Barr exclaimed.

Her hugs were the absolute best and always made me feel like I was home.

"Oh, I missed you beautiful girl! How is Pennsylvania? Not better than Maryland, I am sure."

"No not at all, but I do like it. I am meeting some new people, which is hard. I met this boy. He's super cute."

"I heard; Melinda told me some of what's been going on. She told me that Lucy finally got the mom title from you. I am happy honey, and I know your mom would want you to be happy too. Lucy is a good woman, and she adores you and the girls. How are they by the way?"

"They are good, they have like the biggest room in the house I swear." We both laughed and she didn't seem surprised.

"Ok, well let me get back out there so we can get back before rush hour. Traffic was so bad on the way down."

"Ok, kiddo. Be careful. It was so good to see you!"

The ride back to PA was a lot of fun. We all talked the entire way, Lucy just smiled and listened to us, I am sure she thinks we are crazy teenagers, which we probably were, but we had a fun time together every time we were together.

When we were driving down one of the roads, the girls saw one of the farms, and were flabbergasted.

"Dude, when did a farm get here? I don't remember that from last time." Mel asked.

"Yo, wait it that a bull?" Gabs said with her eyes wide.

"Yep, that's Henry the Bull. And yep, there's always been a farm here, there's another one on that side too."

Both looked to their left and their mouths dropped.

"Dude, you moved to the country."

We all laughed about it, because I was a water girl and now, I am a country girl.

"All right ladies, we are here!" Lucy informed us.

"Woo hoo!" we all yelled as we got out and grabbed their bags from the trunk, to get them settled into my room right away.

<h1 style="text-align:center">CHAPTER 24</h1>

It was so awesome having my girls with me, we picked up exactly where we left off. When we talked about Sandy's accident, they could understand why I thought the ghost that I have been seeing was her. And I told them about Lucy and Avery seeing her too.

"I wish I could talk to her. Like, to see what she is trying to tell us."

"What if you could?" Mel asked.

"What do you mean?"

"What if we did a séance?"

"Uh, absolutely not." Gabs was way to scaredy cat for something like that.

"Why not? It'll be fun."

"I think I have to agree with Gabs on this one. I am not ok with that especially since I don't even know what else is here. What if we wake up something sinister or evil. No thank you ma'am."

"Fine, you two are boring." Mel said.

"Hey girls! What are you thinking for dinner? Your dad's gonna be home late tonight, Justin is going out with Rachel, so you girls get to pick!"

"Wanna do Chinese?" I asked them.

"Yeah, sure that works."

"Can we do Chinese, mom?" both looked at me cockeyed because they had never heard me call her that before. "What?" They both shook their heads like it was nothing.

"Yep, I'll get the menu so you can write down what you want."

"Thank you!"

"What about this Rachel? Is she cool?" Mel asked.

"Yeah, she's cool. She is the absolute opposite of any girl she has dated in the past. I like her. And she makes a big deal about the girls when she is here. I know Lucy and my dad really like her."

"That's good, one day he will realize he should be with me though." Mel was so infatuated with him; it was gross but whatever.

"Ew, stop."

"What if we did the wegie board?" Gabs asked.

"You mean the Ouija board? So, let me get this straight, you won't do a séance, but you'll play with a Ouija board? You are so confusing and weird." Mel said, asking her head.

"It's not real, so I can do that."

"Oh ok." Mel said mocking her almost.

"I would be cool with that. Justin has one, I can borrow it anytime she said. I never wanted to because, uh I am not doing that by myself. But I would totally do that with you girls."

"Awesome! Tonight?" Mel was eager.

"Yeah, that's cool. We have plans tomorrow night re-member?"

"Oh yeah, with the new beau." They enjoyed picking on me about Chris.

"He is not. Even though I would like him to be!" I said scrunching my nose and laughing.

I went to the hallway closet to grab the board game; it wasn't there.

"What the heck? Hey mom? Do you know where the *Ouija Board* went?"

"I think Justin took it to Rachel's house tonight."

"Ugh, ok."

I went back into my room, "Sorry girls, Justin has it. Anything else you wanna do?"

"Well, it's pouring so we can't go outside. Any movies we can rent from *Blockbuster*?"

"Oooo, *Wes Craven's New Nightmare* is out. We could see if it's in, which it should be since it came out in March. I'll ask if we can swing by there before, we grab dinner."

Lucy yelled to us when it was time to go, and we all sprinted to the car, so we weren't completely soaking wet from the rain. It was so awesome being able to spend that weekend with them, had I known it was going to be the last time I spent a weekend with them I would have done some things differently.

When we pulled up to Blockbuster, it was packed. I was so hoping that the movie was in, so as soon as we walked in, I ran over to the horror section so see.

"Jackpot baby!" I yelled as I held it up to the girls. "Mom, is it ok if we get this? It's the new one I was telling you and dad about." It came a lot easier for me to call her mom, I know her, and dad were happy too.

"Yeah sure, just make sure you girls wait to watch after Avery and Vi go to bed. I don't want them having nightmares for the next week."

"I promise we will! Can we get snacks? I know we have popcorn and drinks at home and were getting Chinese, but this could be for dessert!"

"One thing each, no more. Got it?"

"Got it!"

We went over to the candy racks, and I grabbed a bag of *Butterfinger bb's*, Mel got her usual *Hershey* cookies and cream bar, and Gabs grabbed a tube of sour ooze, blue raspberry. We got some skittles for the girls, that was always their go to snack. The Chinese place was two stores down from *Blockbuster*, so we walked under the awning to get the food.

When we were pulling into our driveway, I thought Lucy was going to crash at first. There was someone standing there, just out in the middle of the driveway.

We all screamed; it scared the daylights out of all of us. And then POOF, they were gone as soon she drove through.

"Is everyone ok?" she asked.

We all were too afraid to speak, so we shook our heads and hoped that we didn't just run someone over.

"Mom. What was that?"

I remember her face, literally she had seen a ghost, we all did. "Um, I'm not sure sweetheart, but I am going to get out first and I will come and get you when I know it's safe. Stay in the car."

I wanted to look in the mirror but was too chicken to do it.

"What the hell was that, Letti?" Mel asked.

I shrugged my shoulders, "I have no clue. But I am glad you both saw that and even more glad that the girls weren't in the car."

Only about a minute or two later Lucy came back to the car and let us know it was ok to get out now. I know I didn't want to turn around when I got out, but something told me to. Again, same thing I saw a few nights ago. It just disappeared behind the big pine tree. I knew right then and there it was Sandy. I think she was trying to tell me something, and this time I was determined to figure out what.

We didn't talk again that night about what we saw, honestly, we were all too afraid to bring it up again. Dinner was delicious, we hung out a bit with the girls, and then it was our time. Movie time.

"Ok, we can all sleep on the bed, but I am not in the middle this time. Gabs you get the middle."

"Ok, I guess it's my turn anyway." She said.

She was the most laid-back friend I ever had, her and Mel total opposites. I was bummed that the other two girls couldn't be there, I am getting there with what happened, I just wanna tell my story so everyone knows how much love there was shown to me and that one day someone will figure out who did it.

The movie was outstanding, one of the best so far. *Dream Warriors* was still my favorite, but this one was a close second. We stayed up most of the night and talked about what was happening in Maryland, what was happening here. I was telling them what the place was called that we were going to tomorrow, and who all goes. They were as excited as I had hoped they would be.

CHAPTER 25

"Letti, mom's making bacon and eggs, wake up!" Avery always made sure to wake me up when I had the longest nights ever.

"Ok, ok. I'm up! Hey," I smacked my pillow on the two of them, "get up."

"NO" Mel was grumpy when she didn't get enough sleep.

"I am, I am." Gabs were a bit nicer.

I could hear that everyone was already out in the kitchen, talking about who knows what.

"Morning everybody!" It smelled so good, loved the bacon so much, especially because dad would make the eggs in the bacon grease and toss it over the eggs oh it was so good.

"Morning Letti! Got your eggs ready right here." Dad was the best.

"Mmm Mmm, thank youuu!"

Mel and Gabs walked out from my bedroom right behind me, they both preferred scrambled, which Lucy had that ready for them. "And here you go girls, scrambled, sausage, toast, and OJ."

"Thank you, Ms. Lucy."

"Girls, call me Lucy. You know I don't mind."

"It's just a respect thing, that's all." Mel said.

"Oh, I know, and I appreciate that. Ms. Lucy is just fine then."

"Justin, did you have fun last night? You took the Ouija board; we were so bummed." I said to him.

"It was all right. She really wanted to play, and so the whole group of them joined in. They are into all that stuff."

"What stuff?" Violet asked.

"Nothing kiddo, scary stuff that you and Avery don't wanna hear about." He always shook her hair when he spoke to her, she adored him.

"So, what time are you kids going out tonight? And Justin are you taking the girls?" Lucy asked.

"I think we are leaving at seven, and yes, I am taking them with me. We are meeting everyone else there."

"I am kinda nervous, are you guys?" I was hoping everyone else was.

"A little, but it's because we literally know no one. You at least know a few people who will be there." Mel noted.

"True. But it'll be a cool experience to share with you two!" I said enthusiastically.

We spent most of the day trying on clothes and not liking anything we put on. We ended up wearing almost the exact outfits we would any other day. I put on a pair of bibs, overalls, Mel had her jean shorts on that she made from an old pair of jeans, and Gabs put on one of her dresses that her mom made. We were so predictable.

"Letti, Mel, Gab, I am ready. It's time to go." Justin was yelling from the front yard.

"It's showtime girls! You ready?" anxiously I said.

We all hopped in his car, and I needed to get back to the comment he made at breakfast.

"Big bro, what did you mean by they are into all that stuff? Like witchcraft and stuff?"

"Yeah, it's weird dude. They do this like, voo-doo hoo-hoo, bah humbug crap. Rachel thinks it's weird too, and the two of us just kind of watched and I don't know. It was weird. Just do me a favor, stay away from that group. I know they are the cool kids and all, but just steer clear of them, and stick with Chris, ok?"

"Ok." I had no interest in hanging out with them, but I appreciated him looking out for me. Honestly, I only wanted to hang out with Chris anyway.

As we were driving down the winding road, it was pitch black and eerie, I had this awful feeling in the pit of my stomach, and I wasn't sure why. I thought it was just nerves at first, but it was something else. Eventually I would find out what. But not tonight, tonight I got to have fun with my friends, like a normal teenager would.

"We're here. Everyone out!"

I could see Chris waiting on the side of the road, with some of his friends, I assumed.

"Oh, good. Your boyfriend is waiting for you," Justin loved to tease.

"HAHA!"

He and Chris hooked hands and did their bro thing, and Justin walked off to find Rachel. The girls and I walked over to them, and now I was nervous.

"Hey girl!" He said silly like.

"Hey yourself."

"These must be the friends from Maryland. I remember seeing you both at the shop. I am Chris in case you forgot. This doofus right here is Joey, and that one there it Rob."

"Nice to meet you." We all said at the same time, and of course started laughing.

"So, what do we do here?" Mel asked.

"Well, most of the time we go swimming and shit like that, but the waters up too high so it's dangerous."

"Oh, that blows. But cool, what else. We drinking tonight?" Mel's tone was more of an assumption than a question.

"Yep, we got plenty of that. Follow me."

Mel and Joey walked off together, while Gabs and Rob sat on the trunk of Justin's car. I was with Chris, and we were joking back and forth about who pop liked more. I believe it's me, but he disagreed.

"You, know, it's because I am prettier than you, that's why he likes me more." I said jokingly.

"That I can't disagree with." He said.

Uh, ok I was not expecting him to say that, hoping but never thought he would. I didn't think he thought that I was, but apparently, I was wrong. I am so cool with that. I know my face was beat red from blushing, and there is no doubt he noticed. We kept talking, and Mel and Joey had four cups with them.

"What do we have on tap tonight?" Chris asked as he took two of them and handed me one.

"Natty Light," Joey said with a sour face.

"Well, it's better than nothing right?" Chris said laughing, looking at me.

"If you say so," I took the cup from him. I didn't drink, ever. And I really didn't want to look like a complete loser, but I really didn't wanna drink. So, I just held onto it and when no one was looking I would pour a little out when their backs were turned. I know I shouldn't give in to peer pressure, and I didn't entirely if you think about it.

"Letti, are you drinking a beer?" Gabs was surprised when she saw me.

"Just one, nothing crazy." She knew by my tone that I was not drinking it but had to say it to save face.

"Gotcha. Rob and I found a beautiful spring over that way," she pointed behind us to the left. "Do you guys wanna go there?"

We all started out walking to the spring they found, and I realized that night how vastly different it was here. Mel seemed to get along just fine, Gabs was good with talking about God knows what with Rob, and I felt like I was out of place, for the first time ever.

"What's up? You, ok?" Chris asked.

"Yeah, I'm good."

"That's not very convincing. You can tell me."

"Ok, to be honest I don't feel like I fit in here. I see everyone hanging out and having a good time drinking and smoking, but that's not me. I mean even Gabs is hitting it off, and she's usually the one who doesn't talk much to anyone. You think I'm a loser?"

He took the cup out of my hand and laced his fingers into mine, and looked down into my eyes, "Scarlet, you don't have to do anything you don't want to. If you don't wanna drink this, don't. I would rather have the real Scarlet than someone who is pretending to be what she thinks she should be. Does that make sense?"

I nodded my head yes, "yeah. But do you think I am a loser?"

"Oh, yeah hundred percent." He wrapped his arms around me and chuckled, "Not even a little bit Scarlet Adams."

Oh my God, for a second, I thought he was going to kiss me, and the little voice inside my head was freaking out. He didn't but damn did I want him to. I think he knew I wanted him to kiss me too, because he smiled and then took my hand, and we walked back to the group.

The rest of the night was a blast, I didn't need to have anything to drink for them to want to hang out with me still. Let me tell you, being a teenager in the nineties was hard as hell. Peer pressure was not fun, and if you weren't drinking, smoking cigarettes, pot, or having sex, you weren't cool. I did none of the above, and when I was in Maryland, no one cared, we didn't do those things. But here, what a reality check.

I wasn't a prude or anything, I only had one boyfriend so far and the other stuff was available where I lived. Well, like I said, it could've been I just was never introduced to the stuff.

One promise I made to my mom before she passed away was that I would never let anyone put me in a position that made me uncomfortable, and I wouldn't do things just because everyone else was. Nowadays that was getting harder and harder, but I try to keep that promise every time a situation like this presents itself.

"Scarlet, if you don't mind me asking, but what happened to your mom? I know she passed away, but that's all Chris told us." Rob asked.

"Cause it's all I know doofus.' He said.

"She had cancer. It was quick, but it sucked."

"I'm sorry. I lost my mom to cancer too, but my dad wasn't nice enough to stick around. I live with my Aunt Sarah."

"Who also happens to be the judge around here. Literally." Joey said.

"Oh, that's cool!" Mel chimed in.

We were all confused by what she thought was cool.

"Melinda, are you drunk?" Gabs asked.

"No."

Yes, she was. She was slurring, rocking back and forth standing there, and kept closing her eyes. Ugh, I did not need this and knew Justin was going to be pissed at me for not watching her better.

"I think she was talking about your aunt being the judge." I assured them.

"Yeah, I wouldn't say that's cool of his parents. God, I am not heartless you know."

Oh, she was going to be a peach when we got home tonight. As long as she didn't throw up, I would be allowed to go out again, if she did, I was most likely grounded for the next eighty years.

"Ok, I think she has had enough. Let's just get some water from now on." I directed Joey.

"Got it. Be right back."

Apparently, she had two beers, so I knew it had to wear off soon, and hopefully way before we had to leave. Our curfew tonight was eleven and it was only nine thirty, so we had plenty of time.

CHAPTER 26

There were more people arriving as the night went on. Chris and the other two seemed annoyed when a Jeep pulled up. I could see that it was a bunch of guys, and I guess I didn't know what the big deal was, until I did.

"Chris, who's that?" I asked.

"That's the guys that ruin the night for all of us. They are preppies, and we don't get along well with them. They are supposed to have Friday nights, but I guess since it was raining, they assumed it was cool to come tonight. If there isn't any trouble, then we will be fine. Just stick with me, ok."

I took his hand and held it tighter, and of course happily agreed to stick with him. Justin and Rachel joined us in the meantime, apparently, they all try to hang with their own school.

Chris started to tell us how the rules are here. There're six different schools that party here, and they all had an assigned weekend and day for that weekend. This was the best way to keep things in order and no trouble. Until tonight. Everything was calm for the remainder of the time that we were there. We all started to make our way to the cars, when we heard someone say Mel's name.

"Melinda Barr? It can't be." A male's voice said.

I knew it immediately and stood frozen for a second. Chris turned back to see why I stopped walking.

"Scarlet, what's wrong?" he asked.

"No way. Scarlet Adams. What the hell are you two doing here? No shit, there's Gabriella Clark. My eyes must be deceiving me."

"Richie Greene, we could ask the same about you," Mel said.

"You know this guy, Scarlet?" Joey asked.

"Yeah, we grew up together." I answered him.

"I just can't believe you three are here. Why are you here?" He questioned.

"Scarlet moved here with her family. Why are you here?" Gabs asked.

"I go to school up here. Remember when my parents sent me to a special school? Well, it's quite elite and impressive."

"Clearly by the ridiculous outfits you are all in," Rob said.

I could tell that the guys were not thrilled about the idea of talking to them, so I tried to just say hello and goodbye. Luckily, Justin walked back to us, and it wasn't until then that those guys finally walked away.

"Is there a problem here fellas?" Justin was intimidating with all his tattoos and how big he was. He worked out pretty much all the time and was not afraid of a fight.

"Nope, we were just saying hello." Rich said.

"Well, then say goodbye now." Justin urged.

"Good to see you Letti," can you believe that he walked over and kissed my hand. The nerve of him.

"Dude, are you joking?" Chris was angry now.

"Well, you obviously weren't going to do it." Rich said arrogantly.

Chris went to go after him and I stepped in front of him, hoping he would stop. Luckily, he did.

"He's not worth it. Trust me. Let's just go."

We got into Justin's car and the guys got into Chris', and we went to my house since dad and Lucy didn't mind if we all went back there to hang out for a bit.

"Letti, was that the loser you were dating when my mom and your dad started dating? Damn I'm glad you upgraded to Chris. He was about to get a beat down, and if he starts his crap again, I won't hesitate next time."

"Believe me, I was young and dumb, and apparently had no taste in guys when I was thirteen."

Even though I was only fifteen I knew I had changed since moving, and since he just up and left. Looking at him I questioned what I ever saw in him in the first place. And why was I not surprised that he ended up at the preppy school that Chris talked about tonight. He would end up there.

When we pulled up to the house, Chris was right behind us. Dad and Lucy met us outside, to make sure everything was ok. Justin assured them that we were all fine, we were just going to hang out in the back if it was ok. They would rather us home anyway, and they enjoyed that the house was being used as the hang out house.

"I can't believe all the people we run into here and it's him. God, I hated him back then too, I am so glad you didn't end up with him Letti." Mel was much more sober now.

"I know right. What an ass. And wow I thought he was cute." The three of us laughed.

"Dude, what's their deal? It got tense when they showed up, I don't mean with just you guys but like everyone that was there from Weston." Justin asked.

"It's a long story, and I don't even know if I know all of it," Chris began to tell us, "I think it was like five maybe six years ago, my brother Jay and a bunch of the other kids from Weston were down there. Everything was cool, until two of them, the preps, showed up randomly. Now, there were a ton of Weston kids so they knew it would be cool, but they didn't wanna waste their time on these two nitwits. Anyway, he said about an hour later and someone heard a girl screaming. Of course, everyone was freaking out and stuff because no one knew what was happening. My brother and his boys were running around with everyone else looking for this girl. They didn't find her because there was no girl.

The assholes from St. Charles had a radio behind a tree and put a tape in of Halloween music and played the screaming girl. Here they distracted Weston kids from their partying and when the kids came back their cars were egged, and all their beer was gone.

They knew it was weird those two showed up alone, but once they came back and saw what happened they knew it was them. So now everyone is on edge when they show up. Like they are entitled."

"Wow, that's crazy. Thank God there wasn't a girl though, cause damn that would've sucked. And yes, I know Rich his daddy is the chief of police back in Havre de Grace, and he always acted as if he was entitled, so I am sure they are all the same." I needed him to know that.

"I don't wanna go back there again Justin. I know my sister will, but I don't want to. That was the first time I've been there since sophomore year, and now I remember why I don't go." Rachel said to Justin.

"We don't ever have to go back there." He assured her.

"What about you? You, ok?" Chris asked me.

"Yeah, I just hate that I had to see him again. I was so messed up after he left without saying a word. Even his mom was weird to me when I would see her. Sorry you had to deal with that."

"Don't be sorry, he should be lucky I didn't knock his ass out, I was definitely not a fan. Guess there weren't as many options down there then there are up here?" jokingly he said.

"HAHA, yeah because I have so many options up here. Well, I know of two guys that are into you."

I looked at him like he had three heads, "What? Shut up, who?"

"Well, me, and Matt."

"Matt, that boy I met at the waterfall. Doesn't he have a girlfriend?"

"Yeah, Kim." Chris said.

"Kim? She's wacky, sis don't get mixed up with that crowd, ok?"

"You don't have to worry about that big brother, they were nice, an no offense Rachel but they weren't really my type of crowd."

"Oh, no no, none taken." Rachel said.

"Good, because they were the ones doing all that hoodoo nonsense, I was telling you about from last night. They are trouble."

The rest of the night was a lot of fun, and sadly this would be the last time I saw the girls. They both had vacations and camps, and I had a job this summer working at one of the produce stands in the town over from us. Mrs. Burns got me the job, forgot to mention that, because it was the same day I was talking with pop. It seems like things are moving fast, right? Well, they did, but the rest of the summer gets even faster, so hang on for this roller coaster.

CHAPTER 27

Around two o'clock Mrs. Barr pulled into the driveway, which made us all sad, since we knew it was going to be a while before we saw each other again. I could hear her and Lucy talking in the kitchen and Lucy was going to show her around. That meant we had a few more minutes together. I knew they had to leave soon, Gab started her science camp tomorrow, something she did every summer, she was a counselor's assistant this year and she was excited for it.

I wasn't sure when I would see them again, once school started back up, August for them and September for me, we wouldn't have any time at all. When Mel's mom called them to say that she was ready, I felt sick to my stomach. I felt as if this would be the last time I saw them, not by choice but distance and time.

We hugged for a long time, and none of us wanted to let go first. We counted to three and we let go at the same time, I felt as if part of me left with them that day.

After they left, I was in my room for the rest of the day, it was raining, and I was depressed.

"No one bother me, please. I just need to be alone."

No one bothered me at all, until it was time for dinner when Avery came in to check on me and see if I wanted to eat. I was starved so I got myself up and headed to the kitchen. I thought a lot about growing up with them, and what it would've been like to grow up here. It was nice here and I really liked a lot of the people I have met so far; it was just different. Not bad or good, just different.

"Sorry everyone. I know I was sulking in my room all day, and there were other things that needed to be done. I just feel like that's the last time I am going to see them. I don't know why."

"Scarlet don't apologize sweetheart. We knew this was going to be hard for you, and we all just wanted to give you your space. We will just have to make it a point to make plans with them for your birthday, this way you know you will see them again before next summer. Sound like a plan?" Lucy asked as she was finishing up putting dinner out for us all.

"That would be great. Thanks mom."

Dinner conversation was based around the weekend and the upcoming week. When I was starting work, the girls were starting an art camp at one of the local art studios. George had some other camp; Justin was working all week. Dad was on second shift at the museum, which I am still not even one hundred percent I know what he does there. He comes home every happy though, so that's a plus.

We were all most excited for Lucy, she starts at the hospital tomorrow. She seems nervous but she hasn't said so. She was the best nurse, and the kids at the hospital are going to love her.

"If you'll excuse me for just a minute." Dad got up and walked out for some reason. The girls were giggling, like they knew something was about to happen.

About a minute later dad came walking back in with the most beautiful bouquet of flowers I have ever seen. There were roses, greens, sunflowers, baby's breath, all throughout. The red from the roses and the yellow in the sunflowers were perfect together. She was surprised and started to cry. Happy tears of course.

"What is this? These are beautiful!"

"They are for you and how amazing you have been this whole time with this move and the change and starting the new job tomorrow. We wanted to show you much you are appreciated."

He gave her a kiss, and we all clapped and cheered for her. She was amazing, I cannot believe how lucky I was to end up with two fantastic moms. I remembered how dad was with mom and how he would do random things like this for her too. I guess that's why I have such high expectations for any guy that comes into my life. My dad set the bar high.

We all knew life was going to get busy real fast, so we had schedules that we went over after dinner. We all had a color, it was so confusing, I had orange which was my favorite color. I looked at it and just gave up trying to understand it, I know to just look for orange and that's me.

Luckily, the art studio was within walking distance from the house, so I was in charge of walking the girls there this week, and then started work on Wednesday. I looked at the time and it was almost eight, we watch Sunday night movies every week.

"Hey guys, it's almost time. Come on!" I yelled to everyone.

"All right, we are coming." Dad hollered back.

The movie was spectacular, exactly what I was hoping it would be. Oh boy did I fall in love with Benny the jet. He was so bad, and so cool, he reminded me of Chris in some ways.

I am sure you already said it in your mind "You're killin me smalls," and you guessed it we said it all night, it was great. Dad would say something, or Lucy would, and we all say "You're killin me smalls." They laughed at the first ten times, but I think they got annoyed by it after like the twentieth time of us saying it, so we knew it was time to stop. Just for the night though.

That night while heading to bed, I noticed something out of the ordinary, which wasn't really different I guess because

I have seen a lot of things like that since we moved in. I was walking into my room, and I saw something glistening from the floor in the far corner. I walked over to it to see what it was. It looked like jewelry of some sort, but I couldn't quite reach it. I grabbed one of the wire hangers from my closet and used the hook to dig in to grab it.

I pulled it out and it was a ring. I looked at the sides, I read it out loud. "Class of 1976" looks like a pom pom, and some kind of megaphone, and a torch, whatever that means. I looked at the inside and on it was Sandra Mae Lawrence, engraved on the inside.

I dropped it without even thinking because it scared the daylight out of me. What is her ring doing here? Wouldn't she have had it on, or had they put it on her? This is all too much. Why are you giving me all the signs? What am I supposed to do?

Of course, I knew she wouldn't answer me, but I really had no idea what I was supposed to do. Like, I didn't know anything about this town and had no idea what I could do. I thought for a few minutes and thought maybe she wants me to help her. Maybe I can start to get a journal going this week on details and things that have happened and stuff like that. I know I am telling dad and Lucy about the ring so maybe then can call the Lawrences about it and I am sure they will want it.

Bedtime for me, tomorrow is going to be a crazy, wild day.

CHAPTER 28

When I woke up I had about fifteen minutes before I had to walk the girls to camp. No time to eat so I would just get some cereal when I came back home, but I'll grab an apple for the walk down. The girls were frustrated with me that I woke up so late, I didn't wanna hear it. I would get them there when they needed to be, they were worried for no reason.

"Ok, I am ready." I told them, even though they were standing waiting impatiently at the door for me. "And apparently you two are too."

It wasn't raining, thank God, and the day was beautiful. The sky was an arctic color, the clouds were fluffy, and there were so many birds here. I was not a fan of birds, but they had cool little guys. They were yellow and looked like they belonged in a house, but I don't know exactly what they were. The houses were a little different here than they were in Maryland. They were small, and very old. Pop had told me that some were over a hundred years old, which is a lot like down there.

It was very different with not having all the people from out-of-town vacationing, this was just a small town that was filled with blue collar workers. Most of the men, pop said, worked at the refineries and many of the women had jobs as bus drivers, or at the delis in the area. The fire company was near us, but I didn't pay much attention to that.

When I got back to the house Murphy was waiting for me, wagging his tail knowing it was time for his walk.

"Hey buddy! You waiting for me? All right let's get hooked up, but this time don't pull my arm out, ok? It still hurts from last weekend." He looked at me and barked. And who says dogs can't answer us, ha. He knew exactly what I said to him, all the time. Well maybe not all the time but he knew.

I wasn't taking him back to the waterfall this time, just up and down the block a few times, and he was happy with that. I didn't see Mrs. Burns' car in the driveway, but pop was on the porch hollering at the squirrels to get away from the bird feeder. I waved up to him, and he called me up to say hello.

I walked up the stairs and let Murphy go. He loved to run through their yard, since it was fenced in, I didn't have to worry about him getting out.

"Hey Pop! What a beautiful morning huh?"

"Yeah, it is. Deat yet?"

"I'm sorry, what was that pop?"

"Did you eat yet? You know food, stomach."

"Ohh, I got it now. I don't quite have the lingo down yet for here. Guess it'll take some time."

"Yeah, but you'll get the hang of it. I'll teach ya some too. Sure, my grandson will also." he winked.

"Yeah probably." I laughed.

"Why don't ya go in and make us a few sandwiches?"

"Ok, what would you like?"

"Ham and cheese is just fine."

"Coming right up."

As I walked into the kitchen, I needed a few minutes to remember where everything was, when I was in here with Chris, I was not paying attention to anything but him. As I was making his sandwich, I could hear a car pull up, and saw it was Mrs. Burns. They both reminded me of my grandparents, on my mom's side. Their witty banter back and forth, their sense of humor, the stories. I was kind of nice to feel a little at home here.

I heard three of the doors shut, and was hopeful Chris was from one of them. Lucky for me he was. I could hear pop outside saying something, and then a minute later Chris was in the kitchen with me.

"What are you steaking my job now?" He walked over and hugged me.

"Maybe." Yes, I was flirting, so what.

"Hey pop, I quit! You got yourself a much better-looking personal chef now."

I knew he was kidding, and pop agreed with him. He was so handsome, and the more I got to see him the more he became so.

"What do you have in store today, Miss. Adams? I know it is not hanging here with pop."

"I have to walk back down and pick up the girls around twelve-thirty, and wanted to take Murphy, but with my arm I don't know if I can do both."

"Well let me come with. It'll be fun. And I would love to meet them." Chris insisted.

"Really? You wanna do that? Don't you have stuff to do here?" I questioned.

"Nothing pressing. Hey pop, I am gonna go with Scarlet in a bit to get her sisters from camp, cool?" He replied.

"Whatever." Pop was so nonchalant about everything.

"There ya have it. It's settled, I am coming along." he said happily as he put his ballcap on the table. Pop taught him, and the rest of his grandsons, that it was rude to wear a hat at the dinner table, even if it was breakfast or lunch.

"Ok, who am I to argue!"

We stepped out and ate with pop, and talked about the weather again until it was almost time to head out.

"Oh pop. I almost forgot. Lat night when I was getting ready for bed. I saw a sparkle on the floor." I proceeded to tell him what I found.

"Huh, that's odd. I thought they found that, and she was buried with it on. Do your parents know?"

"No, not yet."

"Hold onto it. I'll be talking to Ron this week, let me ask about it first. Ok?"

"Sure pop."

"Is it ok if we swing by my house quick? I gotta grab an envelope to drop off at the studio that I forgot this morning." I asked.

"Absolutely!" he replied with a smile. His smile had one dimple on the right side, and it was so attractive.

We said goodbye and started toward my house; dad was outside attempting to cut the grass. A little about the topography of my house, we have a gigantic hill and trees everywhere, so it made it near impossible for him to cut it.

"You know I can cut that for him, I do that when I am not working at my parents' shop. I'll tell your dad." Chris reassured her.

"Is there anything you don't do?" I wondered out loud.

"Probably, but I don't wanna tell you just yet," he winked at me, again, and jogged over to my dad.

"Hey, Mr. Adams! You know I can do that for you. Me and two of my buddies cut grass and do landscaping during the summertime, and we don't charge much at all. If you want, I can come back tomorrow with them, and we can get this looking nice for you. I used to do it for Lawrences, so I am used to how to cut it. Also, the back yard too. Probably only thirty bucks for the entire thing, cut, weed whack, and clean up."

"Chris, that would be spectacular. Thanks for helping an old man out." My dad said, trying to catch his breath.

They shook hands, so I assumed they worked out a plan. Murphy ended up laying down and did not want to go with us.

"Ready?" I asked.

"Where's the furry one?" He answered with a question.

"He passed out and had no desire to come with."

We all laughed, as Chris and I started to make our way down the road to get my sisters from camp.

"So, tell me about this place. The people, what it's like growing up here. I wanna know it all." I really wanted to know.

"Hm, ok. It's quiet, we don't have anything crazy happen ever really. There's a lot of town involvement."

"What do you mean?"

"Well, we have a lot of events, for all the holidays. Maybe since the fourth is coming up you would wanna go with me to the high school to watch the fireworks? I mean, of course if you don't have any other plans."

"No."

"Ok. I figured I would ask."

"I mean, sorry, no I don't have any other plans. Yes, I would love to go!"

"Cool! Uh, so a little more about this part of town. This is the oldest section of town, so there's a lot of historical stuff that goes on. They do reenactments of beck when it was all Mills back in here. My oldest brother, Jason, started getting involved with the Historical society a few years back, so he has implemented a lot of cool events, parades, holds stuff at the old school lot. The old school burned down in the fifties; I think. We have the best fall festival in the county. Everyone comes here for it. Since we have so many farms down here there's a lot of room to have them. We should go to that too, it's a lot of fun. Oh, and have you ever ridden a horse?"

"That sounds pretty cool. What do you do there? I can't say I have ever had the chance to ride a horse."

"There are hayrides, pumpkin carving, pie eating contests, you name it it's there. There's horseback riding on the trails, that's nice. There's also a Miss. Granny Smith winner."

"Oh, now I have to know more about this." I couldn't help but laugh, I needed to know more.

"So, all the girls between the ages of thirteen and seventeen are eligible. Someone nominates her and sends in a picture and explains why she would make a great Miss. Granny Smith and represent the town for the year. She has to go to all the events for the year and do community service projects, and it's a lot."

"Wow, ok then."

"Yeah, my mom and all my aunts won at one time or another. It's kind of archaic, but the girls love to have a fuss made over them. Well, the girls that get nominated and picked."

"Oh, so it's the really pretty, popular, preppy girls then?"

"You could say that."

"Got it. Definitely do not want that. Have you taken a lot of girls to these?"

"Actually, you would be my first that wasn't related to me."

"Oh, I feel honored that you asked. Even if we are four months away."

"Yeah, you may not even be talking to me by then."

"I hope I am. I like talking to you and hanging out with you."

I know my face was beat red because I could feel how warm it was. I was really hoping that we could do more than just talk sometime, like maybe he would wanna be my boyfriend. I can't say that out loud, and it's been way too soon, but maybe one day.

CHAPTER 29

As we walked along, he took my hand in his, I was never more nervous and equally excited for this. So many cars drove by and honked while waving to us.

"People are super friendly here. They don't even know me."

"No but they know me, and you look like you belong here. You do belong here."

I just smiled looking at the ground as we walked further, kicking some of the rocks along the way. There was a soda can on the side of the road, so I instantly needed to crush the middle down and put my foot in it. I started walking with it and he laughed so hard at it.

"You do that too? We thought we were the only ones around who did that. It's so silly but damn funny. Even as a teenager."

The rest of the walk we talked about other things we had in common, even growing up in different states. We found out we were not all that different than the other. It was fun learning things about him and watching his facial expressions. He was very animated and talked with his hands a lot.

"Here it is!" I could see the girls through the large old windows that faced the street, they had big smiles on their faces. It made me so happy that they were settling in so well. They saw me and started waving from inside.

"There they are! I'll just be a minute."

I walked in and found their teacher and handed her the form that I forgot.

"Letti, is that the boy you were talking about? He is cute!" Avery made me laugh at some of the things she would say.

"Yes, his name is Chris. And don't be weird, ok?"

"What do you mean? We're never weird."

They both said as they walked out of the studio down the stairs backward with their eyes closed. I just shook my head; I knew they would do something. I saw them skip over to him and he crouched down to say hello.

"Ok, thank you. I will see you tomorrow morning." I said to the teacher. "What'd I miss?"

"Oh nothing, we were talking about you!" They both giggled as they danced in a circle around us.

"What did they say?"

"Nothing really, just that you turn into a werewolf when there's a full moon. And that you shouldn't eat after midnight because you're scary." All of them were laughing.

"HAHAHA!" I was not amused.

"Letti, we like him!"

"Great, I am so glad you approve!" Actually, I was glad, because we have been through enough in our short time on this earth. It made me happy to hear.

We made it back to the house and the girls ran straight to the back yard to play. Chris and I sat on the front porch until he said he had to leave for work.

"I am working with your brother today. He's a good cook, and a hard worker. I wish my dad could find five more like him."

"He is the best big brother. He has taught me so much about cars, boys, food, card games. I am a real game shark, so don't ever play poker with me," this time I winked at him.

"Oh, are you flirting with me Miss. Adams?"

"Maybe!"

"I am flattered. Ok, well I have to get to work now. Hopefully, my mom-mom didn't leave me yet." He looked over to see if her car was still there, "Nope, all good. Can I call you later?"

"I would like that."

"Great. I will talk to you tonight then. Probably around eight-thirty."

"Sounds like a plan!"

"Bye, Letti!"

I scrunched my nose up to that; I wasn't sure how I felt about him calling me that. Not because I didn't like it, but because I really liked how he said Scarlet. He said it with a certain smile every time.

"You didn't like that?"

"No, no. It was fine, I just like to hear you call me by my real name."

"Bye, Scarlet."

"Bye, Chris. Go make good French fries!"

He saluted me jokingly as he was walking down my walkway and then ran to his grandparents. I was on cloud nine, I didn't think there was anything that could ruin my mood, until I felt the first rain drop. Rain again, that's all it ever does here. It quickly went from sunny to dark in a manner of minutes and within seconds it was downpouring. The creek behind the house was so high and the girls knew they were not allowed to go near it. The tree house was far enough away so they could spend time there. I ran inside and realized that the girls were not in there. I panicked.

I started yelling their names throughout the house and happened to see them outside in the old tree house. They were terrified and the water from the creek was rising fast. I didn't hesitate, I ran as fast as I could down to them, but the water was getting higher and higher by the minute. I never saw anything like it in my life. We had bad storms in the

Bay, but this was different. It would rise and then fall just as quickly. I was in shock, I froze for a second and then came back to reality.

"Girls, just stay there. I need a minute to figure out how to get you both." I stood there looking around and what I could tie onto myself to get through the rising water. I knew I didn't have a lot of time. Suddenly, I heard a voice from behind me.

"Letti you have to help us. We're so scared." Their voices were breaking my heart.

"Scarlet, stay there. I will get them."

Chris sprinted by me, and to the ladder.

"Girls, I can take you both, but I need you to come to me one at a time, so I don't fall over ok."

"Ok," they were both crying. I was crying. My heart raced as I watched him hold himself up in water against the ladder, and reach out for the girls.

"Violet, you come down first. I got you I promise. Just look at me and listen to my voice."

As I stood there watching him grab her, I inched closer in case he needed my help.

"Ok good. Now Avery, your turn."

She was quick to get down to him. He had them each in his arms and trudged through the water. I walked in as far as I could and took Vi from him.

"Oh, my girls. Are you ok? I know you're scared." I hugged them both so tightly. "Go ahead up, I'll be right in."

I looked at him, and the entire world disappeared around me.

"How did you know?"

"I was walking to mom-mom's car and heard you yelling to them. I saw what was happening and it was an instinct I guess."

"I, I, I have no idea how to thank you. You saved them."

"I believe you would've figured it out. And you did, because if you didn't yell, I wouldn't have known to come down here."

"Whatever the reason, I am so grateful for you." Without hesitation or thought, I leaned up and kissed him right after I said that. Yep, right there in the downpour. I didn't care about the rain, if anyone could see, if he didn't want me to. I didn't care.

"Well, that was unexpected. And happily, accepted."

It was a sweet kiss, not what you see in the movies, we didn't make out. I kissed him for a few seconds and could not wait for that again.

"Ok, now I am really leaving. I am looking forward to talking to you tonight." He leaned down and kissed me. I wanted to scream in excitement and jump up and down, but I had to play it cool, you know. I think I floated into the house. And I was still shaking over the girls being stuck there and that entire awful time.

"Knock-knock. Can I come in?"

They were both in their pj's and robes, sitting on their beds with a blanket wrapped around. Their hair was wet but combed through. They were reading their *Baby-Sitters Club* series books and looked ok now. George took care of them.

"Hi Letti. Wanna read with us?"

"Of course, I do. Vi, why don't you come over here and sit with us, and I will read a few pages to you both."

Violet got up with her blanket and shuffled her way to us on the bed. I leaned up against Avery's headboard and they leaned on my shoulders. I started to read and forgot how much I liked these too when I was their age, and how I wished mom would read them to me, but she was already gone. I was grateful that I could be here for them and do these things I know mom would be proud of.

"Ah, Claudia and the New Girl, one of my all-time favorites! Let's begin, shall we?"

I enjoyed reading to them, I always have, especially when it is a favorite of mine. I read three chapters to them, and then heard Lucy was home.

"It must be three o'clock. Sounds like mom is home."

Dad got home as George was helping the girls get dry. The girls explained to dad what happened, and he was in tears after.

We all got up and went toward the kitchen, saw dad and Lucy kiss, what else is new, and offered to help get dinner together.

The girls had their lunches a little late today, it took them a little while to calm down. So, Dad made them triple deckers. What's that? Just the best sandwich in the world. It's peanut butter, jelly, and fluff on three layers of bread, hence the triple decker. Put some chips in there, oh its heaven on a plate.

CHAPTER 30

As the days went on, I started my new job at the produce stand which was fun most of the time. Mrs. Grogan taught me how to put flower bunches together and make them look pretty. She had them for free in her stand. She was nice, but old, and forgot a lot of things she had already told me.

Chris and I spent a lot of time together when we weren't working. He started cutting our lawn and I very much enjoyed that! He got along well with everyone in my family, and I with his. We never went back to Devil's Hole, after that night. I met a lot of locals, from working at the produce stand, to visiting Chris at work, and just hanging out with him.

Carmen and I started to spend a lot of time together as well. She and a few of the girls had a falling out on the fourth of July and so she and I just started to talk more. She lived right by me, so it was easy to spend time together. We became super close that summer, and I was excited for school to start now since I knew people.

Lucky for us, Carmen and I, our boyfriends were good friends too. She had been dating Ryan Campbell for the past two years. His dad was a Pennsylvania State Police officer, he was very athletic and a well-rounded guy. Everyone seemed to like him, including my parents. Then there was Justin and Rachel, and Joey and Robbie. We all hung out often with each other.

At the end of August right before school was starting back up, we all wanted to have a firepit at my house. We planned it for a Friday night, and we had decided to invite other people as an "end of the summer party," we all agree no drinking or drugs, just good old-fashioned fun and hanging out with friends.

Since I didn't know many other kids our age, I depended on the rest to invite people that would want to just have fun and hang out. Victoria Singleton and Josh Drexler, who were the perfect couple, and I met at the falls when we first moved here, were here. Karen, Kali, and Kerry, they were triplets and were Rachel's best friends, and just as nice as can be. And then us, Me, Chris, Justin, Rachel, George, Rob, Joey, Carmen, and Ryan.

It was the most perfect night for a fire pit. We didn't need all of those "extras" to have a good time.

Apparently not everyone got the memo on that. And a few people showed up that were not invited. We heard a rustling come up from the creek behind us, it was kind of scary actually.

Chris and Justin were on alert immediately, and then Matt and Kim came into view, and behind them were Quinn, Rachels little sister, Brian Peoples, I didn't know him, JJ Masterson, another guy I didn't know, and then a few others that no one knew.

They were carrying six packs, and backpacks.

"Whoa, what's all this? And who the hell invited you guys?"

"Oh, we thought it was an open invite. Are we not included?" Kim was nasty, there was something about her I just didn't like. I wasn't sure what it was, she just seemed to rub everyone the wrong way.

She was also very bossy to Matt, who seemed like a nice guy, just ended up dating the wrong girl maybe. Chris said Matt was a nice guy at one point, he was nice to me when I met him earlier in the summer, but I know Kim was not a fan of me. We spoke maybe two words to each other.

"Come on, loosen up you guys. It's the end of summer, and we need to celebrate." She was very loud.

"Please keep your voice down, I have little siblings and don't want to get woken up by us back here." I demanded of her.

"Oh, I am so sorry," she said to me, I could hear the sarcasm in her tone.

"Kim, let just go to party back at the falls, we don't have enough for everyone anyway." Matt was now pulling her arm to leave.

"No, I want to stay and get to know the new girl. Everyone else seemed to be buddy buddy with her, I wanna see what all the fuss is about."

Her tone was sinister, eerie, it made me uncomfortable. I really wished they would leave just as soon as she arrived. My anxiety was growing now, and I think Justin and Chris could tell. He took my hand and whispered that he would make them leave, just give him a minute.

"Matt we're gonna need you to take everyone out of here now. You all know you were not invited, and you are not welcome. I am sorry it has to be this way, but she is leaving us no other choice."

"She? I have a name, and you know it well Christopher. How quickly you forgot. Let me remind you."

The nerve of this girl, can you believe, walked over to him, and kissed him, right there right in front of everyone. Me, Matt, she didn't care. I stood up without even hesitating.

"Who the hell do you think you are? Get off him!" I said with such anger and rage. I wanted to hit her, but I've never hit anyone in my life. My heart was pounding, I was shaking, I thought I was having a heart attack.

"Ohhhh, well well, now I see why everyone likes you. You're a feisty one."

She walked right up to me, we were face to face, I really thought she was going to hit me. I was so thankful when she did not.

"Never get in my face again, bitch. You have no idea who I am, who my family is, and what I am capable of. Stay out of my way, or you will regret it."

And then they were gone, just like that. I wanted to throw up immediately and run away at the same time.

"Are you all right, Scarlet?" He was rubbing my arms talking to me.

"Yeah, I'm ok Chris."

"Man, I thought you two were gonna throw down. Wow! I have never seen anyone stand up to her like that," Carmen said impressed.

"I am so happy she didn't hit me. I was freaking out in my head wondering what would've happened if she did."

"Oh, don't worry we would have kicked her ass," Victoria assured me.

"Just stay clear of her. Luckily, she goes to a private school, so you won't have to worry about running into her there. But she's always around, and she has friends everywhere. I think it's because they are afraid of her. And when she says her family, we all believe they are part of the mob."

"Well, that's comforting. Geesh, ok."

"Thank you for standing up to her. She is just evil." Chris said.

"What did she mean by that by the way?"

"Oh, Chris didn't tell you? Dude, you should've told her." Joey laughed.

"Tell me what?"

"Kim and I dated for all of eighth grade and half of freshman year. I ended it because she was abusive and mean."

"Oh. And I assume you two had sex?" I asked.

"God no, but we did other things."

"Great, so now she hates me even more because I am dating you and I am sure in her sick and twisted mind she still has some claim to you. Ugh."

"I don't care about her, or that. I am with you, and that's all that matters to me. And should be all that matters to you." He wrapped his arms around my waist while we stood there staring into the fire. It felt right with him.

Shortly after all the hoopla, Lucy came out back to check on us. I worried that they were still lurking, watching as we carried on with the night. It was not a good feeling I had, and unfortunately it stayed with me every day after that encounter.

CHAPTER 31

September 6th, 1995 was a Tuesday and the first day at Weston High School for me and George, Junior and Sophomore. Avery was starting seventh grade at the middle school, and Violet will be staring fifth at Weston Elementary. We were all nervous and excited at the same time, but most importantly hopeful that we would have a great first year here.

Both girls and George had met kids in their grades over the summer, in the camps they were in, plus from the neighborhood. So that was helpful for them, and I was excited for them. Chris was starting Senior year, and I knew we would have no classes together, but hoped we had lunch at least. He was also picking George and I up for school every day, and I couldn't be happier that I didn't have to take the bus.

I was going a little crazy with how I was going to navigate this school. It was much bigger than my old one, and I was familiar with that one since we had many school concerts, plays, and such there.

Chris assured me that it is very easy to get the layout, just tell everyone that I am new there and they will understand. Yeah, I wanna put a pretend neon sign over my head that reads "NEW GIRL" and blinks all day long. No thank you.

Walking into the school smelled like fresh paint, and *Windex*, very different than my old one as well. I would smell salt water and sand when I walked in there. A smell I realized I missed terribly, along with my friends. But now, there's new friends to meet, and ones to get closer to. I am excited for this opportunity, hell many people never get to move out of their hometown, I am lucky yo have moved to another one that is just as amazing as the first.

"So, how was your first day?" Chris asked as he was waiting for me by the stairs, like we planned.

"Confusing, but I will be ok. Most of my classes are on the same side of school, so that's helpful. The only two times I come over here are for lunch and gym. And speaking of that, my gym teacher is like your age."

"HAHA, yeah, he graduated with my oldest brother, he is student teaching. It's weird because so many of us know him, especially the seniors. Must be weird for him too."

George was coming down the stairs, and he looked exhausted.

"Hey little brother. How was your day?"

"I am tired, I had to go everywhere in this building. I even found the basement."

"I didn't think there was a basement here. Huh, learn something new every day."

"What's in the basement?" I was curious now, especially since Chris had no idea there was one.

"A lot of pipes. I felt like Freddy Kruger was going to jump out and stab me. It was scary as heck. You would love it, Scarlet. You and all the scary things you are into."

I laughed because he was right.

"Oh, speaking of scary things. Would you wanna go to the new *Halloween* movie coming out at the end of the month. *The Curse of Michael Myers.* Looks badass."

"YES! Of course, I do! We can get snacks on the way too! Oh, I am so excited!" I was probably a little too excited since it was still almost a month away, but I was really looking forward to this one. I was supposed to be different than all the others so far, and I am curious as to how so.

At dinner that night, we all sat around and talked about how our first day went, the girls went on and on with their day. George and I didn't have much to say because well, High School. While we were cleaning up the phone rang.

"Letti, it's for you!" Mom said.

I put the rag down from drying the dishes and walked over.

"Hello! Ahh, hey girl! My day? Oh, you know, I didn't have you and the rest of the girls there, but it wasn't terrible. Yeah. No, we don't have any classes together because he is a junior this year, and we aren't even in the same section of the building. Yeah. Ok cool!"

"Mel?" mom asked.

"Yep, she's gotta call me back. Her mom needed the phone to call her dad. Which is perfect because I wanna talk to her in my room anyway. Is that ok?"

"Yes, that's fine. I will have George help finish with the dishes." Mom said.

I gave her a quick hug and kiss and ran off to my room, to wait for her to call back. I changed into my pj's for the time being, until it was time to hop in the shower.

I was so excited to talk to Mel and tell her about my day and to hear about her first full week last week. We did not get to talk much because she was grounded for sneaking out one night and she was dumb enough to get caught.

I remember waiting for about an hour for her to call me back, until I decided to get a shower. I asked that someone let me know if she called back and to let her know that I was in the shower and would call her back as soon as I got out. I was in for about twenty-minutes, I didn't want to take too long.

As soon as I turned the water off, I could hear the phone ringing. I wrapped my hair in one towel, and the other around me. I tip toed to the kitchen to see if it was Mel. Justin shook his head no. I was sad when he said no, and then I got worried that something must've been wrong with her dad or someone. I went to my room and wrote in my journal like I do every night, and I wrote about how sad I was that I didn't hear back from my best friend.

The next morning when I woke up, I was still pretty hurt by her not calling back, I told myself I would call her when I got home today and hoped she would answer and that everything was fine.

"Morning sweetheart! How did you sleep?" mom asked, with a concerned tone.

"Morning mom, I slept fine thank you. Is it ok if I just have an English muffin for breakfast? I am not really that hungry."

"Of course. Peanut butter?"

"Yes please." I walked to the fridge and grabbed the OJ and poured a glass.

"Everything all right?" she asked.

"Yeah, I don't wanna talk about it really. If that's ok?"

She patted my shoulder and went on making breakfast for everyone else.

"I have to leave to work in about ten minutes so if you're eating, you all better get in here while its hot." She yelled to everyone in the house.

I didn't say much at all when everyone came out, of course I said good morning, but I am pretty sure everyone could tell I was upset about last night. I tried not to show it because I didn't want to bring anyone else's mood down, but I couldn't help it. She has been my best friend for over ten years, and I know something is off with us. Since the day she left here in June, I could feel it. We haven't talked much this summer either, Jen said that Mel was hanging out with a new crowd of kids, the ones we never talked to much. Heather confronted her about it and apparently Mel flipped out on her.

I knew moving was going to be hard on all of us, but at least I was trying, making sure they all knew how much I missed them and how excited I was to see them for my birthday. I had plans to go to her house for my birthday weekend, but I wasn't sure if that was going to happen now. I wasn't sure of much with her anymore to be honest. I could see that Chris was pulling up out front, so I went to my room, put my shoes on and by the time I came back out he was standing in my doorway.

"Hey gorgeous. I hear you're having a rough morning. You don't have to talk about it, but when you're ready to I am here."

"Thank you!" I gave him a big bear hug and exhaled knowing that it was going to be all right.

"George, you ready buddy?"

"Yes. By mom, tell dad by for me."

I walked over and gave her a hug, "Bye mom. See you after school. I love you."

I thought she was going to cry, that was the first time I told her. I did love her, I love how she was so patient with me, caring she was to everyone in the house. She was an angel and I know my mom sent her to us. I thought everyone was going to cry when I said, you could hear a pin drop in the entire house after I did.

As we were driving to school, I was watching the town go by and realizing that this really was my home now, and even though I had a life back in Maryland, it was one I couldn't go back to. This was my future, as I looked over at him driving and holding my hand. I looked down at our fingers intertwined and let out a sigh.

"You good?" he asked as he glanced over at me.

"Actually yes. I am good!"

We listened to some classic rock, *Kansas* was up first, and we jammed out as we drove into school. It was a great day, one that was burned into my memory even in the afterlife.

CHAPTER 32

The next few weeks were like any normal time in the nineties in a small town. They were starting to prepare for the Miss. Granny Smith nominations and looking for volunteers to help with the Fall Festival. We all thought it would be nice to volunteer, especially since it is pretty much right in our back yard. Mom and Dad were also looking forward to meeting more of the townspeople, they hadn't had many opportunities this past summer to get out much, so this was something they were excited to be part of.

It was mine and Chris's date night to the movies, the time was finally here to go see the new Halloween movie. I had on my black jeans, Dr. Martins, and my new Michael Myers T-shirt that mom bought me from the mall last weekend. I was so ready for this movie, and for my date with my boyfriend.

I think we are boyfriend/girlfriend; we never actually said it or made it official. Something I will bring up tonight. While I was getting ready, the phone rang.

"Letti, it's for you," Avery called for me.

I wonder who that could be? I have already spoken to Chris and Carmen, so it can't be them. I threw my shirt on and walked out to the kitchen. I took the phone from my sister and answered.

"Hello?"

"Hey girly. Long time no talk." Mel said laughing.

"Oh, hey. What's up?"

"Nothing, just wanted to call and chat and catch up. Is this a bad time?"

"Actually, yeah it is. I am finishing up getting ready for a movie tonight."

"Oh, dude are you going to the new Halloween movie? I'm so jealous. I am grounded AGAIN."

"Ohh, that sucks." I was really confused as to why now after weeks of not hearing from her, she was calling me.

"Ok, well I guess I will let you go, since you seem bothered by my call."

"Nope, just have plans is all."

"Ok, cool. Talk to ya later."

"Bye."

Well, that was shitty, I didn't even know what to say. Well not true I wanted to say, "How dare you contact me now after weeks of radio silence, not even calling me back when I called and left numerous messages." For real? Something changed about her, maybe it wouldn't have if I hadn't moved, but who knows. We have no idea what our future looks like, and hers looked like I was not part of it.

It hurt but I knew I didn't wanna be the only one trying, the only one acting like they care. Gabs, Jen, and Heather were all still cool with me, and we talked often, but it was Melinda. She was truly my best friend, the sister I needed when all hell broke loose with my mom, when my dad was depressed. She was it for me, and I was it for her. At least I thought so. That wasn't the case anymore, and it was something I needed to move on from.

"Yep, I will be home by eleven. I promise." I assured mom and dad, who were heading to the community center for one of the fall festival meetings.

"I will have her home before eleven, no worries there." Chris said.

"Ok, you two, have a great time."

We got in his car, and I immediately turned to him, "Are we dating? Like boyfriend/girlfriend?"

He snorted, "Uh, I thought we were. Am I wrong?"

"No. I don't remember either of us asking the other, so I was just making sure."

"Scarlet Adams, would you be my girlfriend?"

"I thought you'd never ask." I leaned over and planted a big sloppy kiss on his cheek, as he scrunched up his nose and laughed.

"So, now that were official, I guess I should tell you, I am a serial killer."

"HAHA!"

He wasn't don't worry, he was an amazing boyfriend and an all-around great guy. I was lucky to be in his life and to have him in mine. We hadn't kissed much, so I was hoping that would change, but he knew I was taking things slow. I told him about my promise to my mom, and he wanted to respect that. Which I appreciated greatly.

When we pulled into the lot, we could see Ryan's car parked already, and he and Carmen were standing out front of the box office. She saw us and started waving like a mad woman, we started laughing and Ryan was shaking his head smiling at her. She was such a fun person to be around, it was never a dull moment with her.

"Heyeee!" She yelled as we were walking up, and she hugged me.

"Hey!"

As we were waiting in line for the concessions, I felt someone staring at me. It made me uncomfortable; I looked around but couldn't see anyone who I knew that would be.

"You, ok?" Chris asked.

"Yeah, I felt like someone was staring at me for a minute there."

"Ah, well that's probably because Kim and Matt just walked into the theatre. I didn't wanna say anything and ruin our time. I'm sorry I should've said something."

"No, it's ok. I am just glad I wasn't going crazy."

"Nah, not yet anyway." He smiled at me and kissed my forehead, probably my favorite thing that he would do.

He was so much taller than I was, and he always made me feel safe, no matter where we were. We were lucky enough to get four seats toward the back of the theater, but unlucky for us that Kim and Matt were in the very last row, and I knew I would feel her eyes on me the entire time.

"We can get seats closer up if you want to?" Carmen bless her heart, was so sweet and always accommodating to everyone else.

"No, its fine. Thank you!"

The movie was not even close to what I expected, and I was not really a fan. I liked the guy in it though, he also played in Clueless. Other than that, it was a weird premise for it.

"So, what'd ya think?" Ryan asked.

"Eh, it was ok. Not really what I thought it was going to be at all."

"Really? It scared the heck out of me," Carmen exclaimed.

I just shrugged my shoulders, and Chris wasn't really a fan either. It was a shame because the original and the second ones are my favorites, that's usually how it goes though. It was only nine-thirty, so we ended up going to Donnie Mac's Diner. A local establishment that most teenagers would frequent on a Friday or Saturday night.

It was my first time coming here, and it did not disappoint. The food was greasy, the waitresses were miserable, the cigarette smoke bellowed in the air, teenagers were everywhere outside the building waiting to be seated. No wonder the staff was miserable, I would be too if I had to wait on all of us every weekend. The food was cheap enough for high school kids to afford, that was probably the best part of it all.

We hung out and talked, laughed, and told stories. They were very curious about life in Maryland, so I told them a lot about what it was like living there and the summers.

They were intrigued by me living in a beach town, and the people that would vacation there. I never thought of it in any other way except home to me.

When Chris dropped me off that night, I was the happiest I have been in a long time. I never expected him but was grateful for him. I was grateful for all the new people in my life.

I walked in and mom and dad were watching a movie in the upstairs living room, the kids living room is what we called it, waiting for me to get home.

"Hey kiddo, how was the movie?"

"Disappointing."

"Oh no, you were really looking forward to that too. I'm sorry sweetheart."

"It's ok mom. I had a blast though. We went to Donnie Mac's, and it was everything you would expect it to be."

We all laughed.

"What are you guys watching?"

"20/20, it's just ending, so perfect timing. Chris was right, he said before eleven. I like that boy."

"Me too, dad!"

CHAPTER 33

October 21st, 1995 was the Fall Festival, and my entire family was volunteering in one aspect or another. I was helping Chris and the rest of the group from DiMada's in handing out food. His dad made so much food, BBQ Chicken, Pulled Pork, Sausage Scallopini, Roasted Veggies, that he got from Mrs. Grogan's produce stand. Fresh apple cider, lemonade, sweet tea, and bottled water were available, it was literally a smorgasbord.

I have never seen so many desserts in one place, the decisions were endless. My parents were handling one of the game booths, there were a ton of them as well. They got the baseball booth, something my dad requested. Speaking of, we couldn't get to a Phillies game this year, which really bummed me out. But with dad's schedule it just wasn't possible. They didn't do nearly as well this season anyway, and I knew next year I could see my guy play. #4 Lenny "Nails" Dykstra, boy did I love him. My dad couldn't understand it, he said he was slob but could play for sure, I didn't care in the least if he was a slob, he was my favorite of all time.

It was the best time, the fall festival, we all really enjoyed helping and attending. I rode a horse for the first time in my life, that was interesting.

And luckily for me, Chris did not nominate me for Miss. Granny Smith. Nope Carmen was the lucky winner of that contest. I was happy for her, she most definitely embodied all that Weston was, and everyone surely loved her.

I was looking forward to the next weekend though, Ryan was having a Halloween party and bon fire, and I had never been invited to one before. This was my time to shine with the costume. I was going to be *Michael Myers* and Chris was going to be *Jason Voorhees*, it was going to be epic. Even though everyone told me I should be Chucky because I was so short. I did not find it that funny, they all thought it was hilarious.

I had not spoken to any of the girls really over the past few weeks, they were busy with school and homecoming, and after school activities. The last time I spoke to Jen though she had told me that Mel was getting into some bad habits, and even got arrested.

Chief Greene called Mr. and Mrs. Barr and asked what they wanted to do, they told him to have her stay the night in the holding cell and see if she had learned her lesson. According to Jen, she didn't. We talked about her meeting someone, another girl on her fall ball team from another school.

I always knew Jen liked girls; I was just waiting for her to figure it out. She told me all about her, and that she couldn't wait for me to meet her when I came down for my birthday.

"Yeah, About that. I don't know about coming down now."

"Why not? Cause of Mel? Stay at my house." She said.

"I mean I could do that if your parents are ok with it. I know they strict with sleepovers."

"For you they would totally make an exception!"

So, we planned for me to come to her house instead, and since I still hadn't spoken to Mel since mid-September, I was under the impression that I would be staying at Jen's. So, when I got a call from Mel on the twenty-fourth of October I was floored. Like I said it had been weeks since I talked to any of them, let alone her.

"Hey, so you're staying with Jen when you come down next month. That's messed up. I thought you were staying here." She yelled through the phone.

"First of all, I haven't heard from you in over a month. Second, don't yell at me. Third, why would I want to go there when all I hear about is how much trouble you are getting into. I don't want that, and I don't want to be around that."

"Oh, little miss perfect you are. Wow, Pennsylvania has made you soft."

"What? What is that even supposed to mean? Me moving has nothing to do with your behavior, and don't try to blame me for it either."

"I wasn't blaming you; I was blaming where you moved to. If your dad never met Lucy, you would still be here." "If only your mom," she said with a mean tone in her voice.

"Don't even finish that statement, Melinda Barr. Do not bring up my mom in this conversation, never bring her up again."

"I'm sorry Letti."

"And don't call me that. Only friends get to call me that, and I don't think we are that anymore. I must go. Goodbye." I hung up before she could even respond, and you know what I didn't feel bad at all about it.

She is making decisions on her own, I won't let her blame me for the mistakes she was making. And I'll be damned if I ever let her speak about my mom again.

Now I know in twenty minutes the phone will ring and it will be Gabs, Mel would put her between us all the time. But I believe Gabriella wasn't going to get involved this time. All of us were fed up with Mel and how she was acting, and now I know she was blaming me for all of it.

I wrote in my journal everything that happened so when she calls me again in the future so I can come back to it and remind myself of this conversation. She will call as she always does, and she always makes me feel like it was all my fault and then I end up apologizing for everything that happened. Not this time, I won't allow it.

The phone did not ring at all tonight like I thought it would. Maybe she didn't try to put Gab in the middle, I know she won't talk to Jen or Heather about it, because they would just hang up on her.

I won't lie, it makes me sad to see my once best friend going through something, something that I cannot fix for her.

We were friends forever, and the more time I spend away from her the more I get to look back and see just how messed up our friendship was. I feel bad for myself that I allowed it for as long as I did, but truly I didn't know any better.

I remember my mom and I were talking one night, before she got sick, about friends and family, and the future. She had said something that I didn't understand then because I was only eleven, but I think I do now at fifteen almost sixteen.

She said, "Scarlet, my first born. I know you may not understand this now, but one day you will. There are people that come and go in your life as you grow older, let them go and let them in. You were not put on this earth to be a revolving door, so the ones who need to go, close the door behind you when they leave, and the ones who come into your life, hold the door open for them with a smile. You will know who is who."

Mel, Rich, Kim, Matt, those were not supposed to be in my life. I closed that door behind me, and I will not open it again to anyone who will treat me like that. And for the future ones who do, I will open and close it again. I know I have some amazing people in my life now, ones who make me feel good about myself.

One thing a lot of people my age doesn't understand is that when you lose a parent, especially your mom, it changes you as a person. It changes your soul, it makes you jealous at times to see other daughters with their moms going to the mall, movies, and getting ice cream. I will never have that with my mom, of course I have Lucy and she is the most wonderful stepmom I could have ever wished for. But she's not my real mom, and I know that may sound harsh, but it is a fact and sadly one that no one can change.

So, with Mel acting the way she is, I cannot feel bad for her, she is taking advantage of having her mom right there with her. She is being so selfish, and I cannot be part of her life anymore. I must move on from her, and me going down to Maryland for my birthday is not a great way of attempting to move on. I will call Jen and let her know I will not be able to come down and explain to her why. I will try to see if maybe the three girls can come up here and stay the night, I mean it is my sweet sixteen and I would like to be able to be with all my friends that weekend.

CHAPTER 34

Thursday when I got home from school, I was planning on calling Jen to explain what I would like to do for my birthday. I was just hoping she wouldn't be mad like Mel was. I knew Jen had softball after school so I had to wait until later tonight to call, in the meantime I would just catch up on homework and finish up the final touches on my costume for Saturday.

"Scarlet, is that you honey?" Lucy called out.

"Hey mom, yep, it's me. I didn't know if you were asleep or not, I know you worked overnight, so I didn't want to wake you. I am sorry if I did."

"Oh no sweetheart you did not. I woke up about an hour ago. How was school?" She was in the kitchen now making a sandwich.

"It was good. I have a lot of homework this week and I want to try to get it done before tomorrow so I can go with Carmen and Rachel to get the rest of their costumes and ice cream. Wait, is that ok? I didn't even ask first, sorry."

"Letti, why on worth would you apologize? If you get all your work done of course you can go."

"Sweet! Thanks mom."

"MmmHmm. Letti, could you come out for a minute I need to talk to you about something."

Uh-oh, I did not like the tone of her voice at all.

"Sure." I walked into the kitchen, "What's up mom? Everything ok?"

"Mrs. Barr called me this afternoon, I just got off the phone with her before you got home."

"Ok, what's up?" I had no idea what she was going to say.

"Melinda ran away yesterday after school. She had called here to see if we heard from her or knew anything. Have you? Do you know anything?"

"What? That's crazy. I talked to her on Tuesday night, and we got into a fight. I told her we weren't friends anymore. But I have a lot of reasons for that."

"I heard you girls on the phone. I know she brought up your mom. I'm sorry sweetheart, I didn't know she was not such a nice friend to you all this time."

"It's ok mom, I mean it's not because she hurt me all the time and I didn't realize it until I left there. But I don't wanna think about anything bad happening to her or anything like that. What should we do?"

"Nothing sweetheart, we are too far away to help. And if Mel wants to be found she will be, and she will most likely come back home. If she ends up here, which I doubt, I will call her mother and take her back home immediately."

"Ok mom. If you hear anything will let me know? I hope she is ok."

I went back into my room and tried hard to focus on my APUSH work. This class was probably my favorite so far of all high school, and my teacher Ms. Martin was the absolute best. As I sat at my desk doing my work, I felt as if someone was standing behind me. I started to just go along with it because I knew it was Sandy. I typically would say hi to her and go on with whatever it was I was doing.

Today though, I spoke to her, out loud. I am sure I sounded like a crazy person, but I just needed someone to listen.

"I really hope Mel is ok and doesn't do anything stupid. She is prone to make bad decisions especially if I am not there to guide her in a different direction. What am I going to do if she's not? What if something happened to her? The last time we spoke I was so mean." I went back to my work and still felt her presence. And then it was like a lightbulb went off in my head.

"You're right, she is probably just doing this to get me to be her friend again. That would be something she would do. Ugh, I am sure she's fine, she is just looking for attention."

About an hour later the phone rang, I had the cordless in my room with me, but I didn't want to answer in case it was bad news on the other end. I heard mom on it and heard her say "Oh thank God, that great news, I will tell Scarlet." I felt calm again, like the anxiety just floated away and I didn't think Sandy was with me anymore.

Mom knocked on my door, "Scarlet,"

"Come in mom."

"Hey sweetheart, that was Mr. Barr, Mel came home, and she is in big trouble, but she is safe."

"I heard, that's great to hear. Now maybe she will knock this crap off. Whatever it is she is trying to prove."

"I hope so, for her sake and her parents. Did you wanna come to help with dinner? It's your favorite, Beef Stroganoff!"

"Yes, give me ten minutes and I will be right there. Are the rest home yet? It's awful quiet today."

"Yes, you had your headphones on, so you probably did not hear them when they came in. Your dad is laying down, he is not feeling well. I told him it's probably just a head cold."

One of the pluses of having a stepmom for a nurse was that she pretty much always knew what was wrong with any of us. Head cold, poison ivy, bee sting, pink eye, you name it you can diagnose it.

"Awe, poor dad. Let me just finish up this paragraph on *The Civil War* and *Dorthea Dix* and I will be right out." I didn't even realize how excited she would get when I told her what I was working on.

"*Dorthea Dix*? Is that the topic?"

"Oh, no its my midterm project. We had to pick some-one from American history that we admired and feel made a huge impact on the country for the good of the country. So, I picked *Dorthea Dix* for this half of the year and *Louisa May Alcott* for the second half next year."

"Oh, my sweet girl! You make me so proud!" She walked over, hugged me, and kissed my head.

"Thanks mom. Nurses are probably the most impressive individuals to me. All that you and the others did for my mom. And the way you personally treated me and the girls, I think you were meant to be in our lives, and I think you are the best I could've wished for. Because I did wish for dad to be happy again, and then you came into our lives again."

She was crying, and said they were happy tears.

"But I do have a question. When are you and dad planning the wedding? It's been almost two years since he proposed, and I haven't heard you guys talk about plans at all. I kind of want to be a bridesmaid and wear an awesome black dress."

"Black huh?" we laughed, "We have been talking about it and I think we were going to talk to the Carlins about possibly having it at their farm up the hill. When we were there prepping for the festival you dad, and I got to walk around and found a perfect little area where we could hold it. It wouldn't be anything big, just us and some close friends and family of course. We were thinking about next spring. What do you think?"

"I say yes! It is so cute up there, except that bull, he's a mean dude. So, no black dress then huh?"

"No black dress, but you can accessorize with black any-thing. Deal?"

"Deal."

"Let me get back to dinner, and if you have any questions about Ms. Dix just let me know!"

"Thanks mom, I will. I'll be out in a minute."

She walked out and suddenly, I knew why Sandy was there, all the times she was there. They all stemmed around encounters with Mel. Every damn time. I went to my journal to see if I was right and for the most part, Mel was either here or I was on the phone with her, and Sandy would make herself known. I am not sure why, but I could take a hint. I think she was trying to tell me to close the door, like mom had warned me about years ago.

I wanted to tell pop, I finally figured out why she was here. I called over to Mrs. Burns to see if it was ok if I came by after dinner, around seven. She said of course.

"Hey mom, would it be ok if I went to see pop after dinner. Around seven? I won't be long; I have to tell him something that I finally figured out."

"Sure," she said questionably.

"Thank you. Now what can I help with?"

She gave me tasks and I went to work helping with dinner. Justin walked in shortly after and Chris and Jason were right behind him. I was never happier to see him.

"Hey ma! Do we have enough food for the guys? Oh, and Rachel?"

"Hello son. And my adopted sons. Yes, of course. Where is Rachel?"

"Hi mom," they both said.

"She'll be here soon. She had to let the dog out."

"Crap, thanks Justin I forgot take Murphy for his walk." I heard Murph whimper as soon as I said walk.

"I will take him Letti; you keep helping you mom."

"Are you sure?"

"Yep. Hey Murphy! Wanna go for a walk buddy? We can swing by and see pop; I saw him on the porch sitting there."

Murphy did not hesitate to jump up, well slowly get up. Poor old guy was getting up there in age, he was eleven now.

I don't even know how old that is in people's years. I know he loved Chris, and when he saw Pop, he would give him treats. Which was why he was getting chunky.

"Just don't let pop give him too many treats. He's getting chunky and the vet was upset he put on five pounds."

"I will try my dandiest, but I am sure you know how impossible it is to tell that old man anything."

"Two peas in a pod they are," referring to Murphy and Pop.

"Indeed, they are. Ok, let's go Murphy."

After they left mom walked over and spoke softly to me, "I really like him Scarlet."

I smiled and blushed, "Me too mom. He's pretty perfect for me."

"I agree sweetheart."

CHAPTER 35

When Chirs and Murphy got back, he asked why I was going to pops. I called him into the living room where no one else could hear. I told him about Mel and why I think Sandy was there at those times. He didn't look at me like I was nuts, he actually agreed that that was a valid reason. So, I wanted to tell pop and see what he thought.

"Can I tag along?"

"Of course, but don't you monopolize the conversation damn it. You always do that."

"Sorry, I will try. You do know who my grandfather is though right?"

"Yeah yeah."

After dinner we cleaned up and walked down to pops, without Murphy this time. I needed pop to focus on me and not be distracted by him.

"Hey mom-mom, long time no see." Chris laughed.

"Hello grandson, where's my beautiful neighbor? Oh, there she is! You hungry, wait no you just had dinner. How about dessert? I made apple pie." Mrs. Burns greeted.

"Mmm, yes please." I answered.

"Warm, with vanilla ice cream?" she asked.

"Is there any other way?"

"Oh, I like this kid!" she yelled out.

"Me too mom-mom!" Chris hollered into her.

"Ok, what's up kiddo?" pop asked.

"Pop, I know why Sandy has been hanging around and why I see her sometimes."

"Ok, shoot." I had his full attention.

I began to explain the events and such that occurred when I saw Sandy and all about Mel and what my mom had said before she got sick.

"That makes sense. SO, what did you learn then?"

"That Mel is not a good friend and to keep my distance."

"And to close the door like your mom said."

"That too. So, I don't sound crazy? Sandy wasn't trying to tell me anything else right?"

"I knew Sandy well, and I will say that if you see her again know that there is some kind of danger or negative thing that is about to happen. So, always be on the lookout for her. That's my advice."

"Right. That makes absolute sense pop. You are the best. I knew I needed to tell you because I knew you would help me figure it all out."

"Mom-mom that smells amazing. And looks even better."

"Well, you didn't want a slice remember?"

"Can I change my answer?"

"Lucky for you I had made a plate for you, because I know you too well."

It was the most delicious apple pie I had ever had, and apparently, she won awards across the county for them. She said she had secret ingredients, that she never told a soul about, and that's what makes them so good. Whatever it was I didn't care, it was so good. The ice cream was not homemade though, she said no one has time to churn ice cream and that's what the supermarket was for.

We headed out and said our goodbyes. He helped me down their stairs because they were steep and hard to see at night in the dark.

"I gotta get over here and replace that bulb for them. Mom-mom told me about earlier."

"I could wait if you wanted to do it now."

"No, it's ok I'll do it Sunday."

"Chris, what if she needs to go out at night for something? She won't be able to see. And what if she fell, that would be terrible."

"You're right. I'll be right back."

He went back in and shortly after came back out with a new bulb. Mrs. Burns came up beside me put her arm around me and said, "Scarlet, you bring out a side of my grandson that we have never seen before. We are so grateful to you and happy you and your family moved to this street. I know he graduates this year, but I don't think he is going to go any-where now that you are here."

I didn't know how she meant that, like did he have plans and now suddenly won't follow through because I am here. Or will he stay here just because of me? I am so confused.

"What do you mean mom-mom?"

"He wanted to get in his truck and drive across country to work in California and live on the beach. I could never picture him doing that. I think he just wanted to move as far away from here as possible because there was nothing truly keeping his heart here. Until you came that is." Her smile was so big, and I knew she meant nothing but kindness with the words.

"Thanks mom-mom for telling me that. We have never talked about after graduation, maybe we should do that."

"Well, whatever you do kiddo don't spoil the great thing you have by over thinking anything. Enjoy each other's company, and let fate tell you how things are going to work."

Not terrible advice, but I still needed to know what he planned on doing after graduation. If moving to California was still an option.

"All set. Bye again mom-mom."

"Goodnight you two. Be careful walking home."

"Hey, so your mom-mom said something about you wanting to pack up and drive to California, is that still something you wanna do after graduation?"

"I did, but not anymore."

"Because of me?"

"Well partly yeah. But I was going to tell you this after the party this weekend, my dad offered me a partnership with him. He wants to expand and open a second location in Braxton, where Devil's Hole is. Well not right there but the town that it's in. He wants it to be mine." His face lit up.

"Oh my God! That's amazing! I am so excited for you babe!"

"For us. This is a great thing for you too. And for Justin, I am going to ask him to manage it for me."

This guy really was absolutely everything I could've asked for and more.

"You are the best!" I stopped.

We held each other and stared into one another's eyes. Wait, is this it? Is this going to be "the kiss", the one I have been waiting for? We kissed but not like the movie kisses.

We leaned into each other, and our lips met. I thought the world disappeared before, nope it had melted away. It was just him and I. Sparks went off, my knees went weak, my back was doing some weird thing. He put his hands on my cheeks, and I was putty in them.

Ok, moving on now, that's enough of that.

The next day he was there promptly at seven in the morning, walking in the house because he would not dare to beep the horn. He said it was rude and no woman should come running to a guy beeping his horn. He was too good to be true sometimes. He asked if everything was ok, it was, it was that time of the month, and my cramps were the worst they have been in a long time.

"Say no more."

Thank God, because I didn't want to talk about my period with my boyfriend and my brother in the back seat. When we walked into school that day it felt different, like something was off. He and I walked past the office and saw her there. KIM! Panic came over me, and Chris could feel my hand tense up in his.

"What the hell is she doing here?" he asked out loud.

"Good lord, I have no idea. But I hope she's not staying."

Crmen and Ryan walked up about a minute later.

"What are we looking at?" Ryan asked.

"Not what. Who." Chris nodded toward the office.

"Jesus, what the hell is she doing here?" he said.

"Who knows?" Chris replied.

"Oh, no. That's not gonna be good." Carmen chimed in.

We went on our way and waited until lunch to see if anyone had heard anything. As I was walking to the cafe, there she was standing by Matt's locker hanging all over him. Please God, tell me she's not going to school here. PLEASE, PLEASE, PLEASE.

"Scarlet, hi." Matt said.

"Hi Matt. Kim." I didn't want to acknowledge her, but I was not rude.

"Matty, tell Scarlet the great news."

"Kim is going to school here now. Today is her first day."

What the hell? He is not serious.

"By the look on your face I am going to say you don't believe it," she got right up into my face I could smell the juicy fruit gum she was chewing, "Well, believe it princess because it's true. And stay the hell out of my way Adams, because if you don't, I will crush you into a million pieces."

I hated this girl so much, she didn't even scare me, she annoyed me. I loathed bullies more than anything, and I was not going to let her bully me in my school.

"You don't scare me, Kim."

"Well, I should. You have no idea what I am capable of, and what my family is capable of. Stay the hell out of my way." She pushed past me and drug poor Matt along by the hand behind her.

Grrrr, I wanted to scream but instead I made my way to the caf so I could tell the others.

"You guys. She is going to school here. And she just totally threatened me too." I relayed everything she said to me, and Chris was mad.

"Where you going?"

"I am going to the principal's office to tell her what she just said to you. She can't just threaten you and get away with it."

"Listen," I grabbed his hand, "she doesn't scare me, Chris. People like that expect people like me to go tell on her and then she makes my life a living hell here. I don't need it. I won't stand down to her, but I won't put myself in a worse position either. Please just sit and eat with us."

He hesitated for a minute and then took his seat.

"I hate her."

"We all do buddy. Everyone will see just how much of a bully she is. She won't have many friends here. But it does make you wonder why she came here. Wonder what happened at the private school she was at."

"I'll ask Quinn and see if she knows anything. They haven't been talking as much lately. She said that she has been doing weird seances and stuff, worse than before. She is scary. I'm afraid of her." Carmens voice was shaky.

I didn't see her the rest of that day and was thankful it was Friday. I was focused on one thing, and that was Ryan's party.

"Ok, I'll call you when I get back from the mall with the girls."

We kissed each other bye and I went in to get ready for my night with them. I was so excited to have a girl's night, and that they were so cool to hang out with. We were getting pizza while we were there, so I didn't have dinner with everyone else. Rachel and Carmen came into the house to get me.

"We are heading out mom and dad. We will be back around sevenish. Love you guys!"

We hopped into Rachel's VW Beetle, of course that's what she drove. I will never understand the dynamic between her and my brother, but it worked, and she made him very happy. The two were very different than the girls back in Maryland, not in a bad way just different. I enjoyed spending time with them, and how girly they both were. I used to dislike that the most about Heather, but now having a serious boyfriend, I have become to love it. I like dressing up in the styles of the day, and he seemed to enjoy it.

"I wanted to check out the new store *Wet Seal*, after we get the rest of our costumes. Ok?" Carmen asked.

"YEP!" we both answered.

It was a very different experience going to the mall with just friends, then it was going with your mom and sisters. Believe it or not this was the first time I went without them; it was cool and felt good to be just a normal teen.

"Ooo, you guys can we stop at *Orange Julius*? I have been dying for one." I asked.

"Absolutely! They have the best soft pretzels too, with cheese sauce. Oh my God to die for!" Rachel dramatically said.

There were so many kids from our high school there, which they said was typical since Devil's Hole was closed for the next few months due to maintenance on the quarry portion of it. I did not see that part when I went, and I heard it was very high up and there were not many attempts to jump in from that point. There is a lower level that everyone jumps off, I didn't see that part either and from what I hear I don't think I was missing anything by not seeing it.

Our last stop was *Wall to Wall*, only the best music store around, to get some new tapes. I was looking forward to buying *Jagged Little Pill* by *Alanis Morissette*. It came out this summer and every girl I knew would jam out to *You Oughta Know*.

"Hey, can we listen to your new tape in the car, Scarlet?" Rachel asked.

"Yes, I thought you'd never ask!"

I took the wrapper off but kept the sticker and made sure I put it on the case cover in case I needed to take it back for some reason. *Wall to Wall* was so awesome about that.

"Do I stress you out? My sweater is on backwards and inside out and you howwwww appropriate..." we sang our asses off in the car that night. That would be another time that makes me angry that I am not here anymore to share in. I guess that's just the way it goes.

We pulled up to my house, and got out to head in. I could see Ryan's car there, so of course I hoped that Chris was here also. We could see the glow of the TV coming from the window, and the lights were off. I was sure they were watching a scary movie without me.

"Hey!" I said as we walked in. Lucky for me Chris was here, it was like a triple date now.

"Hello lovely ladies!" Ryan the forever charmer greeted us.

"What are we watching?" I asked as I took a seat by Chris.

"*Halloween*," Justin answered.

"My favorite!"

We all sat together and watched the rest of the movie; it was truly my favorite movie ever. *Jamie Lee Curtis* was the best actress for horror movies. It was my favorite time of the year, and I think they all realized just how obsessed I was with it.

After everyone left, I went to my room to settle in for the night. The moon was a cool crescent shape that I could barely see from my window. I felt the presence of Sandy again, but I didn't see her. I called out to her, but I still didn't see anything that would tell me she was there with me. I assumed it was just me being tired and was so used to the feeling of her being there, that maybe she really wasn't, and everything was going to be all right.

I don't even remember falling asleep, but I do remember the dream I had. It was like a premonition more than a dream though. I remember I was near water, but dirt was all around me. There were female and male voices that were muffled, so I couldn't hear them. It was dark, pitch black, and cold, I think. It seemed so real, I felt as if I could touch the walls and they would be cold and smooth.

I was a bit disheveled when I woke up and felt like I was running from something. My heart was racing, and I could feel it pounding from my chest, I could see it too. It was not a nightmare, but I know it wasn't a positive dream. Maybe that's what Sandy was telling me, that I was going to have some weird dream that I couldn't figure out? I don't know, whatever it was I am glad it is over.

CHAPTER 36

Today was the day! Ryan's Halloween party, I have been looking forward to this since I got the invite. I had no idea what to expect, as this was the first real Halloween party I was ever invited to. Of course, I went to ones in Maryland, but they were either at my house, or one of the girls and no one else was invited. So, basically it was like any other day for us there.

"Mom, could you help me with making sure my hair is under this bald cap? I don't want any of it to be seen under my mask."

"Yep, come sit down. Do you have bobby pins? I will need them."

I ran into the bathroom and grabbed a few.

"Ok, now when I put this on, you can't mess with it ok. Because it will fall out if you do."

"Got it!"

I had everything on but the mask, the jumpsuit was huge on me. I looked ridiculous. Why I didn't try it on sooner was beyond me. Dad even told me I should try it on to be sure it fit. He was right.

"Ugh. This is so big; I look like a joke."

Mom walked in, "Oh, sweetheart. I thought you tried it on before this?"

"No. I can't go looking like this. I will be the laughingstock of the party. I can't embarrass Chris like this. What am I going to do, mom?"

I flopped dramatically on the bed, knowing damn well this was my fault.

"I have an idea, if you're willing to hear it?"

"Anything, I am desperate." I muffled my pillow.

"Well, you love Halloween we all know that. *Jamie Lee* is your favorite. You have a lot of similar traits to her when it comes to looks. So why not go as her?"

She was a genius, why didn't I think of that.

"MOM! YOU'RE A GENIUS!"

"Thank you!"

"Umm there's one problem I don't have any clothes that would really scream seventies. Can you help me figure something out?"

"I can do one better. I have all my clothes still from the seventies, and I was about your size then too. And many of the outfits are very similar to the girls in the movie."

"Mom, you're an angel you know that?" I could kiss her I was so happy and relieved.

I know Chris was going to be surprised when he showed up and I was in fact not Michael Myers, but instead Laurie Strode.

"One last thing, do we have a pumpkin I can borrow for the night?"

She chuckled and pointed to the outdoors. I would grab one then when we were to leave. It was almost time now for Chris to show up. Justin and Rachel were going as *Bonnie and Clyde,* how original. Carmen and Ryan were *Danny and Sandy,* go figure. I wasn't sure about anyone else, so it would be fun to see who all ends up as whom.

Ryan said the only rule for the party was you had to come as a famous person, or couple. They were going to be so surprised when we walked in, and I was not what they thought I was going to be. Now I have to try to convince Chris to go like *Michael* so we can be a couple.

I heard his door close and was giggling when he walked in.

"Hey Murph buddy. Hi there everyone!"

"Hi Chris. She is waiting in the living room." Dad said.

"Well, hello there. Did we change our couples costume and I don't remember?"

"Be happy you missed the debacle of what was supposed to be my costume. My dad was right, I should've tried it on before tonight. I looked ridiculous. So, mom gave me the idea to dress as *Laurie Strode*. Annnnnd"

"And, what?"

"I was thinking since we have to go as couples, Jason and Luarie are not a couple. But" I gave a huge smile and batted my eyes at him, "Michael and Laurie are!"

"Where's the costume!"

"Oh, that was so much easier than I thought it would be. You are the best!" I ran into my room and grabbed the entire costume and brought it out to him quickly.

"I'll be right back."

I sat in the living room while he went into the bathroom to get changed, without complaint, into the *Michael Myers* costume that I swear was made for a giant. Mom and Avery were sitting with me, as he walked out.

He filled out the costume quite well, I may note, a lot better than I did. He did not put the mask on, and I was ok with that.

"Well, that suits you quite well." I said in a flirty tone, mom and Avery giggled.

"Thank you, my lady," he curtsied and modeled it.

It was time for us to head to the party, we said our goodbyes to everyone, and I promised I would be home before midnight. He opened the door for me, like usual, and we headed out to Ryan's. We pulled up to his house and there wasn't much in the way of parking already.

"So many people are here already. We aren't late, right?"

"Nope, just everyone looks forward to this party every year. His older sisters started it about six years ago and he picked up planning it last year. It gets better and better evert year. You are going to have a blast, Scar!"

With that we got out of the car and headed up the stone path to his front door. By the time we got there he was standing with it open, Carmen next to him, greeting everyone.

"Oh, we changed our costumes I see. However, I think Chris may have been able to pull off *Laurie Strode.* Now that would have been a sight to see."

"Oh, you're a funny guy." He said shaking his hand and giving the side bro hug.

The two did their handshake and we walked in, there were tons of people there. I don't think I knew a quarter of them. A lot of older people, I assume that have graduated. There were kegs, party balls, cases, wine coolers, you name it, it was there.

I have never been to a party like this. First his parents were on a cruise, but it seemed his one sister was over twenty-one so that would explain the alcohol. I have had maybe two beers in my entire life, one I threw up almost immediately after I drank it and the other was at Mel's before I left to come here. This was going to be something.

"Psst" I waved Chris over.

"What's up?" He whispered.

"I don't drink."

"I know this, remember we went through this already. The sodas are in the blue cooler. What would you like?"

"What's in there?"

"*Coke, Sprite, Fanta.*"

"*Coke* is perfect please."

"Coming right up."

I was looking around his living room and seeing all the accommodation that his father received from being on the job.

"Impressive huh?" a female voice said from behind me.

"Very." I replied.

"Hi, I am Jacklyn, Ryan's older sister. You must be Scarlet. I have heard a lot about you."

"Hi. I am. It's nice to meet you."

She walked over to a crowd of girls and started dancing with them. *Another night by M.C. Sar* was playing on the radio, nothing could ruin this night, usually famous last words. But truly nothing ruined the night. We had such a wonderful time, all of us. No one crashed it, like we were all worried about.

Chris and I did not win for best couple, but we did win for best vintage costume. That was cool, I had never won anything before. Even if it was just among us, it was still great that he and I won. We stayed for a while after to help clean up, found some not-so-great treasures left behind by some of the guests attending. I walked away from those and let someone else handle them.

"Thanks, guys, for staying and helping clean up. I appreciate it bro." Ryan thanked us.

"Anytime buddy. But we are gonna head out 'cause I gotta get Scarlet home by midnight."

"Does she turn into a pumpkin?" he laughed.

"Maybe. All right buddy, I'll see you tomorrow."

I hugged Carmen and Ryan and said goodnight.

The ride home was fun. We talked about the entire night, and how I met his older sister, and a bunch of upper-class students. It was perfect, in every sense of the word. When I said before that I was in love with Rich, I had no idea what I was talking about. I am madly in love with Chris. He is everything you could ever want in a boyfriend. He is kind, loyal, handsome, trustworthy, well-rounded, he is all of that and so much more.

That night when I went to bed was unlike any of the other nights so far in the house. It was scary what happened while I was in bed. I was looking out the window, the sky was so dark it was almost glowing. It was about one in the morning, and something was keeping me from falling asleep. I sat up thinking someone was there with me, but I couldn't see anything, it was so dark. I leaned over on my nightstand and flipped on the black light, that was the dimmest light I had in my room. As soon as I turned it on, I could see her, standing there. It was as clear as day, she was a ghost.

I wasn't scared at first, because she didn't look like a movie ghost. She looked like just a person, that was almost translucent. She didn't say anything, she just stared at me, like she was staring through me. It wasn't until she lunged at me that scared me to death. I jumped back on my bed and then she was gone. It was so insane, and surreal at the same time.

I didn't know what to do or what that meant. The times I have seen her before Mel was always around. But maybe that wasn't it this time, maybe it was someone else she was warning me or something else at least.

I did not sleep well at all, I was up and down all night, and that was tough because we had a trip planned to the corn maze with the girls the next day. It was about an hour drive, in Lancaster, so I was hoping I could just take a nap while we drove. No such luck though, I am sure you can imagine,

The girls talked so loudly the entire ride, as if they knew I did not sleep well.

"Letti, are you ok? Did you not sleep well last night?" mom asked.

"Not at all. I had a very real nightmare, so it had startled me enough to where I couldn't sleep well at all."

"I'm sorry sweetheart. Girls, how about we quiet down just a little so your sister can maybe take a nap on our ride. Ok?"

"Ok, mom." They both said.

"Thanks mom."

She just smiled at me, turned the radio up a little and I fell asleep. The next thing I knew, we were there.

"Yay! We're here! Letti, wake up!" Violet said with excitement.

"Hey mom, can I talk to you really quick?"

"Of course, sweetheart, what's up?"

We walked to the back of the car so the sisters couldn't hear.

"I saw her last night. But this time I really saw her. Her face, everything. I was scared."

Mom hugged me and started brushing my hair with her hand.

"Ok, was it a negative interaction?"

"I mean, no. she stared at me and then flew through me. Literally."

Moms' eyes got really wide when I said that.

"Ok, kiddo. Well, that would be scary for anyone. Let's see if we can try to get your mind off it for a little bit. Ok?"

"K."

It was a lot easier said than done. I couldn't help but think about it. Everywhere I walked in the maze I felt like she was following me or watching me. I was not comfortable with this visit from her. I felt it was the start of something that could be bad. I would just have to wait and see, I guess. I knew I needed to tell her, because if I have it right then something just might happen. Mel may show up or wait. I don't know why I didn't think of it before. Kim. Every time I have seen or felt Sandy, Kim has been around or talked about.

So, wait, where was she last night? She wasn't at the party; I would've seen her. Was she in the woods? Is that who felt staring at me? No, that's not possible. I am just making things up now. She's harmless, just like Mel, just like all the other teenage females of my day.

CHAPTER 37

School on Mondays was pretty much the worst, we had an assembly it seemed every week. The only upside was that I got to sit with Chris and the gang. Of course, I am sure you can guess the topic of conversation was the party. While we were sitting down, I could feel the weight of the stare again. I looked around but didn't see anyone, I even asked Chris if someone was staring at me. He didn't see either.

In the far corner of the gym, I could see a mist of some sort, I knew it was Sandy. But it was weird because I didn't think ghosts could leave their permanence. I guess I was wrong, and she in fact did follow me everywhere.

So, it explained a lot, that maybe it wasn't a Mel thing after all. Across the bleachers I could see her, her eyes were piercing green, almost white. She was stroking the back of Matt's head and had this evil grin on her face. I could see she was looking right at me, and if looks could kill.

It was alarming to me as to why she felt the way she did. I didn't understand. I knew she and Chris dated, but that was over, and she was with Matt. What did she want from me? What did she think I was going to do? Take her man from her, not a chance, I had no desire to, I was not interested in him in the slightest. I was madly in love with Chris. Or was that it, she was still in love with him.

She had to have been pissed at me for coming along, maybe she was trying to figure out a way to get him back. Maybe I should just ask her what her problem was with me. What did I do to her?

I decided that I would ask her, she couldn't do anything to me at school, so I'll ask her here. I have 5th period lunch and she has 6th, so I will wait and just get a tardiness for Photography. I will ask her today what her deal is.

I waited after lunch by the main doors and saw her coming.

"Kim," I yelled out.

"I'll catch up guys. Yeah?" she replied.

"Got a minute to talk?"

"I'm standing here, aren't I?"

"Why do you not like me? You don't even know me."

"Who said I didn't like you?"

"No one. No one has to either; I can tell you don't. You give me dirty looks all the time. You're always staring at me with dead eyes. Like I did something to you."

"Well, sweetheart you did. You came here from, wherever it was, and thought you could just walk in and take any guy you wanted. You think you're all that. I can see it. You think you're better than everyone here. That's why you acted the way you did when we first met. Back at the falls. You can't have him too; you already took one from me."

"Kim, you have been dating Matt now for months. Chris has moved on, and it's not fair what you're doing to Matt."

"Mind, your business," she was so close right now in my face, "stay out of my way. Don't even speak to him. You have no idea who I am. You're right, I don't like you, and by the time I am done with this school and telling them about you, no one here will either."

"What could you possibly tell them about me. You know nothing about me."

"I don't have to. You're new here, and my family has been here for generations. Whose story do you think they will believe? Me or you?"

She walked away right after that. I stood there dumbfounded at what she said. I couldn't imagine why someone who didn't even know me would be that full of hate. I truly had no idea what she was capable of, that was obvious, but I realized that day not to cross paths with her again.

I decided that I would do my own research on her family. She kept mentioning them, so I should know who they are so I can steer clear of them as well. I also decided that Sandy shows up when something bad or negative is about to happen. So, I keep a look out for her, and know that when she shows up that I better watch my back, front and both sides.

I mean how scary is that? You wanna talk about the biggest bully you have ever met, times that by ten for Kim. The funny thing is, she was just a little taller than I am. That's why I need to know who her family is. I needed to talk to Chris more about her and them. There had to be other reasons for her disdain toward me, and I was determined to get to the bottom of it. Even if it was just to educate myself better and make myself more aware of their importance.

"Chris, can you tell me about Kim's family. She brings them up a lot and I obviously have no idea who they are."

"I can, I just don't like talking about them. They are weird. We can talk tonight if you want. I can come over after dinner. I have to go to pops to change over his new hospital bed. So, like seven. Is that ok?"

"That would be great!" Honestly any chance I got to spend time with him, I was ok with.

"I'll see you tonight." He leaned over and kissed me goodbye.

As George and I were walking into the house he said something that was very out of character for him.

"Letti, I see her too. All the time when I am in the back yard picking up the bugs. It's like she watches over the house and us. She doesn't scare me anymore, but she used to when

I first saw her. I asked her what she wanted, and she pointed at you as you were walking on the deck talking to mom a few months ago. I don't know if she wants you or if she's here because of you. I just thought you should know."

Um, ok, what. What the hell? Could he freak me out anymore than that. Holy crap.

"What George? She pointed at me. When was this do you remember?"

"Yeah, it was the night you had the bonfire before school started."

I know my eyes were wide and I probably looked like I had seen a ghost, and without the obvious of course. That was the night Kim crashed the party with the rest of them.

"Sorry, I didn't tell you before. I just thought you knew."

"Thanks George. If you see her again, can you let me know?"

"Of course."

I had no idea what to make of that information. I guess I needed to head to the library and check out some books on ghosts and why they hung around. I didn't even know what I was looking for, but I knew I needed to get answers. She couldn't give them to me. Could she?

CHAPTER 38

In a way I was hoping that I would not see her tonight, especially after George told me what he had seen. But then the other part was expecting to see her since George told me. I didn't know what I wanted, I just knew I wanted to not have to worry about Kim and her crazy family. When Chris came over, I knew I would get more answers about what I needed to worry about.

I didn't talk much at dinner, since all my thoughts were on Sandy and Kim, and what the two had to do with each other.

"Scarlet. Is everything ok?" dad asked.

I was in deep thought, so I did not hear him at first.

"Letti?" he said a little louder.

"Yeah, sorry dad. What did you say?"

"Is everything ok? You seem like you're not with us tonight. What's on your mind?"

I was not about to tell them what happened at school, or what George had told me after school.

"Oh, yeah. All good, dad. Just got a lot going on at school."

"Ok, kiddo. Just making sure."

I saw mom's face, and I knew she didn't believe any of that, but she didn't say anything which was a relief. It was hard enough that I was trying to figure out what this damn ghost wanted and why some girl that doesn't even know me wants to beat me up. To try to explain to my dad all of that was not easy at all.

Dinner was over and it was mine and George's night to clean up. I washed and he dried. I could hear Chris's car pull up, and his door closed. My heart skipped, like it typically would. We heard the tap of a knock, and he came in.

"Murphy!" He exclaimed.

"I think you come here for the dog more than me." I was joking of course.

"I don't know, maybe I do."

"HAHA."

I hugged him and asked if he wanted to go to the living room to talk. Mom and dad were downstairs for the night, and the girls were already heading to bed. Justin was, yep you guessed it, out with Rachel, and George was in his room.

"Ok, tell me about her and this family she keeps talking about."

"So, you know how we had said her family was part of the mob? Well, I think that is a fact. When she and I were dating, I remember one night I was over, and I went to use the bathroom.

When I walked downstairs, I remember seeing her dad and all these big Italian looking dudes sitting around a table there was a lot of money in the center. Like piles of it. At first, I thought they were playing poker or cards or something. But then I could see a gun sticking out the back of one of the guy's pants. Mr. Allen saw me, and they all got really quiet, like I walked in on something that I shouldn't have. I said hi and hauled ass to the bathroom. When I was done, they were gone. It was like they were never there. I was in there maybe three, four minutes. So, I knew something was up then. They are also related to the Grayson's, and they are the wealthiest family around. They do a lot of shady stuff, and I would hate to meet any of them in a dark alley, that's for sure."

"Ok, well that's not crazy."

"No, but when we first started dating, we were out and saw Mr. Lawrence, and she chuckled in almost a witch like fashion. I asked her why she was laughing or what was she laughing at. She said, and I quote, "Oh, poor old man will never know who killed his daughter." The way she said it was like she knew who did but didn't say she knew who did it. Does that make sense?"

"Totally. So, do you think her family did it?"

He shrugged his shoulders, "I don't know. I just know I didn't like her response, and especially since pop is so close to them. And all my aunts and mom, being so close to her growing up. It just gave me an uneasy feeling."

"Understandable. So, who was the cop on the case?"

"That would be Detective Miller. He is a miserable old man. But Ryans dad even says he is one of the best detectives he has ever seen. He lives on the other side of town, over on Pine Lane."

"That sounds like it's supposed to be scary," I laughed.

"No, just not a street I go to often. Lots of trouble over there. Which is funny cause you would think there wouldn't be because of him living there. But the cops get called there a lot, to the lane not his house."

"So, did it go to like a cold case or something?"

"I think so. I really don't know actually."

"Hmm. Maybe I could talk to him."

"Why would you wanna do that?"

"Because I see her all the time. And George told me he saw her too. And he asked her why she was here and apparently, she pointed at me. So, I don't know what that is supposed to mean, but I think maybe if I can talk to him and see if I can help in some way. Maybe, it would answer some questions."

"Fair enough. Maybe we can stop by there one day."

"Wait, you just said you don't ever go there because it's a bad area. Why would we just stop by there then?"

"I don't know, I was just thinking of ideas. We could always go to the police station and ask."

"True. I was thinking more that way also. Could we go tomorrow since we have an early dismissal?"

"Sure. I don't know if he will be there, but we can go. If he's not there maybe, we can leave a note for him."

"You're the best! Wanna watch *Drew Carey* with me?"

"I love that show! Mimi is my absolute favorite. She just doesn't care what anyone thinks of her, does she?" he asked while giggling.

"No, she does not. The obsession she has with the troll dolls, though. I don't know, that's a little much for me."

"Yeah, they are creepy things."

We sat and watched the show together, it was only on until nine, so that was good enough for me, since I got ready for bed at nine anyway. It was like he and I had known each other forever with how well we clicked. But, sitting here with him made me miss Maryland and my friends from there. I knew it wouldn't be easy, and I knew Mel was going through something. I was sad for her and was hoping she would figure her crap out soon so we could be friends again. I know I said I didn't care, but I absolutely do and worry about her and the decisions she has been.

"What's up? Your body just changed."

"I was thinking about Mel."

"You miss her?"

"Yeah. A lot."

"So, call her babe. She is your best friend."

"Was."

"No, you say that now because you're mad at her. I understand why, but maybe she doesn't know how much she is messing up. Maybe she is just temporary lost."

What he said made sense, but I still wasn't going to call her first. I don't care how stubborn it sounded; I wasn't doing it.

"Yeah, but I didn't do anything wrong. She is the one who is doing all of this. I just stood up for myself for once."

I wasn't mad at him for saying those things, he wasn't wrong. But I was not calling her first. That was steadfast on.

"All right beautiful. I am gonna get out of here. I will see you in the morning. And I am looking forward to going to talk to Detective Miller tomorrow. I always wondered what he sounded like."

"What he sounded like?"

"Yeah. Like, I picture him having this dark and raspy voice. He has smoked his whole life I heard and drinks a lot. So, I am curious."

"Oh!"

He left and I got into the shower and did my nighttime routine. When I got out, mom was in the kitchen. I know she was waiting for me.

"Hey ma!"

"Hey kiddo. Wanna talk about it now?"

"Yes." I proceeded to tell her everything, I knew she wouldn't tell dad. I told her everything that we were going to do.

"I love that idea. Want me to go too?"

"If you want to."

It was settled, she would meet us there after school tomorrow.

CHAPTER 39

Sitting in his car waiting for my mom to get there, I watched as the cop cars pulled in and out of the lot. I wondered where they were going. To help an elderly woman who locked her keys in her car. Or a child who was found but his parents were lost. Who knows? I was curious as to if any of them were Detective Miller. There were older men standing all around outside, smoking and talking. The ground had cigarette butts all around, the clouds of smoke were thick and all around their heads.

I saw my mom's car pulling into the lot and was all too excited to jump out of Chris's car.

"Yay, she's here! Ready?" I know I probably looked like a mad woman with the look on my face, I didn't care.

"Yep!"

"Mom!" I hollered to her and waved.

"Hey sweetheart! Hey Chris! How was your half day?"

"It was fine, the teachers had a seminar or something. I am so excited right now."

I may have been a bit overboard for wanting to talk with a Detective about a cold case. But I was excited to hopefully get some answers for Sandy, and Mr. and Mrs. Lawrence. I had no idea what I was going to say when I walked in. I was hoping mom would help in that department. I only ever spoke to Rich's dad a few times; he was the only other police officer I have ever known.

"Mom, how do we go about this? Do we go in and ask our questions? What are you thinking?"

She laughed, "Well, kiddo, I would say let's go in and see if he is even in."

"Good plan!" I gave a thumbs up and we made our way in.

Walking through the clouds of smoke and coughing dramatically as I did. Chris opened the door for us, mom and I went through and were greeted by an older woman sitting behind a desk.

"Good afternoon. How can I help you?"

"Good afternoon. We were looking to speak with Detective Miller. If he is in."

"Oh, I am sorry he is off until next Monday. You can come then if you'd like. I can also leave a note for him."

"Oh no no that's not necessary. We will come back another day then. Thank you so much."

"You're welcome. Have a Happy Halloween. Be sure to come by and get some candy, kids. We always have someone here to hand it out."

"Well, that stinks. I was really hoping to talk to him. But like you said, mom, we can come back another day. The secretary seemed very nice."

"That's Mrs. Smitham. She has worked here since my dad was young, I swear. If you wanna know what is going on in town she's the one who knows. She knows everything about everyone. Except you guy, I am surprised she didn't ask more questions."

"Oh, a busy body huh? I am sure if I gave her the opportunity, she would've asked some. But I have known many women like her, I could tell she likes to know what's what and who's who."

"That sums her up."

I was really bummed about that, but I now have a little more time to ask around to the neighbors about Sandy, and now Detective Miller.

"Chris, could we drive by his house? Would that be, ok?" I asked.

"Sure, if you really want to. I don't really think we should just stop by and knock up though."

"Oh of course not. I just want to see where he lives, that's all."

"Sure. It's not far from here."

I had not been to this part of town much, and honestly, I don't think I was missing anything. Chris was right when he said it was not such a great part of town. There was a lot of trash on the sides of the roads, kids were playing in the middle of the streets and didn't seem to care if anyone hit them or not. The homes were a lot smaller over here, a bit more run down. I wondered why it was so different over here than it was over by my house.

It was almost like we were driving through a completely different town; it was hard to believe that it was the same though. There were similar areas in Havre de Grace, and I guess I didn't think much of those since I was so used to them. There really was no difference I guess from down there and right here, just the names and faces.

I was not sure what to make of his house when we pulled past it. It was much bigger than I anticipated, and not some dark, ominous building that I expected it to be. It was set back on the hill, most of the homes on that side of the street did it seemed. The porch was open and had one rocking chair and a small side table next to it. There was an old Cadillac in the driveway, and the yard had Halloween decorations in it.

"I really expected something completely different. He has a fake ghost and a pumpkin man made of old clothes and leaves. Why did you say he was miserable?"

"I mean every time I have ever seen him, he was. But maybe that was just because he was having a bad day." Chris said.

"Maybe he has grandchildren, or maybe he likes Halloween and the kids coming to his house trick or treating." Mom said.

"Could be, I guess." Chris acknowledged.

"Wanna come here to trick or treat?" I was joking but I wanted to see what Chris would say.

"I mean if you really want to. I am not keen on the idea, but its wherever you wanna go."

Good answer!

"No, I was just kidding. We have way too many by us that I promised I would stop by. Especially your grandparents' house."

"Oh, good. I would totally do it, but I am glad you were not serious."

Pulling up to the house I could see that everyone else was home now, even my dad. He was on the night shift for the next five days since the Fort gets very busy at Halloween, due to the haunted tours they do. Dad said next year I could go; he thought it would be more fun for the family to go together. I agreed, I always enjoyed doing those things with him, although it had been a while since we did anything with just the two of us.

He was getting us *Eagles* tickets for Christmas, which I wasn't as excited for because I am more of a baseball and hockey girl. Everyone else was super excited about it.

When we got out of the car mom was walking up to the porch ahead of us.

"Chirs did you want to come for dinner later? We are all home tonight, which is rare." Mom said.

"I am closing tonight but thank you Ms. Myers."

"Of course, you know you're always welcome at our dinner table."

"I appreciate that!"

God, his smile was so amazing, he is amazing. I was smiling and didn't realize it until he said something.

"What's that smile about?" he asked as he walked over and put his arms around me.

"Just you."

"Me huh?" He leaned down and kissed me.

"MmmHmm."

Justin was working as well, so he wouldn't be home for dinner, but I wondered if Rachel would still come. Mom and dad always expected both Chris and Rachel to be there so there were two added chairs and place settings. It was sweet that they are so welcoming of them, and I know that Justin and I appreciated it. I was helping mom clean up from dinner, and we talked about school, Halloween, and how things were with the wedding plans. I was most excited for that next year. They decided on an April wedding, which was a beautiful time of year here in Pennsylvania I am told.

My stepmom, who has become so much more than that, involved me in most all the plans and I happily agreed to go with her whenever and wherever she needed me to. As the maid of honor, I had a lot of responsibilities, not that I knew what any of them were yet. Helping her with important decisions like flowers and such was a very serious job for me, one I did not take lightly.

The girls were going to be junior bridesmaids, and my Uncle John was dad's best man, the boys were his groomsmen, it was going to be spectacular for the family. My mom's, my actual mom, family was going to be invited also. They called often to see how we were and were coming for Thanksgiving this year. I was excited to see them since it had been since June when I saw them last.

Halloween has arrived! It was the best time of the year, for me at least. The ber months, and the three greatest holidays of all time were approaching! Starting with Halloween, then my birthday, then Christmas. I liked Thanksgiving, but it wasn't my favorite, I was always so tired from the turkey after we ate. Then we would go to bed and get up super early to go shopping for deals on black Friday. It seemed like a lot of hoopla for one or two days.

At school some kids dressed up, I had a *Michael Myers* shirt I wore every year but that was the extent of my dressing up for school. It was that night that I made it the big deal. We didn't do much in our classes, since most of the kids were distracted by the fact of what day it was. Most of us just talked about where to go and who gave out the big bars, the popcorn balls, soda cans and bags of chips.

I didn't care much about most of that, since I was going out with Chris, he knew all the places we were going. I was secretly still hoping that we could stop by Detective Miller's, but I don't think he was keen idea at all. A girl could hope though, right?

Getting home after school I knew I didn't have much time to get my costume ready. I couldn't wait for everyone to see who I ended up dressing up as no one was going to expect it. I think it was probably going to scare the hell out of some people, and some may even turn me away. Mom was the only one who knew, and she was helping me with the makeup.

"Mom, I'm ready when you are." I called out to her in the kitchen for her help.

"Ok, sweetheart I will be right there."

She was getting dinner finished, *Ellio's* pizza, for all of us before we went out. She didn't want us filling up on snacks and getting sick, so she had to make dinner. We were fine with that, we all liked *Ellio's*, the cheese was like we were eating molten lava and was probably worse for us to eat than the candy. But it made her happy, so we ate it, and then of course planned on eating a bunch of our collections before we came home.

Mom was taking the girls out around our neighborhood, me, Chris, George, Rachel, Carmen, and Ryan, would be going out also, here, and so many other places. Justin was closing tonight so we would meet up later. We heard some kids would be back at Devils hole tonight, but I don't believe we were stopping by there. It was cool out, not super cold like you would expect it to be for Halloween in Pennsylvania.

Mom said it was fifty-three degrees out, which was mild. So, I knew my costume would be fine and I wouldn't freeze my butt off.

Finished! I looked in the mirror, and holy hell Mom did the best job ever on my makeup.

"Mom, this is so perfect!" I hugged her.

"I hope so, you look scary to me. I hope everyone loves it. Careful you don't mess your makeup up."

I pulled away and shook my head yes. I heard the car pull up and George was pacing upstairs, so mom went to check and see if he needed help. Then she had to help the girls finish up. I was worried they would be scared when they saw me, so I kept reassuring them that it was still me and I was only in makeup.

"We know, Letti. It's fine. Let us see you."

I walked into their room, and they looked terrified and then started to laugh uncontrollably.

"Why are you laughing?" I asked them, confused.

"We think you look amazing, and we were not expecting that at all. It's not funny, it's just funny how we were wrong with who we thought you were going as."

"Oh. Well, who did you think I was going as?"

"We thought it would be one of the typical slasher movie guys. But this, this is so much better!"

"Ok cool! So, it's good? You like it?"

"YES!" they both exclaimed.

"Awesome! Ok, have fun with mom. Get lots of candy. And I'll see you later or in the morning! Love you guys!"

CHAPTER 40

"WOW!" Chris reacted as soon as he saw me walking out of the girl's room.

"You like?" I showed off my face like *Madonna* did in her Vogue video.

"It's epic actually!"

"Thanks!"

I could hear George coming down the stairs now and couldn't wait to hear his reaction.

"Yo! That's so cool Letti!" he said.

"Thanks, little brother!"

"I love that you went the *Exorcist* route this year. Regan is so iconic, and you nailed it."

"Well, mom did my makeup, so she gets all the credit for that."

Chris and George both looked at her surprised.

"Nice!" they said at the same time.

Chris was *Hulk Hogan*, no surprise, and George was *Inspector Gadget*. I couldn't wait to see what everyone else was going as.

"Ok, are you all ready to head to my grandparent's? Scar, mom-mom may be a bit scared of your costume, but pop is going to love it."

"Ok! Oh, wait. Mom, do you have the rosary?"

"Jesus." Chris said.

"Exactly!" I replied.

He just shook his head and laughed.

"Fabulous, we're all set I think." I corralled everyone together to head out.

There were already kids out trick or treating, and dad was staying back to hand out candy. He was just getting home, so he hadn't seen my costume yet. I couldn't wait for his reaction too, he was gonna lose it. It was his favorite scary movie, and he is the one who gave me the idea. I knew he was going to be excited for it. I was happy he could enjoy a night off since they didn't have tours tonight. I couldn't understand that it seemed on Halloween of all nights that is when you would want to do it.

After making our rounds on my street, we hopped in Chris's car and headed toward Carmens house first. Rachel and Quinn were meeting us there, Ryan was already there naturally. They were all standing outside getting pictures done, Carmen's mom was that mom, you know the one who takes pictures of every occasion. They all looked fantastic! Carmen and Ryan were Sandy and Danny, from Grease again. Rachel and Quinn were tweedle dee and tweedle dumb, and they looked perfect in their costumes.

"You guys look amazing!"

"Holy shit Scar," this is a nickname my new friends started, "you are scary looking." Quinn said in awe.

"Thank you, I was hoping for that!" I was so proud.

"Oh, my, Scarlet. That is a scary costume. It looks so real." Mrs. Carter said she was there to hand out candy with Mrs. DiAntonio.

"My mom did my makeup, didn't she do great with it?"

"Yes, she did."

"Ok, we ready?" Chris and Ryan were getting impatient.

"Yep!" We all agreed and started to walk down the street toward the sea of teenagers, little kids, and parents, all walking around like a school of fish. I had never experienced this before, Havre de Grace was a bit more reserved with

Halloween, not that they didn't celebrate it, it was just lower key than this. This, this is what I have been missing my whole life.

I know my eyes were wide at some point, and Chris would look at me and smile. Like this was the first time I was experiencing Halloween or something, in a way it was.

We all had our pillowcases, some of us brought a backup just in case. I got so many compliments on my makeup and costume. We all did, and no one even bat an eye that were teenagers, many did in Maryland when you were "too old" to be trick or treating.

We were out for about an hour, and Rachel asked if we could head back to the house so we could meet Justin. None of us minded and made our way back to Carmens.

We could see Justins car as we were walking up, he was outside talking with Mr. DiAntonio.

"Look at this motley crew walking up here." Justin said laughing.

"Hi babe!" Rachel was the cutest ever with him, and she brought something out in him that we could all get behind. They gave each other a kiss and hug.

"You kids have fun?" Mr. DiAntonio asked.

"A blast dad! We are going to head to the other side of town now. Is that ok? Or is it too late?" she asked.

"No that's fine. It's only seven." He replied.

"Great! See you in about an hour." She kissed his cheek and we all piled into the vehicles.

"Wait, are we going?" I asked with such excitement.

"Yeah, we are going. I told everyone how badly you wanted to go over there, and they all said we should go." Chris replied.

"Yay!" I squealed and smiled with my whole face.

Chris and George laughed at me, and I know they thought I was ridiculous for wanting to go there. But I needed to see him, I needed to at least see him, so I knew what to expect. I don't know why I needed to do this, something told me I did. Could it have been Sandy? I don't know, I just knew.

Turning onto Pine Lane, finding a parking spot was next to impossible, let alone three of them. We all just parked where we could find a spot, which was close to one another, and met at Justin's car since that was closest to the end of the street which was a dead end.

"You ready for this?" Justin asked.

"Oh yeah I am!" I answered.

I could barely see the lights from his yard, we were far down the street, and with each passing house I became more and more anxious to get to his. Everyone on this street was over decorated for Halloween, and I loved it. I could see his house now; I could see the many kids running up and down the driveway. I was so hopeful he would be outside handing out candy, as we got there, I could see that he wasn't there. There was just a big, black, plastic cauldron on the porch with a note indicating us to take a piece.

"Ugh!" I sounded like *Charlie Brown*, with my dramatics.

"Sorry Scar. I had a feeling he wasn't going to be here. He never has been. I think he is going to take his youngest daughter out. He has like ten kids, I think. The one he had with his mistress, that was a scandal my mom said."

"I would like to hear more about that," I said.

"My mom said he has been married twice and had a mistress while being married to the last wife. He has a few kids, who are older than all of us, with the first wife. The second wife I think they are your sisters ages, and then the mistress who herself was like twenty-four he had a daughter with and she's three I think."

"Wow, this guy's sucks." Goerge said.

"I think he sounds pretty great," Justin commented.

Rachel was surprised he said that "Really?"

"Yeah, he obviously didn't want to settle, so he went from woman to woman before he found the right one."

"Uh, no. He cheated on them all, well except the mistress. But, ewe, the mistress should've known better." She was so disgusted by what he said, we all could hear it in her voice.

"Babe, I didn't mean to upset you. I am just saying that he is obviously the type of man that doesn't want to settle. How great for the women because who wants to be with someone who only wants to settle for them? You know?"

She rolled her eyes, "Fine. But don't think I won't remember all of that, Justin Myers."

He grabbed her and kissed the crown of her head. "So, what we are doing now?"

"Anyone wanna go to Devils hole?" Ryan asked.

"What time is it? We have to be home by nine-thirty" I said as I pointed to myself and George.

Chris checked his watch "It is eight fifteen, we should have enough time. We're just going to go check out the scene, right?" he asked Ryan.

"Yeah, for sure." He answered.

"Ok, well let's go then." Justin replied.

We all piled back into the cars and started off for Devils hole. I had an uneasy feeling about it, I was sure I was going to see Sandy there. I wondered if George would see her too, since he is sensitive to her appearances.

"Letti, what's wrong?" George asked from the back seat.

"I just have a bad feeling about going here tonight. Not sure why." I answered him as I looked out the window.

"Yeah, me too." He said.

"We don't have to go if you two don't want to. I can turn around right now and not even miss it." Chris told us.

"No, its fine. Just don't leave me or George, ok?"

"You got it." He wrapped his fingers in mine and kissed my hand.

I felt a little better after that, and I know he knew why we felt the way we did, but I was going to be on high alert with everything around me.

There were tons of cars parked everywhere, and I became almost sick to my stomach when we pulled over on the side to park. We had to park far away since there was nowhere close to park. It was more of the windy section of the road, a lot more dangerous for sure. There was a low guardrail on one side and nothing but a steep, rocky hill, and the tallest trees I've ever seen on the other.

I was nervous walking along because if a car came down there was nowhere to go to get out of the way of it.

"Scarlet, here take my hand, and George, take Scarlets. We can walk up this way together." Chris indicated a little path the was on the steep hill that we could take. It was above the roadway just enough where we could see other people walking and cars driving past. We could see the rest of our group walking and Chris hollered down to them to wave them up to where we were.

Now we were all together and I felt a little more at ease, until I didn't. I turned back to say something to Carmen, and I saw her standing down on the road, right near where we parked. It startled me at first, but I told myself I was going to see her tonight. I stopped in mid-sentence, and then kept talking so I did not draw attention to myself.

I turned back to make sure I was going to trip over anything and when I looked back again to Carmen, I could see that Sandy was no longer there in the road. I wanted to say something, but I didn't want to sound crazy. I wondered what she was telling me this time. As we were walking, I heard what sounded like a boat driving down the road. It wasn't a boat, but the brakes needed a change, the squeaking sound was obnoxious, and the muffler kept backfiring as it drove along.

"Jesus, that's an old ass car." Justin observed.

"That's Eugene Grayson's beater. He should've gotten rid of that car back in the seventies after he hit the tree down a way from the curve there." Ryan said.

"What did you say Ryan?"

"That car that just drove past down there. It's one of the people who own this whole area here. They have a lot of money. My dad told me that I needed to be extra careful, well all of us had to be, anytime we came here. He drove around and didn't care who was in the way. So, get the hell out of the way when you hear his car coming."

That's it, that must be who hit Sandy. Holy shit, I have to talk to Detective Miller now. I got it. I cracked the case. It had to be him.

Five days I would wait to meet him, which sucked, but it gave me an opportunity to get all my thoughts and facts down on paper.

Also, it will give me time to talk to pop and tell him my theory. As we walked down the path to where the first opening was, we heard the crowd of kids, the music was blaring, there were beer cans on the ground and the smell of weed and cigarette smoke wafted across my nose. I sneezed, I was allergic to smoke, and I had awful asthma.

There were so many different schools there, and of course Rich and his friends were there. They were listening to something different than everyone else, some dark stuff for sure. They were all dressed in these goth-like clothes, their nails were painted, and they had fake blood coming down the sides of their mouths. It was repulsive, but I didn't have much room to talk since I was dressed as a possessed girl.

This was different though, something I didn't expect I guess from him, not the same guy I knew when. Enough about him, he nodded his head to Chris and didn't associate with any of us. Thank God for that, I don't think I could handle him and his friends and the drama that could come along with it.

The scene was not really for any of us, so we hung out for a bit and then said our goodbyes. The walk back to the car had us on our toes. The cars that sped by us came a little too close to hitting us a few times, but we all made it safe and sound.

As soon as we got in the car, I couldn't keep quiet.

"I saw her. George, did you?"

"Nope, but I wasn't looking for her either."

"Damn. Also, can we talk about what Ryan said about that creepy car and the guy driving it. I mean seriously couldn't that be the one who hit Sandy and your aunt? Like, think about it that just makes sense, right?"

"I mean yeah, but don't you think he already thought of that?"

"Not necessarily. But I need to talk to Pop and pick his brain. I am sure he has to know who may have been questioned since one of his own daughters was involved. Right? I don't sound too crazy, do I?"

"Not at all. It makes complete and total sense. We can go see pop tomorrow after school fi you want. I don't work until Saturday. Ok?"

"Yes! You're the best! George you wanna come too?"

"I would like that, Letti."

George didn't get out much, so we were trying to change that and make him more sociable, luckily, he was willing to be also.

We pulled up and the outside light was off, typical on Halloween night when a house is done handing out candy. But it turned on as soon as dad saw the headlights.

"Ok, beautiful. I will see you in the morning. Good night, George!" Chris said.

"Night Chris. Thank you for taking me with you guys tonight. I had a fun time."

"Night babe." We kissed a quick kiss and I headed into the house.

I was exhausted and needed to wash this stuff off my face still. Mom came in as I was wiping it off.

"Did you have fun tonight?"

"Mom, I had a blast. The best time ever! George did too!"

"Good. I have some news I need to tell you."

I did not like her tone at all. It worried me.

"What's wrong?"

"It's pop. He is in the hospital."

As soon as she said his name my heart stopped for a minute it seemed and the world around me went black. I don't remember what happened, I just remember dad picking me up off the floor.

"Sweetheart. Are you ok?" mom asked concerned.

"Why is pop in the hospital? I need to call Chris."

"He fainted, and they weren't sure why. The ambulance came and they took him there for some tests. I haven't heard anything since. You should call him."

I grabbed the cordless and went into my room. I called his house; it just rang and rang. I didn't want to keep calling so I asked mom if we could walk up and see if anyone was at the house. No one was there, which we expected, but it was worth a shot.

"I'll call him in the morning. I don't want to bother him."

I laid in bed wondering if the reason I saw her was because of the car or now because of the news of pop. He told me she shows up when bad things are going to happen, and this was the worst thing I could think of happening right now. I was confused and started to question everything about tonight and seeing her. Part of me wished she would show up right now, but she didn't and the next thing I knew I was waking up to my alarm clock.

CHAPTER 41

I woke up at six am when my alarm clock was blaring at my head. I had the most restless sleep I've had in a while. Calling him was the only thing on my mind, I ran out to grab the phone, saw mom and dad sitting at the table drinking their coffee. Their faces seemed forlorn, and I was even more concerned now.

"Mom, dad, what's wrong?" I slowly took a seat at the table with them.

"Scarlet, pop is not doing well." Mom said.

"Like how? Not well how?"

"He is in a coma. I'm so sorry my sweet girl." Mom held my hand and tried to hold back the tears as she told me what happened overnight.

"I need to talk to Chris." I didn't because he was walking in as we were sitting there.

"Oh my God, Chris. Mom and dad just told me, I am so sorry." I immediately got up and hugged him with a huge bear hug.

"Me too Scar. We love him so much, and he loves you for sure. He's gonna be ok, he has to be."

"Scarlet, I called you out of school today, so you can be with Chris and the family. Ok?"

"Thanks mom," that's when I started to cry. How lucky I was to have her, all these people in my life. And now one of my favorites was down, I needed to see him.

"Chris, is anyone allowed to go see him?"

"Yeah, but maybe later. I am so tired I was just going to head home and get some rest. If you want to go to their house, my mom will be there. She said she would enjoy your company and could use your help. If you want too of course."

"Yeah, without a doubt. I will get dressed and eat and then walk over. Go home and get some rest, call me later ok."

"Ok. I'll see you all later on."

I knew how sad he was, I could see it on his face. It brought up so many emotions for me with my mom and watching her go through all she did. I tried to think of what made me happy during that time, and what other people could've done to help with that. It was not as easy though this time, because he couldn't talk to him. I could at least talk to my mom; he can't even talk to pop right now.

No one could.

Going to help his mom was going to be a big help for him and the family and mom being the sweetheart that she is, was making them some food for the weekend so they can eat, reheat, freeze whatever they wanted.

Dad had off this weekend, so he was around to take the girls wherever they needed to go and help with whatever needed to be done. He even volunteered to fill in at the hoagie shop, since everyone would be preoccupied with pop and his health.

"Mom, I am ready if you are. What time do you work today?"

"Ok sweetheart. I am in at three, why? Did you need something?"

"No, I just wanted to make sure you had enough time to go to with me, is all."

"Ok. Yes, I have plenty of time. You are just ordering pizza tonight, so no need to worry about dinner. The dinners I am making for them are in the two crock pots and the baked ziti I made up already, it just has to cool." We started to walk down the lane, "if you wouldn't mind bringing the dinners down later, I would appreciate it."

"No problem mom. I am so worried about them all. Pop is such a huge part of their lives, of so many people's lives. I am scared, mom. Do you think he's going to pull through this?"

"I don't know sweetheart, I hope so. I am sorry you have to go through this, I know how hard this must be for you."

She gave great hugs, just like my mom did, and I felt so much love from them every time.

"I just wanna be there for them all. Whatever I can do to help them."

She shook her head yes at me, knowing damn well I was heartbroken but putting on a brave face. We walked up the stairs and I could see Chris's mom in the kitchen. We knocked and she welcomed us in.

"Hey. Thank you so much for coming down, it means so much to us and of course Chris and pop. Scarlet, would you mind helping with this? My mom said you make the best." She handed me a bag of lemons and sugar, and the pitcher.

Smiling, I happily agreed and started to make the lemonade. I did notice that there were multiple pitchers out on the counter and wondered how many I had to make up.

"Mrs. DiMada? How many pitchers of lemonade would you like?"

"Oh, just one. But if you wouldn't mind making the rest of these up with iced tea, fruit punch and tang that would be wonderful." She looked so sad, and I knew how hard she was holding back the tears."

"Sure thing." I went to work on making drinks for the people coming this weekend, at least I assumed that was why there was so much.

Mom and Mrs. DiMada were talking in the living room, folding towels, and bed sheets. I did not want to be rude, but

I wanted to say something to her before people started to show up.

"Mrs. DiMada, I wanted to say something."

"Ok Scarlet, go ahead." She said with a voice as soft as an angel, like my mom's both of them.

"It's ok to cry. You should cry, because when everyone gets here you will not be able to hold the monsoon back. Trust me, after going through what I did with my mom, I wished I had cried more and not held in it. It also turns to anger, and I don't want to see you mad."

She looked at me, and within a few seconds of me saying this she started to cry. She let it all out, and mom and I were there for her. Mom hugged her and I held her hand, I remember how mom, Lucy, did the same for me when I was having a tough time one day with all of what was happening with mom Ramona.

This went on for about twenty-minutes, she pulled her face away which was beet red, and her eyes were puffy, she said "Scarlet there are many reasons why my son, dad, and entire family are fond of you. This was just another to add to the long list. You're a good kid, and please don't let anyone tell you differently. Don't let that spark you have dim, my sweet girl."

I started to cry immediately and was taken back five years to when my mom, Ramona, said almost the exact same words as she just did. They hurt my heart, like someone literally took a thousand pins and stabbed just the outer portion of it. The sting in my chest was burning and I knew she had no idea why I was crying the way I was.

"Scarlet, I am sorry. Was it something I said?" she asked and was so concerned.

"It's ok. My mom, Ramona, said almost the exact same thing before she passed."

"Awe, I'm sorry." Mom said walking over to hug me.

Both of them were hugging me now, and we all started crying. I am sure if anyone saw us, they would say we lost our minds, but it was long overdue for mom and I and much needed for Mrs. DiMada.

"Ok, ladies we need to get control of ourselves." Mom said giggling.

We all started to do that silly giggle you do when you're crying, and you know you need to stop but you're still kind of crying still.

You know what I am talking about, we have all done it. I went back to making the drinks for the day, and mom and Mrs. DiMada continued talking while folding the sheets and towels.

I asked if I could walk back to the house and get Murphy, so he wasn't home alone and was able to run around while we were there. Neither had any problem with that, so I walked out and headed toward the house. Of course, you guessed it, she was there. Standing right outside on the street. This time it startled me, she had never been there before, or at least I didn't notice before. As I got closer, she wasn't disappearing, and the fear was real.

Why wasn't she going away? I stopped dead in my tracks and was confronted face to face with her now. I was hoping no one would see me standing out here looking like a mad woman. However, I was mostly hoping that she didn't take over and possess my body, I have watched too many scary movies to know what happens when they take over.

I didn't want to look in her eyes, I heard if you did you can get possessed, or I don't know just something.

"What? Why are you here? What do you want? I am trying to help you." I said, which now I know I looked like a mad woman.

The next minute terrified me more than any other time I had seen her. She walked right through me, and when she did, I had a vision. It was from my point of view; I think it was anyway. It all happened so fast; I don't even know if I was seeing things correctly.

Just as fast as she went through, she was gone. And I was still standing there trying to make out what she just showed me. I felt disoriented and dizzy, almost sick to my stomach. I leaned up against mom's car, since that was the closest thing near me, and so I didn't fall over. I heard dad's voice from the opened front door.

"Letti. Are you ok?"

I didn't answer right away since I was trying hard not to throw up right there. I took a deep breath and finally was able to answer him.

"Yeah, I'm all right Dad. I just got really dizzy and nauseous for a minute. I'm ok now." I was not ok, but I didn't know how to explain to him what just happened.

I thought I was losing mind, like officially losing my mind. I needed to talk to pop because he was the only one who would understand me, well mom would too but she was busy. I knew it would be a while before I could tell him, so I ran into the house to write it down in my journal. This way I wouldn't forget a single detail.

I was trying to rush, so I could get back with Murphy and help some more, when I felt her again. I turned around and this time she was looking out the window, in the direction of pop's house. God, I hoped it wasn't another sign she was trying to give me. Like he was dying or something. I knew I had to get Murphy and get back as soon as possible, and I wanted to get as far away from Sandy as I could right now.

As I was walking back up with him, I could see Chris's car on the side of the lane, and my heart skipped a beat. He saw me through the window walking down with Murphy, and he met me out on the macadam.

"There's my favorite girl. And boy!" He leaned down and rustled Murphy's face and hair, and of course Murphy immediately laid on his back.

"He's such a ham. Ugh, you know you're ridiculous right?" I said staring down at him, as he rolled around like a crazy man.

"Oh, he knows it." Chris stood up and kissed my cheek.

"Any news?" I asked.

"Not yet, I think the rest of my aunts and uncles are on their way here. That's why I came back so soon. The shop is closed, my dad just left. He had some orders to fill and deliver. Which Justin did him a solid and took care of those for him. You have such a great family Scar; I am lucky to have found you."

Hearing him say those words gave me butterflies in my stomach and chills up my back. I think we were both lucky. When we got to the yard, I let Murphy off his leash, and he ran free like he always would.

CHAPTER 42

Over the next few hours most all his family was at the house, and Murphy was quietly enjoying all the attention he was getting. Dad came up with some brownies he made, three different flavors. Mom was pleased that he did that on his own. This was the first time we met ninety percent of them, and it was a bit overwhelming.

I don't believe I remember all their names, but I was trying hard to keep up. They were all loud, friendly, and talked over one another. I looked at my parents a few times, wondering if they thought the same things. I had no idea how they could keep up with any of the conversations going on.

Chris walked over and asked if I wanted to go down to the game room. I was grateful for the break.

"Yes."

We went down, he turned the TV on, and we just sat there holding hands watching TV. There was nothing on during the day except soap operas, and reruns of *People's Court*.

He stopped on *Days of Our Lives*, and neither one of us had a clue what was happening. It was a nice break from all the chaos going on upstairs.

I wanted to kiss him, but I knew it was not the time nor the place to do it. So, I just sat and was content sitting there with him holding his hand.

Upstairs was a bit of a different scene, his Aunt Michelle and Aunt Katelyn arrived, with his cousins. They started a bit later in life with having kids, and I remember pop saying that he didn't know why they waited so long because they were going to be like their grandparents instead of parents. The age was quite a big gap for them, he said by the time they graduated high school the two would be in their sixties. Chris said he exaggerated a bit, which I believed when I finally met the kids. They were not much younger than we were, in fact his cousin Jessica was my age.

We hit it off right away. Same music, style of clothes, hair color, and were totally into horror movies.

"I knew you two would hit it off," Chris said laughing.

He wasn't wrong about her and I. The rest of them were boys, and around Chris's age too, so I laughed to myself that pop would make such a false statement about his aunt.

I think he just wanted her to have kids sooner than she did, so he could be a pop sooner than he was.

I know they were all anxious to hear from Mrs. Burns to see if there were any updates on his status. Around one-thirty the phone rang, everyone went silent, and Mrs. DiMada answered the phone. We all quietly and quickly went upstairs so we could hear what was going on.

"Ok. Ok. Yeah mom, of course. That's good right? Oh ok, good. Yes, I can have Jason come grab you if you want. Ok. Love you too. Bye."

She hung up the phone and we were all waiting for her to tell us what she said.

"Ok, so dad seems to be coming to a bit. He moved his fingers and is blinking his eyes even though they are shut. So, they know there is brain activity, and he is fighting whatever is going on. Mom wanted to get picked up in about a half hour so she can come get a shower and changed, but wanted to see if Christian could come up and sit with him." Everyone looked at him, they all knew he was his favorite.

"Uhm, yeah of course I will. Is it ok if Scarlet comes with?"

"I don't see why not. Is that, ok?" She looked at my parents.

"Yes, that's fine. Whatever she and we can do. We will take Murphy home later, and dad will bring the food up. Go, be with Chris and pop."

I gave her a hug and we walked out to his car. I knew he was concerned, hell so was I. The hospital is only a few minutes up the road, so it took us no time to get there. His uncle was waiting to leave to pick up his grandmother, to make sure someone was always sitting with him in case he woke up unexpectedly.

When we arrived at the hospital parking lot, he placed the car in park and let out a long exhale.

"Damnit. Why did it have to be pop? He doesn't need this crap too. Damnit." He was angry.

I just caressed his back; I didn't know what else to do. I wanted to say something, but I didn't know what.

"I'm sorry. I know how hard it is, and I know he doesn't deserve this. You just have to be strong for him, and the family. I am here with you." I grabbed his hand and tried to ease his mind.

"Thanks Scarlet. You are the best and I am lucky. Ready?"

"As I'll ever be."

We got out and walked into the hospital, entering the elevator there was an elderly woman by herself.

"Hello, ma'am." I said.

"Hello." She replied.

Chris looked down and grinned at me. I flirtatiously shoved his arm away from mine, and he chuckled. The doors opened to the third floor, we exited and made a left down the hallway toward room thirty-one twenty-two. The door was partially opened, and we could hear voices from inside. We assumed it was the nurse and were pleasantly surprised to see that pop was sitting up and Mrs. Burns was talking to him, while feeding him some ice chips. Chris began to cry; his emotions just took hold of him in that moment.

"Hey boy, get in here!" pop called to him. His voice was hoarse, and dry.

Chris quickly walked over to him to hug him.

"All right be careful now," Mrs. Burns cautioned.

"Pop! When did you wake up?"

"About ten minutes ago, I guess. The doctor will be right back." He answered, "Who's that behind you? Is that my Scarlet?"

I was never happier to hear him say talk, especially those words.

"Hey pop!" I walked over and gave him a hug as well.

I think he could tell that there was something I needed to say, but I wasn't going to push it right now. He was in no condition to hear my nonsense. I told no one yet, I didn't think it was the time.

"Scarlet." He said in a stern voice.

"Yeah pop?"

"What's on your mind?" he asked.

"Nothing."

"Don't lie to me. I can tell when something is going on with you, we've been talking long enough."

He was right.

"Nothing that can't wait."

"Ok, well see I knew it was something."

"We can talk about it another time, pop. You just started to wake up."

He threw his hands around, "Oh, I was fine. I was just dehydrated. I am fine, they were a little dramatic."

Mrs. Burns rolled her eyes, "Yeah yeah, we were the dramatic ones."

Pop was insistent on me telling him what happened, but I did not want to talk about it with Mrs. Burns there. Honestly, I had no idea if she knew about our Sandy talks.

"Is it about our girl?" he asked.

I sat there shocked at first and looked over at Chris. He was looking for an answer too.

"Uh. Yeah, you could say that."

"Well, tell us. Come on." Pop egged her on.

The three were all eyes on me now, and I knew I had no choice but to tell them what happened. I proceeded to tell them the details of what, and how. Their eyes would get wide as I told the story, and excited at other parts of the story.

"So, I have no idea if she was telling me that you were ok, not ok. If Kim was around. I really don't know this time. I know the scene, or premonition I had when she went through me was something I will not soon forget."

"Wait. What happened there?" Chris asked with some concern in his voice.

"So, when she walked through me, I saw water, dirt, darkness but stars were bright, um. Let's see. It felt warm, like the weather. It seemed like the sun had just set, because there was still an orange glow in the darkness. Other than that, I have no idea what it meant, or when or where. It was scary and I don't want that to happen again."

They could see how scared I was, and Chris stood over to give me a hug. I loved that he knew how to make me calm and feel safe. Pop sat up, the look on his face was questionable.

"Pop, everything ok?" I asked.

"Yeah, yeah. I just, uh, wonder what she was trying to show you. It was not how she was killed so I don't think that was it. Maybe, hm oh I don't know. I am glad you told us though because that is not something you should keep inside all to yourself. That's why you have us, especially the three of us." Pop reassured me.

"I didn't know Mrs. Burns knew about it."

"Honey, I have been seeing Sandy since a few weeks after that damn accident. I never knew what it was she was trying to do or say, but since you came along, we are certainly getting answers aren't we?"

"Are we though, mommom?" Chris asked.

"Well, I think we are closer than we were two years ago before Scarlet moved here." she said sarcastically.

"True."

CHAPTER 43

The last of the nurses came in and now we were just waiting on the doctor for Pop to be discharged. Mrs. Burns called home, to let them know we would be coming home within in an hour or so, and to make sure that his bed was ready in the room and for someone to make sure that the electric stair chair was working ok. It was giving her a problem last week, and she didn't want any issues for him and getting him in.

"Will you stop making a fuss over all this. I am fine, there are plenty of men that can help me up the damn stairs when I get there." Pop said annoyed.

"Pop, stop. You know she is not going to let up and I won't either so let's just get on board with her. Ok!"

"Fine."

Pop was a stubborn man but did have one leg and now was even more down for the count after this incident. We all knew that she was right, and pop knew it too.

It was time for us to take him home, and the smile on his face was priceless. Chris opened my door for me, as he closed it behind me, he leaned down into the door, whispered my ear "You are the best part of my life and I hope one day we get to where they are."

I almost threw up right there, I had no idea how to respond to that. I mean I was only turning sixteen and he was going to be eighteen in January. I wanted to be with him forever for sure, but to hear him say that to me made me sick to my stomach.

All I could do was smile up at him and plant a big kiss on his cheek.

"Come on you two love birds, let's get him." Pop yelled out from his uncle's car.

"Jesus, pop. Really?" I could hear Chris say as he walked around to the driver's side of the car.

The drive back to the house was quiet in my end, he on the other hand was talking up a storm. My thoughts were spinning with what he just said, the fact that pop is ok, the fact that I still need to talk to Detective Miller.

"Babe?" I heard Chris say.

"Yeah, I'm sorry. What was that I missed it."

"I was talking about next week."

"Oh, what about it?"

"Going to see Detective Miller. We are still going, right? Now that pop is ok."

"For sure, I was just thinking about it."

"That explains why you went into Lala land for a minute." He said jokingly.

"Sorry. I was just thinking about a lot, but yes that was on my mind. I didn't want to mention anything until later, since we're still dealing with pop and all."

"All right good, I am excited to play detective with you!" he said with the wink of an eye.

I rolled my eyes, shook my head and chuckled. We pulled onto my street and cars were parked everywhere.

"You can pull in front of my house." I directed.

He pulled over and put the car in park, "You, ok?" he asked as he leaned onto the wheel.

"Yeah, that was just a lot to take in. I am not sure I am able to comprehend what she was showing me. It just was all too much, and I don't want to keep talking about it because of pop just coming home after his medical thing and I don't know." I knew I was rambling, but I just kept going.

"Ok, ok." He said calmingly. "It's gonna be ok. We will figure it all out. Just do me a favor, write it in your book. This way if something happens in the future we can refer back to this day and what happened."

"Already on it!" I said smiling.

We got out of the car and started walking up to their house. I could hear Murphy whimpering from inside the house, I assumed mom or dad brought him back home.

"I'll catch up. I need to run back and check on Murphy."

"Ok. Do you want me to come with?"

"No, that's ok. Go be with pop and the family. I'll be right there." I gave him a quick peck on the cheek and ran back to my house. It was cold, and my asthma was acting up, so running was probably not the best idea right now. I walked in and called out for Murphy; he didn't come. I walked around the house calling for him, still nothing.

I know I heard him, maybe I didn't. I looked out the living room window and I could see him running around with Chris outside at pops. What? How is that possible? I am sure you can imagine how freaked out I was at this point. I took my jacket off and threw a hoodie on instead. As I was pulling my head through the top she was there, and so close she could've smacked me in the face. I jumped back and fell onto the bed, she stood at my feet. I could see her face better than ever before, I could see her mouth moving, as if she was trying to tell me something.

"What? Sandy, what is it?" I said to her.

"Snow."

That was all she said, and she was gone. What did that mean? Snow? Snow what? I wanted to say, No. And you stop jumping into my body, yes. May you stop scaring the hell out of me, yes. I quickly grabbed my journal again and wrote down that too. I don't know how much more I can handle before I start to believe I am losing my mind.

This was getting out of hand now and I did not know what to do with it all. I knew that she was telling me something. Hearing her talk to me was enough to make anyone go crazy. Her voice was almost hissing, and it was low and echoey. God, I sound nuts I know. I walked out as fast as I could so I could go back there.

As I was walking up Chris pointed down to Murphy and put his hands up to the air. I shook my head, not having any idea why I heard him, which was a lie because I knew why I heard him. She made it sound like Murphy so I would come back into the house.

"Murphy. I thought I heard you in the house. I am glad you're here buddy!"

"What was it? Anything?" Chris asked.

"Yep, but I don't wanna talk about it right now."

"Ok. Nuff said." He grabbed my hand and we walked into the house together.

Everyone was sitting by pop, surrounding him and I know he was not keen on this. He was a very private man and did not like all the attention they were giving him.

"Scarlet, can you bring me some of your lemonade. I heard you made it." Pop asked.

"Of course, pop!"

I think everyone knew that he was a bit overwhelmed and finally they all started to disperse from the living room. He finally was able to relax, I walked into the living room to hand it to him, and he smiled.

"Thanks, dear."

"You got it pop!"

"Anything you wanna talk about?" he asked, as if he knew something.

"Nope, not really."

"Ok. Well, Chris tells me you guys are heading to talk with Chick next week. That's good, just be careful he's an old man like me, just not as handsome or nice," he laughed quite a bit at that.

"I am looking forward to meeting him and telling him what my theory is. I just hope he doesn't think I'm nuts after I tell him what I've seen. I know it's not the easiest thing to understand. Heck, I don't even understand fully."

"I have known Chick for quite a few years now, and while he is rough around the edges. He is also a reasonable man, he has been here many times in the past, and I told him before about my experiences with Sandy. He did not think I was crazy, probably because he already knows I am. HAH!" he almost cackled when he laughed.

"I wish you could be there pop. I know you can't because of all this, but it would be so much easier since you know him and all." I said.

"Who says I can't go? As long as my grandson is here to pick my butt up, I can go. Christian, you hear that?" he looked at Chris for affirmation,

"Yep, I got it pop. I will pick you up."

"Then it's settled."

"What's settled?" Mrs. Burns asked as she walked into the living room.

"Scarlet asked if I would accompany her to talk to Chick next week."

"And let me guess, you thought it was a great idea and told her yes? Am I right?"

I snickered.

"Yep!" he said proudly.

She shook her head, "Well, I don't want to hear it if you start to feel like crap. Got it?"

"Yes ma'am." He saluted her as she walked out of the room.

I knew it was time for Murphy to eat and the girls would be home from school soon, so I needed to meet them as they got off the bus.

"Ok, well I better get Murphy home and wait for the girls to get off the bus. Pop, I am glad you are home. I will see you tomorrow, I am sure. Enjoy the dinner my mom made; I think its chicken casserole."

"MmmMmm. One of my favorites from her. Scarlet, it's gonna be ok. We will get to the bottom of all this eventually." He grabbed my hand as he was talking.

"Thanks pop." I leaned down and hugged him. Walking in the kitchen I said goodbye to everyone who was there. Opened the door to the outside and yelled for Murphy, who was around back with the kids getting all the attention. As he came running around the side, Chris was walking out too.

"Let me walk you home."

"Ok."

Wasn't arguing, I knew he was a lot like his grandmom and wasn't going to take no for an answer. He took Murphy's leash from me and walked down the stairs behind me.

"Thank you!"

He just smiled at me, and I knew he needed to get out of there for a while.

"A little much for you today?"

He let out a long exhale, "You could say that. I love my family, don't get me wrong, but all I ever hear is, are you really going to run one of the shops for your dad, why don't you want to go to college? Blah Blah Blah, same stuff different day with them."

"I can only imagine. I have no idea what I am going to do next year, I know we can't really afford college and I don't know if my grades are good enough for any real scholarship offers. So, I'll most likely go to community college and then figure it out from there."

"I will need workers when I open in May. I would love to have you come to help manage the place. Especially since summer will be right around the corner. And it's after the wedding so there won't be any added stress. And you get to work with me all the time!" he smiled.

"You are very charming, sir."

"Sir, oh I like that."

"Oh, stop it. You know what I meant."

"I heard Sir. I am sticking to it."

We both laughed as we walked to the end of the street to the bus stop to wait for the girls. It was turning out to be a much better day than it started. I know he was tired, as was I, but I appreciated him staying with me for the evening. I don't really want to be alone, but it was nighttime that I was dreading now. I thought about sleeping in the girl's room, since it was Friday night, it wouldn't be unheard of for me to do that.

I just didn't want them to ask so many questions, I didn't want them scared too. I will just suck it up and sleep in my room but keep the connecting door open. I typically don't do that because I don't want them to come in at all hours of the night, especially on a school night. Tonight, would be special though, and I know they like it when we do that.

I didn't understand why I still had to wait for them to get off the bus, they were both plenty old enough to get off by themselves. But mom insisted that someone was there for them. They both would roll their eyes when they saw me standing there, but if Chris was with me, they would sprint off the bus.

Walking back up the street to the house, the girls had a million things to talk about, Avery was talking about trying out for the play and Violet was talking about what the new game was at recess.

"Wish we had recess." I said laughing in a sad way.

"Right!" he agreed.

The girls just kept talking over one another all the way up to the house, and continued on even when we walked in.

It was a lot sometimes, but I love them and so did Chris. It could've been worse, I reminded myself of that often.

The phone was ringing as we were walking in, I picked it up from the receiver. It was Justin looking for Chris.

"It's my brother he was looking for you."

"What up buddy? Sure. Yeah, no problem. Thanks buddy."

"What's wrong?"

"Nothing, he asked if I could grab George from school. He has a chess match at some school, and they should be back around four. I can grab some pizza on the way back if you want. I'll get *Pizza hut*; I know the girls prefer that."

"That would be awesome. I don't know if mom or dad left any cash though."

"I got it."

The girls were waiting in the living room for Chris to come in and sit down so, yep, they could talk some more. He really was amazing and very tolerant of them.

I started my laundry while he kept them occupied for a bit, fed Murphy, and was even able to start on some notes for Detective Miller. Which I wanted him to look over when I was done. I needed to make sure I didn't miss a thing.

It was close to four and he was heading to pick up dinner and George, I had told the girls to get showered and all so they could stay up a bit later tonight and watch TGIF all the way through. Typically, mom has them in bed by nine, but I didn't mind their company a little longer.

CHAPTER 44

The weekend came and went, a little too fast, I think. Nothing crazy happened since Friday, and pop was doing much better. We were planning for Tuesday to go see Detective Miller. Mom suggested not going on Monday since that would be his first day back. We all agreed that would be best.

School was boring, everyone seems to be in their own groove now, Kim hasn't bothered me since I confronted her that day. But I heard she and Matt broke up and she was dating Brian Peoples now. I felt for Matt, he lost so many friends because of choosing Kim over them, that now he just sat by himself and didn't do much at all.

I asked Chris if we should invite him over to our table, he said it was not a great idea because we didn't want Kim's wrath. I didn't care, she didn't scare me. I walked over and invited him over to join us. I don't think he thought I was serious at first. I could feel everyone's eyes staring at me, almost burning a hole in the back of my head.

He grabbed his food tray and followed behind me. The cafeteria was chaotic as usual, but many watched as he and I walked to my groups table.

"Thanks guys." Matt said quietly.

"Yeah, no problem." Ryan responded annoyed.

I knew they would all look at me with the eyes, and cocked heads, but I didn't care. No one should ever have to sit alone in the cafeteria. George told me stories of his old school and how he sat alone more times than he could count, so, I was not about to allow that for someone else. I saw the sadness in George's eyes when he told me, and I saw that same sadness in Matt's today.

I knew no one would really talk much to him, and that was ok with me. I just didn't want him alone, whether that would end up backfiring on me was not my concern. Meaning, Kim would retaliate somehow. The bell rang indicating that the period was over, and we all made our way out the door. Literally walking like penguins down the hallway, it was pretty tight in some parts.

"Thank you, Scarlet, for that. I really appreciate it. You don't have to worry about that again though, I will find somewhere else to sit. I know they were uncomfortable with me there."

"You're welcome. You can sit with us for as long as you want. They will get over it," I smiled at him and ran to catch up with Chris.

As I approached him, I was pulled back by my schoolbag and brought to the ground. I don't remember much at all, except black hair, all around my face and what felt like cold stones being smashed again and again on the side of my head. There were people yelling and screaming.

I was finally able to see that it was Kim, literally straddling me and kicking my ass. I had never been in a fist fight before, and boy was I about ready to pee my pants. I was terrified, I had no idea what I was supposed to do. I had never hit anyone before, everything was flashing before my eyes. I could hear people chanting "FIGHT! FIGHT! FIGHT!" The next thing I knew I was able to get my arm free and hit her with all the force I could muster.

The next few minutes were just as much of a blur, but she rolled off me and onto the cold floor. I know it was cold because I was just held down for a bit on it. I hit her so hard, her nose was gushing blood and looked like it was falling off her face. It wasn't, it was just broken.

Three teachers stepped in to break it up, I was looking for Chris, but he was nowhere to be found.

"Let's go Miss. Adams and Miss. Allen. To the principal's office you both go."

She was complaining and fighting them the whole way to the office, I was not. I was not feeling well at all, and unfortunately, I threw up right in the middle of the hallway. Great, is all, I think.

"Scarlet, look at me" Mr. Brinton said, as he was inspecting my eyes.

I looked at him but couldn't focus and needed to throw up again.

"Jesus, we need to get you to the nurse, I believe Miss. Allen here gave you a concussion. Will you let Principal Holman know I am taking her there?"

"Mr. Brinton, I think I have to throw up again."

"Ok, let's stop right here." He pulled one of the trash cans over and took the top so I could use that. He stopped one of the kids and directed them to go to the office and have them call for the janitor to clean up the hallway behind them.

"I'm sorry." Is all I could say.

He rubbed my back and told me it would be ok. Once I finally stopped long enough to walk into the nurse's office, Mr. Brinton was nice enough to stay with me while they called my mom.

"What were you thinking? You're one of the good students, Scarlet." He brushed my hair back so I could see.

I really was having a hard time with all function at this point.

"I didn't though. She pulled my backpack from behind and to the ground I went. She was hitting me so hard with I swear a stone or something."

As the nurse was writing things down and calling my mom, she heard me say this and got up immediately from her desk.

"Scarlet, can I lift your hair up really quick?" Nurse Vaughn asked.

"Let me help," Mr. Brinton stood up and helped prop my hair up.

I heard them both gasp. Now I was even more upset because I couldn't imagine how bad it looked.

"This is not good," she said to him.

"No. I will be right back." He stormed out of the office.

"Am I in trouble, Nurse Vaughn?"

"No no, sweetheart. You were defending yourself." she reassured me.

She grabbed some ice packs from her freezer and told me to put them on each side of my head. That was even more painful than when Kim was hitting me.

"Ouch. That really hurts. Can I see what it looks like?" I asked.

"I'll walk you to the mirror, you should not be on your own moving around."

She helped me up from my seat and I got dizzy as soon as we moved. She could feel my body lose balance and put both of her arms around me to keep me up. Man, I was a mess right now, and still had not seen what I looked like.

We made it to the mirror, and I started to cry instantly.

"Oh my God. What did she do to me?"

I have not felt this sad since my mom got sick. I wanted to run away and hide so no one would see me. I was embarrassed, in excruciating pain, sad, scared out of my mind, and still wondering where my boyfriend was.

The bruises were already starting to show, I had welts the size of golf balls on either side of my head. My ear was double its size, and it looked like I was even missing some hair on the right side.

All I could do was cry.

After about fifteen minutes my mom was there, I could hear her yelling at someone outside the door. As she threw the door open, she saw my face, sprinted over to me, knelt down and hugged me.

"Oh, my sweetheart. Let me see you."

She pulled up my hair as well, a lot gentler than Mr. Brinton, and started to tear up.

"Mom, its ok. I will be ok."

"No, it will not be. Where is Principal Holman? And where is this girl that did this to my daughter. And why the hell is there not an ambulance here or on its way?"

One thing I learned about my future stepmom was that she did not mess around when it came to her kids, and especially when it was something medical related.

"I will see what is taking him so long." Mr. Brinton left again.

"Mrs. Adams, I did call the ambulance we are just waiting for them to arrive. We have been following protocol the entire time with Scarlet, I assure you I have been taking care of her."

"She has mom, even Mr. Brinton has been so nice, He helped with my hair, with me throwing up. He's been great. They both have."

My mom seemed a bit uneasy when I said that about him, but she could tell that I was fine, and it was really going to be ok. Now, not knowing much about concussions, I knew that they could be bad. I was not allowed to fall asleep, which I was trying hard not to, but I was getting more tired by the minute.

"Nurse Vaughn, the ambulance is here and the EMT's are on their way back to you." We heard from her speaker on the wall.

She walked over to the door and opened it for them.

"She is right in here." She directed them.

While I was talking to the EMT's, and they were doing their assessment, Mom and Principal Holman were having their own conversation. I remember hearing "I will press charges against her. How did she get her hands on those?" That was all I could hear.

"Scarlet. Scarlet. I need you to wake up for me sweetheart. Come on, wake up now." The Paramedic was shaking me.

When I came to, I didn't remember passing out, but I do remember this shooting pain behind my left eye. It felt like someone was stabbing me from inside my brain into the back of my eye. If you've ever been punched, then you understand.

"Ok, I think we are ready to head to the ambulance. Mrs. Adams, are you following us there?" The paramedic asked,

"Yes, I am." She answered.

They wheeled me out into the hallway, and everyone was saying "Get better soon." And shit. As we rolled by the office Chris was sitting there with an eye pack on his eye and he stood up so fast, I could hear the secretary yelling at him to sit down, obviously he didn't.

"Scar. I am so sorry. Oh my God, baby are you ok?" he looked at me up and down, "Jesus Christ, what did she do to you. What the hell did she hit you with. I won't let this go. Ok, I won't."

Mom stopped to talk to him and assured him she would keep him updated but he should come by the house this evening to be with me.

I knew my mom wasn't even close to being done talking to the school, and that she would not tolerate this violence. I learned quickly that I did not like being in the back of an ambulance, especially sitting backward. I threw up the entire way there and apologized every time. It was really just awful.

They wheeled me into the Emergency Room, shouting out all different things to the nurses who were going to take care of me from here on out.

"Feel better Scarlet," the ambulance crew said.

"Uh, thank you. Sorry for the whole throwing up thing the entire ride."

"Eh, don't worry about it. We are used to it, kiddo."

Mom went to the registration desk and took care of the things she needed to while the nurses took me back into a room for a cat scan. I wasn't sure what that was since I have never had one. I heard about my mom getting them done when she was sick, and mom talked about them because the kids needed them at the Children's Hospital. Other than being tired and wanting to throw up every five minutes, I was fine. Yeah, I had pain, but I knew that would go away eventually.

The nurses brought me back to a room now, mom was there waiting.

"Hey sweetheart. How are you feeling?" mom asked.

"I still feel tired and like I'm gonna be sick. But I think I'm going to live!" I wasn't trying to be funny; I just needed a little levity right now.

"Oh, Scarlet. It's not the time to be funny."

"I know mom. I am sorry."

She sat right by me that entire time, she never left my side. Even when dad walked in, she didn't leave my side. I was reminded once again of how lucky I was to have two absolutely amazing moms in my lifetime.

Mom explained to dad what happened and of course you could guess he was pretty pissed. They were contacting the Superintendent to request a meeting on what they were going to do with the girl, Kim, and to make sure I didn't get in any trouble. I was still concerned as to what happened to Chris, but I knew I had to wait to see him tonight before finding out anything.

"Mom." I touched her elbow. "Do you know what happened to Chris?"

"I do. I spoke to him briefly when I was in the office looking for you. He got into a fight with some boy, a few seconds after that girl did what she did to you.

That must've been Brian, I don't like him. He's a creep. I was anxious to talk to him now and was hopeful he was ok. I hope he kicked his ass because he deserves it.

I hate to talk like that, but I was tired of this from her and now he gets involved. This is ridiculous. It was unfair just because of who her family was, no one ever wanted to do anything about her and how much of a bully she was.

I hoped that would stop after today, but that will remain to be seen. Later that evening there was a knock at the door, I could hear dad but couldn't quite turn my head to the door to see who it was this time.

"Hello there..." was all I could hear from a man's voice.

"Scarlet, you have visitors." Dad said.

"Huh. Ok."

"Hey there. How are you feeling? We wanted to come by and check on you."

I was flabbergasted, it was Mr. Brinton and Nurse Vaughn. They had a bouquet of flowers and a card in their hands.

"I'll be all right. Thank you both so much for making sure I was ok today. It was really great having you both there."

"It was fate I guess kiddo!" he said with a smile.

We chatted for a little while, and mom told them what was going on with the detectives and the incident. They didn't stay much longer, but it was so nice they did come by.

CHAPTER 45

All my tests came back clear, I did in fact have a concussion which sucked. I also knew that we weren't going to talk with Detective Miller. I was so angry; I did nothing to this girl for her to treat me the way she does. It was finally time for me to go home, I was never more relieved to do so either.

I had so many restrictions and rules to follow from the doctor, and mom. I didn't care, I just wanted to be home in my own bed waiting for my boyfriend to get there.

When we pulled into the driveway, there was a strange car parked out front on the street. I thought I recognized it at first, but I was wrong. Dad pulled in right behind us and ran up to open the door and help me out. Justin came running out of the house too, with a gentleman coming out the door behind.

I did not know who this was. "Mom, who's that?"

"I'm not sure sweetheart. I will find out though."

She walked up to Justin before he made it to the car, I know she was telling him that we didn't want company right now. She turned around and looked at me, then back to Jsutin, then she waved to the man standing on the porch.

He was older, I couldn't quite make out much because I couldn't see that great from the concussion.

Mom walked up the hill to greet him, Justin came over to help dad with getting me into the house. I had to stay down-stairs with them for the next few days, so they could monitor me. I wasn't allowed to do any stairs, or anything. I was going to live a very boring life the next few days, but that gave me a little more time to think of more questions for Detective Miller.

I was settled into the recliner in their small living room now, when I heard mom's voice and then a voice I did not recognize.

They stepped into the room, conversing, while I was staring at them both wondering what was going on and who this was.

"Here she is." Mom said.

"Hello Scarlet." The man greeted and shook my hand.

"Hello, sir."

"Scarlet, this is the officer who will be taking your report so he can relay everything back to the detectives assigned to the case." Mom said.

"Hello!" I said again.

"I hear there were some issues at school today. Can you walk me through what happened?" he sat down and started to ask his questions.

"Ok, so why am I here? Well, Miss. Allen's family is pressing charges against you Scarlet for breaking her nose, and right cheek bone."

All of us were shocked and then an uproar broke out.

"What? Are you kidding me? She attacked me, I was defending myself. She hit me with something, I don't know what. But punches cannot do this to you." I lifted my hair and showed him the welts and bruises that she left.

His face winced; he knew that was painful for me.

"Oh gosh. I am sorry she did that to you. Listen, let me talk to the school administrators and any of the kids that are willing to come forward to put in a statement. I will get back to you all. Is there a number I can call that's best?"

"Yes, you can call here at the house." Mom gave him our number.

I didn't want to talk to him about anything now, I was so mad. How dare she turn this around on me. Like this was my fault. I was seeing red at this point. I could not wait for Chris to get here so I could tell him what she was trying to pull now.

Dinner was ready, everyone was nice enough to eat downstairs with me, Murphy was here too. Nothing from Chris though, not a word. It was unlike him not to call at least.

"Chris hasn't called right?"

Everyone shook their heads no.

"Ok." I sighed sadly.

It was not until nine o'clock that evening that I finally heard from him. The phone rang and George brought it to me.

"Hey. Are you ok?"

"Hey babe. Not at all. I had Detective Schaffer here at the house when I got home from school. That douchebag Peoples is pressing charges against me. I told the detective all the details and what happened, and he is looking into the school now. What the hell. Are you ok? Is it too late for me to come over?"

"Are you serious? You're never gonna believe there was a detective here, at my house. Kim is pressing charges against me too. I'm ok. Let me ask mom, hold on?"

"Yeah." Lucy replied/

"Hey mom, is it ok if Chris comes over just for an hour?"

"Sure, honey."

"Mom said yes that's fine. I'll see you soon."

We hung up the phones and I started to tell my parents what he had just said.

"What? That's asinine. I'm calling Charlene. This is not acceptable."

Mom's voice was different, she was a different kind of mad. She walked over to me and grabbed the phone so she could call her.

"Charlene, hi. I know," she trailed off because she left the room.

A few minutes later Chris was walking in. As soon as he saw me, he started to cry.

"Jesus, what the hell did she do to you? What can I do? Are you in pain?" He was kneeling next to the chair on the ground.

"I'm ok. I promise. It hurts but I think I'm too mad to feel it right now. You look fine though." I chuckled.

"That dude tried; I did kick his ass. Pretty bad too. Probably why he wants to press charges, that and I crushed his ego. I have hated that dude since we were kids. He's always pretended to be a tough ass but he's not. Not even close."

Neither one of us knew of Brian's home life, not until much later anyway. It's a sad story, one that no one should ever have experienced. There were more secrets in this small town than anyone ever knew. When the detectives started their investigation into this incident it raised a lot of concerns. Mainly, how could a kid go his whole life being abused physically, mentally, and verbally, by his father for his entire life, go unseen by others.

Chris called me about an hour after he left, which was not typical since he was here. It was eleven o'clock and luckily, I had the phone sitting next to me, so it did not wake anyone up.

"Hello?"

"Babe, I'm sorry it's so late. Did I wake you up? Or anyone else?"

"I don't think so, and no I was awake. what's wrong?"

"You're never gonna believe who was just here. Who was waiting for me when I got home from your house."

"Brian?"

"How'd you know that?"

"Just a lucky guess. What did he want?"

"It was weird. I pull up right, and he's leaning against the driver side door of his Nova. I walked up of course on edge cause seriously why are you here when you're pressing charges against me."

"MmmHmm,"

"So, I was like Yo, what's up? What are you doing here? He says *"I'm sorry. I don't wanna press charges, I was just doing what Kim told me to do. My dads pretty pissed, so I am going to the station tomorrow to drop them and take back my statement. Dude, I'm sorry"* I was flabbergasted, babe. Then I felt bad, cause like why is your dad pissed. It was a fight, you lost." He retold what they said.

"That's probably it babe. He lost. I heard someone say something at school one day. I was walking into Art, and he was heading to Shop class, and someone said look he's worn that outfit twice already this week. I felt bad, and he just ignored them and rushed into the classroom."

"Ok, so what's that gotta do with his dad and saying that?"

"I don't know, maybe he's abusive? His dad. Do you know about his life? Like is his mom still in the picture?" I asked.

"Shoot, I don't know. Honestly, I never took a minute to talk to him. I never cared to. But yeah, a lot of how he acts makes sense and could explain why. His dad probably is that way. Damn, babe, what if that's true? I just added to that abuse. Damn."

"Don't get too down on yourself babe, he had it coming unfortunately. You can't jump someone, especially someone your size, and think that they are not going to fight back. I am more upset that Kim is once again using another guy to her advantage. Like, what will it take for her to stop. I still wish I knew what she hit me with."

"That's another thing, Scar. I know what she hit you with, Brian has it. He is going to give it to the detectives when he goes there tomorrow. Baoding balls, that's what she had in her hands. That's why the damage is so bad."

"What? That's crazy, but I knew she had something in her hands. Why would she do that? It's like she planned it, she wouldn't just have those lying around. Babe, she probably wanted to kill me, I think if I didn't hit her as hard as I did, she could've."

Now I was terrified, thinking someone wanted to hurt me that badly. I didn't know why, what her reasons were. Because I was dating Chris, that can't be it, it's been over a year that we have been together. I don't get it. I was grateful for Brian coming forward and telling the truth and giving them the balls. Typically, I would laugh at that, but this was serious, and I fully believed that she wanted me out of the picture permanently.

Trying to fall asleep was nearly impossible. I had to sit up, and this recliner was old and had a spring popping out in my back. This was the worst. I was hoping to see Sandy, but she never showed. Weird. She was there for so many other incidents, but this one is the one where I need her the most, she is nowhere to be found.

I don't remember falling asleep, but I remember the wicked headache I had when I woke up and the sun was shining right into the tiny hole in the shade. It was like a beacon shining in my face.

Mom was next to me, checking all my vital signs. Nurses!

"Mornin, mom."

"Morning sweetheart, how did you sleep? How do you feel?"

"I don't remember falling asleep, and I feel groggy."

"That's normal. I heard you talking with Chris late last night. Is everything ok?"

"Oh, let me tell you this story. You're never gonna believe it."

I sat and told her everything Chris said, and her reactions were just as shocked as mine were.

"I think you're right Letti. About the abuse. When I was talking to Charlene, she said something along those lines. She told me his mother died when he was very young, his father claimed it was an accident but there have been questions over the years. There were numerous 9-11 calls for the police, for domestic violence. It seems very sad for this boy, and my heart breaks for him. But what he did was not acceptable, and he should not have done what he did to Chris. I am very grateful that he did go talk to Chris and can only hope that he stays true to his word and goes to talk to the detectives today. We will wait, I guess. I am sorry you didn't get to talk with Detective Miller, maybe after all this blows over you will."

"Maybe. That's sad to hear about Brian, I am very lucky I never had to worry about that. How did no one know?"

"Unfortunately, when you shut down the way he has, it just happens. It is not right, nor an excuse and someone had to have known that his home life was not good. How are you feeling, do you want to eat breakfast?"

"Yes, I would love some breakfast, mom."

"Coming right up. How about a half a bagel and some OJ?"

"Sounds good to me."

I did nothing for the rest of the day, just waited for everyone to get home from school and for Chris to call me. I knew he had to work today, but he told me he would call before he went in. I was also hoping that someone would let us know what was going on with the charges. Maybe the detectives would call, or something.

Mom said she wasn't sure if anyone would call today or not, since it could take some time to question Kim. Since Brian was going to the station today though, we were hopeful that we would hear something before they went home for the day. The phone rang so many times, most of the calls were people checking in on me and seeing if there was anything they could.

All I cared about was hearing from Chris, with some good news hopefully.

CHAPTER 46

Chris called as soon as he got in from school, he said the school day was different. There were teachers posted at every bathroom and double the number in the cafeteria. Everyone was asking how I was and hailing me as a hero for doing what I did to Kim. Many said she had it coming, and they were tired of her being a bully.

I think the part that blew my mind was that she broke up with Matt and within a week or two she was with Brian. I think she had been cheating on Matt for a while to be honest. Chris said she did the same thing to him, she had been dating him for a while, broke up and then almost immediately was with Matt. I know the situation was different because Chris broke up with her, it was still very fast that she ended up with Matt so quickly.

Oh, why am I rambling. You all have been so patient with my story so far, and soon enough you will all know the horrid night that I endured. But let's get to my birthday, and through the holidays. Also, you must find out how close I became to the Detectives, and how I helped them solve Sandy's case.

Ok, let's fast forward to that evening, Brian did in fact go to the station. All chargers were dropped against me and Chris, Brian got in a bit of trouble. But the police knew his situation, so they took it easy on him. Kim, however, was nowhere to be found. They went to her house, and everyone was gone. Chris said she was not in school either. That was reason enough for the detectives to drop the charges. They asked if my parents wanted to press charges against Kim, and I did but I didn't. I just wanted it all to be over, and for everyone to move on from it.

My head was still pounding, it was worse today than it was yesterday when it happened. I knew I was tired, so I asked if I could go to bed and put this day and yesterday behind me. Chris wanted to come by when he was done closing, but I told him I needed sleep I was exhausted.

That night, Sandy came to me. This time she was in my dream; it was like she was real. I could hear her voice, see her in color. We were in the back yard, under the willow tree, she was swinging, and I was sitting on the log bench. She said things to me that I would never forget.

Scarlet, there is danger coming to you. I don't want to scare you. I want to help you. I cannot stop the danger; I can only warn you of it. Please be careful and stay alert. Some-one who you think you can trust, you cannot. This person will approach you a few times, and one night will be the last. Stay alert. Stay safe. She swung high enough to where she could jump off and as her feet landed on the ground, I felt myself fall.

I jumped awake, thinking I was falling out of the chair. I sat there in a daze, not knowing what to make of what she said to me. I needed to write it down, my journal was on the side table, and I felt so dizzy I couldn't stand up just yet.

I said the words over and over in my head, so I didn't forget them. These were important ones I needed to remember. I looked at the clock, it was three fifteen, and I knew everyone was asleep in the house.

I sat up feeling as if someone was staring at me. Not like the times before when Sandy would show up, this was differ-ent. This felt ominous, brooding almost. I couldn't get up so I couldn't check the outside to see if anyone was there. I yelled for my dad, twice I did, and he ran into the living room.

"Letti. What is it? What's wrong?"

A few seconds later mom was in there too, tying her robe around her waist.

"I think someone is outside."

Dad and mom looked at one another and dad quickly went to the light switch and turned it on. He couldn't see anyone, so he grabbed his baseball bat, and a flashlight, slipped into his shoes and tossed his jacket over his shoulders.

We could hear him yelling outside.

Mom sat by me, hugging me. "I am so sorry sweetheart that all this is happening to you. This is not fair."

"I hope no one's out there. I don't hear dad anymore."

As soon as I said that dad walked back through the door.

"Someone was out there all right. They parked across the street, I couldn't see the car, or them. I heard footsteps pounding on the pavement when I started yelling. I couldn't even tell if it was a man or woman. I am calling the police." He said as he was picking up the phone.

Mom and I looked at each other, terrified. Who could that be? Brian was ok now; Matt didn't have a car. I don't want to be here anymore; this place is the worst. I want to go back to Havre de Grace. God, I haven't talked to the girls in so long. I needed to tell them what happened, and to make sure they were still coming up later in the month for my birthday. I had not talked to Mel, I did miss her, but she had her own things to figure out still. I didn't need any more drama or trouble in my life right now.

"Ok, police will be here soon. Damnit. If I was just a little faster, I may have been able to at least see the car, that would've certainly helped."

I could tell dad was really getting down on himself, which he had no reason to, but he was dad and that's what he did.

"Honey, this was not your fault. We are just grateful that you went out there and saw or heard something. That was heroic." Mom said with an endearing smile.

"I guess so."

"Thanks dad."

The police officer showed up about twenty minutes later, I was half asleep when he knocked at the door, Murphy alerted to him first now that he was downstairs with us. I wished he was there earlier when whoever was outside, maybe he would've alerted then too.

"Ok, I think I got everything I need. I will make sure I get this to the detectives tomorrow before I leave my shift. Have a good night. And if anything, else comes up call us again and we will be out."

"Thank you, officer."

That's the last thing I remember hearing before falling asleep again. I was abruptly awakened by a hard knock at the door.

"Hello Detective. Please come in."

"You must be Scarlet. I am Detective Schaffer. I got the report this morning from Officer Michaels, and I wanted to just follow up. Also, to give you some updates about the attack on Scarlet from Miss. Allen."

I was wide awake now. Petting Murphy on the head, I was trying to get up. This time was much easier since I was not so dizzy and could function a bit better than I could a few hours ago. I was happy that I had to be down here for a few days, because the girls did not have to deal with all this. Hell, I didn't wanna deal with all this, but here I am.

"So, I wanted to let you know that we have received multiple complaints about a possible peeping tom, in the area. So, while we are gathering more information on this, we ask that everyone be diligent here and keep their windows closed at night, and do not get changed in front of any open windows or doors. You know, just make sure you're aware of your surroundings. And of course, if it happens again call immediately. Now, as far as the incident. I don't know if you have all heard, but the Allen's seemed to have relocated. We are unsure of the whereabouts as of now, but rest assured we will have officers driving by their residence throughout their shifts. We have also asked for the cooperation of the neighbors up there, and if they see anyone entering or exiting the home to give us a call right away. I know that's not the solution we were all hoping for."

"At least I don't have to worry about her jumping me again at school."

"Oh, we have an officer now at your school, all day. We are possibly going to post a second, but that is still in the works. And Chris explained that he picks you up and drives you home, which is good. That's good."

"Detective did the young boy hand over the things that she hurt my girl with?" dad asked.

"Yes, in fact he did yesterday after school."

As he went on to tell my parents, my mind started to wander, I needed to think of something other than the incident and overnight. I wanted to go back to solving Sandy's murder. I must call it that because you don't just hit someone and drive off and it is not considered murder. Right? I thought so too.

"Detective Schaffer? Is Detective Miller in today?"

"He is, he is at your school getting the remainder of the statements from the faculty and students. Why? Was there something you needed?"

"I need to get my mind off everything going on, And I know it's going to sound a bit crazy, and I promise it's not the concussion talking. But I think I know who killed Sandy Lawrence."

His eyes got wide like an owl's, he gasped so loud, and even jumped back in the chair. I wasn't expecting that response.

"I'm sorry, what Scarlet. Sandy Lawrence?"

"Yes, you heard her correctly. She has had some experiences since we moved here, we all have. I know it probably sounds off, but I can assure what she has to say is fact and her experiences are real." Mom said with such confidence.

"Well, I think Chick, sorry Detective Miller, should hear what it is you have to say then. I do as well. Mind if I page him?"

"Please," dad directed him to the phone on the wall.

"What is your number here?"

"555-8557" mom said.

"Thanks."

He hung up the phone as soon as he was done, and we waited now for him to call back.

"Are you close with the Lawrence family?" He asked.

We shook our heads and dad replied "No, I mean we are friendly with them, but we have not seen them since we moved in."

"Do you mind if I take some notes down?" he asked as he took out his pad and pen from the inner pocket of his jacket.

"Not at all. I have pages of notes if you wanted to look at them?" I handed him the notepad I was writing in; I was not about to hand him my journal. No way!

"Wow, yeah that's great thank you Scarlet."

He started reading them over when the phone rang. Mom got up to answer, "Yes, Detective Miller, hold on please. Detective Schaffer, it's for you."

He was not paying the slightest bit of attention, mom had to nudge his shoulder. He was so enthralled with my notes, I think.

"Chick. Yeah, I am at the Adams residence, and uh, I think you may wanna come by here when you're done there at the school. Ok. Yep. Sounds good." He put the phone down on the receiver and went back to the notes, as if we weren't all sitting there.

"Um, Detective?" I questioned.

"Oh, God I'm sorry. He will be here in about twenty minutes or so. He was just finishing up with your teacher, Mr. Brinton."

"Ok. Good!" Now I was excited.

"So, you see her?"

I was afraid to answer, but mom looked at me with encouragement.

"Yes. Since the first time my dad brought me here with my friends, before we officially moved in."

"Huh. And does she speak to you every time you see her?"

I shook my head no.

"Ok. Is it a negative encounter when you see her? Like does it feel evil, or bad?"

"No, not really. The only time was this past Friday, you'll see that on the second to last page."

"Ok." He said as he continued reading.

We heard the screen door open and a knock on the door after. Dad got up to open it, we all knew it was him. The man I had been waiting for, Detective Miller. His voice was not as harsh as I expected. I could see him much better now, he had a scruffy beard, bright blue eyes, wrinkles in the corners of his mouth that had a permanent frown.

His eyebrows were not well kept, neither was his hair really. He smelled like cigarettes and cologne. I wasn't sure of the cologne, but it actually smelled pleasing. He dressed nicely, slacks that were a dark grey, almost black, a collared shirt with the top button undone, his badge was on his belt. His shoes were worn down, definitely needed a new pair. He was probably an attractive man to women his age, and I could see why he had multiple wives in his time of being an adult.

My mom even seemed a bit giddy with him there, which was weird. Dad took to him easily; he was an easy-going guy. Until he told me what he was doing there.

"Morning everyone." He greeted as he nodded his head to us all.

"Good morning. Can I get you a cup of coffee or anything?"

"No thank you Ma'am. What was so urgent that couldn't wait until I saw you later at the precinct."

"You're gonna wanna hear what she has to say. I think you should take a seat and maybe take Mrs. Adams up on her offer."

"Uh, ok. I'll have a seat. So, tell me what is going on Scarlet." He inquired while taking a seat across from me.

"I believe I can help you solve the Sandy Lawrence case." I figured there was no need to beat around the bush and just come out with it.

He was frozen, his face, his body, it was like he became a statue. He didn't say a word, Detective Schaffer handed him my notepad. It wasn't until after that when he woke up it seemed.

"Ok. I'll bite. Lay it on me." He said almost in a rude tone.

"I think you should look over her notes, I think you might find them interesting." Schaffer urged.

He let out an annoyed sign, as he started to read over the first page. He looked up at me a few times, and around the room at everyone else. Almost as if he was seeking validation that we all knew what was written on those pages.

"Scarlet. You see her? Tell me what she looks like."

I told him every detail, even down to the right ear having a second earring hole but the left one didn't. I didn't know what that meant, but I figured it must have some meaning. He was hanging on to every word I said and agreeing with me the entire time.

"Ok. Well, looks like we got ourselves a Junior Detective to help us out here. Can I take this with me? I would like to make copies if that would be all right?"

"Sure, but you need to give back as soon as possible, because I never know when she is going to show up again."

"Of course. Actually, Detective Schaffer would you mind taking these to the station and making copies and heading back here when you're done. I have some more questions for Scarlet, and I wanna go over a couple of things about the case that no one knew, stuff that she has written here."

"Yep. On it." And he left.

"So, I want to tell you a few things about me, and about this case in particular. The Lawrence family is a great family, and Sandy's death hit them, and well all of us, pretty damn hard. Excuse my French. Many have claimed to have seen her a few times here and there, and I have not but I do believe those individuals one hundred percent. I believe you, too. Mr. Lawrence claimed to have seen her many times, typically once a week. He never knew what she wanted I don't believe, so I don't think he made a big deal about it. At first, he thought he was just seeing things, but when Mr. Burns told him he saw her one evening, outside in the front yard, well he knew he wasn't seeing things. I guess what I need to know is who do you think did it? I don't see that written here. Just some names, one in particular stands out."

"Ok, so hear me out." I began to tell him about Devils hole and when I saw that car and heard it, about Sandy about all of it that night.

"We always thought it could be him, but he stated he had an alibi and his mother confirmed it with us."

"Don't you think they could have been lying?" I asked.

"Well, yeah of course. But we had to go with the facts. And we had no evidence to link him to the scene."

"Maybe you didn't ask the right questions?" I was not trying to be rude.

"Maybe we didn't. So, what do you think we should've asked?"

"Well, I think that Chris's mom should've been asked if she heard any strange noises. The car, his car, makes a distinct sound when it is driving, and according to some of the kids around, apparently it always made that sound. Maybe it did that night too, but she didn't realize it because they were all used to hearing it."

He looked down at the notepad, and he looked as if he agreed with my theory.

"We checked his car though."

"But when, that night?"

"I am pretty sure it wasn't until the next day. And when we did it was covered in a barn, and looked as if it was in pristine shape."

"MmmMmmm, that gave him and his family plenty of time to come up with an alibi and fix any damages that may have occurred to it."

"Has she ever given you anything that could tie him to the scene? That would be helpful."

"I mean, not that I can think of."

We sat there in silence, all of us thinking of what could be a sign from her that this man hit her.

"When you saw her in your dream, where was it you were at?"

"Um, we were outside. I thought it was our backyard, but maybe it wasn't."

"Ok. Devils hole?"

"Hmm, maybe. I don't know a lot of the area there, so it could've been."

"Ok, well how about this, when you are feeling better what if we took a ride out there and I took you to some of the places that maybe look like your back yard? Maybe that might trigger it?"

"I think that could work."

"Ok, well in the meantime if anything else comes up or you see her or whatever. Page me or Detective Schaffer and we will call or stop by, and you can get us the new information. How's that sound?"

I shook my head yes, "yeah, I can do that."

"How is everything else? Your head? Your boyfriend?"

I touched the left side and winced when my hand brushed up against one of the bumps.

"Er, still hurts bad. I know it looks worse than it is though. He is ok, he didn't get a scratch on him. He has been trying to figure out how he can help Brian get into a better situation. I think he is going to offer him a job, or have his dad hire him rather." I exhaled longer than I should've, "I don't think it's a good idea, but you know he is a nice guy and wants to help him."

"He is a good kid, from a better family for sure. I think that's commendable for him to do that for Brian. Brian's life hasn't been easy, and for Chris to recognize that is great for him."

"I think so too."

I really was not keen on the idea, but I also was taught by mom, Ramona, to give people second chances. Not Kim though, not a chance on that.

"Mom, later on can I give the girls a call, they don't know what's been going on and I wanna fill them in since they will be here in two weeks for my birthday."

"Of course, sweetheart." Mom answered.

"You stay in touch with your friends from Maryland? That's great."

"I try too, my one friend, Mel, well she's been going down a bad road and I don't know what's going on with her. The rest of them are the best, and I miss them all a lot. I miss being there a lot. I never had to worry about any of this anyway," I said as I pointed to my head and face.

I could see mom and dad and how disappointed they looked when I said that. It was the first time I said it in a while. I felt bad but I knew I wasn't wrong in saying that. I really did miss being there, I loved everyone I met here and all the new friends, but I truly never had to worry about someone trying to kill me in school, or anywhere for that matter. That is what I believed in my soul that Kim was trying to do, she was trying to kill me. Fortunately for me she failed.

CHAPTER 47

Later that evening mom reminded me to call the girls, we had just gotten three-way calling on our phone, and she wanted me to try it out. I was excited to do it since I could talk to Gabs and Heather at the same time. I didn't have a clue how to use it yet, so this was going to be a hoot.

"The phone company gave us a manual to set it up, so hopefully that will help us. It's me and you kiddo!"

"This is gonna be interesting," yes, I was being sarcastic again.

"Hey, we got this." She was much more optimistic than I was.

"Why don't we get George, he's a genius at this kind of stuff."

"Hmm, that's not a bad idea." She agreed.

She left the room to go upstairs to get him. My thoughts went back to the "peeping tom" that was here the other night, and I was praying he didn't come back. How creepy is that? I don't even wanna think about it. As long as he didn't come back here, I was good. Knowing that the detectives wanted to listen to me, and my theories, was probably the only good thing that came out of this whole nonsense. My bruises looked the worst today so far, didn't hurt as bad though. Makeup couldn't even cover up what this looked like, and today it looked like I was a bruised apple.

I was happy to have my notes back, so I could add anything new that might happen, which deep inside I had hoped nothing would happen tonight. I just wanted a normal night's sleep. I could hear them coming back down the stairs now.

"Letti, we are going to try it out with your friends, I think I know how to set it all up. Can you dial which ever one first." He handed me the phone.

"Yep, I'll call Gabs first." I dialed the number, and she picked up. "Ok, she's on. Now what?"

"Letti, what are you talking about?" she asked.

"Oh, shoot sorry Gabs. We got three-way calling, and we are the guinea pigs for it." We both laughed.

"Ok, now hit the dial button one time. You should hear a double tone." He spoke.

"Ok." I did that and heard it. "Got it."

"Now, dial the next number."

"Ok" I dialed Heather's, it started to ring. Her mom picked up and gave her the phone.

"Hey!" I said.

"Ok, now hit the dial again and both of them should be on there."

I hit it, "Hello?"

"Hi" Gabs said.

"Hello!" Heather also said.

"Oh my god, it worked! You're a genius George!"

"Wait is that Gabs?" Heather asked.

"Yep! We got three-way calling! This is the coolest!"

"So cool!" They both exclaimed.

The three of us talked for about an hour, I told them what happened, and they were filling me in on everything down there. We needed to hash out the plans for my birthday but were still torn as to whether Mel should come.

"I know she's going to be so pissed at me if she's not invited, but honestly, I don't know who she is anymore, we have talked only a few times, and she blamed me for all the problems she is having. I don't wanna deal with that."

"We agree. We were talking about it with Jen the other day. We can get the ride up there if someone can take us home on that Sunday. Is that possible?" Heather asked.

"Shouldn't be a problem!"

"Good, my mom is dying to see Lucy. She misses her so much. We all miss you guys. I don't like the new people in your house. They are snobby."

Now that was a bold statement coming from Heather, her family were the snobbiest group of people most have ever met. But we loved them, regardless.

While I was talking to them, Chris walked in the door. I was very happy to see him. He had a bouquet of flowers too, and a box of chocolates. This guy couldn't be more perfect, right? His parents most definitely raised him right. Even though I am pretty sure that pop had a lot of influence on his upbringing. And of course, Mrs. Burns too, she was a feisty woman and ran the show in that family, without a doubt.

I said goodbye to the girls, but not before we planned our next call so this time Jen could be there. There were only a few weeks left before my birthday, so we wanted to get everyone on the same page. Plus, I wanted to hear her voice and catch up. I hung up as he waited patiently for me, he walked over and handed me the gifts.

"I know you're not big on flowers, so rest assured they didn't cost much," he said with a grin, "but the chocolates on the other hand, you don't wanna know what I spent on them!"

"Oh, I am so honored to have them. Both."

"There's one more thing." He said it in a weird way.

"Ok."

He took off his jacket and placed it on my lap.

"I would be honored if you were to wear my jacket."

Now, I know this sounds silly, but when a boy gave you his sports jacket, or letterman as they called it, it was a big deal.

Like, huge. It showed the world that you were his, and he was taken. Yes, we have been going out now for quite some time, but this was what sealed the deal.

"Are you for real?" I asked.

"For real, for real!" He said with a smile. That dimple, got me every time.

It was the best feeling, being his girlfriend. I never imagined that it was as good as this.

I couldn't be happier to have his jacket and wear it with pride. Most of us girls would have our guy turn our class ring to "lock it," that was how we showed our devotion to them. Maybe a bit archaic but, it's what we did back in the nineties. I told you we did a lot of stuff back then, and what I am telling you isn't even half of it.

I would be getting my class ring in a few months, and had every intention of him locking it, which he would be the ninety seventh one. See, you have the number of people turn it to represent the year you graduate. Since I graduate next year in ninety-seven, I'll have ninety-six people turn it and then him lock it. It was a rite of passage for us.

Ok, so back to the story. I know that there is so much that you are asking right now, mainly am I really dead? Yes, I am. I have been telling you this story from my journal, that Detective Schaffer is retelling to you. I hope he is doing a good job, and that you come forward to him so my family can finally have peace. What they have endured is not fair, and what you did was evil. I am waiting for you to meet me here because I believe that we will meet again.

In the meantime, I have been silent in the face of evil but am lucky to have someone willing to tell my story.

CHAPTER 48

Chick and Mike have both been keeping me updated on the progress of opening Sandy's case back up. The Lawrences have been by a few times, here at the house, to get my side of everything. They both seemed happy, and almost relieved that someone was bringing new life into their daughter's cold case. We are on a first name basis, because of how much we have been working on this. I look over things that they write down, because I technically can't see the actual case, and then I compare what I've experienced.

They are both so busy, they cannot commit fully to the research, but I can. Plus, their cold case unit is just as busy, and they got permission from their Chief to allow me to help in some way, and honestly since then I have not seen her. Which was helpful because I wasn't distracted by her appearances.

The time I have been spending with all of them has been rewarding. I have learned a lot about unconditional love, whether here or not. The Lawrences still love Sandy as if she were here today.

He confided in me, the many times he saw her and spoke to her. He explained she never showed him many signs or spoke a word, but she was always there he said.

He could feel her presence everywhere he went. Of course, everyone assumed it was because she was his daughter, but now the ones who know, know the real reasons. Sandy was speaking to us from beyond the grave.

Sounds like a really good plot for a scary movie. Doesn't it? Well, you haven't seen anything yet.

My birthday had arrived finally, my sweet sixteen! I had no big plans for a party, just the girls coming up from Maryland and my new friends from here. Mom was making a cake; dad was making his famous homemade pizza. Famous to us anyway. The Violet and Avery were helping me decorate, Justin was making appetizers, and George was setting up music. It was going to be the best birthday to date for me!

A knock at the door came around four o'clock, on Friday November seventeenth news came that would rock my world forever. It was Chick and Mike, and they had a new development in Sandy's case.

"Scarlet! Just the person we are looking for. Boy, do we have some news for you. Can we come in?"

Of course, they could. I stepped out of the way and invited them in.

"What's up? I am nervously excited for whatever it is."

"First Happy Birthday!" Mike handed me a gift bag that he was hiding behind his back.

"Aww, you guys didn't have to. But thank you! Tell me what's going on?"

"Well, because of your notes and endless research and reading what you could. We believe we are ready to make an arrest."

"Ok, ok, well tell me. Don't leave me hanging here."

"You wanna tell her?" Mike said looking at Chick.

"I don't care who tells me, just tell me. I am losing it here."

Please say Eugene, please say Eugene.

"It was Eugene."

"Ha! I knew it. I knew it was him. Did he admit to it? Tell me everything."

"Slow down, we can't tell you everything just yet. We still must notify the family and get a full confession from him. But you connecting the dots between his car and the fact that it was in the body shop, his cousins, the very next day after the hit and run before we were able to get a look at it. Well, his cousin told us everything we needed to hear. Explained the damage the fact that it seemed like there was blood, the fact that there was hair. He was told it was a deer he hit, so his cousin didn't question it. I am sorry for interrupting but we are so grateful to you and all the help you gave us. Hence the gift."

I opened it and it was a badge, a legit badge that read "Honorary Investigator for Weston Police Department."

"Now, it has no authority or power, but the Chief had it specially made for you. And the other thing in there is from us," Mike pointed to Chick and himself.

I pulled out a *Ty Beanie Baby.*

"Aww. It is so cute." It was cute, it was a ghost, called spook. How fitting!

"We know it's a little kiddish, but we felt it was perfect for everything you did and what this case was about."

This was absolutely the best birthday, I helped find her murderer.

"Mom! Dad!" I yelled.

They walked downstairs quickly, worried, I think. They didn't know the two of them were there.

"Oh, hi gentlemen! What do we owe this honor?" Mom asked.

"Scarlet. You wanna tell them?"

"Oh my god, mom dad, we did it. We actually did it."

"Did what sweetheart?" dad asked, while mom stood there with tears falling down her face.

"We solved Sandy's case. It was Eugene all along. Just like I said it was."

"Oh, Scarlet that is the best news. Do the Lawrences know yet?" mom asked.

"Not yet, we are heading there after we are done here. We just wanted to tell Scarlet in person ourselves and to give her a birthday gift."

Mom was looking at the badge now and laughed.

"You can't pull anyone over with this, ok kiddo!" We all laughed.

"I know!"

"Scarlet, did you want to come with us to speak with the Lawrences? I mean, if it wasn't for you who knows how long that would've taken for us to solve. It's already taken all these years."

"Mom, dad, can I? I know everyone will be here in a little while, but I am sure they would understand this."

"I mean, just have her back by six, ok?" mom demanded.

"Yes ma'am."

As we were leaving Chris was pulling up.

"Wait, can Chris drive me? This way you guys can stay however long you need to, and he was a huge part of helping me with this."

"Yeah, that actually may work out better." Chick said.

Now I know what you're probably thinking. "How can this girl figure out this hit and run in just a few months? Well, it literally fell on my lap. Partly because of Sandy and the other because of everything else falling into place. From Pop to Mr. Lawrence, to the redacted files, and the ones that I was permitted to see. I could just see it, the sound was really the biggest thing of his car, I mean that was obvious.

But we knew they were waiting on a solid piece of evidence. That was the biggest thing. So, when I brought up about how she only had one of her second holed earrings in, they meaning the detectives asked the cousin if he saw one. He did not. But, when they searched Eugene's house and bedroom, they found it in an envelope in the back of a drawer.

When we pulled up to the house, they didn't get out right away. We walked up to their car and could hear Chick on the radio talking to the station. It was one of the other officers letting them know that he was in custody and was in the process of writing his full confession.

"10-4. Thanks."

They high fived each other and smiled. They saw me at the driver's side door and celebrated with me.

"Ok, now we go in." Chick led the way.

He rang the doorbell and in a split-second Mr. Lawrence was already opening the door.

"Detectives, Scarlet, Chris. I sure hope this is a good visit." He said.

"May we come in?" Mike asked.

"Please." He welcomed us in.

Mrs. and Mr. Lawrence took a seat in the living room, invited us to take a seat as well.

Chick started to explain everything to them, they both started to cry and hug one another. I was so relieved for them, and sad at the same time. Sad because even though they will have closure now, they still lost their only child.

"Oh, Scarlet, I know you had a lot to do with this. Thank you, sweet child, for being you and never giving up." Mrs. Lawrence walked over and hugged me so tightly, which hurt a bit.

"I knew you could do it kid. I knew there was a reason you were sent here. My, our, Sandy sent for you to save us and her. We will be forever grateful for you, and you will always be part of this family." Mr. Lawrence said.

It was such a beautiful experience to be part of, and the fact that it was on my birthday was I can't even explain.

We were ready to leave so I could get back to the house when they stopped me.

"Scarlet, hold on one minute ok." I saw Mr. Lawrence walk into the kitchen, and Mrs. Lawrence was smiling through the tears.

He walked out with a small, wrapped gift.

"Happy Birthday. It's your sweet sixteen, and we wanted you to have this."

He handed the box to me, it was wrapped in shiny iridescent paper, with a beautiful silver bow on it. I sat down and placed it on my lap. As I opened it, I could see a velvet box, like a jewelry box of some sort. The lid was hesitant to open at first, but I could see it as soon as it started to open. It was her class ring on a sliver chain. I immediately started sobbing sitting right there in their living room.

The meaning behind this was more than anyone could ever imagine. Yes, I found it in our room, but I know it meant so much to them because they thought it was lost when the hit and run occurred. Them giving this to me was their way of accepting me as one of their own.

I hugged them both and promised I would be by to visit soon.

Chirs and I walked out to his car, and I sat in it for a minute and cried. He just sat there and held my hand, while I did. It was sweet.

When we got to my house no one was there yet, which was good because I wanted to tell mom and dad alone and show them my gift. I know mom would cry and dad would be so proud. It was one of the happiest days of my life.

CHAPTER 49

The weekend was the most wonderful one I had in a long time, my face and head were fully healed. The cold case for Sandy was solved, I was helping my parents plan their wedding even if we weren't too far in just yet. I was on Honor Roll at school, there were so many things looking up. Nothing could go wrong... yep, I said it.

Sunday around six o'clock there was a knock at the door, Murphy was whimpering, and I hadn't seen him do that in quite some time. The only time he did it was when Mel was around. Speak of the Devil, and she shall appear.

I opened the door and all I could smell was her perfume wafting in the kitchen. I wasn't sure why she was here, well, other than because it was my birthday weekend.

"Hi." I said with hesitation.

"Hey! Happy Sweet sixteen!" she said with a huge awkward smile on her face.

I could see a car parked on the street closer to the end near the stop sign and was kind of curious who it was.

"Someone with you?" I asked.

"Oh, that's just a guy I've been seeing for a little while now. I didn't want him to come up since you know, you don't know him, and I didn't want him to be uncomfortable. Or like weireded out."

Oh, she didn't want him to be uncomfortable or weirded out. Ok.

"Oh, gotcha. So, you're not staying long then. I assume."

"No, I can't I just wanted to drop off your gift I got you. I didn't want to come Friday or yesterday so I figured I would come up when I knew the girls were back home, sorry back in Maryland."

"Huh, ok. Well, thanks."

"Oh, here." She handed me a pretty large gift bag, "Please don't open it now. If you could just wait til I leave that would be awesome."

"Um, ok."

"Ok, well happy birthday Letti. Sorry I've been such a shitty friend."

And she just ran off, I couldn't respond or anything. She was so quick to get in the car, which I might add drove off like a complete ass and peeled wheels the whole time up the hill. I just rolled my eyes, because why wouldn't she have a guy like that.

She made me sad knowing that she had changed so much, as I am sure I have as well. This change seemed to happen so fast for her, like it was there the whole time, she just didn't realize it. So, I guess this would be the last time I spoke to her, I felt in my gut that this was it. It sucked, not gonna lie, but I think it was for the best. When I turned and closed the door my dad was standing there curious as to whether I was ok or not.

"You good Letti?" dad asked.

"Yeah, dad. I will be anyway. Just a lot of years of friend-ship gone in the blink of an eye."

I could feel my throat starting to develop a lump in it and knew that it was just a matter of seconds before the water works started.

"Ok, well I'm gonna head to bed. Night dad. Love you." I said as I gave him a hug.

"Night kiddo. Love you on purpose."

Here they come. I quickly walked to my room so I could let the tears come freely, that was the first time I heard that since my mom, Ramona, said it. She would never say I love you too, she said it always sounded like people said because they had to not because they wanted to. She decided that I love you on purpose sounded better and had more meaning, I agree.

I cried into my pillow, until it was soaked with tears and became uncomfortable to lay on. So many thoughts raced through my head while lying there. My birthday this weekend, my family, Sandy, Mel, my mom. Even after the wonderful weekend I had I been still so very sad. I missed my mom immensely, and my best friend just left and for good.

I knew I just needed to fall asleep.

Waking up to my alarm clock was the last thing I wanted to have happen. I felt like I was hungover but didn't know what that felt like, so I think this is probably what it felt like. I was groggy, and cranky, through no one's fault but my own. I heard footsteps coming toward my door and then a quick knock.

"Letti, mom wanted me to make sure you were awake." Violet said.

"I am. I'll be out in a little bit." I looked at myself in the mirror as I got out of bed and my face was still so puffy. I had to pull it together, so I didn't get a million questions when I walked out there. I don't wear makeup really, so that wasn't going to help cover this face. I just had to go out there and face the music.

I heard another knock at the door.

"Morning sweetheart. Can I come in?" mom asked softly.

"Of course."

She came in and sat down on the corner of my bed. I wasn't sure what she was going to say, I couldn't read her face.

"Scarlet, are you ok? I know that couldn't have been easy last night having to say goodbye to Mel, again."

"It wasn't, but it was necessary. She is so different mom, like I don't even recognize her at all. Did you see her?"

Mom shook her head no.

"She had so much makeup on and was in all dark clothes. I can only imagine what the guy looked like that she was with."

"Well, people change. You both went your different paths, and honestly it is probably for the best."

I just agreed. I knew it was for the best, she made me feel bad about moving here since we moved here. She never wanted to hear me, ever.

Chris pulled up to pick up me and George, I still hadn't told him that Mel stopped here. And I never opened her gift either. I wasn't even concerned about it to be honest. George got in first and then pulled the seat back so I could get in.

"Hey!" I greeted my guy.

"Hello beautiful!"

"You guys know I am here, right? Like every day I am here. Just reminding you."

We both laughed.

"Sorry buddy." Chris apologized.

"So, you're never gonna believe who came to see me last night."

"Who?"

"Well, that was no fun. You're supposed to guess," I laughed.

"Umm, Matt?"

"What, why would you guess him? Of all the people that's who you guess. Ugh"

"Ok. Umm, Carmen? Rachel? I don't know babe, tell me."

"Mel."

His eyes got wide, and he was just as shocked as I was last night when I opened the door and saw her.

"Yeah, I know."

"Why? I mean, obviously because of your birthday, but she wasn't invited."

"I know. She gave me a gift."

"Did you burn it?" he chuckled uncomfortably.

"No. But I didn't open it. She was so goth, like even more than any of Justins girlfriends from the past. It scared me a little."

"How did she get here?"

"Her new boyfriend drove her."

"Oh," he laughed, "What was he like? I am sure he was a real winner."

"I don't know. She said he would be uncomfortable meeting me."

"Jesus Christ, that doesn't surprise me."

We didn't say much else on the rest of the ride.

"Wait, you never said what she gave you," George said from the backseat.

"I didn't open it."

"Oh. Why not?" he asked.

"I didn't care to."

"I understand."

"I don't. Just throw it away then." Chris said, sounding a bit frustrated.

"Are you mad?" I asked him.

"No not at all, babe. But if you don't care then just throw it away. If you can't I will do it for you."

"No, I will probably open it. I just don't want to right now. I am still hurt by what she said to me in the past, so just don't want to right now. OK."

"Ok. Ok. No problem, babe. Just trying to help."

He took my hand and rubbed his thumb along my knuckles and smiled at me.

"Thank you."

This was my first day back since my concussion, and a bit overwhelming. As soon as I walked in Mr. Holman was there to greet me, I think he was terrified that my parents were going to sue the school, but they agreed that it would only be hard on me if they did. Chris and Geroge had permission to help me go to any classes I needed help with. Mr. Brinton was also very helpful; he was going to help me get back on track with my classwork. He was our class sponsor, so it was part of his duties too. Mondays and Wednesdays we agreed on, and that worked for Chris too because he had basketball practice on those days and George had Mensa. It was a win win for all of us.

Mr. Brinton was very helpful to me, and I didn't know how to thank him. I asked my mom if we could bake him some cookies for my next tutoring session which was when we came back from Thanksgiving break.

CHAPTER 50

The days just flew by, we had some cold weather come through and by the time Thanksgiving came around it was snowing. I loved the snow here, the nature looked so beautiful, and it was peaceful at night especially. We heard that Devils hole was finally reopened, which I didn't care much about that, I did want to take the ride out there now that I got my license. Mom and dad said I couldn't take any long rides, really was just allowed to stay in town. They told me I had to wait at least a month before I could go out of town, especially to Devils Hole.

I didn't have a car yet anyway, so it's not like I could go anywhere even if I wanted to. Mom and dad said they were working on getting a third car, and have Justin do the work on it, but I wasn't pushing it. With the car, however, I needed a job. So, I started work at DiMada's too, I worked as many shifts as possible with Chris and with Justin. I wanted to contribute as much as possible to getting a car, and to save up for gas and such.

The agreement was if I paid for gas and any simple maintenance they would pay for the insurance and anything big that needed to be done. I was totally fine with that deal, who wouldn't be. So, in the meantime Chris and everyone else just drove me wherever I needed to go. December third was Heather's birthday; she was an entire year older than me. So, she and the girls came up that weekend to go to the Holiday Bingo Bash with me, mom, Avery, and Violet. Avery's birthday was December twenty-second, but everyone always tried to make it special for her. So, we agreed that the bingo bash would be part of her birthday celebration. Mom had so many fun plans for her, twenty things in twenty days, this was the kick-off.

Heather got a bad ass VW bug for her birthday, so naturally they would come here to spend a weekend with me. I was jealous, I won't lie, but also not surprised. I was more surprised that she didn't have it last year. Her parents bought her everything and anything she wanted. I still loved her, even though she was spoiled rotten!

"B- five." The number caller, who was the Chief of Police, called out the numbers. It was hard to hear over the women all having their own conversations. I swear I had Bingo like ten times already, but I couldn't hear all the numbers.

"I- nineteen. I- nineteen"

"BINGO!!!" Violet yelled out.

We all cheered and laughed. She walked up to the front to check her numbers.

"We got a winner!" Mrs. Smitham exclaimed to everyone in the hall.

Everyone clapped and cheered for my little sister, her face beamed as she walked back with her prize. The prizes were wrapped so no one could see what they picked, you had to unwrap when you got back to your seat.

"What did you win, honey?" mom asked as Vi unwrapped the box.

"A mini crockpot," she was disappointed, you could tell.

"Oh, how nice! You are not happy, though. I can't say I blame you. That's a boring gift for a soon to be thirteen-year-old.

"Well, if one of us wins we can switch if you like that one better. Would that be ok, Vi?" Heather asked.

"Yeah, I would like that. What am I gonna do with a mini crock pot." She shook her head.

"Ok, let's get a new sheet out and start the X bingo."

This is where you have to make an X on your sheet. Let me tell you what the scene looked like in this room. These women came to play and meant business. They had lucky hats, troll dolls, food, drinks, it was insane. But man were they having a great time.

The table behind us was most of Chris's family, and then the other side next to us were my girlfriends and their parents. We shared food and drinks; it was such a blast. I am sure many of us missed numbers, but we were having so much fun it didn't matter.

Mom looked over at me around eight-thirty and I knew it was time for the big surprise. Heather and I got up to pretend we were going to the ladies' room, but really, we were going to the kitchen to get Violet's cake, so we could all sing happy birthday to her.

"B- eleven is what Miss. Violet Adams is celebrating this month! If everyone could join me in singing Happy Birthday to this lovely young lady!" Chief Masters said happily.

I could see her face; it got beat red, but she was smiling. Heather and I walked out with this gigantic sheet cake, it had fun bright colors on it kind of like splattered all over. We lit thirteen candles, but they looked so small because the cake was so damn big.

"Happy Birthday to you..." the singing continued, "Happy birthday dear Violet, happy birthday to you!"

"Woo, yay, yeah!" Whistles, cheers, and exclamations all rang out from the crowd.

I have never seen Violet happier than she was in that moment.

"Make a wish little sister." I said with a smile holding her hand.

"Make a wish little sister." Avery said while holding her other hand.

This moment would be burned in everyone's memories for ever. Sadly, this would be the last birthday I would spend with Heather and Violet, the last big event. It wasn't the plan obviously, but it was fate I guess you could say.

As we were leaving everyone was wishing Violet a happy birthday and saying good night and drive safely.

Apparently while we were at the event there was a lot of snow sticking to the ground. Which makes it hard to drive around here, there's so many hills and backroads that don't always get plowed right away.

We talked about the night and how much fun we all had and couldn't wait for the next one. This was Friday December first, the start of a fantastic weekend with my friends, from Maryland and Pa. Chris told me there was going to be a bonfire at Devils Hole tomorrow night, and reluctantly we planned to go there. Heather was stoked about it, I was not keen on it, I was never really interested in going there. The place creeped me out, and I was not the partier like everyone else was that went there. And I saw Rich every time we went, ugh I did not want to see him again.

When we woke up that morning, the snow had stopped, the roads were clear, and the girls were ready for Devils Hole tonight. I just got a new pair of snow boots, so I was ready, and a cute new sweater for under my coat. I outgrew those flannels I used to wear and had more of a preppy, emo look going. If you can make sense of that, ha-ha.

I agreed I would ride with Heather and the girls, and Chris would carpool with Ryan and the rest of the group. This way we didn't have as many cars to find parking.

As we drove up the hill, the glow of the bonfire was illuminating the sky. It was clear, cold as ice, and pitch black except for the orange glow from the bonfire. We could hear everyone, music playing, as we walked up to the clearing. It was a pleasant surprise to see just the group from our high school. I knew I could relax a little this time. I even considered having a beer, or a wine cooler which was probably more my speed than a beer.

I let lose a bit, we talked about everything they all had questions for my Maryland friends, since every time they've been here there's been a ton of people and never a chance to talk. It was cold but the fire helped a lot, and Chris of course. It was a great night, one that we will all cherish, especially me.

Within the upcoming weeks, you will see what is changing around me, who is coming in and out of my life, and how I met my untimely demise. It will not be easy for any of my family, friends, or the town as a whole. It may not even be easy for you, because I have given you so much of me for you to think of me as a living being at one time, not just someone you are reading about.

You know I have lived a great life; some unfortunate things have happened like losing my real mom as a young person, or getting the crap beat out of me causing a two-week long concussion. But I had some great things happen too. I helped solve a cold case homicide, met the greatest boy ever, developed friendships to last a lifetime. So much I have to be thankful for.

But now this is where I tell you what happened to me, and where. I cannot tell you why, or even who, because everything is a blur to me, I think I know who, but I am not sure why.

On December twelfth around seven o'clock we received a call from Justin, his car broke down way out past Carriage Ford, which is where Devils hole is. It's a twenty-minute drive on a good day, and since the roads were always a bit worse out there it would probably take a little longer to get out there tonight. It was also the first time I would be driving alone, so I was a little nervous about that.

Our parents were out to dinner, Chirs was closing the shop, and no one else seemed to be around. So, I guess it was up to me to go get him. He gave me the address of the house he walked to, so I knew where to go. I just needed to look on the map for where it was in relation to devils' hole.

Ok, it looks like it's about a mile and a half north from Devils Hole, I can handle that.

"Hey girls, if mom or dad call, tell them I had to go pick up Justin. His car broke down and no one was available to get him. I should be back in about an hour and a half. Ok?"

"Ok, Letti. Be careful."

I pet Murphy on his ears and gave him a kiss on his head, "See ya good dog!"

"Bye girls, I'll see ya later!"

"Bye!" They both called out.

I got into the driver's seat, my hands were shaking a bit, and my heart was pounding. I was ok driving with other people, but driving by myself and all the way out there made me more nervous and put a pit in my stomach. I haven't felt this way since the last time I saw Sandy. I knew I wouldn't see her though because I haven't since that night in my living room during the concussion.

The roads were clear leaving town, so I knew I was in good shape. Until I hit the backroad to get to Carriage Ford, then it was a bit tricky, there was black ice everywhere it seemed. I slid a few times, but I was driving slow enough to not get into an accident. As I was coming up to the top of one of the many hills, I could see headlights on the left side of the road. The lights were dimmer than headlights should be, I slowed down as I approached the car. There was a man leaning into the trunk of his car.

"Hello. Do you need help? Are you ok?"

"Oh hey, well you see I am not sure actually. My car is doing this weird thing and I think it might be the battery.

You wouldn't happen to have jumper cables in your car, would ya?"

I had no idea what was in this car, but I did know that Justin would've had some in his car.

"Um, I'm not sure. But I am on my way to pick up my brother and he works on cars. I bet he has a set in his car and could help."

"Oh, all right then thanks anyway."

I was confused at his response. His voice sounded familiar, but he looked different, it was also dark so that made it harder to see anything let alone a person.

"Are you sure? He's only just up the road a little way. It won't take me long to come back with him. His car broke down too, so I needed to come get him."

Now I knew not to let a stranger in the car with me, and I knew not to get out of the car, so I was smart I promise. I spoke to him from my window, and I knew I was safe.

"Look, it'll only take a second, if I can just look in the back to see if there is a set, it won't take long and you'll be to your brother in no time."

I knew I shouldn't, but he seemed harmless, and it would only take a second to check the back, so I had to help him. Plus, he had some type of cane or something he seemed to walk with.

"What happened?" I nodded to his cane.

"Oh, nothing. I just need it occasionally."

PART TWO THE INVESTIGATION:

Detective Frank "Chick" Miller

There was nothing more that I hated than being on call. I had some of the worst luck with this shit. I always tried to convince someone else to take it, but Mike was a pain in the ass and always insisted that he would handle anything that came in.

Tonight was the exception. I heard my pager vibrating on the desk in the other room, I was reluctant to get up to check it. But something was telling me to get my ass up and look. Obviously, it was the station, so I walked over to the phone and called down there.

"It's Chick. What's up?"

"Detective Miller, Chief said he needs you to come in asap. Like no joke, he said get your ass down here. I already spoke to Schaffer," Sergeant MacNeil demanded.

"All right. I'll be down in fifteen. I gotta get my shoes on and shit."

"10-4, I'll let Chief know."

God damn it, I can only imagine what the hell I'm being called down there for now. Why the hell did it seem like every time I was on call that shit went down.

Where the hell are my car keys?

As I was getting my stuff together, I saw something out of the corner of my eye but brushed it off as a passing car's headlights reflection.

Damn, it was cold out, colder than a witch's tit that's for sure. I knew the car wouldn't be warmed up before I got to the station. I drove a *Caprice Classic*, and it was a beast on the road. Probably not the most practical of vehicles, since I have a six-year-old, and my ex isn't keen on me driving her around in it. I do it anyway. I have three ex-wives, but I am still madly in love with the first one. I messed that up really good. I have seven kids, four with the first wife, two with the second and one with the last one. That's a story for another day though.

The roads were clear, the stars were bright as shit tonight, the town was quiet, almost deafening. There were a lot of cars at the station for it being nine o'clock at night, I can only imagine what the hell was going on. I got out of my car and started walking up to the side door.

Is that Chris's car? He had a distinct vehicle, a metallic blue Chevy Nova, a pretty bad ass car. Huh wonder what he's doing here.

I walked into the station and could hear a lot of voices, female, male, everyone was talking over one another.

"What's this?" I said as I walked to the desks.

"Chick, it's Scarlet. She hasn't come home." Joe Adams told me.

"What? Where was she?"

"She was coming to get me." Justin said.

"Ok, and where were you?" Man, I had no idea what the hell was going on.

"My car broke down past Carriage Ford. I walked to the closes house I could find. And called home, no one was there she said, and I assume she couldn't get ahold of anyone else. So, she took my mom's car to come get me."

"When was that?"

He gulped, "I think it was around seven."

"Shit, and only now I am hearing about this. Why did it take two Damn hours?" I was mad now.

"Well, I had to get a ride. The old guy at the house I walked to drove me home. When I got there around eight-fifteen my mom and Joe were walking in from their dinner date and then…" I knew he was having a hard time, but so many questions needed answered.

"Then we called her friends first since we saw the car was gone. Until Avery came out to us from her room, it wasn't until then that we thought she was just at a friend's. Avery, can you tell detective Miller what Letti said?" Joe was visibly upset, so I was trying to take it easy on him.

"She said that she was going to get Justin, that he broke down near Devils Hole and she would be back in about an hour to an hour and a half. Told Murphy he was a good dog and said bye to me and Vi." Avery was hysterically explaining what her sister said to her.

"Ok. Ok. I think we can all say this is rattling us, so what we need to do is just calm down and. Was anyone out there yet? To where Justin's car broke down?"

"Not yet. When I got back to the house and saw the car was gone, and my parents were pulling in just a few minutes later. I don't know, I should've had the old guy take me right there. God DAMNIT" he yelled, rightfully so.

"Ok. Justin, this isn't going to help anyone. We know you're upset; this is not your fault." Schaffer tried to calm him, but Justin was a hot head and protective of her.

"If I had known she was going to end up coming out I wouldn't have allowed that. I told her where I was so she could get someone to bring her out there or tell someone where I was at least. Jesus, this is my fault mom, dad. I'm so sorry." He started crying into his hands. His girlfriend Rachel was rubbing his back, she was crying as well.

Christ, who am I kidding we were all a damn wreck right now.

"So, we need to get out to the car. What roads would she take?" MacNeil asked.

"Um, I would guess the only way she knows. It's the only way we've ever taken out near there. Ellson to Main, to SpringHill to Chesterfield, to Carriage Ford. That's how we would go out there." Chris said.

"All right, we have a start. Let's get someone out there and check it out." Chief Masters told two of the patrolmen.

"Yes, sir." They left.

"So, we know she left after seven, were the roads bad when you were out there Justin?"

"Not that I remember, I broke down because the battery died. It was struggling to get up the hill, and as soon as I crested it, it just stopped. So, I was able to drift off the side. It's still in the road a little though. I can't believe no one called yet about it."

"Well, they might've but that Statey territory so we may not get that call for a while."

"I could call my dad, Detective. If you think that'll help. He's working tonight." Ryan offered.

"That's all-right kid, we will get ahold of them if we need to. We try not to have any alarms called out unless necessary." MacNeil answered him.

This guy is a pompous ass. I rolled my eyes because I knew what was coming next.

"What does that mean? Lucy asked concerned.

There it is. Asshole. He tried to respond but I beat him to it.

"Lucy, we will call them if we have to. We are going to just stay calm here and wait for the patrol to get back to us. Ok." Man, I never thought I would be the one calming down a family.

Shit, I was typically the one who got them fired up and pissed off, most of the time. But Scarlet was special, she was a great kid. We, me her and Schaffer, became close over the last month. Damn, if something happened to this kid, I'm telling you. I gotta stay positive, not just for them but for me too.

It was about a half hour, and we had not heard from the patrol car yet, and I could tell everyone was getting more on edge with each passing minute.

"Avery, I heard you guys went to Bingo for your birthday. Did anyone win?" I asked.

"Violet did, but no one else did. She won a mini crock pot." She laughed, which made everyone else laugh.

It was a moment that needed to happen. Shortly after we heard patrol over the radio, "Car 82 to station,"

"Go ahead," MacNeil answered.

"We're gonna need more vehicles out here."

Oh, shit. I looked around the room and saw everyone's faces and how the smiles and laughs went to panic and gasps.

"10-4. We will get some units out there. What's your twenty?" he asked.

"Just about a half mile south of Devils Hole on Chesterford." Justin looked confused.

"Justin, what's wrong?" Schaffer asked.

"That's not where my car broke down. I broke down after Devils hole."

I know everyone was panicking now, and I had to defuse the situation before it exploded like a bomb.

"Ok, we don't know anything yet. Let's get some other units out there and we will see what we are dealing with. Mike you and I will take the ride out, ok." I knew if we went the family would feel much better about this whole thing.

"Oh, please Chick that would be best if you went. Because if she's hurt, she will know you and Mike and she will be ok. She's ok. She's ok." Lucy reassured herself, while hugging Avery and Violet.

"Chief were gonna head out there. If you guys can get the PSP out there too, and Mrs. Smitham can you stay here with the family until we get back? Lucy, Joe, I promise we will find her."

"We will get every available unit in the area, Chick." Chief said.

"Of course, Chick, I am not going anywhere." Mrs. Smitham assured him.

"All right, Mike lets go."

I could hear them crying lowly as we were leaving. I think we all felt that same pit on our stomachs once the radio call came over.

"What the hell, Chick. What are we gonna do?" Mike asked.

"I don't know. But we gotta do our job, no matter what."

The drive there was silent, as we came up to Chesterford we could see lights everywhere.

"Jesus Christ, this better not be a crime scene." I didn't even realize I said that out loud.

"You think so, Chick?"

"I sure as hell hope not."

As we pulled up to the roadblock where one of the state police officers were, we pulled over. I knew one guy, Officer Hamlin, and my son were in the academy together.

"Officer."

"Detective Miller, the guys told me to have you go right up."

Well, that's not comforting. Mike and I both looked at each other knowing that something had happened. What? We didn't know yet, but we were about to find out.

We could see her mother's car on the right side of the road. The driver's side window was down, that was all we could see at the moment.

"Chick. Come on over here." Lieutenant Campbell hollered and called over.

"Howie, tell me some good news, please."

"I don't know what we're looking at yet Chick. Your two guys got here, didn't touch anything to my knowledge, and told us that this is what they found when they pulled up. They also told me who was driving the vehicle. Chick, we gotta find her."

I shook my head yes, "Yeah, we do. I'm gonna walk it ok."

"Be my guest, I expected you to. That's why we haven't done anything yet."

"All right, what if we get some guys canvassing the hill over here, look for shoeprints, footprints, hell any kind of prints right now. We gotta start somewhere, call out her name, and stay silent for a minute in case she is injured and it's hard for her to respond. Just start looking."

I needed a minute to compose myself, this case was close to me, so I needed to have a level head to ensure that I did my job right and effectively. There was no snow on the road so looking for anything there is useless. So, let's look at the car itself. Why is the window down, the driver's side window?

"Mike, why is the window down?"

"Maybe she saw something or heard something. Maybe she was talking to someone."

"Bingo. Ok, anyone check the other side of the street?" I yelled out.

"I don't think so yet." Someone called back.

"Good, don't. Mike go over there and check it out. Whatever you can find, tracks, footprints, paw prints. I don't give a shit what it is, everything is important right now."

"On it."

I let out a loud exhale, wiped my hands across my face and knew it was time for the detective in me to kick in.

"Where are my two patrolmen?"

"Right here Chick." One answered. Shit I didn't even remember their names.

"You, what's your name?"

"I'm Reid, detective."

"Ok, I need you to get me some tape and tape off from about ten feet behind, in front, and side to side of both sides of this street. I don't want anyone touching anything, breathing on anything, unless they come to me, that man right there," referring to Mike, "or that big fella over there," referring to Howie, "Got it?"

"Yes sir." He ran off and did as I told him.

Mike walked back over, "Chick, there was definitely another vehicle here, some footprints but they seemed to have been shuffled around."

"What does that mean?"

"It means I can get any impressions. I took pictures but I don't think they are gonna be worth anything. I am just going to keep taking pictures. Let me know when you're ready for me."

I couldn't understand why the driver's side window was down, now we know. There was another vehicle here.

"Mike. Look for any oil drips, cigarette butts, anything."

"Any sign of her at all?"

"Not yet." Someone yelled back at me.

"Keep looking, and I want a group on that side of the street, do not pass the tape. Go behind it. If I see one footstep over or under it, I will kick someone's ass. Watch where you are walking. Keep yelling for her, but again give her a second in case she needs it to respond."

I waved to Howie so we could start in her mother's car.

"All right Howie, you take the passenger side, I will start here. You got your recorder?"

"Right here," he pulled it out of his arm pocket.

"How do you wanna handle this? Technically its yours." I said.

"Well, why don't we work this one together. We both have an invested interest in the outcome of this."

"Agreed."

"December twelfth. Tuesday, it is now twenty-two thirty-seven hours. I am Detective Carl Miller; I am here investigating a nineteen ninety-three Buick Century Wagon. When arriving on location, it was noted that the vehicle was on the Eastern side of the road, Chesterford Road to be exact. There were no vehicles other than this one. The driver's side window was down, let it be noted that the vehicle was not running when patrol cars arrived. I, Detective Mike Schaffer, and Pennsylvania State Police Lieutenant Howard Campbell are taking control of the investigation of this scene. As of now we are unsure if this is a crime scene, or a freak accident, we will treat it as a crime scene until we find evidence telling us otherwise. At first look, the driver's seat is in the upright position. The steering wheel does not look like it has manipulated. The key to the vehicle is not in the ignition. Note we must search for that."

"Yo, we are also looking for the keys to the vehicle. It may also be just one key. So, anything that catches your eye yell out," I yelled out.

"Mike, how tall is Scarlet?"

"Uh, probably only about five two, five three."

"Seat looks to be in the position to fit an individual of the five feet to five-foot three height. We will have exact measurements on this once CSI arrives. Also, have them dust for fingerprints immediately. We will have all the people who could have prints in this vehicle and rule them out. Shit."

Howie looked up at me, "What's wrong?"

"Reid!"

"Yes Sir."

"Come over here."

He ran right over.

"I'm gonna need you to go back to the station and speak with the family. This is exactly what I want you to say. Write it down."

I wanted him to grab his notepad and pen.

"Ok. We have found the vehicle that Scarlet was driving. We are searching for clues as to what may have happened. There do not appear to be any signs of an accident. So, we are hopeful that she will be around the area. Ok, stop writing. I also need you to get those guys who are standing around with their thumbs up their asses to drive to all the homes in a three-mile radius. Check and see if she may be at one of those."

"Yes sir."

Shaking my head, I went back to recording.

"Howie do you want to start your recording?"

"Yeah. I am lieutenant Howard Campbell of the Pennsylvania State Police, and I am conducting an overview investigation of the vehicle that is believed to be the one that Scarlet Adams was said to be driving. I am on the passenger side of the vehicle and there seems to be nothing out of the ordinary. Her handbag is on the seat, with the contents inside and sitting upright. The window was closed, and there is nothing that is standing out that would be considered unordinary."

"Shit, Howie, what the hell happened here."

We both stood looking around, but it was pitch black and the headlights actually made it harder to see anything.

"Anyone have any flares? I want to turn off these lights that are directly on the street here."

"Theres some in my trunk, Johnson, grab the flares for me." Howie directed.

"Let's turn these off. Keep those shining on the hills and the woods, but I wanna turn these off. I feel like we're missing something but can't see shit because of these headlights. Here follow me kid."

I led him to the areas I wanted the flares to be set up. He was a rookie, and he looked green in the face.

"You all right kid?"

"Yes, sir. This is my first crime scene, and I don't want to mess it up."

"Good. Congratulations. Now, don't mess it up. Got it?"

I was too old to deal with the rookies, but I know I had to work side by side with Howie's guys, since technically it is his scene. At sixty-five, I was not looked at as the young hip detective, or even the middle aged mature one. I was known as the asshole. But who am I kidding, I've been known by that since the late sixties when I first became a detective.

I was young, a lot like Schaffer, when I was promoted. I worked in Lannister, a city not far from Weston. It was hit hard with Civil Rights riots and protests; weekly we were getting calls from business owners about the colored community invading their space or causing them to lose business by being there. It was getting old fast, and I knew there was a better way for me to help and use my talents of investigating skills.

I won't talk much about that because it's a time that the country showed its evil side, and since I was never on the receiving end, I have no right to speak about it. I will tell you quickly of a call that came in and this is ultimately how I was promoted to detective.

It was a hot summer day in sixty-eight, and a mother called from one end of Lannister stating that her daughter had not come home yet. No one wanted to take the report from the mother, so I had the balls too, so I did. I went to her home, she was not welcoming by any means not that I could blame her, but I had a job to do, and I made a promise to uphold the law by any means necessary, regardless of race, gender, religion, or ethnicity. So, right there no one liked me. I didn't give a shit either. I loved my job; I loved that I was able to help people when they were in need and put the bad guys away when they did wrong.

When I knocked at the screen door, I could hear jazz playing, the blades on a fan clicking, and a woman humming along.

"Hello. Lannister Police Department. We received a call from this address. Anyone home?" I yelled in.

"I cannot believe my ears right now." And older, heavy woman said as she was getting up from a chair in the living room.

She walked to the door with a cigarette in her hand, smoke encircling her head, and she was a large lady for sure.

"Afternoon ma'am. I am Officer Miller from Lannister Poilc..."

"I know where you're from. What the hell took ya so long to get over here."

"Ma'am?" I asked confused by this.

"I called yesterday morning, evening, and this morning. I gave someone a report on account that my granddaughter has not been home since Saturday evening. It is now Monday eleven thirty in the afternoon. I can only assume that some-one must've misplaced my call and only now just found it. So, tell me Officer Miller, what happened?"

"Ma'am, I only just found out this morning about you calling and I knew I needed to come over right away. I do apologize for no one coming out to you yesterday, I cannot speak for them. I can only speak for me, and I am here now, and I would like to help you if you'll allow me."

Now I know you're thinking, ok this does not sound like the same guy I've been reading about. And, you would be right, but it is me. This is the call that caused me to become the way I am. There were things that happened with this call and a lot of really dark things. It was not a happy ending; I will tell you that. That's all I'm gonna say right now, and I'm gonna get back to the case in front of me.

"Howie, we hear anything from my guy yet?"

"Which one Chick?"

"The one I sent to the station?"

"No, not as of yet. I will holler too you as soon I hear him calling."

"Thanks."

I knew I needed to get this group together, because I don't know if we are doing this search as effectively as we can.

"Howie, can you call everyone back and have them meet me behind the line back there." I pointed behind her car.

"Everything all right Chick?" he asked.

"Yeah, I just think there's a better way we can do this search."

"You got it. All right everyone I need all bodies back up here behind the line and the vehicle." He called over the radio.

I could hear and see them all walking back toward the car, and I stood there thinking of how I was to handle this. Schaffer walked over to me.

"Chick, what are we thinking. You want a better way to handle this? You wanna call it a night? What do you wanna do?"

"No, we are not calling it. I just need a minute to get my thoughts. I'll be right there. Tell Howie I'll be right there."

All right Chick, get ahold of yourself. I was quickly starting to lose hope that we were going to find her. First, it was freezing cold out here, the terrain was unfamiliar to her.

Second, I need to know what the other car was doing here. Was it here when she was? Was it someone who passed by and saw no one in the car? What the hell. I could not wrap my head around what the hell was happening here.

"All right everyone. Listen up. I need to talk with the family, I am going to head back to the station. Lieutenant

Campbell and Detective Schaffer will be in charge until I get back. I'm going to confer with them, and they will let you know shortly what the plan of attack will be. Thanks everyone so far for your cooperation so far. It is imperative that we find her, or any sign of struggle, you know the drill."

"What plan would you want? Be detailed Chick, I don't want to miss a damn thing. We have a lot against us tonight, its pitch black out here, the temp is dropping every hour, and we have no leads. CSU should be here any minute, I'll have them dust for prints, and do a full search of the entire car."

"Good. I want a few guys down the riverbed further, looking for prints, anything. Shit look for a god damn blood trail."

Schaffer and Campbell both winced when I said that.

"I know that's not what we want, but we cannot rule anything out. I'll be back in an hour or so. I gotta go talk to them personally."

I played over the conversation in my head on how this was going to go. It was not one I ever imagined having to have with this family. Damn, this girl better be ok. I hope I pull up and she is there waiting for me. Her with her quirky smile she always had. She's a good kid. I drove pretty slow in the area with my take down lights shining on both sides of the road just in case.

Every few feet I would stop and look as far as the lights would shine, but I couldn't see any evidence that anyone or thing was in that area for a while. Not even deer prints, which wasn't odd for the weather tonight. This day was just an all-around shitty day.

I finally got results from some bloodwork that my doc wanted. Which of course was bad news. I gotta go in on Thursday for a consultation with him. Which was a nice way of saying I have some type of cancer, I'm sure. Would explain why I feel like shit every day, and why I feel like I have an elephant in my lungs. I just gotta focus on finding Scarlet, that was crucial right now.

I pulled into the station lot and could see more vehicles now. Curious as to who's they all are. I hesitated for a minute before getting out of the car, so I could calm myself. I didn't want them to see the concern on my face. All right here goes.

"Good evening, everyone." I greeted as I walked in the door.

"Chick. Oh my god, what is the word. What is going on?" Joe and Lucy were both trying to stay as calm as possible, but I could hear in their voices they were losing hope.

"I don't have any word yet. I assume she's not here. Is anyone at home in case she goes there."

"George and the DiMada's are there. We knew someone should stay in case she did come home or call."

"Ok, so no call yet either I assume."

They both shook their heads no.

"Ok. I need a detailed list of what she was wearing. Justin, I need you to write down exactly what you two said on the phone. Girls, I know this is scary and confusing, but I'm going to need you two too also write down everything you remember as she was leaving. We can't miss anything."

"Ok." They all agreed.

"Chick. What can I do? Can I go out there, maybe all of us, go out there and help with the search. It's a huge area and we know it well." Chris said as he looked around at all the teenagers in the room.

Their faces were desperate to help somehow, I couldn't tell them no.

"Yeah, ok. I need everyone's parents to give permission, I can't just let everyone go, unless they're over eighteen."

"I'm on it Chick, I'll make sure we get that." Chris walked over to the group and told them what they had to do.

He came back a few minutes later.

"They all said OK. They are going to go home and get some warm clothes on and get their parents' permission. This was a good time for me to talk with the family, now that the majority were gone.

"Chick, just be frank with us. Ok. Tell us what do you think's going on?" Lucy asked me with such sadness in her tone.

"Ok. This is the deal. The car is fine, but we cannot find her yet. I am going to be fully transparent with you both, ok. Well, all of you." I forgot there were still the rest there. "There is no evidence of a struggle, or anything that would indicate that she is hurt or anything like that. So, that is promising. But my concern is that she had some car trouble and tried to walk back home. Now being out there is dangerous, it's cold, dark as a cave at night. Did you have any flashlights in the car or anything that would help her to see?"

Lucy and Joe both shook their heads no and looked at each other with heartbreak in their eyes. They knew something was wrong, and between the weather, and the darkness, it was making it nearly impossible for us to do the job we needed to.

Every time I get one of these cases it puts me in a bad headspace, honestly, I don't know if you ever truly get used to it. I have been a detective for over twenty years now, and I know I haven't. All the cases are hard, but this one was going to be the hardest so far, even harder than the first one I worked when I was first a beat cop. But like I said, that's for another day.

"Lucy, Joe, Chris, everyone. I am going to head back out to the scene. Chris, when your gang gets back here just lead the convoy out there, I'll make sure, and officer is aware that you're all coming. Ok?"

"Of course, Chick. I am going to head to my house really quick to grab some stuff too. I can stop by the house and check on my parents. Murphy and George."

"Chris, hold up a second." I yelled to him before he went out the door.

"Joe, do you think Murphy would be helpful right now. He knows her scent better than anyone or anything. I know that K-9 will be on the way, but that could take an hour to three. I don't want to wait any longer than we have to on resources."

"I mean it's worth a shot, right?" Joe asked me.

"I think so. Chris can are you able to get Murphy too?" I asked.

"Hell yeah!"

I just shook my head; I don't know what this kid is so excited for. He has no idea what we could have in store or us. Christ, she could be anywhere at this point. It's eleven thirty now, and every minute that passes makes it that much harder to find her. I still don't even know if she is alive if she is lost.

Damnit, why this kid.

I grabbed my keys and jacket to head back up to the scene when Lucy stopped me.

"Chick. Please find our girl, I know you can't make promises to bring her home, but I don't care how you have to bring her home, just bring her home."

Lucy was hysterical, and Joe seemed to be in a daze. I had three officers stationed here and two of the detectives were coming in also in case she showed up here.

"Lucy, Joe, you know I will do everything in power to find her. We don't know anything yet; we just know she is out there somewhere. I will promise I will bring her home."

I know I shouldn't say that, but I wasn't kidding nor was I breaking my promise. If it was the last thing I did, I would bring this girl home. Whether alive or dead, I wasn't going to quit until I found her.

Driving back, I had this terrible feeling in the pit of my stomach, I was starting to doubt that we were going to find her tonight, but I wasn't giving up. Going over and over the scene so far in my head, there had to be something I was missing. What was it? The snow looked a little off, there was a disturbance in the snow where the other vehicle seemed to be. At the time I didn't think anything of it. But now that I am replaying it, I think I've seen it before.

I'll figure that out when I get back home, I got to go through some old case files. I could be completely off, but I know I've seen that before. As I pulled up, I could see light everywhere, and uni's wondering around like they were lost.

I exhaled and got back out of my car, saw Schaffer, and went right to him.

"Chick, how are they? The family?"

"They are as good as can be expected. A damn wreck. Chris has a team coming up to help with the search. They should be here in about twenty minutes or so. He is also bringing Murphy."

Mike looked at me confused.

"Hey, no one knows her scent better than that dog. He's the best chance we have right now of possibly finding her tonight."

"Fair enough. So, this is what we have got so far. Up over there," he pointed beyond where the tracks of the other vehicle were, "we found nothing. Some deer prints, maybe a fox, but it's so cold out here they could be from a week ago. The ground is pretty frozen up there. I can see the Grayson's quarry and all in the distance. It could be worth a shot to talk to them, see if they have had any problems with anything. I don't know, I feel like I'm grasping at straws right now."

"Did anyone go to Mr. and Mrs. Brinton's? They live about two miles down the road. I know someone went to the elderly couple just up the road." I asked because I wasn't sure if they knew that the Brinton's were the Grayson sons' grandparents.

"Chick, no one would make that far, especially in these conditions." Mike replied.

"So, I'll take that as a no. Shit." I ran my hand through the little bit of hair I had left.

"Why is that imperative we go there?" Mike asked.

"Because the Brinton's are the Grayson's grandparents. And also, the parents of her teacher that was taking care of her when she had that concussion." I know I sounded like an asshole, but I was pretty pissed now.

"Shit is right. I'm on it."

"No, we will go together." I stopped him.

"Howie, there's a bunch of the kids coming up, they are going to help with the search. I am going to the Brintons with Mike. No one went there yet."

I could see Howie's reaction, and he was just as pissed.

"Damn, I didn't even remember they were there." He said.

"Yeah, we all tend to forget about them. Which is why I want to get there as soon as possible."

"Chick. It's after midnight, you think they are going to answer the door?" Howie asked.

"I don't give a damn what time it is." And this is another reason why people don't like me, and I don't care much either.

"Mike, let's go, were taking that marked unit. Grab the keys. I'll meet you there. I got to talk to Howie really quick."

I jogged down to where he was and excused myself, "Howie, can I talk to you for a minute."

"Give me one minute everyone. What's up Chick?"

"Listen, when Chris gets here keep him with you, please. I don't want this boy to be the one to find anything. That's the last thing we need. I know you know what to do, I don't have to tell you."

He shook his head at me, "Yeah Chick, I got ya. Now get going were wasting time." He said to me with a cocky grin.

"Yeah, yeah." I ran back up the hill to Mike. Damn I am out of shape.

Winded I got to the unit, and hopped in.

"All right let's go. No lights or sirens. Let's not piss them off any more than we are already going to."

As we drove down the road, I was working on a game plan for the morning and how to approach the Grayson's. I knew that they were supportive of our investigation into Eugene, but I don't know how they are going to feel about us walking around their property. That is of course if we don't find her before that. The Grayson's owned about eighty-eight acres of land, so the odds of her stumbling into a part of it were likely.

"How do you want to handle this?"

"I think you should be the first at the door. We have a little history, and I don't believe I am one of their favorite people."

Mike rolled his eyes at me, seemingly unphased by my statement. It was never really a surprise when I tell people that someone doesn't like me, or when people hear that someone doesn't like me.

"You don't seem surprised." I laughed.

"Chick, nothing surprises me anymore with you, buddy. When we pull up, I will gladly walk up first. But how do you wanna handle it?"

"Tell them we are searching for a young girl; we are sorry it's so late. Um, ask if they happened to see her. Something along those lines. You know what the hell to say. What are you asking me for?" Yeah, I was annoyed. But this was also his first real missing person case, so I was trying to be patient, but I don't have a lot of that.

"I didn't know if you were looking for them to say something in particular. That's all I meant. I know how to do my job. Now, if you'll excuse me, I'm going to go do it right now. Are you coming?"

Damn, I didn't know Mike had it in him. Good for him. I wouldn't take my shit either.

"I'll follow your lead."

We got out of the vehicle, as we walked up, I was taken back to a time before I was detective in Lannister, I was just a beat cop. The first time I wanted to be a detective was because of this one call. This call also led me to The Brinton's, but there are many of them around. They have a huge family, not just the Grayson's. So, coming here I knew they wouldn't be thrilled with me.

Mike hit the doorbell, and we could hear it all the way outside. It helped that it was so quiet and still out here, hell you could probably hear a deer fart it was so quiet.

I could see a light come on from a room just to the right of where we were. If I remember correctly, it was the sitting room back in the sixties. We saw a shadow coming toward the door, and the chain lock sliding from one side to the other. The knob creaked when it turned and there was a very elderly man standing there. His robe was worn, he had on large thick glasses, his hair was a bit disheveled, and he had on slippers that I know I heard dragging on the hardwood floor as he walked to the door.

"Can I help you?" he said with an unfriendly tone. Almost annoyed. Can't say I blame him.

"Good evening, sir. I am so sorry to wake you at this hour, but we are looking for any help any of the residents here may be able to give us."

"Ok. What's the problem?"

"Well, we are looking for a missing girl. Sixteen years old, she was driving..." mike didn't get to complete his sentence before Henry interrupted him.

"Wait, I remember you. You're that pompous detective that tried to put one of my grandsons away for some murder of some colored girl back in the day. I don't have anything to say to you people. And you took one of them away recently because of some nonsense cold case murder. Now get off my doorstep and take your search elsewhere. There is no young girl here."

And he slammed the door.

"Jesus, Chick, what did you do to them?"

"He wasn't lying. But that's a long story, and one we're not getting into right now. I will fill you in another day."

"All right. But this is gonna make it tough. If we run into more people that aren't fans of you, we are gonna have a hard time finding Scarlet."

I knew he was right, and I also knew that yeah, we would be running into more people out here that weren't fans of mine. That wasn't stopping me though. Hell for all we know she found a cave to hide in until the morning came. We just got to keep looking.

The search party was well underway by the time we got back. We met up with Howie and Chris and got the rundown on how they were sending out the crews.

"Howd you guys make out?" Howie asked.

"Don't ask." Mike said, like a smartass. Ha I was rubbing off on him.

"Let me guess. The Brintons were not really happy to see Chick at their door?"

"Bingo."

"Ah, Chick. What are we gonna do with you." Howie said laughing,

"Listen." I started to say.

"Nope, no time for that tonight. Let's focus on the issue at hand. Finding Scarlet." Mike interrupted.

We joined in with the search, the hills were very icy and dangerous and did not look disturbed at all. We had small fluorescent yellow flags that were placed in every location that was searched, this way we never get turned around as to where was checked. The snow was still deep, but the winds here blew much of it onto the creek below. The creek was mostly frozen everywhere, so we knew that would be the last place we searched and would wait until some daylight before we started that.

I knew the time would come when we had to speak with the Grayson's, and I also knew that they would know by then that Mike and I were at their grandparents. I remained cautiously optimistic that they would allow us to search their land. When I looked at my watch last it was one-fifteen, I didn't realize that it was already three-thirty. I knew I needed to regroup with everyone and get a new crew out here so these guys can go get some rest, and so I can send these kids home.

I called on the radio for everyone to meet at the start of the scene. I could see how exhausted and freezing cold most everyone was as they came from everywhere around me. I was exhausted, mentally, and physically. I wanted to find Scarlet, I was trying not to make it personal, but it was. I know this girl, her family, what they've been through over the years. This is why I was determined to find her. I don't want to think about anything bad happening to her, but I was beginning to lose hope.

No one found any signs of anything. How? How is that possible? Where could she be? I was convinced that someone had to have kidnapped her or abducted her. Because in my soul I did not believe she was here anymore, at this location.

I had no idea how I was going to tell the family; I was hoping that they at least went back home to try to rest. Chirs brought Murphy home hours ago, it was too cold for him out here and I don't know what I was thinking with having him bring him out here. The k-9 arrived around two I think, and searched the area around the car, where the other car was and the surrounding area. He seemed to have got a scent near where the other vehicle was, but he lost it about a half mile up the road.

We continued our search up that way, which was bringing us back toward Weston's direction. This also could take us to a hundred different ways the vehicle could've gone. Standing there thinking about past scenes and shit, I knew it was time for me to go back to the station and get my head straight.

"Howie, can you have a unit or two stay here for a few hours? I think we all need to get our heads on straight and take some time away from here. We can't do much else yet. The sun will be up in a few hours. We can start over then, plus this will also give us some fresh eyes out here. You good with that?"

"Yeah, I think that's the right call for now. I'll meet you back here around six, that's about three hours from now." Howie said.

"Mike!" I hollered. "Were heading back. Let's go." I waved to him to get moving.

By the time we got back to the station it was almost four-thirty, I hadn't had a long night like this in a few years. I was certainly getting too old for this, and apparently too sick also. I felt more tired than usual, a bit nauseous, and overall drained. I knew I had to call my doc back and let him know that I was not going to make the consultation on Thursday, and I will have to reschedule, if we don't find her by then. I swung by my house on the way back, to get changed quick, grabbed one of the case files boxes from the basement. I couldn't remember which case it was that triggered my memory, but I knew it was sometime between eighty-two and eighty-three.

Of course, I could not find those case files, and did not have the time to go searching through every box I had. My game plan was to meet at the station and have whoever was on head out and get a new search going, me and Mike would go to the Grayson's with Howie and hope they would cooperate.

I was unsure if Joe and Lucy were still at the station, I had not heard from anyone there in a few hours. Pulling into the lot I couldn't see their vehicle, so I assumed they went home. The station was full since it was day shift, and Mike was already there waiting for me to get back.

"Are they here still?" I asked him as he stood with the door open.

"No, I sent them home to try to get some sleep."

"Good. I got to make a call to my old partner at Lannister. I swear I've seen that disturbance in the snow on the side where the track was from another vehicle. I couldn't find my case files from the year I believe it was from." I said all this while picking up the receiver and dialing his number.

I sat with it held against my ear, as it rang a few times, finally Tom picked it up. Our conversation went as follows:

"Tom, its Chick. How the hell are ya?"

"Chick! What is up buddy? How are you?

"I'm good, I'm good. How's Judy and the family?"

"Everyone is good. Jackie had twins back in August. Two boys."

Tom had three girls, was all he ever wanted was a boy. So, there was no doubt in my mind he was ecstatic to have two grandsons. I could hear the excitement in his voice. Unfortunately, my kids stopped talking to me a few years ago, except for Chloe but she's only six so she hasn't learned how to hate me yet and I am truly trying to be a good dad to her. Her mother, that's a different story, she hates my guts.

All my ex's do, well maybe not the first wife, but definitely the other two. Now I am just too old, too overweight, too broke, and probably too sick to find someone new. The only one I found who doesn't mind putting up with my bullshit is Mike, and I am pretty sure he doesn't want too either. He doesn't have a choice though since he gets paid too.

"That's great news Tom! Congrats."

"Thanks Chick. Now what's up? I know you're not calling just to say hi."

"You know me too well. I need your memory."

"Ok, well I am just as old as you are, but I will try. What do you have?"

"We worked a case back in eighty-two or eighty-three, I think. It was a kidnapping, young girl I think seventeen, over on tenth street. Snow was coming down fast, but there was something particular about the disturbance in the snow. It was like."

"Someone wiped it with a broom but no bristles evidence. That one?"

"Yeah, that's the one."

"It was eighty-three, her name was Rose Blandon."

"That's it. Thank you, Tom, you are a life saver."

"What, do you have a similar case?"

"Not sure yet. The snow was disturbed like Rose's case was. But I couldn't find my files at the house to be sure."

"I'm sure it's because you haven't gone through anything in years buddy."

"Yeah, that's also true. All right let me get back here. Good talking to ya Tom!"

"You too Chick, don't be a stranger."

As I hung up, I could hear some talking from behind me, I turned to see what was going on and who was talking. It was Joshua Grayson, looking for me apparently. One of the uni's was talking with him getting some information. I did not want to miss my chance to talk with him so I got up as quick as I could and headed toward him.

"Mr. Grayson. What can I do for you?" I asked.

"Detective Miller, good to see you. I heard you paid a visit to my grandparents earlier this morning."

"I did, my partner and me. I know your grandfather was not happy with my being there."

"I mean rightfully so; you wrongly accused his son of murder years ago. Did you think they were going to be welcoming to you?" he laughed like the arrogant ass he is.

"What can I do for you?" I asked.

"I hear there is a young girl missing. I wanted you to know that your department along with the State police are free to search our grounds as you find necessary."

"Thank you for that. We appreciate it. I know Lieutenant Campbell from PSP was going to be stopping by this morning, so I will give him a call and let him know that we have your permission to search."

"All I ask is that you leave my grandparents alone. They are too old, they do not need any added stress in their life so if you could leave you search to just the eighty acres, that's minus their eight, then we will cooperate with anything you all may need."

I didn't like the sound of that, but this was a gift he was handing us right now. If we needed to search their part, then we would revisit that later. I will take what I can get right now.

"I am sure we can accommodate that request for now."

"My brothers and I, sorry minus Eugene since you already have him in custody, will be at our respective businesses. When you all arrive, please come to the main office at my building, we will give you any maps, layouts, whatever it is that you would need to help."

"Will do."

He left, but that was too easy. It's never that easy, that meant they had nothing to hide or everything to hide. I will go with the latter until proven otherwise.

"Yeah, this is Detective Miller from Weston PD, I'm looking for Lieutenant Campbell. Thanks."

Mike walked over to see what was going on, since the conversation with Joshua was so brief, he did not get to hear what we discussed.

"Howie, listen Joshua Grayson was just in here. I don't know either. He gave us permission to search on the eighty acres, but not the eight that his grandparents are on. I told him that would be fine for now."

"What was that all about?" Mike asked, seemingly annoyed that I did not tell him right away.

"Well, you heard what I said to Howie?"

"Yeah, but why did he come here?"

"That's what Howie asked also. I don't know, probably because of the history I have with the family. If you couldn't tell by earlier this morning, I am not well liked by them."

"Yeah. I noticed. So, what does that mean? I mean it's a little suspicious to me that he just shows up here. Makes me think they are hiding something."

"I thought the same thing, Mike."

Working in Law Enforcement, especially the investigative division, you think that people walking in like that man did would be a positive thing. On the contrary, we are trained to pay attention to every single detail of every situation. That's a huge reason why I am single. We look for body language, eye contact, speech patterns and context.

When someone is all too willing to give up information or something like what Joshua did, we see red flags all over and we all get suspicious as to why they are so willing.

"Chick, you should go home, get some sleep. I can go back out and get the search started again with Howie. I'll call if anything turns up."

I knew I should, but I was hesitant. I did not want to let the family down, but I knew I was no good to anyone in the state I was in. I was exhausted.

"Ok, I'm gonna swing by the Adams' first, and just let them know what is going on."

"All right, see you later this afternoon."

When I pulled into their driveway I could see cars everywhere, looked like they were having a party, but I knew that wasn't the case. I figured most of the neighbors would be there and even some of the teenagers. There were people outside smoking, and one rushed back in, I assume, to let them know I was here. As I got out of the car, I saw Joe coming out the door to meet me.

"Chick. Any word?" The desperation in his voice was obvious.

"Not yet. I wanted to come by and let you know we have another search party starting shortly, and the Grayson's have given us permission to search their land as well. Which is a big help."

"Wow, ok. Yeah, if you say so, then that's great news. Lucy is laying down finally, and so are the kids. We were going to go get Justin's car, but we figured we would wait to see if anyone came by."

"I can have one of the units stop by and grab his keys, I'll get it towed to Luigi's down the road."

"You sure Chick? You don't mind?"

"Not at all. I will be heading back out there in a few hours. Mike is there now with Howie Campbell. I was forced to get some rest for a bit, against my better judgement though."

"No no, you need to be on your best for this. I get it. You need to rest too, you're not superman."

We both chuckled, even though it was lighthearted, and then went silent. I didn't know what else to say, so I just said goodbye and I would keep in touch with any news. I suggested they stay here at the house in case she called or came back home.

I knew damn well I wasn't going to rest when I got back to my house, I had every intention of looking through the files from eighty-three now that Tom confirmed the year and the name. I had to make a call first to the doctors to reschedule this appointment tomorrow. When I pulled on onto my street io could see Lydia's car in the driveway. She is my second wife and hates me more than the other two. I couldn't figure out why she was here, it was not my day with the kids, and I paid her for child support already, so this was going to be interesting.

I had to park on the damn street at my own house, because she thought for some reason, she could still do whatever the hell she wanted. She and I ended on not-so-great terms, she hated my hours and how I devoted my time to my cases. I know I could've been a better husband and dad to them all, but I can admit who I am and never pretended to be anything but.

I also forgot that all of them have a key to the house too, something I should remedy soon.

"Hello second wife." I yelled out as I opened the back door.

"Jesus Chick, can you come up with something a bit more original that line is getting old."

"Yes Lydia. What is it? Are the kids, ok?"

"Yes, they are fine. I heard about the young girl who's gone missing. I wanted to come and check on you. I know these cases always hit you a bit harder. That was all I wanted."

"And her heart grew three times that day," I said in my best Whoville narrator voice.

"HAHA, you're hilarious Chick. I didn't know you went into stand up."

Man, I loved that about her, that sarcasm way she had. She still looked great even at forty-seven. Who am I kidding, all three of my ex-wives looked great. What can I say I'm a real ladies' man. I have no idea what they saw in me. My first wife,

Caroline, was my high school sweetheart, and we all know that usually doesn't last. We were married for seventeen years and have three kids together. Then there's Lydia, she and I were married for four years, and have two kids together, and then there's the youngest of the three and our divorce is not even final yet, Daphne, she was so young, and I had no right even to start a relationship with her. I am thirty years older than her, and we have one child together. I see her most often; she is the youngest of them all. My daughter that is.

"Thanks, though. For coming by. You're right I take these ones a little harder than any others. I guess because when you have kids of your own it hits home. This is the girl that was helping with the Lawrence girl case."

"Oh, the hit-and-run cold case from seventy-six, was it?"

"Yep, that's it."

"Wow, that's terrible. Do you have any leads or know anything?"

"Not really." I proceeded to tell her what happened and where we were with everything now.

"Chick, I really hope you find her. Do you want me to keep the boys with me this weekend? I can if you need to focus on this case."

"I promised them we would watch the Eagles game on Sunday, so maybe I can pick them up Saturday night and they can stay the night with me, we can do a guys thing on Sunday."

"I think they would love that. I won't keep you; I know you need some rest. You look exhausted. Is there something else going on?"

I wanted to tell her about the doctor's consult, but why worry her when I have no idea what it was right now. Hell, it could be nothing and he just wants to put me on meds for something.

"I'm good, just tired. I will keep you updated though."

She walked over and hugged me, something she hadn't done in quite a few years.

"Thanks Lydia."

She smiled and left.

I didn't realize just how much shit I had in this basement. Finding these files was going to be next to impossible, but I had to find it. I knew it would help, somehow anyway. After about two hours of looking through all these damn boxes, I found nothing. I have no idea what I did with them. I knew I needed to walk away before I got even more pissed off and decided that I needed to take a power nap.

I went back up the stairs and took a seat in the Lay-z-boy. I don't even remember passing out, I only remember being woken up by the phone and my pager going off simultaneously. I knew I wouldn't get to the phone in time, since I was half asleep getting up from the chair. So, I grabbed my pager, it was the station with 9-1-1 typed at the end of the number.

This is either going to be a great call or a crappy one, I was hoping it was a good one.

"It's Chick." I said after dialing the station.

"Chick, we need you to head to the scene. They found something."

"I'm on my way."

What the hell could they have found? Was it a body? Nah, he would've said that. Had to have been something she was wearing, showing us some indication on which direction she went in.

This ride there was different, I started thinking about my girls. I have three of them, two of them were grown adults, with kids of their own, and one was just a little girl. I took for granted having the older ones, I never even had a second thought that something like this could happen to them, how foolish of me. How irresponsible. I think of Chloe, and I cannot imagine anything happening to her right now. Man, I really should've been a better dad to my girls, to all my kids. Caroline has told me before that it's better late than never, so maybe I should take her advice on that and try to work on things with them.

After I get this girl home.

"Mike, what do we got?" I said as I walked up the hill to where I could see them.

"We found a necklace, were pretty sure it's hers." He waved me over to the back of Howie's squad car.

"Chick, does this look familiar to you?"

Howie held up a silver chain with a ring on it. I made sure I put a set of gloves on first.

"I'll be damned. This is what the Lawrences gave her for her birthday."

"I thought so, I just need you to confirm." Mike said.

"Where'd you find this?"

"About a hundred meters down the road. As you can see it's been driven over."

"What side of the road? Show me."

I was anxious to see where this was, this could be a huge breakthrough for us. We walked back down the hill where I just came from onto the right side of the road.

"Here. This is where the uni found the necklace. We assume one of us had to have driven over it, obviously without knowledge of it being there, over the course of night and this morning."

"Did you canvas everywhere around here?"

"That's what they are all doing now. I told them we are looking for any being of her being here. So far, they've got nothing other than the necklace. Forensics will be taking the necklace to test for any trace evidence, I don't think they are going to find much since it's been so badly compromised."

"Mike, do you think Sandy is trying to tell us something?"

"No, I think Scarlet is."

When Mike said that I knew immediately that she was no longer with us. Something was telling me he was right; she was trying to tell us something. Obviously, I did not want to lose hope, but there is no sign of her anywhere. It is like she just disappeared, and it's my job to find her, dead or alive.

"You might be right. But let's not rule anything out just yet. Has anyone checked that side where the creek is?"

Checking the integrity of the ice was crucial right now, hell anywhere along the creek bed was critical.

"We checked back at the original location, but I don't know who Howie has on it now. I know we have new guys coming and going, Howie has threatened to call in the FBI to assist, since this is similar to a few cases that he heard about in Delaware and Maryland. Since we aren't far from either border he wants to confer with the departments and see if this is a call to FBI."

"Damnit, I was hoping it wouldn't come to that. That will complicate the shit out of this."

I understood the importance of them, but there was no one who knew this girl better than Mike and I did. We know how she thinks, we have worked with her one on one, we know her family. Christ we just celebrated her birthday with her a month ago. I was not about to give up, but I knew the longer we searched the chances of finding her alive were dwindling. You have to understand how cold it is out here. When it snows here there is nothing impeding it. It falls on the road and the plow trucks would move it off the roadway. This almost caused an avalanche effect on the embankment below. If she went down a path heading down there, who knows what could happen. She could fall into a snow drift, the creek, there's so many things that could happen.

The importance of checking here was imperative, and I knew we didn't have much time left before Howie reached out to the FBI. Dealing with them a few times I know how the locals can get set aside, sure we are able to put our two cents in, but they still do things their way. It works for them, but sometimes it doesn't. What if this was a time when it doesn't. We just got the cooperation of the Grayson's; would they be willing to cooperate with them? Doubtful. Will they treat this like a missing person rescue mission, or will they assume she is already dead?

I don't pretend to be naive; I know there is a high probability that she is gone. I know we are missing something, something that is right under our noses and just can't catch the scent yet.

"Mike, what are we missing? Someone just doesn't vanish in thin air. She must be here. I am not waiting for the damn snow and ice to thaw before I find her. We have to get our heads together, figure out what our next moves need to be. Who has gone to the Grayson's office?"

"Someone from PSP, I don't remember who Howie sent."

"What'd they say?"

"I don't know if he came back yet."

"Jesus, can you get Howie on the radio please."

"Lieutenant Campbell, could you walk down to where we found that piece of evidence."

"Be right there."

"Where we at with the Grayson's?" I didn't mean to bombard him, but I needed answers.

"Detective Goldberg just got back; he was just about to follow up with me. Let me get him down here. If I had known that's what you needed, I would've made you walk your ass up to me."

"You're ten years younger than me, you can handle it." We both laughed.

"Goldberg, what did the Grayson's say?"

"Detectives," he greeted us all, "they said that we have their full cooperation with searching any grounds of theirs.

They gave me a layout of where everything is on their property. Which I didn't realize was so massive, that's gonna take a while to search. You know they got the quarry, concrete, and construction businesses over there? Is there anything they don't do?"

"We know. Who did you meet with?"

"Uh, Joshua Grayson, he said the brothers were all on travel for their companies. He apparently owns the quarry portion, Wes owns the concrete part, and Harvey runs the construction part. Impressive."

"Yeah, makes you wonder where Eugene came from." Mike said with a snarky tone.

"Eugene has a lot of problems; you have to remember he was in the vehicle when their parents died."

"What? I didn't know that."

"Theres a lot you don't know about this family. Which is why I would appreciate not contacting the FBI yet. Howie, you know once they get involved, we will no longer have their cooperation. Right now, they think they have the upper hand and are smarter than we are. Let's let them keep thinking that. This way we always have the upper hand on them. We watch them, we don't let them move or go anywhere without knowing it. Hell, they don't sneeze without us hearing it."

"Chick, are you liking them for her disappearance?" Goldberg asked.

"I'm not ruling them out, that's for damn sure. We already have Eugene, even though I still have my doubts that it was him and wasn't one of the other three."

I stood there staring into the distance, where I could just see the outline of the quarry. I had a gut feeling that they knew something, at least one of them had to. And now with two of them out of town, we would have to wait. For what, I wasn't sure yet. I knew that they were hiding something, and I was determined to find out what.

This investigation has caught the attention of the news media, which was not our plan. The last thing we ever need is the interference of the media, they tend to manipulate the case to what they think the public should hear, not what the truth always is. Luckily, the State Police were handling that, so we could continue with our investigation. Sadly, it was going nowhere. The weather was not our friend, time was long past being on our side, and no one saw anything.

This area is so desolate and rarely driven, unless of course you live here or are familiar with the roads. Which is why I believe it was someone local, the odds that some random person was sitting waiting for someone to stop is slim to none. So, the likelihood that someone would be driving out here was a huge risk.

PSP had a forensics team that was coming out to cast some tracks that were made from the other vehicle. Hopeful that it helps, and they are quick with the results. Nothing is fast in this field, we run tests, we wait, we question people, we wait, it's always a waiting game. Every damn case I have ever worked was waiting.

I stayed in contact with the family day after day, it was now day four and we were finally coming to the end of the search on the Grayson's property and the surrounding areas. We questioned everyone we could find, we stopped at every damn house in a three-mile radius. Why only three miles? Because we knew the terrain and the options she would have to choose from. Christmas was coming closer, but the answers were not as easy. I had no new information for them, we couldn't find anything, and I finally agreed with Howie that it was time to bring in the FBI. We were getting nowhere, and I knew it was unfair to keep this up.

I was running on maybe three hours of sleep a day, and a lot of coffee. We all were exhausted. Scarlet's friends all wanted to continue to help so they made missing person flyers and hung them up all over. From PA, to Delaware, to Maryland. They figured the further they could get the information out there, the better chances they had of helping with a lead of some sort. If it helped them to deal with all this, then we were all for it. Chris was the most helpful, he would come to my house in the morning, with coffee and check in. He would go to school, and then come right back to the scene or the station. I felt bad for him, he was a good kid, and his family was taking this hard.

We all were if we're being honest.

You know when cases like this happen one of two things occur. The first one is we work the scene and what we are given, and if we're lucky we find the person we are looking for either alive or dead. The second is we have nothing, we work day in and day out, and we get pulled to other cases and shit starts to happen in the world that we can't control. The latter unfortunately puts that case on the back burner, or as we call it in the field a Cold Case. I have quite a few, sadly and kind of embarrassingly. I did not want this one to become that, but the reality of it was clear. We had nothing, after days of working round the clock. We had nothing.

I let the family down, I let the friends down, but most importantly I let Scarlet down. I didn't find her, not yet any-way. I wasn't sure if I was ever going to either. Mike kept telling me "Don't lose hope Chick, we will find her," I started to believe that, until I didn't.

SCARLET

I don't remember how I got here; I don't even know where here is. Nothing is familiar. It smells like rotten eggs; it makes me want to throw up. It's hot in here.

"Hello? Is anyone here?" I called out, hoping for an answer.

No answer came though. I got up, I was so dizzy.

When I stood up lost my balance instantly and fell back onto some type of bed. It was so hard for me to see anything.

I decided to just sit there for a few minutes before trying to get up again. I didn't know where I would go anyway. I called out again, I thought I heard a faint cry but wasn't sure. "Hello? Can anyone hear me?" I knew no one was going to hear me, the sounds above were almost deafening, it was no use. I was scared, confused, and anxiety took hold of me.

"Hello?" the voice was low and I wasn't sure if I heard it or if my mind was playing tricks on me. I closed my eyes and tried to just focus on the possible sound of another human voice.

"Hello?"

OH MY GOD! I did hear someone "Hello, Hello" I said frantic and quick, "Can you hear me?" I yelled out.

"Yes," the voice was shaky and so quiet, I could hardly make out if it was a male or female.

"Where are you? Keep talking to me. I can't see anything at all. The light is so dim." As I was yelling out, the loud noises above us stopped. I thought I was hallucinating it at first.

"Hey." I said again now that it was much quieter.

"Hi." The voice replied. I could tell now it was a female's voice.

"My name is Scarlet Adams. What's yours?" I asked.

"Karlie, Karlie Gorton. When did you get here?" she asked.

"Hi Karlie. Maybe yesterday, or last night. Honestly, I don't even know. I don't remember getting here. How long have you been here?" I asked her.

"A long time. Theres a few of us down here. Well, there was anyway. I haven't heard the others in a while. So, I'm not sure anymore."

"Others?" I was even more scared now.

"Yeah, I think there's two or three others down here. One sounded like an older lady, but the others are young. I don't think as young as you though. I am thirty. How old are you?" She sounded so sad and defeated.

"I am sixteen. I just had a birthday last month."

"How did you end up down here?" Karlie asked.

"It's kind of a blur, but I was driving, and I think I was going to pick up my brother. Um, there was a car, I do not remember what it looked like or anything. There was a guy on the side, he seemed familiar I do remember that. But I don't know. I have been wracking my brain since I woke up. I don't even know why I was asleep." I sat down on the ground to be closer to where I could hear her voice.

"Do you think people are looking for you?" she asked me.

I felt a lump form in my throat and my stomach got twisted in knots, "I would like to believe they are." I answered.

"I am sure no one is looking for me." She said.

"Why would you say that?" I was surprised to hear her say that.

She laughed in a way when she responded, "I have been down here for at least six months. My job was not one that people took notice of if I were to go missing." I did not understand what she meant.

"What do you mean? What did you do for a living?" I wasn't sure if I wanted her to answer.

"I was an escort."

"Um, I don't know what that is." I said.

She laughed again, "A call girl."

As soon as she said that I understood, "Oh."

"Yeah, So, like I said when we go missing no one looks for us. I would bet no one is looking for me."

Her and I talked for a while longer until she wanted to lay down. She told me that there were certain times throughout the day or night that someone would bring food down, not one word was ever spoken. The food was left and then an hour the tray was picked up. No lights were on, so she could never see who it was. She said one time she smelled perfume. Not cheap perfume either, expensive stuff. I followed her lead and laid back down as well. There was nothing else to do expect sleep, wait, and talk to Karlie.

DETECTIVE MIKE SCHAFFER

When I got the call that Scarlet was missing, I didn't know how to respond at first. I couldn't believe it actually. There was no way this girl could be missing, right? When I got to the station, Chick wasn't there yet. Which didn't surprise me, he hated being on call. I enjoyed it because I felt that my expertise was best suited for it.

When I walked in Joe and Lucy were sitting at one of the desks, they were a mess naturally. I went and talked with Chief Masters and Sergeant MacNeil before I spoke with the family, just so I could get an idea as to what was going on.

"Brian do me a favor?"

"What's that Mike?" MacNeil asked.

"Don't tell Chick yet what's going on. He may blow a gasket if he is told beforehand."

"Yeah, sure." MacNeil walked away to call him, since he hadn't answered the page yet.

I knew I needed to get more information on the report for the Adams, even though MacNeil started it already. My goal was to have as much information as possible by the time Chick got here, so he didn't have to ask too many questions. I know when he gets here and finds out what is going on he's going to be upset.

We developed a great relationship with this kid, and one thing Chick doesn't do well is relationships with kids. His own don't like him much, except his youngest but she's six so. One of the many things I respected about Chick, was the ability he had to keep his personal feelings out of things. I felt this case would be different.

But I am getting ahead of myself, I had no idea what the scene looked like yet, she could easily be hiding somewhere trying to stay warm and out of harm's way. It was easy to get lost that way, especially if you're not familiar. This was the first time she had driven alone, and to a place she never drove to on her own. I can imagine she is scared, but I also believe it won't take long to find her. Hearing Brian on the phone with Chick, I could hear how annoyed and frustrated he was getting with him.

"Damn, that man." he said as he slammed the phone down.

"Is he talking about Chick?" Lucy asked.

"I am pretty sure, yeah. He has always hated being on call, he says it's because every time a call comes in its always bad." Shit, well I said that before thinking.

Lucy and Joe both looked at me with scared, panicked faces.

"I'm not saying that's what this is. I am just saying that's how he acts. Since I asked Sergeant MacNeil not to say anything, he's probably acting like an ass. That's all."

"Oh, ok." Joe said with a sigh of relief.

I didn't want to make any promises to them, that was one thing Chick told me "Never make a promise to the family. It's a cardinal rule in law enforcement." I took that very seriously and made every effort to never do that.

About fifteen minutes later and Chick was walking in the door to the station, He looked confused already, and I felt a little bad for not telling him before he got here. I knew how he would react though, so it was better. At least I thought so.

After we filled him in on what was happening, he seemed pretty pissed at me. I mean rightfully so, we were partners, and these were things I should tell him. We were getting ready to leave and the last words I heard him say, surprised me.

"Lucy, Joe, I promise we will find her." Chick said it, I wouldn't have believed had I not been standing there.

I didn't say a word to him about it, I just got in the car. I explained a lot already on what we saw when we arrived on scene so I won't repeat that, but I will fill you in on what happened when Chick went back to the station, and I stayed on scene. We were all busy, making sure to look behind every tree, follow any tracks, anything to find her. Unfortunately, there were no tracks. That made it hard for us to do our job properly. I scoured the entire street, hell I even got down on my hands and knees to make sure I missed nothing. If there was something to be found, I was determined to find it. We hadn't known her for long, but that didn't matter.

It was easy to like this kid, she was funny, outgoing, smart, not your typical teenager for the times. We knew what she had been through so far in her life, and all we wanted was to find her safe and sound.

After about an hour, I decided to walk back down the road where we came from, on the side where the tire tracks were found. I walked about a half mile and saw there were some patrolmen there as well.

"Hey guys, anything?" I asked, knowing damn well they found nothing.

"Not yet detective. We got a lot against us tonight, huh?"

"You could say that again. This cold is one thing, but the darkness is making it near impossible for us. All right, well let me know if you find anything at all. Even if you think it has no significance."

"Yes sir."

I walked up the embankment near where we were talking and shined my flashlight out onto the ground. It looked as if it bounced back off the snow and almost blinded me, it was so bright. I could hear the unis behind me talking louder so I turned to see what was going on.

"Everything good?" I hollered down.

"Uh, Detective, we don't know if this means anything, but you might wanna come check it out." One of them said.

Finally, a damn break, is all I could think of. I could see something dangling from his hand, as I got closer, I could see it was a chain, possibly a necklace.

"What is that?" I asked as he handed it to me.

"A ring on a necklace, looks like."

I held the ring up as he shined the flashlight on it, and I'll be damned. It was Sandy's class ring, the very one that the Lawrences gave to Scarlet for her birthday last month. This meant so much, I know the patrolmen had no idea how significant it was eight now.

"Is this something that we should get logged in?"

"Yes. Call for Detective Miller asap, I need him here forthwith."

"Yes sir."

It was flattened, most likely from one of our vehicles running it over. I am curious as to why it is on the road, but also elated to know that she was here and hopefully this was a sign from her. I did nothing with it until Chick showed back up. I did let forensics know because I wanted them on this immediately after I showed him. When Chick arrived back on scene, I showed him the necklace and he had the same reaction as I did. We had no idea if she was still alive, but this gave us both hope.

"Mike, do you think Sandy is trying to tell us something?" Chick asked me.

"No, I think Scarlet is." I replied.

Now, that did not mean I thought she was no longer with us. It meant that I knew this girl, and she knew that her family would be looking for her and this was her clue to let us know she was alive, at least a few hours ago she was. When Chick explained that the Grayson's gave us approval to search their land, I was shocked. I was, however, not surprised when he said we weren't allowed near their grandparents. After that little encounter earlier, I could see why. They were not fans of Chick, which really sucked.

We had no idea if she was there, she could be who knows. All we could do was respect that, and not go there again.

The last thing we wanted was for any hurdles to pop up, so everyone knew to stay away from Mr. and Mrs. Brinton's property. Eighty acres of land we had to search now, eighty. I was still zinging from all the coffee and adrenaline, so I knew I had a few hours left in me. I also knew that when Chick left to go home for a few hours he would not sleep.

Once they started the search on the Grayson property, I was hopeful that it was just a matter of time before we found her, or some semblance that she was there. Howie ordered us to go home, get some sleep and relax for the day. We were to meet later this afternoon, around two o'clock back at his station.

I did go home to get showered and change and something normal to eat, not the crap at the scene. Donuts, cookies, and too much coffee, that's all that was out there. I didn't eat that shit, so I felt like shit from eating it. My two babies were waiting for me when I got home. Rosie and Della, my brindle pitbull and blue coat pitbull, best dogs in the world. I thought a few times to get them and Murphy to play, they would get along great. Maybe I'll mention that after we find her.

Wait, how dumb is that. People don't do that, have their dogs play together. I must be more tired than I thought, and I must've passed out on the couch. The next thing I remember, the phone was ringing off the hook and my pager was beeping. Looking at my watch I saw it was twelve o'clock and jumped up to grab the phone.

"Hello. Damn I missed it."

I checked the pager and saw it was Chick's number. I called him back to see what was going on, God I had hoped I didn't miss anything.

"Chick, sorry I missed your page."

"What were you doing, sleeping?" he asked like a smart ass.

"Actually, yeah, I passed out, I guess. What's up?"

"Get dressed and come over to the house. I wanna show you something."

"Ok. Let me feed the girls, and I'll be over in about a half hour. We still meeting at PSP at two?"

"I think so. I didn't hear any different."

When I walked into Chick's I could hear faint music coming from the back of the house.

"Chick. Yo, where ya at?" I called out.

No answer of course.

I was amazed that his house was so clean and organized, no one would believe that he was a bachelor. Again, ha. I don't have any room, I have been single for six years now, once I started the academy my long-time girlfriend left me. She said that she didn't think she could handle the stress of my job. So, once she left, I decided that I would throw myself into it and prove my abilities and worth to the department.

Chick wasn't thrilled when I was made his partner, he told the chief he worked better alone and didn't need some rookie messing things up.

At first it was always him telling me to just watch and learn and not to touch anything. But after about six months he started to warm up to me, I grew on him. Actually, that wasn't it at all. It was a call we had been requested on; well, he was, I just happened to be his partner, so I was there too. His old department reached out for a cold case from about ten years ago, one he had worked for about eight months before decided to leave Lannister.

He had a lot of unsolved cases in the city, a lot of women of color who were murdered and never solved. Every lead he had was a dead end, every piece of evidence was tainted in some way, if there was any at all. Whoever committed these murders was meticulous in everything they did. His old partner needed his expertise on something, with all the new technology they were coming up with and our area finally getting some of the capabilities to test for things, they believed they found some new evidence. It was a small glimmer of hope they had, but with all the knowledge he had from the cases they knew he would be the best to give his input on what they found.

I helped him as much as he would allow, and together we solved a different cold case than the one his partner called for. That one was also a dead end and the DNA found ended up being hers. They were all disappointed, but because we worked well together, we did solve another one like I said.

After that he seemed to act differently toward me, not as mean as before. It made both our jobs much easier after that case. We didn't have many here in Weston, the cases we dealt with were petty crimes, DC's, curfew calls, it was relatively quiet for a small town, which is why Chick wanted the change. I was born and raised here so I knew it would be a great steppingstone for me and my career. My goal was to get into the FBI or Secret Service, whichever accepted me first. Not all our plans end up how we expect though, right.

When I walked down the stairs to his office, I say that loosely, there were papers, folders, post it's sprawled out everywhere.

"You didn't leave any space unused huh?" I laughed.

"What? Oh yeah, uh I got into some old files. That one over there on the buffet, get that one and read it. I want to hear your opinion on it."

"Ok." Very unlike Chick to want my opinion about an old case.

As I read through the pages, and documents, I asked him, "What am I looking for?"

"Look at the pictures, toward the middle of the file. Tell me if it looks familiar."

Oh, I got it now. He said something similar before about the fact that he knew the snow disturbance looked familiar. Damned if he wasn't spot on. Right, there are the tire tracks, and the weird swipe almost of the snow. Looked as if someone was trying to cover up tracks, footprints most likely.

"Looks a lot like what we saw last night. How long did they say it would take for the pictures to be developed?" I asked.

"Probably when we get back up there, they should be ready. Make sure you bring that folder with us ok."

"You got it. Is there anything else you found in your great big boxes of everything?"

"Maybe, I don't know there's so much shit here. I don't know why I kept some of this stuff. I guess I thought it would be important at some point. None of this has ever helped."

He seemed a bit defeated, which I couldn't blame him. We found nothing except the necklace and that's going to take a while before they get anything, if anything, off it.

Nothing new on the scene, we were there for hours again. Howie had us pull back a bit, he knew we had other cases to deal with, but Chick and I weren't ready to give up. We knew there were ways we could help, but once he called in the FBI, I knew it was going to be this way. To say I wasn't disappointed would be a lie. I felt like we were giving up on her, giving up on the family.

Days went by and we made sure we would keep up with the case and check in with Joe and Lucy every chance we could. Chris and her friends wanted to help, even her friends from Maryland, so they made flyers and posted them all over from

Pa to Delaware to Maryland. They figured it couldn't hurt to get her face seen to anyone and everyone.

I remember one day at the station Chris walked in, he looked sadder than usual. It was the day before Christmas Eve, he was carrying a basket that his mom had put together for us which was a nice gesture.

"Hi Mrs. Smitham."

"Hello Christian, how are you?"

"I'm ok. My mom asked me to bring this in and wish everyone a Merry Christmas."

"Well, that was very nice of her. Please tell her I said thank you on behalf of us all."

He tried to smile, but I could see the sadness in his eyes that he was trying to mask.

I walked over to him to strike up a conversation, "Hey Chris. How's it going?"

"Hey Detective Schaffer. Oh, you know. It's going."

"You wanna sit and talk?"

"Nah, that's ok. Thanks though."

My heart was breaking for this kid.

"Chris, sit with me. Talk to me. I can see something is going on. I know the obvious, but I've never seen you this sad."

"I don't know. I don't know anything anymore. It's been, what two weeks, that's it. I feel like it's been an eternity.

I know everyone looks at us like we are just kids, and well I mean technically we are. But she made me feel like I mattered to this world. She had a way of calming me, like she was a cloud that would just fall around me and make me feel safe. I know you and Chick got to know her; you can see how this is hard for me. For all of us. She was a pure person, someone who just saw the good in the world. Even when you guys' arrested Eugene, she was sad for him. Almost, like she felt bad. She knew he was different, special, and she didn't know if he could do it on purpose after she got to know the family."

"Yeah, she is great. Wait, what do you mean after she got to know the family?" Now I was concerned and curious. Chick always had a suspicion that it could be the Grayson's.

"Oh, she was hanging out with umm one of their daughters. She got a second job, over in Innerborough, at some coffee shop. His daughter works there too, she's a senior at Carriage Ford High School. They were hanging out some after their shifts. She's nice, not at all what I expected when Scarlet first told me who her family was."

I was speechless when he told me this, I never knew any of this. I am guessing that Joe and Lucy didn't know either, at least not who this girl's family is. I waited until he was finished talking before, I reached out to Chick. I felt he needed to know this right away. I contemplated calling Howie as well, but I knew Chick would be pissed if I did.

The phone rang at my desk, I knew it was Chick calling me back.

"Schaffer."

"You page me? What's up?"

He was especially cranky today.

"Chris was just in, he told me something that I think you will find interesting. Are you heading in soon?"

"Yeah, I'll be in in about a half hour. Can it wat 'til then?"

"Yeah, that's fine."

"Why are we just hearing about this? Why didn't anyone say anything before this?" Chick was irritated by the news of the Grayson girl.

"I don't know. Maybe they didn't think it was important? She was only working there for about a week or two, so maybe they didn't think there was any connection. That's my best guess."

"You didn't ask him?"

"No, it was hard enough for him to tell me and quite frankly I didn't want to chase him off by asking so many questions."

"That's your job." He got louder.

"I know what my job is."

"Do you?"

"You're unbelievable sometimes. I sit here and take your shit, your low blows, your smart-ass comments all the time. I will not sit here and allow you to discredit how I do my job."

I stormed off after that, I was irate at this point. I had never really stood up to him before this, and although it felt great it was also another hurdle for us to get over. The outburst caught the attention of everyone in the station, including the Chief. Now, I did not want to cause a scene, but he crossed the line.

"SCHAFFER, MILLER, MY OFFICE NOW!" the chief yelled with his deep, brooding voice.

We could hear the mumbling under everyone's breath, the whispers from across the room. We knew we messed up, well at least I did.

"What the hell was that all about? You know what, don't answer that. Whatever it was, it better not happen again. I don't need my two best detectives fighting with each other. Do I make myself clear?"

"Yes Chief," I said.

"Crystal." Chick said, which I'm sure the chief did not appreciate his tone.

Leaving the station was probably the best decision we made that day. It was his day to drive so we got in the car and started out to the coffee shop she was working at. We didn't say anything the entire drive out there, we kept it professional while at the shop. Unfortunately, the young girl was not in that day, she was away with her family in *Disney World* until after the New Year.

Great. I was hoping that this could be a break for us, but not likely, at least not now.

"What do you want to do? You wanna tell Howie about this?" I asked.

"We better, if we don't it'll be our asses on the line."

We started to drive over to the State Police Barracks, but we were distracted by something on the side of the road. We were back on Carriage Ford Road, about a mile down from where Scarlet went missing.

"What is that? Is that a jacket?" Chick asked as he started to slow down and pull over just before it.

"Or a sweatshirt." I spoke.

He put the car in park, we both looked at each other and got out to see what it was.

"Put your gloves on and watch where you're walking just in case there's something else."

I nodded to him. We both carefully and slowly approached the object and could see that it was soaking wet and was there for a while. It was green, or even black, we weren't sure yet because of how wet it was. He leaned down and pinched one corner of it and lifted it up slowly. We couldn't make out what it was until he opened it all the way.

"Mike, get PSP on the radio." The tone in his voice was urgent and a matter of fact. I knew in an instant it must be Scarlet's.

He turned it around to show me, it had Chris on the left breast of the jacket and a basketball on the right one. We both knew, there was no question.

I ran to the car and called over the radio for an urgent, immediate response to the scene.

Weeks this was out here. It must've been covered with snow on purpose because it didn't snow that night or even since then. Holy shit, I just stood there staring at Chick holding the jacket. I can't believe this.

"Chick, how the hell did this get here?"

"That's exactly what I was wondering. Did you get PSP?"

"Yeah, they are coming lights and sirens."

"Good. We are going to have to start this all over again. Maybe we might have some answers to help make their Christmas a little less depressing."

No one could believe it when they arrived on scene, they were all just as shocked as we were. We all knew that this wasn't closure by any means, but at least we had something new to work with. The searchers found nothing. Even with everyone spaced ten feet apart, and their directions on what to do if they found anything, absolutely nothing was ever found. We searched for five days, and then were told to take a step back. Then suddenly today, of all days, we find this? It's unbelievable.

I cannot even count the number of vehicles that have driven by this exact spot. How many times we drove by it.

"Chick, Mike. What do we got?" Howie stopped dead in his tracks when he saw what Chick was holding.

He refused to let it go just yet, he did not want anyone handling it until Forensics got there.

"Well, I'll be damned." Detective Goldberg uttered lowly.

"Yeah, that was our reaction too." I replied.

Finding this jacket seemed to breathe new life into this investigation, which was a relief to us.

"Chick, Mike, I want you two to take lead on this. If anyone has questions or anything they will be directed to you two. I am not losing this one, I will contact Agent Graham immediately and let her know that we are back on the case, and we have found new evidence. We will have to work with them, so I need you to put your ego aside, ok?"

We all knew he was talking to Chick about the ego, we all agreed.

Agent Graham was no bullshit; she took none and she had no time for any. She for sure gave Chick a run for his money. He seemed to be impressed by her though, which was comical to me because he didn't seem impressed by anyone ever. We waited for Howie to give us an update on when the FBI would be arriving, I still wasn't sure why they were involved, but obviously it was above my paygrade.

We all talked about how we knew it was the Grayson's but we also knew the uphill battle it was going to be getting anything from Sarah. She is a great ADA, but she is by the book always. There was a lot of history with Chick and her dad, something he didn't talk much about to anyone.

I knew Scarlet was out there, I stared out over the large area that the Grayson's owned and wondered where could she have gone? No one just disappears just like that. It boggled my mind, but as a detective we had a job to do and that was to find Scarlet.

SCARLET

I have no idea how long I have been down here. I was able to wander around the small room I am in, but I only found a door that was locked from the outside and the hole on the wall that I can talk to Karlie through. Someone brings food and water every day, the light gets turned off when they bring it. I can hear when the doorknob turns, it's loud. Once they place it on the floor the door slams closed, and the light goes back on.

It seems as if there's a few hours a day when the light comes on, and then it goes off for good I assume at night. Honestly, I have no idea. I don't know who brought me here, or why.

"Karlie? Are you there?" I had to wait for the noise again to stop, it was so loud but I was starting to get used to it.

"Yeah." Her voice sounded worse and worse everyday. I was worried about her, more than ever.

"You ok?" I asked.

"I don't think so. I am really weak and shaking a lot. I am not sure what's going on. I just am so tired."

"Ok, well maybe you just get some rest. I will sit here and contemplate how we are going to get out of here."

"Ok, Scarlet. I'm just going to lie down for a little bit." And she was quiet.

We never heard anyone else, even though we yelled and called out often, there was never a response.

I don't remember falling asleep, but I was woken up by the slam of the door and someone was standing in the room with me this time. My heart was pounding, I knew they had to have heard it.

"What do you want from us? Just let me go, I just want to go home." I begged them.

"No more talking." It was a male's voice, I recognized it from the night I was taken. He was here in the room with me, I knew he was going to kill me. I stayed seated on the mattress and tried not to speak. Just as quickly as he came in, he went out.

I started sobbing instantly when he closed the door. I tried to feel around for anything he may have left, but there was nothing except the food on the tray.

"Karlie? Oh my god, he was just in here with me." I said.

There was no reply, I knew she had to have been asleep still. I did not want to disturb her so I decided to eat and wait for her to call out to me.

ASSISTANT DISTRICT ATTORNEY
SARAH MAJORS

"I need a better reason than just because, to get you that warrant. Give me something." I said to Lieutenant Campbell.

"I know, I'm working on it." He replied.

I have been an ADA now for a little over four years, I love my job and I hate it at the same time. I have worked on some terrible cases, and not so terrible. This one was one that seemed to be hitting a small town hard. I do not know Scarlet Adams, but I know many people who do, and I was willing to help in every way I could, just the right way.

Howie coming into my office, demanding a warrant to search the Brinton's property was not the right way. I had nothing to validate that it was needed. Not even circumstantial evidence, I needed something solid. Something ironclad.

So, when Howie showed up again at my office, I was skeptical about what he was going to present to me.

"Sarah, I'm gonna need that warrant."

"Howie, I told you already. I'm going to need something rock solid for me to get that for you. Do not waste my time."

"We got it."

"What did you get?"

"The evidence needed. But I need a bunch of warrants."

I was afraid he was going to say that.

"That's wonderful news. Where is this said evidence?"

"It is on its way to forensics for testing."

"And what was this evidence?"

"The jacket she was wearing the night she went missing."

Ok, that is exactly what I was looking for.

"Ok. Where are you planning on going?"

"The Brinton's, and all the Grayson's homes, offices, businesses, and the six other residents directly in the area of where she went missing."

"Christ Howie, that's a dozen warrants, I can't make that happen. I can make it happen for any of the homes that are directly in the same vicinity of where the jacket was found. That's the best I can do. Where does that take you?"

"Well, I'll get the Grayson's and the old couple that helped her brother, the Hagerty's."

"Ok. I'll fax it over to your office by tomorrow. Do not, I repeat DO NOT attempt to go to those locations until you have the warrants in hand. Tell Detective Miller that, and I mean it. If he so much as breathes in their direction, I will pull these in seconds without even hesitation."

"Yes ma'am. Thank you. We are very grateful. I will pass that message along to Detective Miller and we will wait for your fax. Have a great day. I am sorry you must work tomorrow on Christmas Eve. In our field I guess our jobs don't get holidays off, huh?"

"You got that right. Merry Christmas, Lieutenant."

Allow me to explain why I was so adamant about Detective Miller not doing anything until these warrants were in hand. My father and he were the best of friends when they were in school, growing up together. They both enlisted in Vietnam together, both to the Navy. Everything was good between them, until they came home. They talked about what their futures looked like, and what plans they had for it when they were done on their tour.

Four years, which was the time they had to commit to. It was hard for them; I know my dad never spoke to me about what his experience was over there or the things he saw. And being friends with Chick's oldest, Mariel, she said the same thing. One of their assignments was to assist the Apollo eight mission. The story he tells is so cool.

They were in the middle of the Pacific Ocean, and their Commander was briefing a few of the Frogmen for the landing. They were all out on the deck when they could see it come through the sky, he said it was like a meteor coming in. So bright, and fast. Obviously, there were concerns about the impact into the ocean, but they were all ready for the best and worst scenarios.

Everything went exactly how they planned. And when the astronauts stepped onto the deck my dad made his way to them to introduce himself. He was a go getter; he wasn't afraid to out himself out there. Well, Chick was upset with him because he left him behind. My dad said he always would say that. Now, my dad loved Chick, but after this incident Chick became bitter toward him. Dad couldn't understand it, he got nothing from introducing himself to them, all he did was shake their hands. But Chick had it in his head that this would put him in a better situation than him. Didn't make sense to my dad, doesn't make sense to me even now when I'm twenty-seven.

When they came home, they went their separate ways. My dad went to Law School, and Chick went to the Academy. Once they both were established, that's when the real hatred came out, you could say. My dad was a Defense Attorney, which most in the Law Enforcement community weren't fans of. I am an ADA, and I am not a fan of them either, but I understand their importance in the law and order of it all.

I am sure you can imagine how things went when a case came and my dad represented the defendant, Chick would make comments like "shyster" "pettifogger" you name it. I never heard, nor knew, of my dad doing anything shady or illegal or immoral. He was so proud what he did, and his firm was too important for him to end up in a jam.

He never wanted to be disbarred so he was always on the up and up. Chick just couldn't get over an old problem that he had.

When my dad passed away in 1995, part of me was hoping that he would show for the services. He did not, he did send a mass card though, which I guess was the best we were getting. My mom always told me that he was a complicated man, and to not be so hard on him. And that the history was with my dad and him, not me. She was partially right. When I became an ADA, he was the first one there to say how great it was that someone from the Majors family was doing good in the law-and-order community, not being a scapegoat like my dad.

I took that personal, but I was always professional. Plus, like I said, his oldest daughter is one of my closest friends, so I try not to show the disrespect I have for him in front of her. I was curious as to how this case about this young girl was going to play out.

I hoped that he would be able to stay unbiased about the entire thing, and that his head would be clear enough to do his job properly. Not that he doesn't, he is always by the book. Always.

MILLER

I knew going to their home was the best decision I could have made, I needed to tell them in person, and I didn't want to parade them into the station. They deserved better.

It was Christmas Eve, 1996, I didn't have much, but I wanted them to know we found the jacket and it is being tested. We also have a warrant to check the surrounding properties, which include the Grayson's.

I pulled onto their street and could tell that it hadn't been plowed yet. It started snowing early this morning. All I could think of was how ironic we found that jacket at the exact time we were supposed to. If not, it would be covered again, and lord knows how long it would've taken to find it.

I could hear Murphy barking from the door, his typical friendly bark he did. As I walked up the walkway to their porch, I could see them sitting at the kitchen table. I was interrupting lunch and felt a little bad at first. I knocked, and Violet saw me first. She hopped down off the stool at the table and smiled at me. As if she knew I was there for a good reason. It made me smile too.

"Hi Detective Miller. Merry Christmas!" she said in such a sweet voice.

"Merry Christmas to you too Violet!"

"Chick, come on in!" Joe called out.

I was grateful for how nice of a family they were, and they were very understanding. The fact that they did not interfere with anything we were doing was probably the most helpful they could've been. Everyone seemed to be there except Justin.

"How is everyone?" I asked. I was terrible at small talk, Scarlet made it a point to tell me that often.

"We're all ok. Trying to stay positive and waiting to hear from you guys. We got some more posters up in Jersey. And Chris and her friends have replaced any that have been taken down, or damaged because of the weather. It's hard, I won't lie. I am lost without her here, but I, sorry we, are trying to keep everyone positive." Joe explained.

The strength he had to say all that in front of his family is something I have never been able to possess. What a great man. We could all take some lessons from Joe Adams.

"Ok, full transparency here. We found something. It is promising, but it's going to take a few days or so to test it."

"Ok, well what is it?" Lucy asked excitedly.

"It was the jacket she was wearing the night she went missing."

They all looked at one another.

"Chris's jacket?" Avery asked, with tears streaming down her face.

"Yeah, kiddo. That one."

I could see that they were overwhelmed by this, and I knew it was going to be hard for them for many reasons. One there was no Scarlet yet and two we found something that could help us find her.

"I know it's not much, but it is a great thing because this starts an entirely new investigation on her being missing. I do have a few questions. She started a new job at a coffee shop over in Innerborough, is that right?"

"Yeah, I guess she was there for about two weeks before this all happened." Lucy said, confirming with Joe.

"Yeah, that's right. She really enjoyed it there. She was working hard to save up for a car. Oh God, we were too hard on her for that weren't we?" Lucy broke down in tears.

"Honey, no. Don't even think like that. This isn't our fault. It's no one's fault. Look at me." Joe said as he pushed Lucy's hair back behind her ears looking at her. "We will find her; God didn't give her to me for me to lose her so soon. Ramona is watching over her, I feel it in my soul that she is with her. When Ramona was sick, we had a conversation about three weeks before she had passed. She told me that I needed to watch over my girls, but most importantly Scarlet. She said because of her love and compassion for others it could bene- fit her or be detrimental to her. Either way it was my promise to her that day that I would protect our daughter at all costs. So, if anyone feels as if it's their fault, it's me. I broke my promise to Ramona and to Scarlet. I know I sound ridiculous even saying that, but I have been going over and over in my head how different that night should've gone. I should have been home. I should've told her all the time how dangerous it could be out there, especially for her.

I should've told her I love her more often than I did. But I cannot live off should have's because I am not a perfect man. I am Joe Adams, just imperfectly me. I pray to her every night that we will find Scarlet, I know she can hear me. I know we will find her; I have faith."

Standing there listening to him open his heart to his wife and be that vulnerable without hesitation was unfamiliar territory to me. I wished I could be that positive, especially in a situation like this. If it were one of my kids, I would be burning shit down to find them.

"Joe, Lucy, kids, I promise we are doing everything we can to find her. I know it was quiet for a little while there. But finding this jacket is a huge break for all of us. Did Scarlet ever talk about anyone she was working with at the coffee shop?"

"Um, yeah, she had mentioned a girl around her age. Uh, what was her name?" lucy questioned.

"It's Alaina Grayson." George answered.

"That's it. Thanks buddy." Lucy smiled.

"Ok. Did she ever talk about her or what they did after their shift?" I asked.

"She went to her home a few times after because Alaina drove her home. She told me their home was like a mansion, like the ones back in Maryland. She said that her dad and mom were nice, and there were other people there also. I don't know who because she didn't say who. She told me and Chris that she didn't think Eugene killed Sandy on purpose." Goerge was always so matter of fact about everything he said.

"Did she say why she didn't think he did it on purpose?" I asked.

"Welp, she said that the way they talked about him it made it sound like he was slow, or like had a mental problem. I don't know how to say that because I don't want to sound mean."

"That makes sense." Exactly what I thought too.

Joe and Lucy looked at me confused as to why I would say that.

"I say that because his lawyer had a psychological evaluation done on him, and he has a bunch of different things going on with him. And his family knowing that he has this, they probably helped him, so he didn't end up in some hospital. Unfortunately, he is being transferred to a mental hospital to get properly medicated and the care that he needs."

"I don't know anything about this family. Chick, what are they like? Are they a good family?" Joe asked me.

"Well, they don't like me much. Then again most don't." I said with an awkward laugh.

"We like you, and Scarlet just idolizes you. So, give yourself a little more credit, you're not as bad as they all give you credit for."

We all laughed at that.

"Ok, so listen I won't hold you up any longer. I am heading to meet the rest of the team at one of the other homes out there."

"Chick, did you go to that girl's house?" Lucy asked.

"I did, but unfortunately, they are in *Disney World*, so I got to wait 'til after the new year to talk to them. But we have a bunch of other places and people to search for and question. I will stay in touch, try to have a nice Christmas. I know that won't be easy. Merry Christmas."

I got in my car to head out to the scene; I had this dull pain in my arm. I thought I was having a heart attack at first, but I think it was just heartbreak. I really liked this kid too; she gave me a run for my money that's for sure. I had to take a minute to regroup and get my head straight. I could see Chris was walking down the street to their house, I wanted to talk to him too.

"Chris. Hey buddy. How ya holding up?"

"Ah, you know it's Christmas and my girlfriends been missing for weeks, my pop has pneumonia. Doesn't everyone have this stuff happen to them."

I know he didn't mean any of the sarcasm, so I took none of it personally.

"Your pop, man I'm sorry to hear that. Listen, I have some news. We found your jacket that she was wearing that night."

He perked right up, "What? Seriously? So, what does that mean? Are you close to finding her?"

I put my hands up for him to slow down, "Not exactly. We are running tests on it to see if there is any evidence, trace evidence, on it. We also have warrants for the homes in the direct vicinity of the location and we are starting a new search and rescue mission for her as we speak."

He rushed in and hugged me.

"Chick, I don't care what anyone says about you, you're a good man. Thank you for never giving up on finding her. What can I do?"

"Nothing right now. Just be there with the family and with yours. Now is the time to stay positive and be strong. I told Joe and Lucy I would stay in touch, and I will. Please give your family my best, and of course your pop. Merry Christmas, Chris."

"Merry Christmas, Detective Miller!"

He walked away toward their house, and I started my drive out to the scene. The roads were going to be slick due to the snow. I realized I hadn't eaten in the last day; I don't remember the last thing I ate. I decided to stop at *McDonald's* and grab a *McChicken Meal* supersized with a *coke*. I needed something to fill my gullet and keep me going for a while. I wasn't feeling well, but I chalked it up to not eating and my diabetes acting up.

I was called over the radio by Howie to go straight to Harvey's home first. I didn't think that was the most obvious to search first, but I didn't argue with Howie. He was one of the few I didn't do that with. When I pulled up to the driveway, I could see that everyone else was there already, and I knew it was most likely going to be adversarial, and promised myself I would go into this with an open mind and not so much like the typical asshole I was. I knew that wouldn't make it any easier for anyone.

When I came to the beautiful stone hardscape, which wasn't a surprise considering the business they are in, I could see uni's and detectives outside searching the grounds.

The front door was open, as I walked onto the stairs leading to the door, I could see his family sitting in the foyer, scared, and confused as to why we were all there. I could hear raised voices coming from around the corner. I walked around the wall into what I believed was the living room, and could see Howie, Mike, and Harvey in a very heated conversation.

"Oh, great and now the asshole of the century is here." He was obviously not excited to see me.

"Harvey, good to see you too." Yeah, I was a smartass.

Mike and Howie both shook their heads, so I made sure to check that.

"I told you I have no idea who she is, or where she is. You are searching everywhere, I wouldn't hide someone here, that's insane."

That statement right there, you see that. It's things like that which sends up red flags for us detectives and brass. I wouldn't hide someone here. Why would he say that if he wasn't asked or accused of doing so? It will stay on my radar, and I will be sure to note all of what he gives us without realizing it.

"We are not saying that you did. We are hoping that we find her hiding out. We just need to make sure we check everywhere. Unfortunately, your house was first, since Josh is away, Eugene is already in the hospital, and Wes and your grandparents are all being searched as we speak."

Damn, I didn't know that. I would've gone to the Brinton's had I known. Which now that I think of it, that's probably why I didn't know, because the last thing they want is me there.

"What? You're kidding me, right? This is just ludicrous. Do you really believe my family is capable of kidnapping some girl and hiding her here? Get real, Howie. We are a huge help for this community, and this is really starting to make me rethink that."

"Is that a threat Mr. Grayson?" Howie inquired.

"You're damn right it is." A male voice came from the foyer, assuming it was his son.

"Junior, quiet." Harvey demanded.

Well, we know he gets angry, but I knew that already. This is about the tenth encounter I had with him over the past thirty years or so. He was not wrong about how much his family contributes to their community, and even ours over in Weston. But that cannot play a role in this, we must keep our heads focused on the reason why we are doing this. To find Scarlet.

SCARLET

I am so tired down here, still don't know where exactly here is. I am feeling weaker as the days go by. I think I have been here for about sixteen days. Which would make that Christmas time, and that makes my soul hurt, because I am not with my family. I don't know how much longer I can go on. I haven't had food in over two days, I have rationed my water out so luckily, I have that. It smells awful, sadly I have nowhere to escape it.

There are rats who have become the only things that are keeping me going, I feel like Cinderella every time I talk to one of them. I cannot believe that this could be it for me. I refuse to believe that this is how I am going to leave this world.

I am starting to remember things from that night, now that I think I am through another concussion. I remember a man broke down on the opposite side of the road, which I think I was going to pick up Justin. I asked if the man was ok, he said something but that's hazy too. He had a cane I think, and a weird old timey looking hat and clothes. It was like he wasn't from this time, like he was from another century. I wish he would come back in here because now I know what to ask him.

I got out and I saw the car, it was old too. It was familiar but I am not sure why. I did exactly what I wasn't supposed to do. I helped him, and now I am here. I think he hit my head, after I struggled in the passenger seat to take off my jacket and as fast as I could I rolled the window down and thre my jacket out the window.

It was a blur after that, then I woke up here. Alone. I wish I had something to write with so I could leave a note in case I don't make it before someone finds me. God, I am so hungry. I don't smell the rotten eggs right now, I haven't for the past day. I don't know what that means, I just know I don't smell it. I think I hear things all the time, like people talking, or someone yelling. But I know that is just delusions, and I am slowly losing my mind. I hate being alone. I hate being here. I miss talking to Karlie, a lot. I dreamt of my mom last night, it was a beautiful dream, and it was almost as if she were here with me. She kept telling me that I was going to be ok, and that it was ok to sleep now. She said she would be with me as she promised and as I wished.

CONCLUSION OF THE CASE WITH DETECTIVE SCHAFFER

After searching all the properties, we found nothing. We had no reason to believe that anyone in the family was responsible for her going missing. We came to another dead end on the jacket. It was quickly becoming a cold case for Chick and I. Sadly, the Grayson's filed multiple complaints against us, and I was transferred to Internet Crimes. This was a department I was not mentally ready for, especially after Scarlet.

Chick became sicker as the weeks went on, and he ended up taking some time off. This was wearing on him and his physical wellbeing. He finally went to that consult he kept pushing off with his doctor, and he ended up having stage four lung cancer. It was spreading fast, he opted not to do treatments for it. By May, he was in a hospice care hospital and sadly passed away on May eighteenth, 1996. This was a hard time for me in my life. I devoted myself to the job, nothing else mattered after Scarlet disappeared and after Chick passed away. I really wanted to be left alone. I did not want to lose hope, but it was creeping into my thoughts for sure.

The Adams' never gave up hanging and replacing flyers of their missing daughter. Chris decided he was going into the police academy after graduation. I was very proud of him for making that choice, however I could understand why he did. The loss of Chick hit them all very hard, they treated him like family, and were heartbroken consistently for the past year with all the loss they were enduring.

One year almost, and still nothing I don't understand how someone can just vanish in thin air. November 1996, I started in Internet Crimes and I would do my own investigating for her case, crazy enough on the sixteenth which would have been Scarlet's seventeenth birthday. I bought a computer that was top of the line, so I could search anywhere and everywhere, always coming to a dead end but never giving up.

So much time passed by, it was more than a year before anything new would arise.

March 1st, 1997 would be a day that I would never forget. I was sitting at my desk when my phone rang.

"Schaffer."

"Mike, it's Howie. Listen, uh we found something."

I immediately felt sick to my stomach and almost threw up right there at my desk.

"Ok, can you tell me what, so I can prepare myself."

"We found a body in the water."

"Scarlet's?"

"We're not sure yet, we are pulling it out as we speak."

"Wait how are you calling me?"

"They put one of those cellular phones in our vehicles, just the supervisors."

"Damn. Ok, uh do you want me to come out?"

"Yeah, I mean that would be great. I think you should be here for this. I want you on this with me. I already called Chief Masters and is fully on board with you assisting on this."

"Ok, I'll be right there. Give me just a few ok."

"And Mike."

"Yeah."

"Don't tell anyone yet. We're not sure if it's her and we don't want to cause any more unnecessary heartache for her family."

"Understood completely."

By the time I got out there, a lot was going on. The road was blocked off, there were multiple Coroner's vans there, which I found odd. I could see Howie shaking his head in disbelief but still had no idea why.

Then I saw it. I looked down the hill onto the embankment, and the scene was so gruesome and grim. There were body bags lined up, I could count four. But I had a feeling it was more.

"Howie. What the hell is happening?"

"Mike, I think I need to contact the FBI. I think we have a serial killer on the loose."

I couldn't believe my ears or my eyes. I don't even have the words to explain what that scene looked like, but I am sure you can imagine it was not good. Something evil cursed that water, something sinister that you could never fathom. I stood there in fear, anger, rage, sadness, damn every emotion you could think of.

When they finally pulled out Scarlet, I knew it was her. I didn't need anyone to tell me or to do any tests.

"GOD DAMN IT!" I screamed as loud as I could. Everyone looked at me, I didn't care.

"Mike, I need you to stay with me ok. I need you to help me."

"What the hell, Howie. What the hell. How are we going to tell them this is their little girl. What the hell."

"I know. I know. We will, I will be with you. Ok. We will do this together. Chick would want it that way."

They took all the bodies so far and placed them in the vans to take them to the Medical Examiner's office to start all tests on them. Howie instructed them to keep looking in the water in case there were more. God, I hoped not.

There were more, I don't even remember how many. Some were so decomposed it was suggested that they were in there for over twenty years or more. Some were more recent; Scarlet was the most recent. Crazy she was well preserved because of the cold water. So, Forensics wanted to do tests before anyone.

Howie and I drove over to the Adams house, and I still felt like I wanted to be sick. I could see Lucy's car as we pulled up, but not Joe's. I didn't want to tell them unless they were both home, especially Joe since it was his actual biological daughter.

"Howie, can I use this phone?"

"Sure, you want to call them?"

"Yeah, I think they both need to be home to hear this."

"Ok."

I dialed their number, I had it memorized. It rang a few times and Justin picked it up.

"Hello."

"Hey Justin. Its Mike."

"Oh, hey Detective. What can I do for ya?"

"Are your parents' home?"

"Actually yeah. Did you want to speak one of them?"

"No that's ok. I just wanted to check."

Damn, I knew he was going to wonder now. I should've just walked up to the damn door.

"Ok, well I'm pretty sure they will figure out what's going on. Now that I just messed that up."

"Let's go Mike. We gotta talk to them."

I let out a long exhale and got out of his vehicle. I could see that Justin was standing in the door waiting for us. Before we got to the sidewalk, Lucy and Joe were both walking toward us from the porch.

"Did you find her?" Lucy asked with tears pouring down her cheeks.

"We did."

The shriek she let out was enough to make anyone cry, it was so full of heartache, anguish, and despair. I tried to fight back the tears, but I was overcome with so many emotions I couldn't help it. Justin ran out the door and knew immediately what was going on.

"No. No. Nope. It can't be." He was getting angrier and angrier.

"Justin, I know buddy."

"Where?" Joe looked up and asked, as he was kneeling holding Lucy.

"Innerborough creek."

They all looked at me confused.

"But I thought." Justin started.

"I know. We searched everywhere there. And with the water frozen we couldn't access under it, and with the thaw there was still nothing. There were no disturbances to indicate we should look where she was found. We aren't sure why it took so long, but unfortunately water has a crazy way of preserving things and having a mind of it's own. The Medical Examiner believes that either she was placed there after the last thaw or she was there all along and just did not appear until now. I don't know"

"Joe. Lucy, would you be able to come to the Medical Examiner's office to give a positive ID?"

"This can't be real right now; this can't be happening." Joe of course said in disbelief.

"Mom, Joe, I can go if you want to. You don't have to go through that."

"No, we will go together. All three of us." Joe said.

We were set to leave when I saw Mr. Burns outside waving to me. Shit is all I could think. I knew I needed to go to him, but wanted to speak with Joe and Lucy before I did.

"Joe, Mr. Burns is up there waving to us. I can go and speak with him if that would be easier for you?"

"I'll go with you Mike." Joe said.

We both started walking up the street when Mrs. Burns met us at the end of her driveway.

"You found her, didn't you?" she asked.

I looked at Joe and he responded to her, "Yeah they did."

"Oh, Jesus, Mary, and Joesph. Where?"

"Innerborough Creek."

"Oh my God. No." She looked up toward him and shook her head no.

You could hear his cries and moans down where we were on the street.

"Joe, whatever you need. You know that." Mr. Burns yelled down.

"I'll go take care of Murphy, ok." She said.

"Thanks Sandy." Joe replied as we walked away.

The ride there was very quiet, except for the sniffling from all of us in the vehicle, even Howie.

"How are we going to tell the girls, and George." Lucy asked.

"Let's worry about getting to her first, sweetheart."

Nodding her head yes and leaning back into his chest, she was quiet again. Pulling up to the Medical Examiner's office, many of the vans were there. I did not tell them about the other bodies yet.

"Mike, why are these vans here?"

Howie and I both looked at one another and knew we should tell them before they walked inside.

"There were many bodies found before we found Scarlet. We believe that." Before Howie could finish Justin cut him off.

"There's a serial killer isn't there? I knew it. Scarlet has these notes, oh my god why didn't I think of this before. Jesus Christ. She had been following news stories for a year and a half. I don't know." Justin was stunned.

"Justin, after we get back can you show me her notes? Do you know where she kept them?"

"Yeah of course" poor kid was in such a daze now.

"Before we walk in, I want to explain what you're going to see. When you see her, you will see that her body was well preserved in the cold water. Which is yes, very helpful for forensics. It can tell them a lot about the circumstances surrounding her death. Her color may take you by surprise, but that is normal for the conditions that she was in. Please do not pay attention to anything else going on, ok." Howie's explained.

"Take me to our daughter." Lucy stood tall and composed herself.

We walked down the hall past rooms that had bodies covered, and some still in bags. When we arrived at door two, we were ready for the impact this was going to have on them.

"Dr. Hannum, this is her family. They are here to positively ID her." Howie explained to the Doctor.

He didn't say a word, he pulled the blanket slowly down from over her face, and when she was revealed, their gasps were loud, and they were in fact not ready for this. Who the hell would be?

"Thank you. That is her, that is Scarlet." Joe said with a cracking voice.

Standing outside they had a lot of questions, which were to be expected. Unfortunately, some we could not answer right then. Howie explained how the process worked, and they needed to approve the testing from Forensics to be performed. He explained how long the process can take, and that we would appreciate it if they would approve them because that team would find as many answers as allowable from her. They say that bodies in water, cold water specifically, tell a detailed story of what, where, and how the body got there and what it went through before getting there.

"Of course, we want to know what monster did this to our Scarlet. Whatever we can do to help you find them, we will. I know Justin is going to get you what you need from the house, I hope that is helpful for now." Joe said.

You could hear the sadness behind his voice, but also a sense of relief that she was finally found. Now he could have some closure, not full closure obviously but at least they have her now and the questions can start to get answers.

By the time we arrived back at their home, there were many cars out front now, and we all knew that it was time to face them and tell them.

"I can explain everything if you would like." I suggested.

"Yes, Mike. Please. I don't know if I have the strength to do it." Joe agreed.

"Very well."

I directed everyone to the first floor, the biggest space in the house, and I would explain everything at one time to everyone. It went exactly how I expected, many cries, angry outbursts, even a militia was forming to find whoever it was. In the meantime, Howie and Justin were getting her notebook with all the notes she wrote about the serial killer she believed was in the area. I did not tell the group about the other bodies, hell I couldn't be positive that someone in this room didn't do it. So, to cover this case and my ass, I was not bringing that up.

The forensics team took about a week to get all the information and tests done that they needed, so they released the body to the family finally. I know it was what the family needed, so they could have closure. This would mean I had time before I would hear anything about the results. We all went back to our respective divisions and sat in wait.

Late April is when we finally got results from the tests, and guess what? They were all inconclusive. Ha, of course they were. Nothing was easy in this case, absolutely nothing.

The notes she had were handed over to the FBI, with the exception of the journal she kept in the stair's outback at the house, and I have no idea what the outcome was on the ones she had that they did find, if anything. It was placed in the Cold Case unit by June and has been sitting there ever since I started in the division last month. I swear the guys leading that investigation did nothing, every time I asked what was going on and if there were any new news they just always said, "Nothing new." Before you called me, I was losing hope that we would never find Scarlet's killer.

Some of the other victims were identified and those families were able to get closure, and I could sleep better at night. I still had a vow that I made to myself all those years ago, though. I am sure you can guess what that is.

When Violet found her journal, we thought we hit the jackpot, and in some way we did. It gave us an insight into what she was thinking and feeling, from when her mom passed away to moving here. It was all there, her notes on Sandy and the Grayson's, luckily, they weren't all given to the FBI.

I have also started a hotline and an email specifically for the Carriage Ford Road murders. So, I hope this interview will help bring some attention to them because we need answers. Her family, but most of all Scarlet, deserves them.

"Detective, is it true that her boyfriend at the time is now a police officer with the department?"

I shook my head, "Yes, Chris is a standup officer. He is willing to help anyone and is the first to volunteer for overtime. He was actually the one who helped me get this Cold Case back up and active. We have all been looking over everything, just to see what we missed all those years ago."

"Who is we all, if you don't mind me asking?"

"Well, Greenberg, Judge Masters, Howie, MacNeill, Chris, and myself. George is working for the FBI in their Computer Forensics Department. So, we have people everywhere helping to solve this case. There is additional evidence that we have to explore still, but we are waiting to disclose that information."

"That sounds cryptic. Can you share anything with us?"

I shook my head no, "Unfortunately not right now."

"Fair enough, Detective. I want to thank you for coming here and speaking with me and sharing her story with the listeners. I hope you can get the answers that you are looking for and that whoever did this to her and those other people finally get some justice. It must be some kind of monster to do what was done to them."

"So, when you were retelling everything about Scarlet, was all that from her journal?" He asked me.

"Most of it, yeah."

When he said that everything flashed back for me, not that it hasn't everyday since, but this was different. "Damn, Landon. I think you might be onto something."

He looked confused, rightfully so he had no idea why I said that.

"Ok, what did I say?"

"It was a monster that did this. It was a heartless person, but they were careless in some things. I think I need to leave it at that. Thanks Landon, and I hope the next time I see you we are celebrating that we found the monster."

As I sat there, I was thinking of the hoodie she was wearing that night, among other things.

"Detective Schaffer are you ok?" he asked me.

"Yeah, actually I am. Landon I think I have an idea that may open this case wide open. But like I said I can't talk about it right now. I will be back though, and I will keep you in the loop." I stood in the doorway and was blown away by how much he looked like Chick. "Damn, you look so much like him it's like seeing a ghost."

There was a long pause of silence, I exhaled recapping all that I had said, and left. I knew what needed to be done.

"George, hey buddy it's Mike Schaffer!" George and I spoke often so calling him was not abnormal.

"Mike, how are you? How was your birthday?" He knew I disliked my birthday.

"Eh, you know." I replied.

"Yeah, yeah. So, what's good?" George was always to the point, not a lot of small talk with him.

"I need a favor; can you meet me sometime over the next week or so?" Since we were not far from D.C. I knew the drive wouldn't be a problem, plus he was here often enough visiting with the family.

"Yeah, sure I can come up this weekend, if that works?"

"That be great. Thanks buddy. I will see you then." I said.

"Mike?"

"Yeah?"

"Should I be worried?"

"Nah, not at all. I think I have something that may just take us into a different direction with Scarlet's case."

"Ah, ok. I figured it was about that, but I wasn't too sure. You know I don't have anything new, right. All we have is what we had all those years ago."

"I know, I know. But I wanted to take a different approach to it. I want to run it past you, since Agent Graham retired and now you are my only connection there. HA!"

He laughed, because he knew I was right, "Yeah. Ok. I will text you when I am at the house."

We hung up and I knew I needed to have a rock-solid plan on how I was going to approach this. Also, I knew that the one thing that could blow this case wide open was also the one thing I couldn't access.

All week long I sat at my desk sifting through every piece of documentation, evidence, which there wasn't much of, you name it. My floors, walls, and tables were all covered with the shit. I have cork boards with things pinned all over them. There was one name I kept going back to, it was actually just initials. They were KG. I looked through so many old files, and there were thousands of "KGs" in the system. So, I knew I needed to enlist the help of George on this one. I needed him to see if there were any complaints that were associated with the Carriage Ford Road Murders, The Grayson's, or the Brinton's. Anything he could find would be helpful now.

I was early to meet him. When I arrived at the house, I could see the Willow tree in the back taller than any other tree now. Everything still looked the same. Chris purchased his grandparents' home, and he helped the Adams' all the time. We were all so much older now, you could see the gray hairs, the wrinkles, the years of hurt, sadness and heartache were written all over our faces. I had been by for holidays and such over the years, and when Justin got married. The girls were married as well now but moved out of the house and back to Havre de Grace. I don't blame them.

I saw Joe looking out the front door, he was smiling and waved at me to come in.

I got out of my car and started walking up to the sidewalk. The door opened as I stepped onto the porch.

"Mike. George isn't here yet. I am glad you came early though. Come in, have a seat." He was always so welcoming.

"Joe," I hugged him, "It's damn good to see you. Where is Lucy?"

"She is upstairs with the baby. Rachel had to work, and Justin got stuck at the Restaurant, so we are on baby duty today." He said with a huge smile.

"Oh! I have not seen her in a few months. I am sure she is getting so big."

"She is. Lucy will be back down soon, so you can see both!" he said happily.

"Great!"

Joe poured me a cup of coffee and began to talk. "So, you think you have something new?"

I started to nod my head as I added the cream and sugar, "I think so."

"Good. I hope we can help in some way." He said.

"You might be able to. Do you ever remember a person with the initials KG brought up during the case?" I asked.

He looked at me confused, "Hmm, not that I remember. But you know my head was all over the place back then. Why?"

"Well, I have seen the initials come up just a few times as I have been reading over the files. And I just can't seem to find anything or anyone that it would line up with. I am at a loss."

"Well, hopefully George can help." Joe replied.

We heard his car pull into the driveway; he drove a 2014 Mustang GT. Impractical, but I dug it.

He walked into the house downstairs and came up the stairwell. We could hear his shoes clanking on each step, as if they were too big for his feet.

"George!" Joe exclaimed as he entered the kitchen.

George walked over and hugged him, "Hey dad. Good to see you. Where's mom?"

He then walked over and shook my hand.

"She is upstairs with your niece."

"Oh awesome. I am so happy I get to see her!"

He poured himself a cup of coffee and joined us at the table.

"So, Mike. What's up?" George always right down to business.

I exhaled, "I need some help with something that has come up a few times among the files," I pulled out the documents and reports, it wasn't many just a few pages, but I knew it was something, "See these letters? I think they are initials. I can't seem to find anything else though, nothing that lines up with KG."

"That's Karlie Gorton. She was questioned, I think it was a week later or something. I have the files from our end," he leaned into his bag, "here let's look."

We sifted thorough and I'll be damned, there it was KG. Why didn't we know about this? Why didn't the department know?

"George, why didn't the department know?" I asked and was annoyed by this.

He shrugged his shoulders, "We did. It was given to Campbell back then. You would have to take it up with him. I know I have personally looked for her and she seems to be a ghost." We all looked at him when he said that. "Sorry, bad choice if words."

We could hear Lucy coming down the stairs, women always spoke higher pitched when babies, and animals were in the picture.

"Mike!" she greeted me with her arms out wide getting ready for an embrace.

"Lucy, so good to see you. And look at how beautiful you are little miss." I guess we men did the same thing in our way.

Frances Scarlet Myers, that is what they named her. After the two people they admired most. I was so proud of what these kids had become in their adult lives and was grateful that I was included in many of it.

My phone started to ring and crazy enough it was Howie, I left him a message a few days ago but he was on a short vacation visiting Ryan.

"Howie, how was your mini vacation?" I asked.

"Ah man it was good! Ryan is doing well! His ceremony was beautiful, I couldn't be prouder." He said with such pride, and I could tell he was smiling by his tone.

"That's great buddy. Listen I am at the Adams', and I need to know who is, or was, Karlie Gorton?" I was hoping he would remember.

"She was someone we questioned back then. She didn't have much to tell us and didn't know Scarlet. We didn't think she was anything for the case. Why? What's up?" he asked.

"Well, see her initials I have seen a few times in the files, and I didn't see anything else. I guess I wanted to see what the report was from her. Do you still have that by chance?" I was praying he would say yes.

"Yeah, of course. You know I don't get rid of anything. How long you gonna be there?"

I looked at my watch, saw that it was only one-thirty, and replied "I will be here until they kick me out."

He laughed, "Alright, give me a few and let me get the box I have from the attic, and I'll be there soon. Probably about a half hour."

"See you then!" I was feeling so many emotions now, excited, nervous, anxious, nauseous, you name it. Could they have missed something back then? They had to have missed something. I mean why else would I be stuck on this? I knew George would be the right one to talk to and I am relieved that Howie remembered.

We all sat around the kitchen table and caught up on what we have all been up to for the past few weeks, they asked how my birthday was and if I had seen Sarah lately. My birthday was just another day and no I had not seen Sarah in a while.

"Knock knock!" Howie called as he approached.

"Hey Chief!" George said excitedly.

"How is everyone?" he asked as he shook hands and hugged Lucy.

"We are good. Damn good to see you Howie." Joe replied.

"And look at this beauty," he said while he was tickling Frankie's toes, she giggled.

"She is so big right Howie. Like where did the time go?" Lucy said, with tears welling up in her eyes.

I can imagine how hard this was for them, losing Scarlet and then having an exact replica of her born again. It was unreal how much she looked like her when Scarlet was a baby.

"Ok if we get started?" I asked.

Everyone shook their heads; I think they were just as anxious to get this going than I was.

"Alright, so this is the report from when we questioned her." Howie laid it on the table.

I read over it and the first thing I noticed was that a rookie conducted the questions.

"Wait, she was seen walking down Carriage Ford Road approximately three days after the disappearance of Scarlet. He wrote nothing down as to what she was wearing, what her condition was. Literally it says "Spoke to an African American Female, around thirty-three years old, walking toward the Brinton property on Carriage Ford Road. I asked if she was from the area, she stated no. I then continued on my way to the station to clock out from my shift." What the HELL Howie? How was that even allowed?" I was furious.

He was shaking his head, "Mike, I have not looked at that specific report since that day. I went on his word and never even questioned it again. Shit, we missed her. How did we, sorry I, miss her." Howie was the first to admit when he was wrong, and he was wrong on this.

"You mean someone could've seen her?" Lucy asked.

"Not necessarily mom. It just means that the officer did not do his due diligence by asking the correct questions." George tried to reassure her.

She started crying, "Do you know what it is like to wake up every day knowing that she will never walk through these doors again? Do you know what it is like to live with the fact that I was helpless? Do you know what it is like to regret every decision made leading up to that moment she was taken?" It broke my heart listening to hear ask these questions.

"Mom, I know. I lost her too remember. We all did."

"It's not the same. When her mother was sick. I would watch Scarlet and I would see that she held the weight of the world on her shoulders. From having to hide the sickness from her little sisters, to keeping it together in front of everyone, to watching her father become more and more distant from her. I made her lunches, dinners, sat with her, spoke to her. Comforted her. I did those things. The day she called me mom was the best day of my life. Because I saw firsthand the love she had for Ramona, and for her to call me that I knew it meant more than just a word or a name. It meant I was mom, and she made me an equal to Ramona."

Joe took her hands into his, "Sweetheart, I had no idea. I am so sorry."

"You were grieving too. But she was just a child and she needed someone to guide her, to listen to her, to be there for her. And someone took her from me, took my beautiful daughter away. The only thing that gives me peace is that she is with Ramona, something I knew she wished for years before she was taken from us."

We all knew what needed to be done. We needed to find Karlie. George had the best resources for that of course, so we followed his lead.

"I'm gonna make a phone call. Excuse me for a minute." George stood up and took his phone out of his back pocket and started to dial a number as he walked out of the room.

"Lucy, let me say these few things ok. I have known you for quite some time, and I know in my heart the Scarlet loved you as her mother, and that she wouldn't want you to be in this state. She literally recreated herself into that beautiful baby girl over there," Frankie was in her bouncy seat giggling and smiling, "so that is a sign from her if I have ever seen one. And you don't even share the same blood with Scarlet, that is how strong she is. She came back to you." We all looked at Frankie, and she really was the spitting image of Scarlet. It was a little eerie, but it was a fact that none of us could deny.

After about fifteen minutes George was back into the kitchen, "Ok, so here's what I found out. Karlie Gorton is now Karlie Maynes, she lives in Lannister with her husband. She is fifty-four years old and has a few children. She has no record, never been in trouble, seems to live a quiet, peaceful life."

We were all in shock, none of us could believe that she was that close still. All this time she was right in our own back-yard. Now, we had to come up with a game plan to talk to her.

"How should we handle this? You're the Cold Case guy." Howie said.

I knew I wanted Chris with us on this, I sent him a text asking him to come over and sit down with us. He responded immediately and was there in minutes.

I truly had no idea if she had any information for us, but I knew something was telling me we had to try. We couldn't let it go this time.

When Chris arrived, we filled him on everything, and he was just as anxious to go to Mrs. Maynes. Howie and I agreed that George and I should go, and the rest should stay back. We did not want to overwhelm her with our questions, and we also did not want emotions to get too high, so we agreed to just the two of us.

When we pulled down Ford Street I was immediately overrun with my own emotions. Trying to hold it together I looked to George for some solace. "Buddy, I am freaking out. What if she knows something? What if she doesn't? Damn, I am a mess."

He turned to me in his seat, "Mike, I am too. But we need to keep it together for Letti. This woman may not know anything, you might be right. But what if she does? What if she has been the missing link this whole time. Whatever happened to the officer that questioned her? Do you know?"

"He left the department a year after this, I think. He started working for the Grayson's. I remember hearing that he said he wasn't cut out to be a cop and would rather do hard work and feel accomplished every day."

"Hm, makes sense. Wait," he shot me a look that I will never forget, "You said he ended up working for the Grayson's? How serendipitous is that?" I didn't follow.

"What do you mean?" I asked.

"Mike, you know Chick thought it was one of them. You know Scarlet didn't believe that Eugene killed Sandy. You know all this."

"But we searched all over, and questioned them, followed them. Never did they seem to break character." I said.

"I know all that, but I knew my sister better than anyone. She talked to me about things she wouldn't talk to anyone else about. I know she believed it was one of the brothers just not Eugene."

"Christ they would be in their late sixties and seventies by now, and Wes passed away last year. I wonder if we went to Eugene and questioned him. Maybe if he cooperates Sarah can offer him a plea deal. I don't know, I know I sound crazy right now. I have no idea what I'm saying. Let's go talk to her.

As we walked up the walkway leading to her home, there were big wheels and bikes strewn across the yard, toys tossed about. Apparently, she also ran a daycare out of her home, something we did not know before we came. George was the one to knock, and we waited for just about a minute before a young girl opened the door to greet us.

"Can I help you?" she said in a soft voice.

"Hi. My name is George, and this is my friend Mike. Is there an adult home?"

"Mmm Hmm. Gammie, there's two men here." She yelled.

We could see a woman in the kitchen through the screen door, and everything in me told me that this was her.

"Hello gentlemen, can I help you?" she asked concerned.

"Ma'am. My name is George Myers, and this is Mike Schaffer. I am with the FBI, and he is with the Weston Cold Case Unit. We were hoping we could ask you a few questions."

She looked hesitant, weary almost, and I was certain she was not going to let us in. She looked down at the ground, I assume at nothing in particular, exhaled with her eyes closed and opened the screen door to allow us in.

"Please have a seat. Do not mind the mess." She said, and it was a mess.

"No worries, ma'am." I said.

"So, what kind of questions do you want to ask me?" she asked as if she already knew what we were going to say.

"Ma'am, back in 1995 you were questioned by an Officer Judge. Do you remember that?" George asked, I sat by rubbing my hands together. I knew they could all tell I was anxious.

"Yes, I do. Why?"

"We wanted to ask you a different set of questions. Ones that he should've asked that evening. Would that be, ok?"

"I knew that girl."

My heart sank, I instantly was sick to my stomach. I know my face turned white as a ghost. George mirrored my reaction.

"I'm sorry ma'am. What girl?"

"The one you are here asking about. I didn't realize it was her until quite a few years later. Do you mind if I get my tea and I can tell you everything."

We looked at each other as she rose out of her seat to head toward the kitchen. We didn't say a word, we just sat there staring at the other one, speechless.

She came back in with a tray and three glasses of sweet tea, "You know, I still have no idea how any of us got down there."

We were astonished by what she was saying, we just couldn't believe this was happening.

"Us? Ma'am." I said.

"Us, yes. Me, that young girl, an older man, and probably many others. The sound, God I will never forget that sound. The banging over and over, I go to sleep "BANG BANG BANG", I drive down the street and if I hear one loud sound I am immediately taken back to that time. I felt so bad I left and couldn't get to them. I tried to go back, I tried to find the hatch I climbed out of. That is what I was doing that day the officer saw me. I was afraid to tell him anything else. Before I married Franklin, I was a companion for men. I was paid very well, I kept them company when they needed it. I told the old man I would be back with help, I tried to tell the young girl, but she never answered me. I called out to her, but I knew I had a very short window to escape."

"Karlie, what are you saying? You were kidnapped?" I asked.

She took a sip of her drink, "Yes, I remember I broke down at the Allen's Gas Station. I asked the attendant if he had any-one that could help me with my car. He came out and I don't remember anything after that. I went to search for my car at the station, but it wasn't there. I asked a young girl that was working at the counter if she had seen a Chevy Cavaliere, metallic blue. She said no. I went to my home here in Lannister, I told my mom and dad what happened. They told me not to get involved, because if I went back whatever it was would probably kill me. They would be waiting for me, because I escaped. It has haunted me every day since. Then when the bodies were found, I wanted to go to the police again and my father told me that I would be in more trouble because I didn't come forward sooner. Listen, I am sure you are fine police officers, but I don't look like you so my trusted my dad and his advice. I wanted to come forward so many times."

"Karlie, how do you know it was the young lady we were looking for?" George asked.

"I remember she told me her name; I didn't remember at first though because my mind was a mess. When I realized it was her, I was at the fall festival in 2006, and a woman was talking about her daughters, and then she said how she missed Scarlet. When I heard her say her name it triggered something in my mind. I remember we talked a few times; she helped me live. Oh my God, I couldn't help her. Am I going to jail?"

"No Karlie, you are not., You are a victim as well, and we need to help you and Scarlet and every other victim. We need to find this monster." I explained.

"Monster, more like monsters. There was more than one, I know it."

"How?" George asked as he took note after note.

"I was down there for I think about six months, I am not sure where there is though. I learned the body size from the shadow that would come in to leave food. I am certain it was two, maybe three, but definitely two. They never spoke, and they only came down when the banging was loudest."

"Ok, let's see if we can jog your memory of the place. Would it be ok if you closed your eyes?" George was very good at this part.

She closed her eyes.

"Ok. I know this part is going to be very hard, so when you think you have had enough just say so and we will stop. Ok?"

She nodded her head yes.

George started his line of questions, "What does it feel like? The temperature?"

"It's hot and I my skin feels sticky."

"Ok, good. Is there any other sound other than the banging?"

"Only when the banging stops. I can hear faint voices; I haven't heard anything for a long time. I hear a young girl who sounds like she is right next to me, and an older man who seems a little farther away."

"What does she say to you?"

"She said Hello, then we talked for a while until we both were too tired to talk. There were no lights, just a faint one outside the door and far away."

"Ok. How about the smell?"

"Sulfur. I remember it vividly, and when I smell a match, I get sick to my stomach."

I knew exactly where that could be. Damn, Chick and Scarlet were right this whole time. George glanced at me, and I knew what he was thinking.

"Ok. Let's talk about how you escaped."

"He didn't close the door all the way. The old man started screaming so loud, it sent chills down my spine. When the shadow left the door did not latch, I heard it every time before but not this time. I waited for it to come back but it never did. I waited a long time before I went to the door. I needed to make sure I was safe to leave. I couldn't see anything when I opened the door. The light was so dim, as I said before. I tip toed around, oh the shards of rocks or something under my feet made it so hard for me to be quiet. I had to feel my way to a wall, I had no idea if I was leading myself into danger or safety, but I knew I needed to do something. I said "is anyone here. Can you hear me?" super low, the old man heard me. I told him I was going to get help. I called for the young girl, but she didn't answer. I told the old man to tell her I will be back with help. I couldn't help her, or him. I walked so far, the further I went the less light there was.

I remember I was shuffling my feet and banged my toe so hard into something even harder. I broke my big toe, but I knew I needed to keep going. It felt like steps when I reached my hands forward. I climbed up them and hit my head on a metal door of some sorts. It was pitch black everywhere. I felt around and could feel a latch of some sort, and I knew it was a hatch to either the outside or another building. When I opened it, it was just as dark. I closed it but I didn't latch it in case they could get free too. I ran, I kept running until I came to a road, and then saw signs for Lannister. And you know the rest." The tears were sliding down her cheeks, and she seemed so ashamed.

Franklin walked in and held her from behind around her shoulders. She cried more. We knew it was time to contact Sarah.

"Karlie, you did amazing. I am so proud of you." George walked over to her and held her hand, "I have one more question. Would you be willing to put all this on the record?"

She looked up at her husband looking for validation, he nodded yes.

"Yes. It is time we all get closure on this. Especially Scarlet."

Hearing her say her name made my heart jump.

We explained what happens now and that we would be in touch soon. I know she felt better getting that off her chest after all these years, and my heart broke for her that she had to live with this nightmare. We sat in the car in silence, trying to wrap our brains around everything she just said.

"You're going to need to call Sarah." George said to me.

"I know," I said hesitantly, "I have no idea what to say right now. I cannot believe that we even heard what we just did." I shook my head and got myself back together.

"Hey, it's me," I called her, "You're never going to believe this. Are you in your office? Ok, George and I are on our way."

Pulling into the parking garage I knew it was now or never to get this right for Scarlet and now Karlie, and all the others. The elevator dinged and we entered, hit the button for the fourth floor. The doors opened and she was waiting for us.

"So, what is it? It has to be about Scarlet or else George would not be here."

"We found a victim." Is all I could get out.

"What? Where, in the lake again?"

"No, a live victim, a witness." George said.

"What?"

We began to tell her everything, and without hesitation she handed me a paper. It was exactly what Chick wanted all those years ago, but this time it allowed us to dig on any part of their property that we needed to.

"Go get those monsters." She said so sinister and scary.

Heading back to the Adams' I asked George if he wanted me to explain everything and he appreciated the offer. Everyone was there when we arrived, so it made it easy to tell them all at once. One can imagine the reactions from them, it was heartbreaking for me and there was not a dry eye in the house. We explained that it would be quick, tomorrow was going to be the beginning of it all.

The next day we presented the warrant to the office manager at the Quarry, the first place I wanted to go to. And we got straight to work. We called out a construction crew to meet us there first thing in the morning. A walking crew was also there to help canvas that area. After about thirty minutes, one of the crew found a door, almost unnoticeable due to the overgrowth of the grounds. I shook my head and knew the reason why we couldn't find this before was due to the snow and how it covered it. We never even thought to look for something like this.

I stared down at the door as the crew member cleared the overgrowth off it and turned the latch. I didn't know what to expect. When he opened it, I descended the stairs. As I got to the bottom my chest felt heavy, I had a lump in my throat, my skin was hot and sticky just as Karlie described. And yes, there was the banging. Much of the crew was there now, setting up strings of lights since visibility was as bad as Karlie explained.

When the lights lit up, they revealed long hallways, doors on every side, shards of concrete on the floor, slow drips of water from above.

"Ok, do not open any of the doors. I need a crew out here that will not compromise the scene. Thank you, gentlemen, I will meet you back up top."

I walked around for a minute wondering where she could have been held, but then I didn't want to torture myself with that.

As I waited for the Crime Scene Unit to show up, I pulled out the gloves from the back pocket of my jeans, opened the door closest to me and was immediately horrified by the scene that was revealed behind it.

"Detective, there's a gentleman up here who is insistent on speaking with you." One of the crew members hollered down.

Good, I got their attention now.

Walking back up the stairs I was greeted by Harvey Grayson, he was in his late seventies and was showing in every way.

"Mr. Grayson. How are you today?"

"I would be better if you told me what the hell this was about. Who do you think you are? You can't just come here."

I interrupted him, "Actually if you go to your office manager you will see that she was presented with a warrant from DA Majors. Any questions, concerns, complaints, can be directed to her office. Now please step aside before I arrest you for interfering with an active investigation."

"This is preposterous. I am calling my lawyer."

"That's probably a good idea. Because if the other rooms show the same as the one room I entered so far, you will need one."

He walked away in a huff, and with force and speed.

"Oh, and Mr. Grayson, you might want to tell your brother that he may want to call his lawyer too." He looked a bit panicked now.

"I guess you thought you would get away with it forever, huh. Well, like my buddy Chick would say if he were here, *doesn't this just blow your wig.*"